TAMARISK BAY

Typesetting and cover design by Formatting Experts

ISBN 978-1-8382227-5-8
Published by Volker-Larwin Publishing

TAMARISK BAY

A NICK FISHER NOVEL

ALEX DUNLEVY

NAMED CHARACTERS

iv

Leftéris . . . . Constable with the police at Chaniá
Leo Christodoulákis . . . . Lieutenant with the police at Chaniá
Manólis Michailídis . . . . Former employee of Alpha Bank
María Papadopoúlou . . . . Mother of Manólis Michailídis
Matej Žagar . . . . Pseudonym used by Ivan
Matej Šuštar . . . . Young Slovenian man
Méli . . . . Stefi's pet goat kid
Michális Spiliákis . . . . Stefi's father
Mr. Tzanakákis . . . . .Archaeologist and MOHCAS official
Mr. Kóstas . . . . Risk Manager for Alpha Bank, Crete
Mr. Arapaï . . . . Albanian pseudonym used by Ivan
Mr. Mákris . . . . Office Manager at MOHCAS
Mrs. Tsesmé . . . . Forestry Department employee
Mrs. Marína . . . . Stávros's lawyer
Náni Samaráki . . . . Investigations Sergeant with the police at Réthymno
Neža Žagar . . . . Pseudonym used by Irína
Nick Fisher . . . . Former DCI with the Met, now living in Crete
Níkos Manousákis . . . . Constable with the police at Réthymno
Pandelís . . . . Constable with the police at Chaniá
Rosalind Kinnear . . . . [aka Roz/Rosie] Volunteer at Tamarisk Bay
Simon Woodruff . . . . Official at the British Vice-Consulate
Státhis Giannakákis . . . . Sergeant with the police at Sitía
Stávros Pagiánnidis . . . . Chaniá estate agent
Stefanos Spiliákis . . . . [aka Stefi/Steff] Owner of Tamarisk Bay
Thanásis Konstantópoulos . . . [aka Thaní] Acting Lieutenant with the police at Chaniá
Theódoros . . . . [aka Teddy] Volunteer at Tamarisk Bay
Vangélis . . . . Constable with the police at Chaniá
Xará . . . . Kostí's daughter

Note 1: MOHCAS is the (Greek) Ministry of Hellenic Culture and Sports
Note 2: Adil, Lékas, Ollie Dunham and Yasir are characters from *The Stone Skimmers*

CHAPTER 1
A CALL FROM HOME

She knocked, then turned the plastic doorknob and entered the prefabricated cabin. She felt sweaty and out of breath. The shift supervisor was sitting behind a plywood desk covered in charts and photographs. He had been smoking and the room stank of it, despite the ceiling fan.

"You wanted to see me, Eric?" she said.

He stubbed out his cigarette and indicated the chair opposite.

"Have a seat, Roz."

Something was wrong. She knew it right away. Eric was Swedish and serious-minded; he rarely smiled. But now an extra layer of gravitas was etched into the lines on his face. Was she in trouble? Had she done something dreadful? She watched as he ran a hand through thinning, blond hair and pursed his lips.

"Your mother called. She's been trying to reach you."

Roz nodded. *Where the hell was her cell phone? Maybe still in the backpack. The battery would need charging now, anyway.*

"It's your dad."

"Oh, no. Shit."

"Your mother is at the hospital. She says it doesn't look good ... I'm sorry."

Roz stared at him for a moment.

"She wants you to go back."

Eric had not said *before it was too late*, but the subtext was clear. Roz reached for the tissue she kept in the pocket of her shorts. She had come to hate that hospital and everyone in it. Maybe they had done their best, but she could not be sure anymore. She and her mother had watched while twelve years of their surgery, chemotherapy, radiotherapy, endless pills and potions had steadily destroyed her father. The last time Roz saw him, he was skeletal, his skin yellowy-grey and blotchy. The morphine doses were so strong now that he seemed to be losing his mind at times and the light in his eyes was fading. He looked twenty years older than he was.

1

"He's dying, then," she managed to say, the words catching in her throat. She could hear the blood, roaring in her ears.

Eric came around the desk and pulled up a chair beside her. Then he took her hand in his.

"I think you *have* to go," he said, "for her, if nothing else."

"I still have another week, Eric."

"You know all you need to know. You're my best student."

"I am?"

"Here. You earned this already."

She took the roll of paper from him. It was her proficiency certificate. She saw the familiar, turtle logo above the text and Eric's sprawling signature below. It was dated the third of July. A tearful grin appeared briefly among the freckles, and she patted Eric's hand.

"That's so kind," she said.

"I dated it next week to avoid any awkward questions. Our secret – okay?"

"Our secret," she confirmed. "Thank you, Eric."

"There's a flight to Glasgow tonight," he said. "I already checked, and they can squeeze you on. I can drive you, but we'll need to leave in an hour. Can you do it?"

"What about paying for it?"

"If you don't have enough, I can lend you some. Don't worry."

"My mum will pay you back."

"Whatever."

An hour was plenty. She could shower and throw her clothes into the backpack in ten minutes. But she was desperate to say goodbye to the friends she had made. Not just the other volunteers in her group, but also the special friend she had made of Daphne, the pretty, local girl who cleaned for ARCHELON. She might be hard to find, though. Roz knew her cleaning shift ended around four thirty. An hour ago. Where would she go?

She found the others in their matching, blue tee shirts on Ágioi Apóstoloi beach. One by one they hugged her and wished her well, knowing they were not likely to meet again.

"Does anyone know where Daphne might be?" Roz asked.

"The girl who cleans, you mean?"

"Daphne, yes. Her name is Daphne."

Irritation had crept into Roz's voice. She heard it herself. Daphne had always been below the horizon for these privileged girls. Roz was her only friend here, maybe in the world. The way she had confided in Roz over the last several weeks, it certainly felt like that. They shared modest backgrounds and a liking for telling it how it is, being open and warm.

"I'm sorry. You mean the pretty one with the gorgeous boyfriend?" said one of the girls, "I didn't know her name. She finished her shift and went off, about an hour ago."

Yes, he was gorgeous, with that long, wavy hair and those startling, blue-green eyes, and he was a hell of a cook, apparently, but he was also poison, Roz thought. One of those guys who puts you on a pedestal and showers you with gifts, to start with. Only then it all turns to shit.

"Did you see where she went? Which way?" Roz asked.

The first girl looked blank but one of the others piped up:

"They have use of an old house, I think. It was her granny's. It's in Lambíni. The only pink house, I remember her saying, and she hates pink; I know *that* much."

"Is it far?"

"Three or four kilometres, no more. Inland."

"I've only got thirty-five minutes."

"Then leave early, get Eric to swing by there on the way."

"Good thinking, girl. Thanks a lot, everyone, and good luck."

*

As Eric drove, Roz was lost in thought. Daphne had been distraught, the last time they met, and she looked awful. She had lost weight and there were dark circles under her eyes. He made her wear unflattering clothes to hide her attractions from other men, but she was still pretty, though she looked older than her years now. Roz asked about the bruises on her arms and Daphne came up with a pathetic lie. To Roz, it was a classic example of coercive control, and she told Daphne so. She told her to get away from him as soon as she could. But had she done the right thing, or was Daphne in even greater danger now?

*

There was no reply at the basic, lurid pink bungalow, but his motor-bike was there, Roz saw.

"They've gone out," a small voice behind her said, in Greek. Roz turned to see a girl of about six with a boy perhaps two years younger.

"Did you see them?" she asked.

The boy looked bashful and was shaking his head.

"He didn't but *I* did," the girl said. "From indoors. That's where *we* live," she boasted, pointing to a modern, concrete house with a shiny car, the colour of baby poo.

"Which way did they go, did you see?"

The girl pointed.

"There's a track up the hill."

"How long ago did you see them?"

The boy screwed up his face. The girl was looking up at the sky as if seeking divine guidance.

"Um," she said, at last. "Not long."

"We need to go, Roz," Eric called from the car.

"Give me five minutes, will you?" Roz yelled and started jogging down the road.

The girl and her brother watched, bemused.

"Why is everyone running today?" she asked him.

"It must be a race," he said.

*

She was halfway up the hill when she saw them. It was just a glimpse, through the trees, but she recognised that hair of his and the turquoise of the dress she often wore. He was lying on top of her, she could tell that much, so, not a good time. She hesitated and then heard Eric,

4

sounding the horn. She glanced at her watch. Her flight left in less than two hours, and they still had to drive to the airport. She would need to check her bag. She looked again, peering through the trees. Nothing seemed to be moving. She was exposed on the hillside, she realised. If she could see them, they would see her clearly, if they were looking. And that would be embarrassing. She thought she heard a soft moan, carried on the wind. *Lucky girl*, she thought.

Turning and heading back down, Roz told herself she would make a point of returning when she was back from Scotland. Chaniá could be reached from Tamarisk Bay. There would be opportunities to see her friend then. And Daphne would be okay with that. It was easy with her; they were already soul mates. And it would only be a few weeks. Everything would be fine.

As Eric turned the car, something caught her eye in the wing mirror. To her astonishment, she thought she glimpsed a figure, racing down the hill towards the road. Was Daphne trying to catch her?

"Stop, Eric, stop!" she cried, leaping out of the car, and turning back. But there was nothing there. Had she imagined it? Or had the figure vanished behind that solitary plane tree, or ducked into the prickly pear field? Had it been her, or him – or someone else entirely? Then it occurred to her; if it had been Daphne, she would have seen a flash of turquoise from that dress. It all happened so quickly; she could not be sure what colours she had seen. But turquoise. Surely *that* would have registered …

She stood there for half a minute, hands on hips. Other than the sheep and the cruising raptors, nothing moved. The only sounds were the sheep bells, the wind rustling the leaves and now a pair of crows, cawing above her head. *They're cackling at my foolishness*, she thought. The edge of the forest was at least two hundred metres away now. She would have to climb all the way back and there was no time left.

"Come on, Roz. What the hell are you doing? You'll miss your flight!"

Eric's urgent call brought her to her senses. She was being ridiculous. She had imagined something, or it had been a trick of the light in the mirror. As for anyone hiding behind a tree, she was being fanciful and silly. Why on earth would anyone do that? She chuckled to herself and shook her head.

"I'm sorry, Eric," she said as she slipped back into the passenger seat. "Let's go."

As soon as he heard the click of her seatbelt, Eric accelerated away, the tyres raising a small cloud of dust. Roz spotted the kids, waving from an upstairs window. She waved back and gave them a nervous smile.

CHAPTER 2
THE BANK

Stefanos Spiliákis felt sick. Not because he was tired from the journey to Chaniá and back, though he was. Nor was it the lurching and buffeting of the boat; he was accustomed to that. No, he knew what it was, from before. It was dread, forming deep in his gut, and – nearer the surface – hot-faced anger and frustration, mostly with himself.

He tugged a bottle of rakí from the freezer compartment and poured himself a generous slug. Then he banged the small glass twice on the tabletop, shouted "Yeiá mas" and downed it in one. He tore the ring pull from a small can of Alfa beer, grabbed a handful of kritsínia in a square of kitchen roll and slumped into the deckchair outside the cabin.

"What is *wrong* with these people?" he asked Méli in Greek, handing her one of the sesame-coated breadsticks. "This is a long-term plan, for Heaven's sake! And it can be a gold mine for all of us. But I must be sure of our team. I can't be dealing with people who flip-flop like this!"

She looked at him with sorrow.

"And no, I *haven't* got all the clearances yet. Of course, I haven't. These things take time here. A lot of time. But why assume the worst? Why on earth *would* there be issues – here, of all places?"

Stefi swept his arm theatrically over the hectares of sandy scrubland, dotted with rocky outcrops and low-level vegetation, stretching from the row of ancient tamarisks behind the shingle beach to the dusty green juniper forest. Beyond, mountains rising six hundred metres glowed dusky pink in the evening sun.

"We're in the middle of nowhere, Méli," he said. "Nobody gives a damn."

Méli's eyes had followed his arm. Now, she came to him, laid her head on his thigh and looked up into his eyes. He selected the best breadstick for her and stroked her head gently as she ate it.

"And I know interest rates are higher now. Much higher. Do they think I have my head up my backside out here? But they'll come down again. And, if they don't, it'll be because inflation stayed high, so I'll be able to charge more. It's not the end of the world, is it Méli?"

He hurled the empty beer can at the trash bucket and missed. It rolled out onto the sand and came to rest against a familiar pair of scuffed, brown sandals.

"You're talking to yourself again," said Dan, in English. "It's the first sign, you know."

"I was talking with Méli," Stefi corrected.

"Oh, dear. Talking to goats is the *second* sign. And I believe it's worse."

Stefi ruffled Méli's honey-brown head and stroked her ears.

"Don't listen to him," he said. "We take a different view, don't we?"

By way of confirmation, she exhaled vigorously, causing her lips to vibrate alarmingly.

"Any more of that beer?" said Dan.

"In the fridge. Bring another for me, please."

The younger man returned, handed one of the cans to Stefi and sat in the wicker chair.

"*Two* beers for you?"

"And a rakí," Stefi confessed.

"Self-medicating, huh? Shitty day?"

"You could say so. You could definitely say so."

"Tell Uncle Dan."

Stefi gave Méli a gentle slap on the rump and she loped off to climb a nearby rockpile. The sun was lower in the sky now, the heat not so fierce with September not far away. It was always their favourite time of day; work done, and a chance for a relaxed chat and a drink before dinner, to the gentle screeching of the cicadas. But the bank visit had disrupted Stefi's usual mood tonight. Dan could see that.

"Okay. First problem? It wasn't my regular guy, Manólis. He's *no longer with the bank* they tell me, which I guess means he's been *let go*."

"Canned, you mean? Not because of you."

"Because of me? No, Dan. Why would you think that? I don't know why. But everything I put into that relationship is now wasted. Kaput. And I liked Manóli; we spoke the same language. Instead, it's now some woman, Anna something or other. And she's the second problem. You know the type: immaculate make-up, high heels, black hair raked back in a tight bun. And wearing pink frames to her glasses for the human touch. Except it doesn't work. There's nothing human about the woman. I think she has a heart of steel."

"Oh, sweet Jesus."

"And now she's in charge, she must conduct a full review of our project."

"And this is the third problem?"

Stefi nodded.

"But the bank made a commitment to support us."

"*Manólis* did. Just words, Dan. And now he's history."

"Wow. We gotta have something in writing: a commitment, a loan agreement … something! Soon we'll be spending big money on land prep, wind turbines, more tree houses …"

"This is what I went there to get but now this woman's dragging her feet, asking about all the formal approvals."

"Which we don't have."

"Which we don't have, yet. And bleating about interest rates being higher than we have in the plans."

"Well, that's hardly *your* fault. More theirs, if anything."

"It's affecting the bank's attitude to risk, she said."

"Sounds like they're going flaky on us."

"They're what?"

"Like they're not so keen, now. Like, they want out."

"What? Well, I'm hoping it's not as bad as that, Dan, but it's not good either. That's for sure. They want me back in a few weeks when they've completed their review."

Dan watched as Méli stretched up into a carob tree to chew some leaves. *It sounded like they were at the bank's mercy now, which was insane. Surely others would be happy to invest in Stefi's plans? They could do some good for the world and make a shedload of money.*

"Couldn't your sister help?" he asked. "The hotel business is booming here, isn't it?"

"Not in Sfinári, it's not. Not yet. It's too far from everywhere else. And we need more than she could ever come up with."

Stefi crushed his beer can in his right hand and looked up at Dan.

"She thinks I'm crazy doing this, anyway."

"She does? Get her down here. Talk her through it. It's a *wonderful* plan, Stefi. And it will make money in the end; heaps of money. I'm sure of it. And it's *doing the right thing*, big time. Don't you remember when we first spoke about it? You were evangelical. How fantastic to be completely self-sufficient: to generate our power from sun, wind and water; manage our forest; harvest the winter rainfall; recycle the grey water; grow our own fruit and vegetables, flowers and herbs. Going back to nature. Living with nature, actually. Dependent on no one. And all that in the context of a luxury, tourist development we would design and build together using sustainable materials, in this remote and beautiful place between the mountains and the Libyan Sea. You lit a fire in my heart that day, Stefi, and it's still raging. So don't you dare go soft on me now. Don't lose the faith."

Stefi stared back at him for several seconds. Then Dan saw his eyes relax and the sparkle of fondness return. Stefi shook a cigarette from a rather squashed pack and lit it, shielding the flame from the wind.

"Okay, man, but forget about Evangelína," he croaked, through a cloud of blue smoke.

"If you say so. What about your buddy, the rich engineer?" Dan persisted.

"Giórgios? He knows everything we're doing, of course. He likes a lot of it, but he's not sure about some of the ideas. He doesn't buy into the whole ecology thing."

"How can he not? We won't have a planet if people like him don't. Doesn't he have kids?"

"He does. Grown up now, of course. Anyway, Giórgios is a clever guy. He'll tell us if he wants to invest."

"You could talk to him about it."

"I could, Dan, but I'm not going to. We're not begging yet. Let's see what the bank comes up with. I haven't quite given up on hard-hearted Anna."

"I think it was *Hannah*."

Dan was wearing that mischievous grin of his, Stefi noticed.

"What *are* you talking about, Daniel?"

"Hard-hearted Hannah, the vamp of Savannah, GA."

Stefi stared at him, big brown eyes widening. Was the American teasing him again?

"It's a jazz tune. From the roaring twenties," Dan explained.

"Man! You and your jazz."

Stefi stared out over the darkening sea in the general direction of Georgia, wondering at a conversation that could touch on a tune from a hundred years ago and ten thousand kilometres away, but that was Dan; over-educated and a touch obsessive but quite delightful, nevertheless.

"It's after seven," Stefi said. "Let's get some food organised, shall we? Is Teddy around?"

"He was checking on the cages. I'll go find him."

"It's our last night to be bad boys," Stefi said, with a wink.

"She's back tomorrow?"

"She is, at last. I hope Teddy hasn't forgotten. I need him to pick up groceries, too."

"We might need wine as well as beer."

"We might. Maybe some food, too."

Dan chuckled and Stefi slapped him on the back as they went inside.

CHAPTER 3
HÁRIS THE BELLWETHER

It was just short of two hours to Chaniá airport. Always. Not like the UK, Nick remembered, where it might take you an hour and a half or it might take five hours. And the girls were due at twenty-two forty, so he had plenty of time. The house was already in good shape. Sofía had given it one of her special cleans; the ones where she finished by mopping all the floors with the stuff that smelled of pine forests. The brand-new, single bed was waiting in the spare room, close to its partner. A little too close, perhaps, but the girls were good friends. He was sure they would cope, and the new air-conditioning unit would help. There were fresh sheets and soft pillows. There was even some scented shower gel, shampoo and conditioner in the bathroom and a fresh bag of muesli in the larder. They would have low expectations of him, being a man, so he must have exceeded them already, he reckoned.

A few minutes after three, the thermometer in his courtyard was nudging thirty-six. If he left now, he could spend two or three hours on his favourite beach, have some dinner at Delfíni taverna and still be in good time.

He had hired a white Suzuki Swift for them, so he left the Jeep behind. It was not well-suited to driving on the National Road anyway. But the Suzuki felt underpowered to Nick and did not live up to its name. It was easy enough to drive, though, and the air conditioning and sound systems worked well, so Nick was appeased. He drove through Plakiás to arrive at Soúda fifty minutes later, feeling fresher than when he left.

The beach was full, even at five pm, but the middle portion was not too bad. Nick grabbed the last remaining sun lounger and, spotting Háris in his usual place at the back of the beach, gave him a wave. Unlike some of these guys, Háris never rushed to collect the money. He would let you change in peace, have your first swim, and then wander over, singing or muttering to himself and chatting to his regulars on the way. Sometimes, he would not even bother to collect money, late in the day.

The water was warm. It was to be expected, at the end of August, but Nick preferred it cooler in many ways. It made for more vigorous swims and the kind of refreshed exhaustion that could justify a snooze under the parasol. In a few short weeks, the tourists would be gone, and, by mid-October, the air temperature would drop to the early twenties. He was looking forward to that.

After swimming steadily across the bay and back, with three or four pauses to roll onto his back, feel the afternoon sun on his face and just float, Nick retrieved his flip-flops and flapped his way up the shingle.

"Is good, no?" called Háris. "Not so much windy."

"It's fabulous, Hári. Water's a bit warm for me, though."

Háris approached and Nick dug into the beach bag for his wallet.

"Né, né. But for me is good. I don't like so much the cold. You on your own today?"

Háris was careful not to say *as usual*, Nick noticed, and he was grateful for it. He nodded.

"Give me three euros. Is okay."

"Are you sure? Didn't you put up your rates a few weeks back?"

Háris sat on the adjacent sun lounger, threw his long, fair hair over his shoulder and pushed his glasses back to the bridge of his nose. *He looked quite Nordic, for a Greek*, it struck Nick.

"I have to do this, Nick. The Dímos puts up the charges I must pay. Like crazy!"

"Inflation is back, Hári."

"I try not to charge too much but I must ask six euros for the set now."

"People will understand. Don't worry. And six euros is still a very fair deal. The money-grubbing bastards at Falásarna charge fifteen."

"What is money rubbing?"

"Money*grubbing*. Greedy."

"Ah yes, I know this. But they have many tourists there. Here, not so many."

"I thought things were picking up, Hári? I'm sure I read something about the numbers of tourists leaping back to pre-COVID levels."

"Yes, yes. But is not the same now. They come. Plenty people, plenty money. But they stay inside their hotels. *All the time.* Big places: pools, restaurants, bars, games for the kids. Much comfort, many, many things to do …"

Háris leaned forward and gripped Nick's still-wet forearm.

"Níko – they never come out of these places! They want to eat and drink and lie in the sun. Nothing else. And they pay big money for this. But they never see our beautiful Crete! And we never see their money. They don't come to Soúda to pay me for sunbeds, that's for sure."

"But the tourist money is still being earned *here in Crete*, isn't it?"

Háris snorted.

"You joke with me, my friend."

He leaned closer, looking sorrowful, and spoke in hushed tones:

"Is foreign money. All of it. Turkish, Russian, Mafia – who knows?"

"How the hell do they get the permissions they need, then?"

Háris tilted his head to one side, adopted a wide-eyed, hangdog expression and rubbed his middle finger several times against his thumb.

"Wha' you think, Nick?"

He stood, spat on the shingle, then began singing to himself as he turned and ambled towards a large, German couple who lowered their Kindles and smiled, like old friends. Nick chuckled to himself. Háris had been here as long as he could remember. He still looked like a hippy, though he was no longer a young man. He owned some olive trees in various places which kept him busy in the late autumn and sometimes he worked evenings in one of the Plakiás tavernas to make ends meet. But in the summer days, he was found here, where everyone loved him and looked forward to exchanging a few wry or amusing sentences with him for the very reasonable price of a set of two sun loungers and a parasol, with a little plastic table if you were lucky.

But Nick was both saddened and angered by what Háris had shared. His second swim was more vigorous as he vented his feelings on the water, carving his way through it like a bull shark. Calmed somewhat, he dried himself off and wandered over to the Delfíni taverna where the owner greeted him with his usual courtesy. Once again, he presented his list of freshly made, traditional specials only for Nick to order his favourite sardélla (panfried, fresh sardines) with the Delfínisaláta and a tétarto (a quarter litre) of the house white. Any more and he would doze off on the long drive to Chaniá airport and back.

CHAPTER 4
A CHANCE ENCOUNTER

As the eight thirty train slid and creaked away from Waverley, Fiona MacFarlane settled back in her front-facing window seat in the quiet carriage, surrounded by what she supposed were businesspeople, and brought out her tablet like everyone else. It would take four hours and eighteen minutes to get to King's Cross. She sat back in satisfaction and thought about what was to come.

She and Lauren had not had a proper girls' chat since before the finals, weeks ago, so there would be plenty to catch up on over a couple of gins. It would be fun. And then all the sunshine and swimming, the beaches, and the Greek boys, too. She checked the weather forecast for a place called Réthymno which looked nearby. It was stuck in a range from thirty-three to thirty-eight Celsius for the next ten days and every single day showed a bright yellow orb with no cloud, though it was windy on some days. There were warnings about the high temperatures and the risk of wildfires but the only report of a fire she could find referred to a place near Rodákino which was well to the west of where they were staying.

After half an hour, she made her way to the buffet car and bought herself peppermint tea, a ludicrously expensive banana and a flapjack. Then she skimmed through The Scotsman before switching to her cosy crime novel. She was fast asleep by the time they crossed the border into England.

*

They had arranged to meet at St Pancras at one pm. That way they could take a direct train and dodge the tube to Victoria altogether. Lauren had trundled through endless Central Line stations to Holborn and now she was rattling a couple of stops up the Piccadilly Line. She was cutting it fine. And she was irritated with herself. Why could she never get organised in good time? She texted Fi and said she might be five minutes late. But at King's Cross, she became confused and then panicky, which never helped. She had not realised King's Cross and St Pancras were separate stations and now she was having to haul her suitcase over the cobbly street between the two, which was not easy as the rubber had started falling off the stupid, plastic wheels and it was making a dreadful racket. She was fretting and cursing now. At St Pancras, she could not see any trains heading for Gatwick and her mind fogged up. Then her phone buzzed insistently. It was a text from Fi: *I'm below the clock. WTFRU?*

She ignored it and pulled up her ticket from the Trainline app instead. She saw it was from St Pancras *International*. She thought she remembered seeing signs for that but why would it be relevant? She was only chugging down to North Sussex, wasn't she? Nevertheless, she retraced her steps and found her way to a different part of the complex. Now fifteen or twenty minutes late, she was jogging, heart pumping, suitcase wheels shrieking in anguish when she spotted a tall, blonde girl waving both arms like a maniac, long before she noticed the giant clock, way above her head. *It must be Fi. Oh, thank God. It is Fi.* As she got close, she threw down her luggage and they hugged.

"How late am I?" Lauren said.

"We have four minutes, but it's okay, the platform's just here."

"Time for a coffee?"

"You've got to be joking, you total nutter."

"Perhaps we'll get one on the train, then."

"Aye. Mebbe."

*

"Was it the case?" Fi asked when they were settled into seats on the Gatwick train, facing each other across a table.

"Was *what* the case?"

"That made you late. Your *suit*case, I mean … It was making a hell of a racket."

"It's knackered. Could be its swansong, I think. But no, I can't really blame it. I was just being my stupid, last-minute self."

17

"I *was* getting a teeny bit worried."

"Sorry, Fi. I'll treat you to a coffee when the little man with the trolley appears."

"Does he exist on this sort of train?"

"Oh, I don't know. If not, I'll buy you a drink at the airport."

"Now you're talking. Start as we mean to go on."

"Right."

Fi was a bit of a good-time gal, Lauren remembered. She had drunk Lauren under the table more than once, but always managed to look so fresh and innocent the next day, damn her.

*

By the time they had made their way to the North Terminal, on the interminable moving walkways and with Lauren's case screeching all the way, it was almost two thirty-five, still over two hours to take-off.

They lined up behind a small, red-haired, young woman with a bright blue rucksack and a large, cardboard box.

"I hope we'll not be standing here for two hours," said Fi.

"It'll start tae move any minute," said the redhead, over her shoulder. "They've people on the desks just now so we're good tae go. Did you come down this morning?" she added.

"From Edinburgh, aye," said Fi.

"You must be well knackered."

"What about you?"

"I came down yesterday. From Aberdeen. Had to get *this* organised." She kicked the box. "I'm Rosalind by the way – they call me Roz."

"Hi. I'm Fi and this is Lauren."

The girls nodded and smiled shyly.

"Off on holiday?"

"Yes. Lauren's dad lives in Crete. We're going to stay with him for a couple of days, then travel around the western part of the island."

"First time?"

"Yes. But not for you, I'm guessing."

"Ach, I don't know it well. I spent April and May working near Elafonísi, in the south-west. Then I was training at Chaniá, for a spell. They tell me the south and west are the best bits, but I've seen nothing else."

"Oh, I've read about Elafonísi," said Lauren. "It looks beautiful."

"Aye, so it is when it's not packed with tourists."

"Is the sand really pink?"

"I believe it is, though I didna notice, to be honest. It's no' as pink as it was a while ago, but the water's gorgeous, like a turquoise lagoon. There's an island, too. You can wade out to it, or swim, of course."

"Sounds fabulous."

"It's very popular."

As they talked, they shuffled forward, from time to time. Lauren had been studying Roz and decided she was interesting but a bit rough. She saw sea-themed tattoos on her arms and neck and there were metal rings through her right eyebrow, her left nostril and several through each ear, in a series of loops. Lauren assumed she was trying to make a statement about something or other. She was short but seemed pugnacious and feisty, and she spoke with a grown-up confidence which made her seem older than her years. The two Scottish girls might look like chalk and cheese, but they seemed to be getting on just fine, Lauren noticed, feeling a flicker of self-doubt.

"So, what sort of work are you doing, in Crete," she asked.

"Four of us are working on this eco-project at a place called Tamarisk Bay. I'll be there for another couple of months, at least."

"Doing what, though?"

"I'm a volunteer, so whatever I'm asked to do, to be honest. Every day's different but mostly I look after the turtles and the goats and help with the guests: clean up, make beds, buy groceries."

"Sounds rather rustic," said Fi.

"Turtles? Why do you keep turtles?" asked Lauren.

Before Roz could answer, the crowd surged forward, and they found themselves close to the self-check-in desk. It was time to dig out passports and pull up QR codes on their phones.

"I might need a hand with this," said Roz, indicating the box, "just to lift it onto the rollers."

"Sure," said Fi. "Gosh, it's quite heavy. How did you manage?"

"With difficulty, and a few nice men along the way."

"What on earth is it?"

"It's a pump for the water pressure, made in Germany. You can't get this type in Greece. They asked me to pick it up."

"For the project?"

"Aye."

"Is that why you came back, then?"

"Er, no. I had to go back anyway. Then I got lumbered wi' this."

Her slight hesitation and the way she avoided eye contact told Fi not to ask any more. A woman from the airline checked some details with her computer screen and then slapped stickers onto the cardboard box.

"There'll be customs duty to pay, in Greece. Did you know?" she asked.

"Aye. A hundred and six euros they told me. Don't you just love Brexit?"

Roz checked in her rucksack and then Fi and Lauren checked in their suitcases too, leaving them all with just light bags.

"Anyone else up for a snack and a glass of something?" said Lauren.

"Absolutely," said Fi.

"Just try and stop me," said Roz.

The three girls spent most of the next six hours together. In the bar, then more queueing at the gate, and then again, on the plane, after Roz contrived to switch seats with the rather weird-looking, older man at the end of the row, to everyone's relief.

Roz was working with three guys, she said. Two were in their twenties, one very bright American called Dan and one rather fanciable Greek called Teddy. The other guy was the owner, Stefanos, a tubby Greek in his forties and his pet goat, Méli.

"He has a pet goat?"

"She's a goat kid, really, just a few months old. Her mamma died, so Stefi adopted her. Méli means honey in Greek," she explained. "Her hide is honey-coloured, but also she *is* a total honey; I've never come across such a sweet-natured creature."

Her owner was sweet, too, but a wee bit haphazard. He might be a wayward genius though, she conceded. Everyone called him Stefi. There were sometimes a few paying guests, but Stefi had big plans to develop the site in an eco-friendly way. There was a nice beach, mostly shingle, but some sand, too.

"Right now, the sandy bit's reserved for the turtles, though," she said.

"You were going to tell us why you keep them," said Lauren.

"Was I? Well, we dinna *keep* them, as such. We – mostly I – look after the hatchlings. They're caretta caretta; loggerhead turtles. It's a protected species. There are three main places they use, in Crete. We're not one of *them*, but we still have quite a few."

"Use for what? Do they live there?"

"No, Lauren. Turtles are aquatic creatures; they live in the sea. But, after they reach maturity, the females come ashore every two to four years to lay their eggs in the sand."

"Oh, wow!"

"And they must return to the place where they were born to do this. It's like, in their DNA."

"So, your beach has been home to generations of these guys?"

"Aye, we believe so. And we want to keep it going, protect them."

"How sweet is that?" said Fi.

Sweet was not the word Roz would have chosen. To her, it was a pragmatic and unsentimental process; scientific methods to correct an imbalance caused by the abuse of nature.

"We have no choice, anyway. It's the law now, in Greece," she added.

"Do you have pictures, Roz?" asked Lauren.

"Ah, no. Not with me. Sorry. But listen, if you guys are coming out west, why not come and see us for a couple of days? Stefi won't mind. He'll put you to work on something, given half a chance. If you're visiting Elafonísi anyway, just let me know when and I'll drop around with the boat."

"Would we see the turtles?"

"Probably not, in real time, but we can show you stuff. We use infrared to video the site each night. This is partly for security, but also, we need to be sure where the eggs are. The turtles cover them over with sand, you see. The mums come in at night, bury the eggs and leave, and the babies hatch six to eight weeks later. That's a few weeks away yet. But you'd get to see the set up and the eggs in their protective cages and we can tell you all about it. It's fascinating. And I could show you the things we're working on elsewhere on the site. It's cutting-edge eco-technology. Interesting stuff."

"So, the mothers never get to see their babies?"

"They don't, no."

"That's sad, and a bit weird."

"They're different from us, Lauren. For a start, each mum lays between twenty and two hundred eggs. I think the average number of hatchlings per nest is about sixty."

"Oh, my God! So how come we aren't overrun with the things rather than having to protect them?"

"Because only one in a thousand hatchlings makes it to adulthood. Many don't even make it from the egg to the water."

"That's terrible."

"It's cruel nature at work; the survival of the fittest. And we humans haven't helped, of course, but we're doing what we can to correct the situation."

"I'd love to know more about what you're doing," she said.

"Then come and see."

Fi was stifling a yawn, Lauren noticed.

"You said you were nearby. Couldn't we just walk around from Elafonísi?" she asked.

"It's possible, yes, but not many try. It's quite tough. Big rocks to clamber over in the heat, scratchy juniper trees. A boat is much easier."

It was settled. They exchanged contact details. As soon as Fi and Lauren had fixed their travel plans, they would let Roz know if Elafonísi was on the agenda and, if so, they'd try to spend a couple of nights at the beach site.

"You can try out one of the tree houses," Roz added. "We're testing different sorts of eco-friendly accommodation right now."

"Right," said Fi, feigning enthusiasm but wondering if they would be testing its ability to remain in the tree. She was not so sure about this diversion, in any event. It all sounded a bit basic. She wanted to be pampered and lie on a beach. She was not clear how keen Lauren was. Maybe she was just humouring Roz …

Almost four hours is quite a long flight. Fi's long legs became twitchy soon after the halfway point. She started thinking about deep-veined thrombosis at the three-hour mark and asked Roz to move so she could escape to the aisle for a good stretch and a stroll to the loo and back. Lauren was more relaxed. She had been staring out of the window at The Alps and then the Croatian coastline with all its beautiful islands as it was going dark. Now, they were approaching Athens and she saw pretty, glowing lights dotting the countryside. *Were they lights or flares? Was some festival going on?* she wondered, sleepily.

*

The girls split up at the baggage carousel. Fi and Lauren's suitcases came through surprisingly quickly.

"You two go on," said Roz. "I have to sort out the duty on the pump, anyway."

They each hugged her briefly.

"Text me if you decide to come. Give me a wee bit of notice so I can get bedding and groceries organised."

"We will," said Lauren. "And you take care. Watch yourself with the young Greek guy!"

"Ach, he's no interested in me. Away with you!"

The girls wheeled their suitcases out of the baggage hall to where Lauren's father Nick was waiting. He was holding bottles of water and what looked like slices of pie.

*

The rucksack finally arrived but not the box. Roz had to hunt around the baggage hall and found it stacked to one side with a selection of other non-standard items. A customs official appeared as soon as she

23

laid a hand on it and told her to follow him.

In the side office, he asked to see her identity card.

"I dinna have one," she said.

"Your passport, then," he said.

He checked the document against something on his computer screen, just like they had at Passport Control.

"You will sign here, here and here and you must pay one hundred and twenty-one euros."

"They told me a hundred and six."

"There is a handling fee also."

She had the money, as it happened, and Stefi would reimburse her. It took several more minutes for the official to complete the paperwork and print out a receipt, densely worded in Greek. She saw several numbers including the ones she was looking for and assumed the others related to tax or duty calculations. *Hey ho.*

The official still seemed to be engrossed in something.

"Excuse me. Signómi. Is that it? Are we done?"

"Yes, yes. You may take your box."

"I might need your help."

"You have car?"

"Someone is meeting me."

The man came out of his office and carried the box to the Arrivals exit where Theódoros was waiting.

"Ah! Signómi. Sas efcharistoúme pára polí," he said, to thank the customs man as he set down the box. The man acknowledged Teddy with a respectful tilt of the head, then gave Roz the smallest of naughty smiles, like his help was their secret and he was not really allowed to do this.

"That was sweet of him," she said after the customs man left. "So, how are you doing, Teddy?"

He said he was okay, and they left the terminal building, the warmth of the night enveloping them. Roz already felt short of breath and thirsty.

"It's quite a weight, isn't it?" she said, as she saw him struggling with the pump box.

"Yes, but the car is not so far."

"Is that smoke I can smell, Teddy?"

"There have been many wildfires. Big news here. I thought you would know of this."

"I've not been following the news."

"No. Of course, not."

She waited while he folded down the back seats of the hatchback and hoisted the box inside, placing her rucksack next to it. When they were all set, he turned to her:

"How did it go, Roz? We've all been thinking about you."

"Ach … I was too late, Teddy. He was already gone."

"I am sorry for this."

"Aye. It's sad we didna have a last shot at putting the world tae rights. But, for Dad, a merciful release. No question."

"He was ill long time, no?"

"Twelve years, since I was nine. It's not been easy."

"And your mother. She is okay?"

"She's sad, of course. He was only fifty-one, you know. But she's also relieved it's over and now she's feeling guilty about that. I told her it was crazy to feel guilty, and that she was entitled to feel relief. We're all relieved – even Dad, I bet – but she's strugglin' wi' that. I'll get her out here for a spell when all the probate shit has been sorted out."

Teddy did not fully understand what she meant but decided to leave it. They were driving now, away from the airport, to join the National Road and head west, past Chaniá.

"You come here quite a bit, don't you, Teddy?"

"To Chaniá? Every two or three weeks, I guess."

"Any more trips planned?"

"I think Stefi will come back to see the bank before too long."

"I might hitch a ride, if that's okay."

"Time for some shopping?"

"I'm not really a shopping kind of gal, Teddy, to be honest."

"Something else, then."

"Aye. Just a friend to catch up with."

She caught sight of a blaze on a hillside, a few kilometres inland.

"*We've* not had any fires, have we?" she asked.

"No. But the forest is dry. And it has been hot. Thirty-five today but it is worse when the wind blows from the south. Where I come from, they call this the *Kadhafi.*"

Roz knew something of this fierce, drying wind from the south. It was like a hairdryer, full on in your face, and tended to blow for several days, pushing the temperature into the low forties and making people and animals fractious and, eventually, quite mad.

"Let's hope the generator keeps going, then," she said.

They exchanged knowing looks. The diesel generator had been troublesome, on occasion, and without it, the air conditioning might struggle, though there should be enough solar energy to keep the lights and the fridges going, at least for a while.

"Do we have any guests, right now?"

"Nothing for a while."

"Okay. Mebbe that's for the best. And how is everyone?"

"Dan's fine. He's been busy, building the second tree house. Stefi, I don't know. He seems distracted. He's not saying much, keeping to himself."

"Well, that doesna sound like him!"

They exchanged fleeting grins.

"I know," said Teddy. "Something worries him, I think."

After half an hour on the National Road, they turned off and headed south from the port at Kíssamos. The road became narrower, meandering and unlit. Roz was feeling tired now.

"How long, Teddy?"

"Not long. Twenty more minutes to Sfinári, then thirty-five or so in the RIB. Less than an hour. Then we party!"

"You what?"

"The boys want to welcome you back. Dan has cooked Stifádo. Stefi has lined up some of the Mandilári."

"It's almost midnight, Teddy!"

"The night is young; I think you say."

She groaned out loud but, in the dark, she was smiling, and rather touched.

CHAPTER 5

THE FORESTRY CLAIM

The next morning, over breakfast, the girls were chatting through their plans with Nick.

"We thought we'd do a round trip," said Lauren. "We could start at Kíssamos. It might not be a very exciting town, but you can get boat trips from there to Gramvoúsa and Bálos. Then we might do a couple of days on the beach at Falásarna."

"Those places will all be busy," said Nick, "but they're worth seeing."

"Right. And then we're thinking Sfinári, which looks quieter."

"Where's that?"

"Yay! We found a place you don't know! It's right in the middle of the west coast."

Nick cleared part of the table and spread out one of his many paper maps. He ran his finger down the far, western end of the island.

"Okay, I see it."

"From there we can get up to Falásarna or down to Elafonísi and there are a couple of local beaches that might be worth a look."

"Hmmm. You want to make sure all those roads are tarmacked. I wouldn't be surprised if some of them are a bit hairy; it's quite mountainous."

"Oh, Dad! I do know how to drive, and pretty much *everything* is tarmacked, these days."

"Yeah, yeah. But you don't want to find yourselves on a precipitous dirt track, believe me. And I won't always be able to come to the rescue."

"We'll be fine. And Fi will share the driving with me."

This did not fill Nick with confidence. She was a nice girl, but she was a bit of an airhead and could well panic in a crisis, he figured.

"Oh, that's all right then," he said, winking at Fi.

*

It was twenty to one in the morning by the time the RIB was bumping up against the little jetty at Tamarisk Bay.

"Hey, guys!" called Dan, blinding them with a huge torch, "Welcome back, Roz!"

"Teddy says you've been cooking," she said.

"Kounéli," he said. "Rabbit stifádo with fried potatoes and spinach."

"Yum! Thank you so much."

"And Stefi has opened two of his best bottles."

"Aye. The Mandilári. I heard."

They had secured the boat. Now Dan helped Roz onto the jetty and Teddy passed her the rucksack. Then he hoisted the box up and passed it to Dan.

"This is my pump? Brilliant. But it's heavy! How did you manage, Roz?"

"I didna, to be honest. But it's amazing how people help when it's obvious you can't cope."

"Oh, dear. We should never have asked you. Sorry."

"It had to be done. Dinna fash yersel."

"What's that?"

"Don't worry."

He grinned at her and gently punched her arm.

"Glad to have you back."

"I bet you were partying every night."

"This is *why* I'm glad! No, seriously, Stefi's not been in a party mood, of late. Teddy and I have been staying out of his way."

"What's happened?"

"He had a tough meeting with the bank, yesterday morning, and now something else has happened. I'll let him tell you, over dinner."

If Dan had not spoken, she would not have known anything was amiss. Stefi seemed his usual self if, perhaps, a little quieter. But Roz was curious now. When they sat back with full stomachs and were well into the second bottle, she said:

"Dan said you had a bit of a rough ride while I was away, Stefi."

He looked up and threw Dan a sharp glance before replying.

"Well, Roz. I had a shitty meeting at the bank. My guy's been fired and now a new woman wants to review our project. They asked me some difficult questions and I screwed up. And then this morning – and *you* don't know this, Teddy – my lawyer called to say the Forestry Department has made a claim on my juniper forest!"

"What do you mean, *made a claim*?"

"It means they want to own it, so they can look after it and protect it, for the nation."

"But *you* own it, don't you? And *you* look after it."

"This will be my argument, of course."

"Then why even bother – and why now?"

"I don't know, Roz. But the bank woman was going on about not having all the clearances I needed – and now this. It's almost like she knew it was coming."

"That's a bit weird."

"It's a pain, Steff, but it's not a disaster," said Dan. "If your lawyer was right, you'll win the case and the problem will go away – or they'll withdraw at some point when they realise they're wasting their time."

"I'd like to believe it, Dan, but even if I win or they withdraw, the *delay* could be a huge problem – will the bank come up with the money we need with this hanging over us? It could be months, years even. We could die waiting."

There was a pause while it sank in, around the table. Teddy topped up the glasses with the last of the wine.

"But wait a minute, Stefi. Who cares *who* owns the frigging forest?" said Dan. "Any plans they have won't change it; they'll *preserve* it. Whoever wins the case will make no difference. The forest will stay the same. Why would the bank give a damn?"

"Maybe it affects the value of the site? And, if they win, these guys don't pay compensation."

"But there's nothing *to* compensate! It's a tangled mess of scrappy, scratchy trees. Thing is, if the Forestry Department owns it, *they'll* have to look after it, not you. It's actually *good* news!"

Stefi laid his hand on Dan's arm.

"You're very sweet, Dan, but I doubt it's that simple."

"I don't know," said Teddy, who had listened intently without speaking. "I agree with Dan. It's like a technicality. It doesn't change what you're trying to do here at all. Worst case, you lose ownership of something which has little or no practical value and you don't have to worry about maintaining it anymore."

Stefi seemed to brighten a little now both of them seemed positive.

"It's odd though, isn't it? Why has this come up now? It's hard to imagine your wee juniper forest, stuck way out here, could be high on the list of priorities for the forestry folk."

"Only time will give us the answer, Roz," said Dan. "Talking of which, it's almost two so I, for one, am going to hit the sack."

There was general assent and Stefi started to clear the plates.

"Great meal, Dan. Thank you," said Roz.

"You are very welcome."

"It's better when there's a woman here," said Teddy. "We don't fight so much."

"I have my uses, then," chuckled Roz and said goodnight.

*

By the time they made it to the beach, after lunch, the wind was getting up again. The taverna owned some sturdy parasols, though, so they decided to hunker down and make the best of it. Nick was hoping for a calmer spell so he could get his swim in. The girls wanted to be left in peace with their phones and not pebble-dashed by flying sand and grit. By four, their optimism was no longer tenable. Most people had already left, and out on the windblown water, they could see mini waterspouts, spiralling into the air. White surf was crashing against the beach shingle, then sucking it back under the water.

"Come on, Dad. You're not going to swim in this," said Lauren and Nick made a rueful face.

They stood and packed their beach kit but not before one of Fi's flip-flops was blown out to sea. To her horror, the gust hurled it perhaps fifteen metres into the waves. It would never be seen again. Even

Nick was not going to drown himself for a flip-flop.

"It's on its way to Libya now," he said. "Never mind."

As they made their way back to the Jeep, he said:

"Don't worry, Fi, you'll pick up some more easily enough."

"But what will I do with poor Flip, now?" she wailed.

"What is she talking about?" Nick asked Lauren.

"She calls them Flip and Flop," said Lauren.

She felt her father's eyes staring at her. He blinked once and raised his left eyebrow.

"Don't ask," she said.

*

Back at the house, the girls made gin and tonics. Poor Flop's tragic demise and the predicament now facing Flip were soon forgotten, Nick observed.

Meanwhile, he was checking the Internet for weather forecasts and wildfires. The girls had decided to set off the next day and he wanted to be sure they would be safe. The fire that had been raging east of Rodákino seemed to be under control now, but he found satellite images of several more fires along the south coast; the return of the hot wind from the south was not helping.

"You should be okay in the north-west," he told the girls. "But watch yourselves when you head south. Check the online reports and stick to the main roads. If you decide to drop in on Roz, ring ahead, make sure everything's all right down there."

The next morning, after they had left, he decided to give Leo Christodoulákis a call. It would make him feel better if the second in charge of policing the Chaniá Prefecture knew about the girls' trip. Just in case. And anyway, it was way past time to check up on his friend.

"Nick Fisher, is it really you?" Leo asked. "I thought you were dead."

"It *has* been a while. Sorry. I've been meaning to call. How the hell are you, Leo?"

"I think the correct English phrase is *on the mend*."

"Still? I thought you'd be a hundred per cent by now."

31

"So did I, Nick, but there were complications. First, the wound became infected, so they had to keep me in hospital, then there was some internal bleeding after the second operation, and it all swelled up. Horrible."

"Oh, dear. I'd have brought grapes if I'd known."

"They would have helped, I'm sure."

"You're not *still* in hospital."

"No, I'm home now and working some of the time."

"Anything interesting happening?"

"Like what?"

"Rape, pillage, murder – the usual stuff."

"I don't know what is *pillage*, but yes, we do have a murder, I am sorry to say."

"And you didn't call me?"

"This one's just local, Nick. Seems straightforward; a crime of passion by the smell of it. We're looking for the boyfriend."

"How recent was this, then?"

"Now you're embarrassing me. The body was discovered two months ago."

"And you haven't found the guy?"

Leo's silence confirmed it.

"We don't know who we're looking for, Nick. No ID yet. Good-looking, long-haired lad with a motorbike. We thought he'd be local, like her, but we haven't found him."

"Embarrassing, indeed. How was she killed?"

"Strangled, we think. No murder weapon. She had been dead four or five days, so putrefaction had begun. Found by a dog walker. All this is confidential, Nick."

"That goes without saying, my friend. Sounds like you've had a bit of a rough time, landing a murder when you're still in recovery."

"Thani's been standing in for me, here and there. He's a good man, as you know."

"So, he's *Acting Lieutenant*, so to speak?"

"Something like that. The captain wants him to prove himself as if he hasn't done it a thousand times already."

"Sounds like he'd better find this guy, then."

"Thaní's not assigned to this particular case."

"Who, then?"

"Anna Zerbáki, my other sergeant. Did you meet her?"

"I think you've mentioned her."

"Anna's very capable."

"And you'll be fit and back to full-time soon, surely?"

"I hope so, Nick, but they want me to be the new captain at Réthymno, when I'm better. Poor Chrístos died six weeks ago."

"Ah. And you want the job?"

"Not much. But you can't say no, Nick. Not really. We're like the military. I will be ordered to take up the position and I will follow my orders."

"Or be shot?"

"Once was enough for *that*, thank you."

"You'll be Náni's boss again."

"Her boss's boss, strictly speaking. Yes. Like old times. It'll be okay, I guess."

"And your wife?"

"I haven't told her yet. It's not official, Nick. You will keep it to yourself, please."

"Will she be okay, making the move?"

"She won't move. She loves Chaniá. We both do. I might commute, or I could find myself a small apartment in Réthymno and stay there some of the time."

"Hmmm. Don't go risking your marriage for the job, Leo."

"And *you* are the man to counsel me on this, Nick Fisher?"

To his surprise, Nick was emotionally winded by that, but he managed to play along with the banter.

"Oooph! A low blow, Leo. But you have a point, I guess."

"My marriage is solid, Nick. We clung to the wreckage together, remember?"

Nick took this as a reference to their daughter's untimely death and hurried on.

"I'm very glad to hear it, old friend. Now, not only was I guilty of denying you the grapes you so richly deserved, but now I must ask you a personal favour."

"Ah! *Finally*, we come to the reason for your call."

It was so true; Nick could only laugh and apologise.

"I forgot you were the ace detective," he said.

Nevertheless, Leo allowed him to explain about the girls' trip and Nick promised to send him an itinerary, as far as it went.

"I just wanted the police to know," he said, "in case anything blows up in those places around those times. It makes me feel better, anyway. All those fires have me worried."

"I understand, Nick. They need to be careful. We'll try to be a good uncle for you, keep an eye on them, where we can. I'll put the word out. I think we owe you a favour or two, after all."

CHAPTER 6
DEAD IN HER TRACKS

The wind was less fierce the next morning and the sun was already hot. Roz put on her straw hat and started walking across the shingle beach. At the far end, almost five hundred metres away, was a more sheltered, sandy stretch, just beyond a jumble of rocks. It was where the turtles came in. Teddy had told her there were four new nests, making seventeen in total. That should be about it, as they were nearing the end of the laying season. The first hatchlings would appear in two to three weeks.

Roz knew Teddy had worked with ARCHELON, the Greek turtle charity, on much bigger sites on the island of Zákynthos. She had completed her technical training now, thanks to Eric. Now she was keen to learn the practical aspects from Teddy before he moved on.

As she came closer, she could see the new cages with the coloured cards and the numbers written in Teddy's Greek hand. All the number ones had long tails, preceding the downstroke. Everything looked neat and organised. She made her way to the oldest nests to check for any hatching activity though she knew it was unlikely, this early. As she crouched down, something caught the corner of her eye. Towards the water. A new rock where no rock should be. It was about a metre long, and well-rounded. She stood and stared for a moment and then gave an anguished gasp. She ran towards the water, shrieking:

"Oh, no. *Please* no. Ach, no, no, no!"

The turtle was about eight metres from the sea and facing inland. It looked like a tractor had emerged from the water by the tracks stretching behind her. Roz realised it was the turtle's trail as it had hauled itself out of the sea, using its flippers. She could see it was a mature female, perhaps forty to fifty years old and probably still carrying its eggs. And she could see it was dead.

"Ach, you poor, brave girl," she said. "Whatever happened to you?"

"What's up, Roz?" called Teddy, who was just coming around the rocks. She did not respond and then he saw: there were tears in her eyes, and they had taken on a pleading, vulnerable look he had not seen before.

"Is she dead?" he said.

She nodded.

"Let me see," he said, and she stood and backed away a little. Teddy crouched down and went straight to the turtle's head and prised open its jaws. He tugged gently on something, then more firmly and it came out a little way. It looked like a blue, plastic bag. She saw him stroking the turtle's head, though he knew it was dead.

"She choked, poor thing. I've seen this many times, and it makes me crazy. She sees this bag in the water, and she thinks it's a jellyfish."

"Just an ordinary, plastic bag someone let blow into the sea?"

"They get tangled up. Not just with bags, but also with pieces of plastic, floating in the oceans. It makes me so ashamed, Roz."

They were sitting cross-legged in the sand now, next to the dead turtle. Roz was stroking its head.

"There was an Australian study not long ago," he went on. "Over half the turtles had ingested plastic – and ninety per cent of the young ones."

"That's terrible. Why so much more with the young ones, I wonder?"

"Because it's getting worse, Roz. Turtles spend the first ten years of their lives out in the open sea, being carried along by ocean currents. After that, they tend to hug the coast more. The ocean currents carry all our shit along with them. But now there's massively more plastic waste out there than thirty or forty years ago when this old girl was a youngster."

"But *she* managed to find plastic even in the coastal waters. Maybe in our little bay, Teddy?"

"Some tourist's food bag, I guess."

Roz stared out over the sea, the sun making her red curls look almost golden.

"These guys have been around for a hundred million years," she said, "but it's taken us no time to screw up their lives for them, has it, Teddy?"

She turned to him and found him smiling at her sadly.

"Come on," he said. "She'll begin to smell bad soon. We'd better get the others. It'll take all of us to get her buried. She'll weigh something like a hundred and twenty kilos."

"What about the eggs, Teddy? Can't we save her eggs?"

"I doubt it."

"Why not? If we do what she would have done, bury them in a nice warm hole in the sand and then cover them over? She got so close, Teddy. She tried so hard."

"I don't know how long they can survive after the mother dies, but I could put in a call to ARCHELON, talk it through."

"Let's do it," she said and squeezed his arm.

*

The problem of what to do with the turtle's body occupied them for several minutes.

"Burying it will be hard work," Dan pointed out. "It wouldn't be so bad, here in the sand, but is that a good idea? We don't want to be attracting predators to the area where the eggs are buried. And anywhere else is going to be very tough digging. You know what it's like."

Roz did indeed know. She remembered admiring the rich, red earth and planning to dig some up for her potted plants, then discovering it was as hard as concrete.

"We could take it out to sea," said Teddy. "It would be the natural thing to do, wouldn't it? A sea burial for an aquatic creature."

"But you've got to get the body in and out of the boat. We'd all have to go, and it could take an hour. That's a lot of time lost, guys," said Stefi. "I say we give her a funeral pyre."

"Burn her?" said Roz.

"Why not? It's quick and it's clean. We'll bury what's left."

"What about the fire risk, Stefi?" said Dan.

"We must take care, of course, but I think we're far enough from the forest here. I'll get a little petrol to start things off. Do you want to gather some brush, Dan? And, if you two want to try and save the eggs, you need to do it now."

Teddy and Roz looked at each other. First, they needed to dig a hole in the sand. They looked around the area.

"It's getting a bit crowded, isn't it?" said Roz.

"I think we could squeeze them in over here," said Teddy. He was at the back of the nest collection and to one side, behind a boulder. "Happy with that?"

"It's separate from the others."

"They won't care. It's protected by the boulder and there's a clear run to the water for the hatchlings. I think it's fine."

She acquiesced.

"Now go and measure her rear flippers. We need to dig a hole that depth, ready for the eggs."

Roz thought he was being overly precise but did as she was told.

"Just under two hands," she said when she returned, splaying her fingers.

"Okay. Then that's as deep as she could go from the pit."

"How do you mean, Teddy?"

"They start by digging themselves into a shallow pit, then they dig down with their *rear* flippers to make a hole for the eggs. Then they get laying, dropping the eggs into the hole."

"Don't the eggs break?"

"No. They're like soft ping-pong balls in a thick mucus at this stage. They don't break."

"So, what do we need to do?"

"I reckon if we dig a hole about three of your hands deep, say half a metre, with room enough for up to one hundred and twenty ping pong balls, we should be okay."

Teddy went off to get some digging tools and Dan strolled over.

"This gonna work?" he asked Roz.

"ARCHELON says there's a chance, according to Teddy. If we can create the same conditions the mother would have created for them. We won't know for several weeks, of course."

"Who's playing surgeon?"

"Teddy. He thinks he knows what to do."

"Let's hope so."

Teddy returned with a trowel and a small spade accompanied by Stefi who was carrying a red, plastic petrol container. Teddy removed his shirt and began to dig a hole in the sand near the boulder. He started with the spade, then switched to the trowel. After about three minutes, he stood back and admired his handiwork.

"I think it looks about right," he said, contemplating the hole, which was about thirty centimetres square and tapering, as it went deeper.

All four of them gathered around the turtle then. Each took a flipper and a grip on the edge of her shell, and they turned her over. Teddy washed around part of her underside to the lower right and then took a large penknife from his pocket and extended the blade.

"May I borrow your lighter, Stefi?" he said.

Stefi passed it over without comment and Teddy flicked the mechanism and walked the flame up and down the blade.

"Why are you bothering? She's dead, isn't she?" asked Dan.

"The hatchlings are not, I'm hoping. I don't want to infect them."

Roz could see Teddy was nervous. He asked the others to move back a little, then took a moment to steady his hand. Then she saw him cautiously inserting the knife into the lower right part of the turtle's underbody, then prising back the tough, outer skin with infinite gentleness.

"I'm looking for the oviduct," he said. "It's around here somewhere."

*

It took Teddy about forty minutes of delicate and messy work to release the clutch of eggs from the dead turtle's oviduct and drop them into a plastic bucket. Three were damaged and oozed their yellow contents out onto the sand, but the remainder made it. He and Roz then counted them as they let them fall into the prepared hole in the sand.

"I make it a hundred and four. A lot of hatchlings, if we're lucky," said Roz.

"They won't all be fertilised. But we might get fifty to seventy if we get any at all."

ALEX DUNLEVY

"At least we're giving them a chance," she said.

"Now, Roz, can I leave you to fill this over with sand, like mamma? I'd better give the guys a hand."

Teddy had seen Stefi and Dan trying to drag the heavy turtle carcass over to the shingle part of the beach, where Dan had prepared a funeral pyre of detritus from the forest floor.

"Why over there?" asked Teddy.

"I figured it would make less of a mess if we did it on the shingle," said Dan. "And I've set up a couple of buckets of water in case the fire starts throwing off sparks."

Dan took the rear flippers while the others each took one of the larger, front flippers and they hauled her around the rocks and seven or eight metres beyond, to where the little stack waited on the shingle. Stefi poured on a small amount of petrol, and they laid the turtle's body, face down onto the pile. They saw Roz scrunching towards them and waited a moment.

"Should we say a few words?" asked Dan, half-joking.

"I think we should," said Roz. "Nothing religious, obviously. But, er, well, I'd like to thank her for her bravery in making it back to her home beach and delivering the eggs, despite everything. It can't have been easy. And I promise her we'll do everything we can to help them hatch."

"And I'd like to apologise on behalf of all human beings for causing her death," said Teddy. "There's not much I can do about the rest of the planet, but I'm going to make certain there's no plastic in our bay. Ever."

This prompted a ripple of applause from the other three and then Stefi knelt and took out his lighter. Roz stroked the turtle's head one last time, saying "Well done, old girl. You rest now."

When she stepped back, Stefi flicked the lighter. There was a whoomph and the flames caught with a crackle that grew to a soft roar. Dan lifted a bucket of water in readiness, but the few sparks were flying no further than the end of the beach. The smell of roasting turtle was not unpleasant, and he wondered, for a fleeting moment, if they should have feasted on the creature. Then he looked at Roz and decided to keep his thoughts to himself.

CHAPTER 7
WILDFIRE WORRIES

Nick was inside the kafenío at Saktoúria, enjoying an Alfa beer with a slice of Xará's spanakópita. Lately, he had observed her emerging from the teenage rebellion years. She was becoming rather useful now and cooked well. She might still be a little in love with him, but now a couple of lads had started hanging around, to Nick's considerable relief; a polite but awkward, overweight boy who was besotted with her, and a skinny one with acne and a motorbike who pretended not to care. *Heartbreak was just around the corner*, Nick thought.

"Eínai téleia, Xará," he called. "Polí nóstimo."

She threw him her heart-melting smile and almost collided with her father, who was carrying a loaded tray to a table of Greek tourists from the mainland. She made a *big oops* face at Nick as she disappeared into the kitchen.

The television was on, as always, inside, where Nick was sheltering from the hot wind blasting red dust over the village. His Greek was not yet good enough to understand the details of the news, but he could see the scenes of devastation well enough. He saw the exhausted firefighters with their blackened faces, the flames leaping across the firebreaks, and the interviewees with bewildered, tearful faces. When Kostí poured himself a coffee and sat heavily beside him, wheezing and lighting another cigarette as if that would cure it, Nick gestured at the television:

"Whereabouts is all this happening, Kostí. Is it The Peloponnese?"

"Óchi, Níko. No Pelopónnisos. Eínai Kríti."

"Whereabouts?"

"The south, the west. From Rodákino to Omalós. Many, many fire."

"What about Elafonísi? My daughter is near there."

"No Elafonísi. Paleóchora, Elafonísi okay, for now."

"Thank God. But why so many fires, Kostí? What's going on? I mean,

41

I know about climate change, and I know it's been dry for a while and now it's hot and windy, but then it often is, isn't it?"

Kostí shrugged.

"Some, I think, are from stupid people. They drop cigarettes, they make fires to cook …"

"A few, perhaps," Nick agreed, doubtfully.

"Some, I know, is not mistake. There are crazy people, Nick. They want to see the flames. They want to be God for a few minutes."

"Or the Devil, more like."

"Yes. Perhaps The Devil. And then some use the situation. Maybe for vendetta?"

"Wait a minute. You're saying some fires are started deliberately, *for revenge*?"

"Yes, Níko. I hear this quite often. Or sometimes it is about land."

"How do you mean?"

"Fire-damaged land is cheap. You want land? No problem. You wait till everything is hot and dry, then you set fire to it. Afterwards, you buy it cheap."

"People do that?"

"I no point finger, Níko. I like my life and I have my lovely daughter."

"But it really happens?"

"Of course."

Kostí stubbed out his cigarette and heaved himself up in response to a raised hand and a call of "Parakaló" from a nearby table. Nick took his phone outside and found a sheltered spot in the corner of the white walls. He sat on the terracotta floor and punched the keys.

"Hi Dad," she said.

"Hi, Lauren. You were going to call, I think."

"I was about to. We're having gin and tonics on our terrace and watching the sun go down."

"Sounds delightful. Where are you?"

"Still Falásarna. But we're heading south tomorrow."

"You two getting on okay, then?"

"Hmmm. Quite often."

Nick concluded from the cryptic response that she could not speak freely.

"Is Fi with you now?"

"Exactly."

"No major rows or bust-ups, though?"

"Oh no, nothing too serious."

"Not too bad, then. Run out of money yet?"

"We have been going a bit mad. There's a fabulous restaurant here and we can't stay away! But, for the next few days, we won't have to spend a thing, so I think we'll scrape through."

"You might need to contribute to the cause."

"Hard work, rather than cash, I'm thinking."

"Hard work – from Fi?"

"Hmmm. Maybe one contribution, then."

"Well, I'm sure the two of you will do what's right. Listen, are you keeping your eyes on the weather – and the fire situation?"

"Er … we haven't been, but we will. There are no fires at all up here."

"Well, there are quite a few, further south and east of you, so check it out, girl. It's scary stuff, believe me, and I don't want you getting yourselves caught up in it. Check the temperatures *and* the wind speeds. Anything over thirty-two Celsius with winds gusting at forty or fifty kilometres or more and you need to be very careful indeed. Make sure you know where the fires are. Every day. You can always come back here, you know. Plenty of lovely beaches here, too."

"I know, Dad, but we want to see Roz again and check out what they're doing, and we want to have two or three nights in Chaniá afterwards."

"I'm not saying change your plans. Not yet, at least. Just be careful. Make sure you're well informed before you set off and stay informed while you're there. It's dangerous, Lauren. You must take sensible precautions."

"Yeah, yeah. I'm not an idiot, Dad. Okay?"

"I know you're not. But you might have to look after Fi."

"Oh, God!"

43

"Just saying."

"I'll be careful. All right? Now, can I tell you about our wonderful boat trip?"

They talked for several more minutes. Nick understood. She was irritated by Fi whom she found unadventurous. She also felt Fi was not pulling her weight, and she, Lauren, had to make all the decisions and then take the blame if she got anything wrong. *It was the usual discovery process when you spent time close to people you did not know well*, he thought. *They disappointed you in myriad small ways and, for a time, you wondered if they were a different person from the one you thought you cared for.*

"She *is* fun, though, isn't she?" he said.

"She is. She was a real laugh on the boat."

"Then talk to her about the other stuff. Not when you're angry, though. Just tell her what you feel."

"I can't do it, Dad."

"You're my daughter. I'm sure you can."

"I *am* your daughter, which is why I'd get angry."

He chuckled.

"Then you're just going to have to focus on her good points and stop finding fault like dear old Dad."

"That's my challenge, is it?"

"Think of it as practice for when you're married."

"I wasn't planning to marry Fiona."

"Glad to hear it. Though I can be surprisingly open-minded, you know."

"Yeah. Right."

CHAPTER 8

OLD MONEY

It was a blustery morning, but clear. Roz found this weather strange. Strong winds heralded poor weather in Scotland but here it was as if the winds were unconnected with the rest of the weather. Gusts that tugged at the roots of your hair and pebble-dashed you on the beach could be coupled with hot sun and unchanging, blue skies. Even the sea remained calm when the winds were offshore as they were today. The wind brought relief from the hottest sun, but it was deceptive. You felt cool, even as you fried. With her red hair and pale, freckly complexion, Roz needed to slap on the factor fifty every morning.

She was alone this morning and enjoying the peace. She would check on the turtle nests, including the newest one, in case their little security fences had been breached. The poor wee things faced quite a list of predators, both in and out of the water. Her job was to keep the eggs safe, as far as she could. When they hatched, it would be a different matter. They were under strict instructions to let nature take its course and not interfere. It was going to be tough. She was not looking forward to watching the gulls and crabs attack her little hatchlings as they scurried towards the water. Perhaps she would not watch at all.

As she made her way across the shingle, something caught her eye. Movement where there was usually none. A flash of colour that did not belong. A green too unsubtle for nature. It was moving, and it was between the turtle nests and the juniper forest, partly obscured by scrub and rocky outcrops. She stopped and stared. Something made her crouch, to lower her profile. It was a person. The size and the movement suggested it was male. She made out a thin, green windcheater and tan shorts. And he was walking towards the nests. She was on full alert now. She pulled her phone from her bag and switched to camera. Using full zoom, she took a couple of shots of him, just in case. But he did not seem interested in the nests and passed just in front of them, staring at the cremation site on the shingle for a moment, before striding along the beach towards her. She moved from a crouch to a kneel and then onto her front. There were a couple of rocks nearby and she slid herself across until she was hidden behind them. She did not think he had seen her.

She thought of taking another shot, without the zoom, when he passed her, but she dared not risk it. The noise of it could carry on the wind and he might hear. And he was quite a big man, in his early fifties perhaps. She would be no match for him. It could all be perfectly innocent, of course, but her instincts told her otherwise.

Instead, she focused on taking in the details of his appearance. He was fair-haired, so probably not Greek. He was the heavy side of medium build and getting on for one hundred and ninety centimetres tall, she reckoned, weighing a hundred kilos or more, but he looked fit. As he moved out of earshot, she took one more picture of him, from behind, then ducked down as he turned his head. He must have sensed something, but he did not slow his stride, thank God. Five minutes later, he was passing below their little settlement and picking up the trail through the trees and rocks that eventually led to Elafonísi.

Roz checked her photos as she resumed walking. Even on full zoom, he looked a long way off and not in perfect focus. The back view was better, but it was only a back view. She cursed herself for her timidity. As she reached the sand, she was relieved to see the turtle nests looking undisturbed. The nest they had created the day before remained unlabelled and she made a note to do something about it on her next visit. She meandered around all eighteen nests, checking. All seemed fine.

*

When she got back to the hut, Méli was there with him, butting his back gently, but Stefi did not seem to mind. Roz patted her rump for her, and, to her embarrassment, the goat turned and nuzzled her groin. Stefi pretended not to notice.

"Can a have a wee word, Stefi?" she asked.

"Sure, Roz. Sit down. Tell me." he said.

"There was this guy on our beach. He's gone now but I didna like the look of him."

"What was he doing?"

"He was walking from the forest to the beach. Then he went off towards Elafonísi."

"We do get the occasional tourist, Roz. Some tough guy will make it across from Elafonísi or someone will drop in with a boat. They might stay on the beach for a while and then they go. They're no trouble."

"This guy didna strike me as a tourist, Stefi."

"Was he a walker, then? The E4 passes near here, remember."

"No rucksack, no poles and he wasna wearing walking boots."

Stefi looked at her for a long moment.

"A casual walker, then. For a fit guy, it's not much more than an hour from Elafonísi."

"Aye. Mebbe. I didna like the hoodie though."

She saw Stefi did not understand the word and mimed the pulling up of a hood.

"What do you not like? Is windy, no? Is good idea to wear this."

"It seemed kind of sinister to me. It's not like he was a teenager or anything."

"He has been and now he is gone, no? He has done no damage, as far as you know."

"Not that I know of."

"Then forget him. It is private land, but we have no signs that say this. I like to keep things open, at least for now."

Roz shrugged but she felt foolish as Stefi went on:

"Now, if the turtles are okay, perhaps you can give Dan a hand? He has finished building the second tree house and he needs your help to fit it out for your guests."

"I don't know if they're coming yet."

"It needs to be done anyway. We will have proper, paying guests soon."

*

Three days later, during a late breakfast, Roz received a text from Lauren.

Hi Roz. Remember us? Hope you were serious about the invitation because WE'RE COMING! We can be in Elafonísi by around three today if it works for you. We can stay two or three nights – and we're ready to help! Lauren & Fi xx

Well, it was short notice, but what the hell? It would be fun, as long it was okay with Stefi. *But he seems very subdued this morning,* she thought.

"Something interesting?" asked Dan.

"It's my girls. They're coming after all – and today!"

"Oh, Lord! We still have quite a bit of work to do …"

"It's perfectly fine *now*, Dan. And they can help finish it off, anyway."

Stefi had been boiling an egg. Now he joined them at the table and sat down heavily before reaching over and pouring himself a coffee.

"Is it okay with you, Stefi?" she asked.

"Sorry, what?"

"Those two girls I met. They want to come today. Is that okay?"

He was tapping the top of his eggshell repeatedly with a spoon, then he looked up and smiled at her warmly.

"Why not! It will be good to see some new faces."

"Great! May I borrow the boat?"

"Teddy will go with you. It is safer."

*

At the hotel in Falásarna, the girls were finishing up their scraps of food in a makeshift breakfast on the terrace when Lauren's phone beeped. She popped the last piece of toast in her mouth and picked it up.

"Yay!" she said.

"What?" said Fi.

"*You'll be very welcome. Stay as long as you like,*" she quoted.

"Who's saying that?"

"Roz, of course."

"You texted her already?"

"You were in the loo."

"We should have discussed it, Lauren."

"I'm sorry. What's to discuss? We agreed we would go there, didn't we?"

"It was an idea. Something you and Roz cooked up on the plane. I assumed we'd talk about it before you leapt in and arranged something."

"Well, you knew we had to leave here this morning. Where the hell did you think we were going? Don't you want to do it, now? It'll be a lot of fun."

"It'll be uncomfortable and probably a bit rough. We'll be expected to work. It's not my idea of a holiday, Lauren."

"Oh, come on. It's just a couple of days, and the place is unspoilt, idyllic. We'll learn a lot. And Roz says Teddy is good-looking."

It was a cheap shot, and she knew it, but it was the kind of thing Fi would care about.

"Listen, Lauren. I don't mind going, okay? Even if I *didn't* want to go, I'd come along if you wanted to, no problem. What I don't like is being stitched up. You wait till I go to the loo, then you text behind my back. First, I hear, it's a done deal."

"I thought it was all agreed."

"No, you didn't. You knew I might disagree, so you gave me no choice."

There was some truth in what Fi was saying but Lauren was not ready to admit it.

"Look, I'm sorry if I upset you, Fi. Do something else if you want. I could drop you off in Sfinári ..."

"Gee, thanks. I'll not be going back there in a hurry."

"It was all right! So, what *do* you want?"

"I want to be consulted on the decisions *we* make, Lauren, not dragged along in your wake."

"Well, that's a bit rich, Fi. I've had to make *all* the bloody decisions because you can't be arsed!"

They stared at each other in mutual disappointment, then lapsed into silence. Fi started clearing away the breakfast things, for once.

*

The icy silence between them was filled with music, on the road south. Lauren was driving faster than usual, delighting in Fi's discomfort as she wound the little car around the hairpins. The road was elevated, the views stunning. At one point, an ambiguous road sign made Lauren hesitate, and Fi waved her arm confidently, indicating right. Ignoring her, Lauren swung left at the last minute, following the tarmac. Glancing back, they saw the right-hand fork was a dirt track leading over the cliff. They exchanged horrified glances, but the incident helped soften things between them, somehow.

"Sorry," she said and gave Lauren's leg a quick squeeze.

Lauren took it as a general apology, rather than just for the cliff blunder, and things began to normalise. She lessened her speed and turned *Bille Eilish* down a little.

"So, tell me about this Teddy," Fi said. "He's Greek, right? Is he from Crete?"

Lauren grinned.

*

Dan had been watching Stefi all morning. He was subdued and he was irritable. He even smacked Méli at one point. This was not like Stefi. Something was wrong. When Dan took the tirópita out of the oven to cool, he made some more coffee and invited Stefi to join him.

"You okay?" he asked, earnestly. "It's not still the forestry thing, is it?"

Stefi stared back balefully over the rim of his cup before putting it down and putting his hands together on the table.

"It is, yes. And something else. I didn't want to tell the others, but it's all turning to shit, Dan."

Dan reached across and patted his hand. He saw tears beginning to well in Stefi's eyes.

"Come on. Spit it out."

"I got this call, yesterday. Some guy from the Ypourgeío Politismoú, the Ministry of Hellenic Culture and Sports, he said. Name of Tzanakákis, said he worked for Chrístos Dímas."

"Who's he?"

"Dímas? Deputy Minister."

"What the hell do they want? Is it some scam?"

"I checked, later. Tzanakákis is the real thing."

"And?"

"He wanted to congratulate me. *Congratulate* me, for God's sake!"

"On what?"

"Some Slovenian tourists took them a couple of bronze coins, Roman sestertii, or something. They found them *here*, on my land. Tzanakákis is overcome with excitement. He sent me pictures."

He pulled out his phone and called up the email attachment.

"Look."

Dan came around the table and sat beside him.

"Are they really that colour?"

"The dark green? Yes. Two-thousand-year-old bronze."

"What are they supposed to mean?" Dan asked.

"This one is the head of Athena, he said. See the helmet?"

"And this one? I can't make it out at all."

"It's not easy. It's an owl, he told me, perching on an overturned amphora. Perhaps the owl drank all the wine? Then he can't be so wise, after all. It's a Roman joke."

"Right. Not exactly a side-splitter, is it? But I get you."

"He said they were from about 100 BCE," Stefi went on, "and it was exciting because no one knew the Romans made it this far west, in Crete. I said: *Neither did I.* He said: *They were in Polyrrhinía, of course, south of Kíssamos, so it wouldn't surprise me if a few made it down there.* But then he told me: coins are rarely found outside Roman towns or cities. And he asked me if I'd seen evidence of Roman habitation here. I said: *No, of course not.*"

"We could be sitting on a city stuffed with Roman treasures. How exciting!"

"Not likely."

"Still, you never know. Some good news, at last, Stefi!"

"You're missing the whole point, Dan. In Greece, people like

Tzanakákis are very powerful. He can order us to stop our development while they excavate. It could hold us up for months, years even. By then, I'll have run out of money and our plans will be in ruins."

"Holy shit."

"And this, on top of the forestry claim, makes me feel like giving up, Dan."

"Hmmm. Where did he leave things, this Tzanakákis guy?"

"He's doing research, reviewing the evidence. Then he will let me know what happens next. Probably a survey, maybe a full dig later. He'll call in a week or two. In the meantime, there must be no building work."

"Well, we didn't have any planned, did we?"

"No, but we do soon. What happens then?"

"Will it affect the whole site, though?"

"We won't know until after the survey if there is one. These coins were found on the edge of the juniper forest, he said."

"Which bit?"

"About a hundred and fifty metres in from the turtle nests. We're not to touch the area."

"Jesus, man. Can't build, can't dig. Gotta protect the trees, gotta save the turtles. For your sake, I hope this isn't becoming a culture ministry, forestry department, turtle conservation clusterfuck."

"If that's your way of consoling me, Dan, it's not working."

"Sorry, Steff, but what a frigging mess! And all this has blown up in the last week or two."

"Yes. Not to mention the bank."

"That's right, the bank too. Do you think they *knew* this shit was going down?"

"I can't imagine how. It's the gods; they've turned against us for some reason, Dan."

"No, Stefi. No way. The gods, should they exist, *must* be on our side. It's just a run of bad luck. We have to stand our ground, sweat it out."

"I don't know, my friend," Stefi said. "This feels like a slow-motion car crash, maybe a fatal one."

*

When they passed the sign for Elafonísi, they immediately hit traffic. The whole place seemed to be heaving with cars and coaches. Signs told them they could drive no further and would have to park in one of the official car parks.

"Okay, here comes the rip-off," Lauren said and threw Fi a look of apprehension.

The second car park on the right was clearly signposted, apart from any mention of price, so they pulled in. A young man guided them to a convenient spot with a little shade and then they left the car and found another couple of Greek guys manning a table near the exit. Lauren braced herself.

"How much is it?" she asked.

"Five euros," he said.

"For how long?"

"Stay as long you want. All day."

"We want to stay for three days."

"Then is fifteen euros, okay?"

Lauren could hardly open her purse quickly enough to pay the money and thank the young man. As they returned to the car, she said:

"I thought it would be four or five times as much! Here we are, at perhaps the top tourist attraction in Crete – a total monopoly situation for them – and yet they charge us just five euros a day. Crazy."

"They're sweet, perhaps a little naïve."

"Not cynical bastards on the make, you mean."

"Or maybe it's all controlled, what they can charge."

Lauren thought it was possible, but she preferred to believe the Greeks were a principled people whose moral code would not permit overcharging guests.

They had been unloading the car as they talked. They each had a rucksack and a beach mat. Their half-empty suitcases could stay in the car. They would also need the big parasol and plenty of water.

"Should I bring the phone chargers?" asked Fi. "Will they work there?"

"It's solar, of course. Is it something you can plug into? I suppose it must be. Bring them along, anyway, and the USB ones. And don't forget your hat."

"I hope it's not far," said Fi as they locked the car and set off, fully laden.

Lauren had been checking her phone.

"She says to meet on the far-left side of the beach and look out for a red-striped boat. And guess what?"

"What?"

"She's coming with Teddy."

"Woah. I hope *she's* not shagging him, then."

"Roz?"

They looked at each other for a second and then exploded in giggles.

They wandered through a vast, sandy wasteland which must have been used for parking before, judging by the redundant signage. *Maybe all of it on the busiest days*, thought Lauren with a shudder. They bought ice creams from a van and walked on. Ahead of them, a large, sandy beach arced out to an island which was end-on to the mainland. The pink-white sand and the pale turquoise water of the lagoon with the darker blue sea behind, combined to make a peaceful and uplifting scene. There were few boats. There were thousands of people, though. Some were lying on the beach, others walking or wading across to the island. Lauren could imagine Lowry painting the scene, had he escaped Pendlebury and headed for Crete.

She had read about Elafonísi but hesitated to tell Fi about the seven hundred or so Greeks, mostly women and children discovered hiding, who had been slaughtered there by Ottoman forces, on Easter Sunday, 1824. Nor did she mention the thirty-eight corpses added in 1907 when the passenger steamer *Imperatrix* sank nearby. She stared out at the sandy, little island with its grassy tussocks. It was one mass graveyard. *And there was enough blood to turn the sand pink,* Lauren thought, though the official line was that tiny, pigmented microorganisms had been consorting with the seaweed …

"Oh, God. Look at the colour of the water," said Fi. "Is there time?"

"We have twenty-five minutes."

"Let's go for it."

CHAPTER 9
AN UNWELCOME APPROACH

Nick was halfway through making a sandwich when the phone started ringing. A couple of flies were buzzing around the kitchen, so he laid a clean tea towel over the ingredients before sprinting into the living room and accepting the call on the fourth ring.

"I've just been watching the news," the voice said, without preamble. It was a voice he recognised. Confident, posh, but tinged with anxiety on this occasion.

"Hullo, Jen," he said.

"It's like the whole island is ablaze."

"It isn't."

"I'm worried about Lauren, Nick. She's not answering my calls."

"I spoke to her yesterday. They were heading down to Elafonísi."

"Where's that?"

"South-west corner of Crete, beyond Paleóchora. They met a girl on the plane. They're going to stay with her. Some remote eco-project down there. There are turtles."

"Where, exactly?"

"It's a boat ride from Elafonísi."

"You don't know?"

"I found it on *Google Earth*, so I know where it is. She's a grown-up now, Jen. I don't need to know *exactly* where she is every second of every day."

"She's come to *your* island, Nick, partly to spend time with her dad. I expect *you* to keep her safe."

Nick could feel his hackles rising but he tried to keep his voice steady.

"I'm sure she's fine. Probably her phone needs a charge, or she can't get a signal. She'll be in touch soon. Try not to worry."

"Do you have contact details for the hotel?"

"Hotel? They're staying in The Wilds of Wanney in a tree house or something. I don't suppose they have neatly printed business cards with contact information."

"There's no need to get aggressive, Nick."

"I'm not. But the nature of the place means they will be reliant on their mobiles. It does have solar power, so I expect they can charge them. I imagine there will be Wi-Fi of some sort, as they have paying guests – or are planning to."

"Are there wildfires around there?"

"Not close by. But there are some inland from there."

"And they're in a tree house? Was that a joke? Are there trees where they are sleeping?"

"I don't know. I saw a line of tamarisks behind the beach. Further in there's a small juniper forest, I believe."

"A forest? For God's sake, Nick!"

"Calm down. There's quite a gap between the two. Must be a few hundred metres. I imagine they're sleeping in the gap."

"But you said a tree house! It *must* be in the forest."

"Not necessarily. I don't have a clear idea of the sleeping arrangements but listen, Jen. The fires were twenty or thirty kilometres away, the last time I looked. I told Lauren to check. She can do it on her phone every day. Even if she's sleeping in a forest, which I doubt, she's perfectly safe, for now. And they're only staying two or three nights, for Heaven's sake."

"You act like I'm panicking, but I'm not, Nick. I just wish you would show a bit more parental concern."

He looked out of the window and saw the swallows swooping playfully in the clear, blue sky, bursting with joy just to be alive and free on such a morning, in such a beautiful place. *Jen had always been irritated that he was not more demonstrative. It was all about her needing to know he was strong, so she could feel safe. He understood but felt no need to prove himself. Not now.* He said nothing. When she spoke again her voice was lower, a little softer.

"What if we don't hear anything?"

"We will," he said firmly.

"And if we don't?"

"Then I'll get over there. I can get there in four hours, I reckon."

"You haven't got a boat."

"I can get someone to take me from Paleóchora or I can hire a boat, if need be."

"Are you sure?"

"Quite sure."

*

Fi was the first to see the boat. It was on a plane, scudding across the waves, bouncing and buffeting its way around the rocky headland.

"Is it them?" she called to Lauren, as they got out of the water. "It's grey, but it does have a bold, red stripe."

As Lauren stared, they saw it slow down dramatically as it came within two hundred metres of the beach area. Now, it was making five knots at most, and Roz was waving. The guy on the tiller must be Teddy. They towelled off and made their way to the left-hand side of the beach where a small promontory provided shelter. They saw Teddy manoeuvre through the swimmers, then he cut the engine and they both jumped down into the shallows to haul the RIB onto the sand.

"You made it!" said Roz, hugging each of them in turn, like they had known each other all their lives. "This is Theódoros, but he answers to Teddy."

They introduced themselves and Teddy shook their hands, smiling shyly and averting his eyes from their bikinis. Lauren could sense Fi going weak at the knees but then he was rather gorgeous.

"I just need to find a loo," said Roz. "You two might want to get dressed. It can be fresh out on the water. If not, I'd put on some extra sunblock."

They chose to remain in their bikinis and lathered themselves with more factor fifty, much to Teddy's delight, Lauren suspected. When Fi asked if *someone* would help with her back, Teddy looked embarrassed, then relieved when Lauren volunteered.

*

The morning after the girls arrived, Stefi was furious. It was a good thing they had met him the previous evening because now he was best avoided. They heard shouting from his cabin and something shattering. He did not appear at breakfast and afterwards, Dan went to him. Teddy and Roz offered to show the girls around the site and check on the turtle nests. They readily agreed, feeling it would be best to be out of the way for a while.

As Dan went in, Méli was looking fearful as she picked her way over shards of pottery, before wriggling past him. Stefi was sitting at the trestle table, his head in his hands. His phone was on the table, his coffee mug thrown in fury at the door.

"What's happened, Stefi? Are you all right?"

"Do I look all right?"

"We're all worried for you. We heard shouting and stuff."

There was a pause and then Stefi looked him straight in the eyes.

"Can I trust you, Dan?" he said.

"You know you can. Why would you even ask?"

"Because someone's been betraying my trust."

"What? Calm down and tell me, from the beginning."

Dan sat down opposite Stefi, laid his hands on the table and adopted what he hoped was an expression of openness and warmth.

"Someone must have told them."

"Told them what?"

"The shit I'm in: the bank, the Forestry Department, the Culture Ministry."

"Told whom?"

"I got a call, first thing. From the estate agent in Chaniá, Pagiannídis. I had some dealings with him over my father's estate. He's a snake, that man."

"I've not heard you mention him."

"No? It's a while back now."

"What did he want?"

"Well, he starts by telling me he's acting as agent for an undisclosed principal who is *minded* to make an offer."

"*Minded*? What the hell does that mean? An offer for what?"

Stefi ignored him and carried on.

"Before he could go any further, he wanted to make *his* position clear. Should this conversation lead to a transaction, he would be acting as *my* agent and charging me a fee for his services. He would email a document for me to sign, accordingly. I asked him what fee and he said three per cent of the full value of the transaction plus VAT."

"But you said he was acting for the other guy."

"He is. It's a total rip-off, Dan. Somehow it has become enshrined in property law here. The estate agent gets fees from both sides."

"Hang on. You must have misunderstood. How can he be an agent for *both* principals in a transaction where they're on *opposing* sides? He'd be more like a double agent."

Stefi spread his hands on the table and shrugged.

"It's just the way it is here. You have to live with it, they tell me."

"To hell with that."

"Anyway, Dan. The reason he called was to sound me out about this possible offer."

"You mean for the plot here, at Tamarisk Bay?"

"Everything I own here, as it is right now."

"But you're only just getting going. You don't want to sell, do you?"

"You know I don't, but with all these hurdles springing up, it might have crept into the back of my mind. And it's like they *know*. That's why I think someone's been talking."

"What was the offer, if you don't mind me asking?"

"Two million Euros, cash."

"It's got to be worth more, Stefi."

"I told him not to waste my time. *It's family land, from my father,* I said. *It's not for sale and – if it were – I'd be looking for more like twenty million.*"

"Attaboy. How did that go down?"

"He said he was sorry to hear it. Said he thought two million was fair, for a clean, cash offer where I could drop everything and just walk away. Said he'd get back to his principals and let me know of any developments. I said you can do that, and, while you're at it, you can tell them to fuck off."

"I bet that went down well. Did you ask who it was?"

"He wasn't about to tell me."

"So, what's the big deal, Stefi? You received a low-ball offer from some mystery man and said *No*. End of story."

"I'm suspicious, Dan. Why would they *imagine* I might entertain such an offer?"

"Perhaps they think it's fair."

"No way. You *know* it isn't. So, why do they think I might accept an *unfair* offer?"

"You clearly have a theory. Tell me."

"Because someone's been feeding them information about our problems. That's why. I think we have a mole, someone working for them."

"Can't see it, Stefi. Sounds like paranoia to me."

"It has to be Teddy if it's not you."

"*If* it's not me," Dan repeated, aghast. "Jesus, man. Haven't I supported you through thick and thin? Didn't I come back this year, like I said I would? Haven't I worked hard enough on this fucking project? What – you think I'd sell you down the river for a few shekels just because the going got tough?"

"Teddy, then. He's been here a while. He knows everything. He makes regular trips out; he could have been meeting people. He could be in their pocket, Dan. And he's moving on when Roz is settled. He's got nothing to lose. I'm going to talk to the bastard. Right now."

Stefi lunged to his feet, but Dan stood and blocked his way.

"No, Stefi. Don't. Sit down, man. I don't want you making a fool of yourself. If you suspect him, watch him. I'm not convinced there *is* a mole, but I can help. We need evidence before we start throwing around wild accusations. You'll just demoralise everyone and end up losing all your volunteers. And then you'll be even deeper in the shit."

"I have to do something, Dan. I can feel my dream slipping away. I'm not sure I believe in it myself anymore. Can we still do it?"

"Sure, we can. We've had a string of bad luck and now someone – *with or without knowledge of that* – has come in with a derisory offer which you've rejected. You need to forget about the offer, keep the bank onside, and square up to the forestry and culture ministry issues."

"Easier said than done."

"Look, I can help, okay? Let's clear up this mess, heat the rest of the tirópita and make some more coffee. Then we'll talk it through, piece by piece. We need a plan of attack."

*

Lauren was impressed. The place was much bigger than she had imagined. The shingle beach would be close to five hundred metres across and then there was the sandy cove where the turtle nests were hidden. There was a row of feathery tamarisk trees right behind the beach which Teddy said were very old.

"They grow slowly," he explained. "These will be over two hundred years old."

He touched the leaves and put his fingers into his mouth.

"Try it."

They did the same.

"It's saltwater," said Lauren, fascinated.

"It kills most trees, but tamarisks thrive on it. They suck it up."

"Wow! So, this is the perfect place for them."

"Dan says they're called *salt cedars* in The States, and they're a pest."

"Well, *I* think they're perfectly lovely."

Behind the beach, the land stretched back several hundred metres to the band of juniper forest. It was sand but dotted with boulders and wiry, wind-blasted trees. The few developments Stefi had made so far were at the Elafonísi end of the beach. They saw the small collection of huts, the two tree houses and a large, rather ugly, concrete shell behind, further from the sea. Beyond, the land rose sharply, perhaps six hundred metres, to the barren-looking mountains.

"What's with the grey concrete thing, Teddy?" she asked. "It's a bit of an eyesore, isn't it?"

"You see many of these in Greece. People put up the frame so they can make a home later."

"Why?"

"It's to do with the property laws here. Especially if you are outside the village boundary, what you are allowed to build on your land keeps changing, so they build it while they can, before the law changes."

"And then, what? They must finish it within five years, or something?"

"I don't think there is a time limit. You finish it when you want."

"So, there are ugly concrete hulks all over the place?"

"There are quite a few, it is true. This one was built by Stefi's father. He planned to complete it for his retirement and have a second home here. But he died too soon."

"Will Stefi finish it now, then?"

"I think he will knock it down. It is not part of the plans I've seen."

They had made their way to the forest now. These trees had dusty, green leaves like the tamarisks, but their trunks and branches looked stringy and spiky.

"These are juniper trees?" asked Fi.

"Wild juniper, yes."

"It's the berries that flavour your gin," said Lauren.

"I know. Maybe we should pick a few basketfuls."

"There are plenty of them."

They worked their way through the trees. It was not easy. The trees grew close together and they were prickly. Some were entangled with each other.

"Okay. We go this way," called Teddy, and they followed a sandy path, tufted with grass until they emerged into the sunlight.

"I think I prefer the tamarisks," said Fi, picking twig shards off her tee shirt.

"Was this a river, at some point?" asked Lauren. She was looking at a dried-up bed that snaked its way along the western edge of the juniper forest and formed a depression in the shingle as it neared the sea.

"It *is* a river. In winter, when the rains come, it changes character. Dan is trying to capture hydroelectricity from it. You should get him to show you some of his projects."

"Yeah. I'd like that," said Lauren.

"Stefi wants the whole place to be self-sufficient and sustainable. We must make our electricity from the sun, the wind and maybe the water too, grow wood for construction and heating and manage the forest so we don't deplete it. We will purify and store our water. We'll grow much of our food, too. He already has many interesting plants from all over the world: vegetables, grasses, herbs and so on. He wants Tamarisk Bay to be a model eco-development."

"But this is for tourists, right?"

"Yes, of course. He wants to lead the way with this, and he expects to make money. Without this he cannot get the bank to lend, you understand. But money is not what drives Stefi. He wants to save the planet and to show us all how to do it."

"That's quite an ambition," said Fi.

"How do you like your tree house, Fi?" asked Roz, who had been silent for some time.

"It's lovely! Quite luxurious. I had no idea such things existed. Sitting on the balcony under the tree canopy with a gin is my idea of heaven."

"Well, there you are. This is the kind of thing we're looking to achieve here. Self-sufficient, sustainable luxury. It *is* possible. And Stefi reckons there's a new generation coming through who will go for this, big time. Have you heard his tagline yet?"

"No," chorused Fi and Lauren.

"*Let nature recharge your batteries*. And it has a second line: *Tamarisk Bay: Greece's first wholly sustainable, luxury destination.*"

"That's quite something," said Lauren.

"I hope he can do it," said Fi.

CHAPTER 10
DAN THE MAN

Dan's structured approach was helpful, but it was not easy for Stefi. He was always happier with the bigger picture and felt choked by detail. They started with the bank.

"Have you shown this new woman the plans?" Dan asked.

"They're on file. I imagine she's seen them."

"It's not the same thing, Steff. We need to *show* her the dream. Let's put a presentation together. Ask for an hour of her time. Blow her away with the concept. Then we'll get into the numbers. *She's* the boss now. You need to forget about the other guy and show the new one the respect she deserves as the new kid on the block. She is the custodian of the bank's money, after all."

"Respect has to be earned."

"We're respecting the *position* she holds, not her. We don't know her yet. But the bank put her in this position, so we respect this. Anyway, it's human nature, isn't it? Show *her* some respect and she'll return it, hopefully. So far, you've assumed she'll take the exact same position as her predecessor, and you've taken the change of faces as a damned nuisance. That must change, Stefi. We need to welcome her, involve her, win her over, make her feel it was *she* who decided to continue supporting the project."

"I did all this with Manólis."

"I know you did. So, do it again. How big a deal is it?"

"It's a pain in the backside, but I guess I could."

"Sure, you could. And I can help you make the presentation snappy."

Dan walked Stefi back through the meeting with the bank and they made a list of the concerns raised. Dan wanted to be sure, in amongst the sales pitch, that those concerns were addressed. There were a few slides from an earlier presentation they could re-use and they added some new ones. Dan insisted they use the new taglines with some inspirational music at the beginning.

"Isn't it too much, for a bank, Dan?"

"Not at all. We need to *inspire* them with the project. They're human beings, too. They are not just lending money to a mid-sized development project; they're helping save the planet! That'll be great for their PR, too."

By lunchtime, they had the full presentation, in draft. Dan said he would work up the slides later, then they should practise.

"Shall we just grab a sandwich and carry on?" he said.

"Sure. I just need to put something out for Méli."

"Doesn't she just eat anything?"

"I try to give her stuff which is good for her, Dan."

"You spoil her rotten, is what I know. Okay, why don't I run up a sandwich for the two of us?"

Fifteen minutes later, they sat down with their lunch.

"She okay?" inquired Dan.

"She's gone off somewhere. I might have upset her, earlier."

"Perhaps she's having a sulk."

"She doesn't do that, Dan. Never for more than ten seconds, anyway. She's such a sweet-natured creature. I frightened her with all my crashing around. She'll be back when she's hungry."

"Count on it."

Next up, they addressed the forestry claim. When Dan asked for details, Stefi said he was still waiting to learn the extent of the claim and the legal basis for it.

"It came from the lawyer. She's sending more detail," he said.

"But you don't have it yet?"

Stefi shook his head.

"We need to understand where they are coming from. It might be helpful to do a little web research."

Stefi was nodding now.

"I can do it. It will all be in Greek, after all," he said.

"We need to understand why they are interested in your juniper forest, and how it fits with their strategy."

"It's hard to believe it does."

"Well, there must be *some* motivation. Are junipers endangered? Or are they trying to buy up all the forestry in this area, for some reason? We need to understand."

"Crete lost most of its forests when the Venetians were here. I think the mission of these guys is to preserve and protect what's left. They take forestry land into public ownership so they can look after it, protect it and allow public access where they can. The land changes from being at risk and inaccessible to being protected and available to everyone. That's the theory."

"Okay, Stefi. So, we have a response. We can *challenge* their claim – what, in law, gives them the right to take it, when you have clear legal title to it? And why do they think it's within their remit? Why Tamarisk Bay specifically – how does it help them meet their brief? And we can *undermine the rationale* for their claim. We can demonstrate effective husbandry – you've looked after the juniper forest and will continue to do so. Your plans *preserve* it rather than bulldozing it. You could even offer to grant public access."

"No one would come, anyway."

"Exactly, so the gesture costs you nothing. You might have to fork out for a few signs and shore up the paths here and there. No big deal. So, unless their brief *requires* them to own it, why on earth would they bother?"

"Maybe because I *haven't* looked after it. I just leave it alone. It's a bit of a mess."

"We might not go into specifics, then."

They exchanged rueful grins.

"Okay, but what about the Ministry of Culture and these Roman remains?" Stefi asked.

"Two coins falling out of some Roman's pocket two thousand years ago do not an undiscovered settlement make, in my book. I doubt it will lead to anything."

"But they are likely to survey, maybe dig, before they can be sure."

"Perhaps, Stefi. We must wait for this guy Tzanakákis to get back to us, but then we must *work with them*. Damage limitation. We try to restrict the area they close off. If we could keep it to within fifty metres of the original find – at least until they discover something else – it would be no real inconvenience, would it?"

Stefi agreed.

"And, if we could put a time limit on the dig of, say, six months?"

"It all depends on what we can get on with, while they're digging away."

"Exactly, so we shoot for a deal where they can dig away happily in this little area for up to six months and we'll carry on with our plans, elsewhere on the site. Only if they come up with a major find will we discuss any changes to our plans. We should get this understood from the outset. Friendly but firm."

"Sounds like a fair compromise to me, but these guys have the power to shut everything down."

"For a couple of coins? I don't think so, not if we try to accommodate their needs."

"I hope you're right, Dan."

Stefi was still making cautious noises, but he was feeling better. Dan had been a big help, talking things through rationally and coming up with sensible responses. It was not going to be easy, and it would take a while, but with his support and by tackling things one at a time, maybe – just maybe – they could still get there.

*

The girls were back in the tree house by mid-afternoon. The weather had turned sultry. They felt sleepy and decided to rest up for a couple of hours. Fi was snoring gently as Lauren lay on her bed, thinking about Teddy. *He seemed quite innocent,* she thought. Or maybe he was just respectful of women. He had not responded to her gentle come-ons so maybe she was not his type. Perhaps he preferred Fi or maybe he was more interested in men? Certainly, he was good-looking enough to be gay. All the best-looking men were, it seemed. What a pity.

Fi woke at ten minutes to six.

"You're just in time," said Lauren. "I'm making G&Ts. Thought we'd preload before dinner."

Fiona rubbed her eyes and grinned.

"Good plan," she agreed.

Ten minutes later they were sitting on the balcony with taramasaláta, olives and spinach breadsticks along with their gins.

"What do you reckon on Stefi, then?" said Fi, stretching her long legs and propping her feet on the balcony rail. "Inspired genius or nutjob?"

"Don't know yet. We haven't seen a lot of him, have we? But the way he was carrying on this morning, I'd have to go for nutjob."

"Aye. But I like the idea."

"Oh God, yeah. It's brilliant. I don't know why everyone isn't thinking this way."

"Oh, they will be. They'll have to. It just takes time, and most people are resistant to change."

"Whereas he's new to it, so he has a clean sheet. He can be radical, do something completely new and different."

"It could make the other places seem uncool."

"Which they are."

"They'll have to get their acts together."

The sun was still quite high in the sky, but it was hazy today and there were clouds on the mountains behind them. They sipped their drinks and gazed out over the sea from the shelter of the tree canopy. Both felt they were at the start of something exciting, revolutionary even.

"We should have asked Roz to join us," said Lauren.

"Aye. Mebbe. Or Teddy?"

"Is he gay, do you think?"

"Teddy? You're joking, aren't you? He's hot, babe. Have you not been on the receiving end of those steamy looks of his?"

"He's not tall enough for you."

"Ah, but he's very good-looking and there's precious little else around here."

"There's Danny Boy."

"Ach. Too serious for me and *he* might well be gay."

"You think so?"

CHAPTER 11
A HUNTING INCIDENT

When they all sat down to supper, which they did as a group whenever practical, there were absentees.

"Where's Roz?" Fi asked Dan.

"She's giving dinner a miss tonight. She might join us later."

"And Stefi?"

"He'll be along," he replied. "He wanted to look for Méli before it gets dark."

"Nutjob," whispered Fi, and Lauren sniggered softly.

"Where's she gone?" asked Fi.

"If he knew, he wouldn't have to go looking, would he?" Dan pointed out.

"You mean she's *missing*?"

"*Gone walkabout*, more like. It happens from time to time."

When the rakí came out after the meal, Dan excused himself and went in search of Stefi. Outside, it was darkening twilight now, the first few stars appearing in the sky. He tried Stefi's cabin first, but it looked exactly as they had left it. He wandered down to the beach, to where he could see the entire length of it stretched out under the rising moon, but there were no silhouettes, no signs of movement other than the sea itself, lapping the shingle.

It was then he first heard it. An animal howl. A wail. It was coming from the forest. It was a desperate, bereft sound. Was it animal or could it be human? He left the beach and started jogging towards the sound. Then he heard it again, quieter but unmistakable. The whimpering of a beast caught in a trap. Or was it human? Could it be Stefi, even?

He found himself sprinting now, trying to reach the sound before it faded. It was very close now but then it stopped. He came to a halt and stood still, straining to catch the slightest sound. The chirping of the crickets, the waves – in the distance now – and then something else.

A faint creak. Rhythmic, consistent, barely audible. Like a boat, straining at its moorings. But another sound, too. Like a muffled sob.

He moved forward hesitantly and became aware of a sweet but sickly smell. Then the moon broke free of a cloud and he saw it, no more than four metres away. There was a relatively tall juniper, on the very edge of the forest. From a high branch, a rope had been strung. He saw an animal's hooves tied. Then he realised the animal was upside down, hanging by its rear legs. The rope was creaking as the creature swung slightly from side to side, head lolling, and, as it swung, something dripping dark on the ground, where a black mess already pooled. It was a small goat he realised, with shock, and its throat had been slashed. He stepped forward and almost tripped over Stefi. He was face-down in a kneeling position, arms protecting his head and muffling the sound of the great, juddering sobs wracking his body.

"Oh, my God. Oh, sweet Jesus. Stefi, are you all right? Let me take you away from here. Right now … No, I'll come back for Méli. I'll take care of her. You need to be somewhere else, buddy. What did you say? No, I don't. Of course, I don't! This could not be one of us. Who would do such a thing?"

Stefi turned away, still on his knees, and edged away from the horror. Dan helped him to his feet and then Stefi glanced back and crumpled.

"Don't look, man," said Dan. "Just don't."

"Cut her down, Dan. At least do that for her," he croaked.

"I will, in just a minute. But she's past caring, old friend."

Gradually they staggered away from the scene, Dan hauling the limp and crumpled form of the older man steadily towards the huts.

*

Later, in the communal hut, Dan described what he had seen. Afterwards, as Fi and Lauren cleared away the detritus of the meal and Stefi sat, walled in silence, nursing a carafe of rakí, it was Lauren who spoke first:

"Could it be poachers, do you think? They would hang her upside-down like that if they wanted her to bleed out. Then, they could skin her more easily." Seeing him flinch, she put a hand on Stefi's arm. "I'm sorry, Stefi. But it's what they do."

"If it was, they'll be back, to collect the carcass," said Teddy. "We could lie in wait for them."

"Hang on," said Dan. "All this is *so* unlikely, isn't it? We hardly get any visitors. When we do get one, he happens to be an opportunist hunter or poacher. Méli happens to be on the loose for once and she happens to run into the guy."

"Perhaps he came here to hunt," said Teddy. "There must be rabbits here, maybe ibex. Then he couldn't believe his luck when he saw Méli."

"She was so tame, the poor wee thing. She probably went up to the guy."

The picture Fi painted of the innocent approaching her killer stunned them all into silence for a minute. Then it was Stefi who spoke.

"Maybe I'm getting paranoid, but it feels more personal. Like someone's trying to get at *me*."

"Do you want us to stake out the area, Stefi, try and catch the guy? Teddy and I can do it."

Stefi glanced at each of them before wiping his eyes.

"What would be the point?" he asked. "It won't bring her back. And, if he thought she was a *wild* goat, he was within his rights, kind of."

"But the guy was trespassing, Stefi. He had no rights *here*."

"There are no warning signs. You know how I feel about that sort of thing."

Dan knew. Stefi was ambivalent about ownership. Perhaps everything had come to him too easily. If he had fought for his land, he would defend it more aggressively. He was the owner, but he would be the last person to tell the rest of the world to keep off. Even putting up a fence was anathema to him. He wanted to share what he had. It was naïve, Dan thought, but it was also rather beautiful, in a way, like some twenty-first-century hippy.

"So, we do nothing?"

"We can leave him a message."

"A message?"

"So, when he returns for her body, he finds the message instead."

"I get it, but saying what?"

"Telling him he is trespassing; he has killed the owner's beloved pet goat and is no longer welcome here."

"I'm sorry, Stefi, but I think he'd just laugh. This guy needs a beating not a polite request to stay away."

"We don't *know* this. And I'm not having you guys waiting around in the dark for hours so you can beat up a potentially innocent man."

Dan and Teddy exchanged glances. It felt like a weak response. Surely, Méli's life was worth more. This might be turning the other cheek, but it felt more like a form of cowardice. It did not feel right to Dan, but it was Stefi's land and Stefi's pet goat when all was said and done.

"What have you done with her?" Stefi asked.

"I brought her back with the tractor. She's alongside number three cabin, covered in a blanket. Teddy and I can bury her in the morning if that's what you want."

"Let me think about it."

He turned to the girls' table and dredged a weak smile from somewhere.

"It's been a rough day. Sorry, ladies. It isn't always like this, believe me! Stay a bit longer, if you can. It can only get better!"

CHAPTER 12
THE GROCERY RUN

It was a slow start the following morning. Thanks to the prevailing mood, Lauren and Fi had experienced their first serious encounter with rakí the previous night and it was leaving its mark.

"What was all the noise, earlier?" said Fi, hair ruffled, appearing on the balcony for the first time.

"Dunno. Dan and a couple of guys were lugging something about."

"Oh, my *God*."

"What, Fi?"

"Was it Méli? Did they come for the carcass?"

Lauren stared at her, looking appalled.

"And there was I, expecting a funeral with full rites this morning, a few carefully chosen readings ..."

Fi snorted.

"And Stefi in a tasteful, black number, I suppose! Aye, it's a bit like that, isn't it? She *was* a sweet, wee creature, mind."

*

Over breakfast, it became clear. Stefi had made a brave decision. Rather than bury her on the site, he had asked Dan to offer her carcass to a rather fine restaurant he knew, in Paleóchora. If they were prepared to come and get her, they could have her body for nothing.

"He agonised about it most of the night, but finally decided it would be a self-indulgence to bury her, so *No*. She should be recycled. Let her body do something useful. Kid is a delicacy here," Dan explained. "The taverna owner was delighted and sent a boat right away. She'll be on the menu tonight."

"Oh, dear. Poor Méli," said Lauren.

"Are we all trooping off to Paleóchora for dinner, then?" said Fi, with a wicked grin, and received a despairing shake of the head from Dan, as he walked away.

"That was a bit crass, Fi," said Lauren. "Don't let Stefi hear you say it."

Fi made big eyes as if to say *I'm not that stupid.*

As they finished breakfast, Roz appeared:

"Hi, Roz. Are you feeling better?" said Fi.

"I was fine. Sometimes I need a little *me* time. Please don't be offended."

"Oh, no, not at all. We're all like that sometimes," said Lauren.

"I've just heard about poor Méli. I canna believe it."

"Tragic, isn't it?"

"He should have kept her safe, in a pen. But you try telling Stefi."

"He might listen, now."

"Aye," she said, seeing the irony. "Anyway, look. It's no' been the greatest start here for you guys. What say we get out of here tonight, just the three of us? I'll buy us some dinner."

"In Paleóchora?" said Fi and she and Lauren had a fit of the giggles. Roz looked puzzled.

"Is there something wrong with that?"

"No, no," said Lauren, trying to keep a straight face. "That would be lovely, Roz."

"There are plenty of good places, but I thought you'd like Cape Crocodile. It's good for meat dishes – especially steaks on the grill – and it's on the front, so a wee bit cooler."

"But you're vegetarian, aren't you, Roz?" said Lauren.

"Aye, but they have things for me, too. Dinna worry."

"Not sure about eating crocs though," joked Fiona.

"The name comes from what they call the headland. They say it looks like a crocodile facing out to sea. Could ha' fooled me. Happily, they cook regular meat rather than reptiles, I believe."

And maybe kid, on special tonight, thought Fiona but she kept her mouth shut, for once.

"We could get a cocktail first, mebbe, if we set off at half five or so?"

"In the boat?"

"Of course, in the boat. How else would we get there?"

*

Roz seemed to know how to handle the boat, they were relieved to discover. Lauren figured Stefi would not have allowed them to borrow it unless he was confident of her skills and their safety. But then he *is* a nutjob, Fi reminded her. It was still light, of course, but it would be dark when they came back and, by then, they might not be entirely sober …

The centre of town was still lively in mid-September. Rock music thumped from one bar and soft jazz floated from another. A narrow walkway meandered between tables and chairs that spread across the streets. They heard many different languages and saw some stylish women, especially the mainland Greeks. They settled in cane chairs with cushions at a bar playing salsa a little further up the hill and ordered cocktails: a margarita and a negroni for Roz and Lauren, while Fi enjoyed embarrassing their rather sweet waiter by asking for sex on the beach. The cocktails looked the part but were not terribly good; too sweet and filled with ice and not enough spirit. Meanwhile, the tables were filling up with drinkers and diners and it was getting noisy. It was not long before they made their way down to the front and found Cape Crocodile, which was quiet, by contrast.

"Most people eat later, around nine," explained Roz.

Lauren glanced at her watch and found it was only twenty past seven.

The waiter was an older man, but he was friendly and charming. He asked them where they were from and then told them he had been to Scotland himself. It took a while for them to realise he was talking about Ullapool after he insisted on stressing the second syllable. He brought them amuse-bouches, little tasters from the kitchen that were on the house, he said, then helped them choose a wine. Lauren and Fi ordered steaks: a sirloin for Lauren and a rib-eye for Fi. Roz went for an aubergine and cheese dish from the oven.

The steaks were outstanding, slightly blackened on the outside, the fat rendered, and bright pink inside but not bloody. *Spot-on for medium-rare*, thought Lauren. They were served with crispy fried potatoes and an interesting broccoli dish which was creamy with a touch of chilli.

"This guy knows how to cook," said Fi, appreciatively.

"He does. The Greeks tend to overcook meat, I find, but this is just right," said Lauren. "Good choice, Roz," she added. "This is really kind of you."

"Ach, it's no' expensive and I feel bad about dragging yous all this way only to find Stefi like a bear with a sore head."

"He's had a lot to contend with. It's very stressful for him. We see that," said Lauren.

She patted Roz's arm.

"He's a grumpy, old bugger. I've never seen him like this, to be honest."

"He's a sweet guy really, Roz. We see that. But he's lost a much-loved pet who was a good friend in very unpleasant circumstances. He's going to have a tough time of it for a few days, at least. And it's okay We'll cope."

Fi then topped up their glasses with Kotsifáli and they clinked them together.

"To Stefi – and what he's trying to do," suggested Lauren.

"Aye. Why not? To Stefi, the poor sod," said Roz.

"Stefi," agreed Fi and they all took generous sips. "I'm glad we didn't end up at the taverna with kid on the menu," she conceded.

Soon after, Roz excused herself and went in search of the toilets. On the way there, it was possible to glimpse the kitchen at work, she noticed. On the way back, she paused for a moment. She saw an older lady, a boy of about fourteen and a youngish man with a dark brown beard. They were all wearing whites and the stainless-steel equipment looked clean and professional. They seemed preoccupied but not rushed. The taverna was only half-full, Roz figured. The older woman seemed to sense her presence, looked up and smiled.

"Étan polí nóstimo," Roz said, and the woman beamed at the compliment.

"Efcharistoúme polí," she said.

The young man also lifted his head briefly and caught her eye. He seemed to frown slightly before turning to the grill, his back to her. He said nothing but the abruptness in his manner left Roz wondering if she had managed to offend him, somehow. The teenager was preoccupied with shooing a cat away from the meat and ignored her completely.

When she returned to the table, she saw the others had cleared their plates.

"Gosh, well done you two!" she said.

"It wasn't difficult," said Fi. "It was fabulous."

"Mine too," said Lauren. "We should thank the chef."

"If it's the one I think it is, he's only a young guy. You see over there? In the corner? You can just see into the right-hand end of the kitchen. He appears every so often."

Just as Roz was pointing and all three were staring, the young man did appear momentarily and glanced in their direction.

"Hmmm," said Fi, appreciatively.

A few minutes later, the waiter ambled over with pieces of marbled chocolate cake and a carafe of rakí with glasses. He set everything out on the table and poured the colourless liquid into four glasses, one for himself.

"We drink to Scotland," he said.

"*And* Crete," said Roz.

"Kríti also," he agreed and drank it straight down before giving a little bow.

"We were wondering if we could meet the chef," said Lauren. "We'd like to say thanks – it was such a lovely meal."

"Chef no work today," said the waiter. "Michális, he cook for you. He is trainee."

"Michális?" said Roz.

"Michális. Is like Michael," confirmed the waiter.

"Yes, I know, but …"

"Well, that was pretty amazing for a trainee," Lauren went on. "Even more reason to meet him."

"You wait, I bring," said the waiter, stacking the dishes from the main meal, at last, and carrying them off on a tray after placing their bill in a leather folder on the table.

They sipped their rakís in silence. Fi toyed with her cake. The waiter reappeared but he did not come in their direction. Instead, he approached a fat, middle-aged man who was sitting on the far side of the restaurant with what appeared to be a Greek family group. Suddenly the man jumped to his feet, demonstrating surprising agility, and they both rushed back into the kitchen. Some shouting ensued. A couple of pans fell to the floor with a crash. The fat man re-emerged, complaining loudly into a cell phone and waving his arms about as he walked. The waiter returned to their table; his face screwed up as if wincing from blows.

"Michális finish," he said. "Sorry." He shrugged.

"What do you mean *finish*?" asked Lauren.

"He gone. Boss not happy."

"We saw. Is he coming back?"

"Who knows?"

"But he's in the middle of a service, isn't he?"

As if to emphasise her point, a small group of tourists arrived, perusing the menus facing the promenade. The waiter spread his fingers and held both hands up. The subtext might have been: *What can you do with these hot-headed young men?*

"I sorry," he said and moved away.

"Well, the chef didn't much like the look of us, did he?" said Fi, chuckling.

"I can't imagine we had anything to do with it," said Lauren. "Not very professional, though, leaving the boss in the lurch. No matter how good he is, he won't get far doing that sort of thing."

They both looked at Roz, but she was busy counting out money from her purse to settle the bill.

*

Before they headed back to the boat, the girls offered to treat Roz to coffee and cake, but she declined, saying she was too full and getting a wee bit tired anyway. It was all of ten fifteen, but they agreed to head back. Fi reminded Lauren they had a small bottle of Metaxá back at the tree house if all else failed.

It was a beautiful night, quite still. Clouds of stars but only a sliver of moon. Their engine sounded loud, bouncing back from the rock cliffs. The lights glowed bright red and green, colouring their faces. The Libyan Sea slapped lazily against the hull.

"It's weird, the echo," said Lauren. "It sounds like there are two engines, one deeper than the other. Listen."

"The sounds play tricks around here. It's just us. No other lights, see."

Roz waved her arm beyond the stern where their wake stretched across a glittering black sea to a paler horizon. Lauren stared into the darkness, thinking about the strange behaviour of their cook.

*

The next morning, the girls met briefly at breakfast.

"I need you to take care of yourselves today if that's okay. Dan's happy to show you some of the things he's been working on, but he might make you work for your suppers."

"It's okay, Roz," said Lauren. "Are you off somewhere?"

"My turn for the grocery run. It's another trip to Paleóchora so it takes a while."

"Paleóchora *again*! Why didn't we all do the shopping last night?"

"There's a lot to get, Lauren. It takes a while. And not everywhere would have been open in the evening. Anyway, it would ha' spoiled our evening!"

"Is Teddy going with you?"

"No, just me this time. I'll be fine. He's helping Dan today, I believe."

This cheered Fi up no end, Lauren noticed. Even the thought of work was not too bad if Teddy was going to be around, it seemed.

"If you have time, ask him to show you some of the turtle videos. They're fascinating."

"Okay, we'll be fine but take care out there. It's a bit blowy today."

"Aye, Lauren. The beers might get shaken up a wee bit, but this is normal. It can be a lot worse than this, believe me."

*

The boat was pulled up on the dry riverbed, where they had left it. Roz checked the fuel, looked in her bag to make sure she had her phone with the shopping list on it and the two hundred euros Stefi had given her, lobbed the cardboard box with the shopping bags in it and the cool bag with the ice blocks into the front of the boat and put a thick, coiled rope on top. It was windy enough for something to blow away, otherwise. Finally, she spread factor fifty over her legs, arms and face with an extra blob on her nose and lips.

The boat hull slid easily enough on the shingle, and she was able to manhandle it into the shallows, spin it around and jump in. She lowered the outboard and the propeller dropped below the surface as it clicked in place, then she pulled the starter cord. It took several pulls before the engine caught, but then she was away, buffeting her way across the water.

The sudden feeling of freedom caused her to break into a joyous smile. Wee Rosie Kinnear, the runt of the class, was living with nature and beauty. She was over three thousand kilometres from the drizzly grey of her home city. It was another beautiful, breezy day and she was a part of something. She was trusted, she had responsibility, and she was helping make a difference. Okay, today it was only groceries, but she was proud of what they were trying to do here, and she cared about it. It felt good.

As she puttered along the beach, she was surprised to see another boat, pulled up on the patch of shingle beyond the turtles' cove and almost hidden by vegetation. It was a plain, dove-grey RIB with a much bigger engine than hers. It looked like a sixty-five horsepower. She closed the throttle and watched but there was no sign of anyone, no movement at all apart from three or four crows harassing a cruising raptor, high above the juniper forest. She cut the throttle completely and drifted into the shore about twenty-five metres beyond the grey boat where a large tamarisk provided some shade.

She put up the prop, tied the rope around a branch and listened hard. Just the hissing of cicadas and the occasional rustle of a gecko on the move. She reached for her phone, but it was not in the bag. She must have failed to zip it and now some things had fallen out. She cursed softly, slipped her feet into the shallow water and made her way to the edge of the shingle where some scrappy grass offered a quieter path. The grey boat contained only a red windcheater; she saw. Beyond, the turtle nests seemed undisturbed. In the distance, on the edge of the forest, she saw a large envelope, pinned to one of the bigger trees. *Of course*, she thought, with a start, *it could be the poacher returning for his carcass. But the envelope was still there, where Méli had died, so where the hell was he?*

She moved softly away from the beach and onto the sandy scrubland behind, searching the ground for any signs of a human passing by. But the sand was too dry for footprints. After another ten metres, she spotted a cigarette end, but it was cold. She had no way of knowing how long it had been there. She wrapped it in a tissue, anyway, and popped it into the pocket of her shorts. Another twenty metres and she was scanning the edge of the forest for movement. Then, she heard a twig crack, like a rifle shot in the stillness. It had come from the small copse of tamarisks behind her, nearer the shore. She spun around, looking in the direction of the noise, and spotted a flurry of movement and then nothing. Was it an animal – a pine marten or a badger, perhaps? She looked for wild eyes staring back through the feathery leaves. There were none, but *something* was there. She sensed it. Edging forward, her eyes adjusted to the light and the shapes became more defined. She stopped in her tracks. A man was crouching in shadow, sideways on and unmoving, just three metres inside the copse. He must have seen her, but he had chosen not to reveal himself. On the gritty sand beyond the trees, she glimpsed an open bedroll with rocks securing each corner. Roz felt her pockets, then cursed silently. She stopped seven metres from the crouching figure, her heart thudding in her chest, her mind racing, panic rising. It felt desperate, but she had to try something.

"Stefi," she shouted into the stillness, "I think I've found him."

CHAPTER 13
THE FIRE

"What are those things, then?" Lauren was pointing to some massive, plastic boxes.

"Batteries," said Dan. "They store solar energy. We need them because we're not on the grid."

"Because you're stuck out here?"

"Basically, yes. It would cost too much to hook us up. And that's a shame because, with NetBilling, if we *were* connected to the grid, we could buy power from them if we ran out, late in the winter, and sell them any summer surplus, though we'd only get half price for that."

"So, without access to the grid, you have to store it in whopping batteries."

"Right. Expensive, whopping batteries."

"And then the power lasts all winter?"

"It's designed to. We have many sunny days, even in winter, so it gets topped up. And we have the old generator if we get it wrong."

Fi was staring at a field of solar panels, tilted towards the sun. Cables were running everywhere.

"Do you need all those?" she asked.

"I'm afraid so, yes. There are twenty-four, so far. We may need to add more, later, as we expand the site. But it depends on the other energy sources."

"They're not very attractive, are they? Couldn't you plant some trees, hide them a bit?"

"Not really. Any shade reduces their performance."

The girls exchanged glances. Any thoughts that renewable energy was environmentally friendly were being challenged by the eyesore all this kit created.

"What other energy sources do you mean, Dan?" asked Lauren.

He grinned and pointed upwards.

"That's one of them, of course."

They followed his arm and saw a row of giant wind turbines close to the top of the mountains behind, and way above, the juniper forest.

"Oh, right. We saw those, but they're not yours, surely?"

"Haha. I wish! But no, those are owned by the power company, but I'm planning to build half a dozen much smaller ones on the edge of Stefi's land, at the back there. See? There's a little one, already. Then, we'll make power when it's sunny *or* windy, which is almost all the time here. I'm exploring a small hydroelectric device for the river, too."

"What river – oh, you mean the dried-up stream thing?"

"It's dried up now, but in winter and early spring, it's a raging torrent. You wouldn't believe how it changes. Tourists have no idea how much rain falls here, out of season. It thunders down, too. And then you have the melting snow, later. All this means there's potential to create power just when we most need it."

"Because the sun's not shining."

"Well, rather less, certainly."

"And the wind's not blowing," Fi was smirking a little.

"Look, Fi, it's fundamentally a solar system, okay? But it will have a lot to do: a complex of luxury apartments, tree houses and yurts, a restaurant, and two pools. It makes sense to integrate a little wind and hydroelectric power. The kind of guests Stefi plans to attract won't appreciate cold water or blackouts. Not at the prices they'll be paying."

"How environmentally friendly is it to produce all this kit, though?" asked Lauren. "And what happens when it comes to the end of its useful life? Is it bio-degradable? I don't think so."

"We don't have all the answers yet, Lauren. I'm just trying to do my best with what's available. I'm sure there will be many changes as time goes on."

Dan wanted to show them his mini hydro station, but Lauren deterred him after looking at Fi's face. She seemed to be impersonating a zombie.

"Why don't you show us what the guests will experience? Pretend we're future customers."

"Sure. Happy to. We haven't built much of it yet, obviously, but I can talk through the plans with you, show you the architect's drawings and so on."

"I'd like that," Lauren said but Fi bared her lip in a snarl of boredom and made big eyes as if to say: *Out of the frying pan into the fire; thanks a lot, girl!* Lauren hoped Dan had not seen.

"Where's Teddy?" Fi asked. "He's supposed to be joining us, isn't he?"

"He'll be along, I guess."

They were heading back to the huts when Lauren spotted a rather different guy.

"Isn't it …?" said Fi.

"Dad. Yes. I've no idea what he's doing here. Jesus."

As they approached the main hut, Stefi and Nick were emerging, looking like old friends. Seeing Lauren's face, Nick raised his hands in self-defence.

"Don't worry, I'm not planning to stay. Just wanted to be sure you're okay. You didn't answer your phone yesterday – or today. Your mum was worried."

"I forgot to charge it, what with everything that's been going on here. Sorry. Stupid of me. And it's probably stone-dead by now. I didn't mean to drag you all this way, Dad. I feel awful."

"Your mum has this mental picture of you both, sleeping in a tree house in the middle of a tinder-dry forest about to be consumed by a raging wildfire. I didn't have enough information to reassure her and – as she's three thousand kilometres away – it was down to me. I thought I'd better check after my police buddy told me the fires were getting quite close and the wind is forecast to strengthen again. So, here I am."

"And you've met Stefi, I see."

"I have. And he's been showing me his plans. Astonishing stuff."

There was a pause and Lauren looked around her, wearing a rather silly face.

"Well, everyone. As you probably gathered, this is my dad, Nick Fisher." She turned to Nick. "You know Fi, of course, and now you've met Stefi. This is Dan, who is an American and a whizz on renewable energy."

"I'm no whizz. Just learning as fast as I can. Hi, Mr Fisher. Welcome to Tamarisk Bay."

Fi glanced mischievously at Lauren.

"*Greece's first wholly sustainable, luxury destination*," they chorused, ending in giggles.

"That's nice. I like it," said Nick.

"You've trained them well, Dan," said Stefi.

"There are two more of us," said Lauren. "You know about Roz, of course. She got the short straw today; she's on the grocery run. You'll meet her this evening. And then there's Theódoros who is Greek, like Stefi. We call him Teddy. Where is he, Stefi?"

"He went to his cabin. Just emails or something. I'm sure he'll be out soon."

"So, that's it," said Lauren, beaming at her father. "Shall we make some lunch?"

"Show me where you're sleeping, first. Then I can call your mum and bring her up to speed. She'll only worry otherwise. You know what she's like."

Nick was looking forward to his lunch. It had been an early start. But, as they strolled across to the tree houses, he saw, with some certainty, that he was not getting any, anytime soon. Bright flames were shooting up from the right-hand side of the juniper forest. There was almost no smoke, strangely, but there was a slight acridity to the air and a distant rustling, cracking sound. Already at least a tenth of the forest was engulfed.

He put out his arm and stopped his daughter in her tracks.

"I assume this should not be happening," he said.

She followed his eyes and shrieked.

"Oh, My God. Stefi! Dan!" she yelled.

They emerged from the cabin behind them.

"Holy shit," said Dan. "Stefi – call the Fire Service now. We're going to need some help."

Stefi returned to the hut to make the call.

Nick was already assessing the situation. If the entire forest went, could the fire jump to the scrubland and across to the huts? It seemed entirely possible.

"Are there paths or tracks crossing the forest, Dan?"

"There are several. What are you thinking?"

"Is there a track that crosses completely, north-south?"

"There is. It's about a third of the way along. It's the route through to my wind turbine."

"Okay. I assume there's no water down there?"

"No. Nearest would be the underground tank for the gardens. You're talking two hundred metres plus."

"Too far for a hose."

"For sure."

"Do you have any explosives here?"

"No."

"How about earth-moving equipment – a JCB or something?"

"There's a mini excavator we use to scoop out the riverbed."

Stefi came out of the hut, looking frustrated.

"They are very busy. They will come with a helicopter, but it might be several hours."

"Did they tell you what to do?" asked Nick.

"Just make sure everyone is safe and wait."

"To hell with that. You could lose the whole place in a few hours."

"You think it could get to the huts, Nick?" asked Dan.

"Would you bet it could not? You must have seen those wildfires on television. They jump gaps, they chuck out burning foliage and sparks ..."

"We have no firefighting kit, Nick. We are at its mercy, I think," said Stefi. "How in God's name did it start?"

"It doesn't matter. It is what it is. And we must deal with it."

"But how, Nick?"

He noticed everyone had gathered around quietly while they were talking. Fi was there, looking scared, and a darker-skinned, good-looking, young man was rubbing his eyes, as if in disbelief. That must be Teddy.

"I have only one idea, but it might just work."

"Go on," said Stefi.

"We use the path to the wind turbine as the base for a firebreak."

"So, we will lose two-thirds of the forest," said Stefi.

"I think that's very likely, Stefi. It has a good hold already. You can see it. As long as this hot, south-east wind keeps blowing, it will move quickly. The firebreak is to save the rest and – more importantly – to stop it jumping to the huts and tree houses."

"What do we need to do, Nick?"

"If the firebreak is to have a chance of working, we need to widen it, clear it and soak it. Dan – I want you and Teddy to get the excavator and get over there. Start clearing the brush and widening the gap where you can. Stefi – how much water is in the garden tank?"

"It holds twenty thousand litres, but it won't be full, not this time of year."

"Check it. If it's half full or more, we're in business. Can you run a hose from the tank? The longest one you have. I know it won't reach, but then we'll need a human chain with buckets from the end of the hose to the firebreak. I hope you have a few buckets?"

Stefi was nodding.

"I guess we're the human chain," said Lauren, looking at Fi. "Rather a short one."

"Stefi and I can help, a bit later," said Nick.

"May I say something?" It was Teddy.

They turned to him, expectantly.

"I'm sorry, Nick, but what the fuck? We only just met you and now you're ordering us all about. Do you know anything about fire control?"

The girls looked shocked at this intervention, but Nick took it on the chin.

"I'm just using common sense, Teddy. If anyone knows more than I do or has a better idea, they are welcome to speak up. In the meantime, we have an urgent crisis to deal with and someone needs to take charge."

"Why not Stefi, then? It's his land."

Nick glanced at Stefi, raising his eyebrows.

"Nick's doing okay, Teddy," he said. "Leave it alone. I'm too shocked by recent events to be much use, anyway."

"Come on, Teddy. Let's make a start," said Dan, striding off. Teddy made a sulky face, threw up his arms and turned to follow him. They saw Dan slapping him on the back a little too hard and Teddy wresting his arm away as they started to jog towards the dried-up riverbed.

"Boys will be boys, I guess," said Lauren, rolling her eyes. "Where are the buckets?"

*

The pressure from the tap was not the best. It took Fi over a minute to fill each bucket with the hose. She managed to attach the hose to each bucket with a clip which enabled her to lug the other bucket fifty or so metres across the scrub to where she left it for Lauren, bringing back an empty one. Lauren's job was to bring each full bucket some eighty metres, to the start of the forest path, and return with an empty one. Stefi formed the last link in the chain, taking the full buckets and hurling the water systematically over the vegetation to the right of the track.

It was a good job they had the six buckets, thought Fi, as she ran, *but would they make any difference?* The path cut through the little forest at what would be its narrowest point, pretty much, but it would still be at least fifteen metres long. Even if they did this for an hour and a half – and, with the fire advancing rapidly and the back-breaking nature of the work, she doubted that would be possible – they would fill less than seventy buckets. Less than five buckets per metre of vegetation. And that's if the blasted clip did not fall off again. She felt hot tears springing from her eyes at the frustration of it all.

Lauren was concentrating on pacing herself. Trying to jog eighty metres with ten or more kilos of water slopping about in a bucket was not easy, especially at thirty-five Celsius with a strong wind blowing. After the third trip, she decided it was both insane and pointless. She would find a vehicle of some sort.

*

When Fi reached the handover point with the fifth bucket, she saw the fourth one still sitting there. She looked around. Stefi was disappearing into the forest. Lauren was nowhere to be seen. Then, a graunch of gears made her turn around and she spotted Lauren at the wheel of Stefi's ancient tractor, bumping and slithering her way across the sandy bush, dodging the rocks. She came to a halt in a shroud of dust and sand.

"Are you crazy?" said Fi.

"I might be, but I think this will be quicker. And I don't think we can keep up the human chain for long."

"It'll slop everywhere on that."

"Let's give it a try."

They loaded up the two buckets onto the floor of the small trailer.

"Now, you get on back and start filling."

"I've nothing *to* fill."

"Shit, of course you don't. You'd better get in."

The drive was doable. You had to avoid the rocks and the places where the sand was too deep, but elsewhere the tractor kept its grip and pushed its way happily through the wiry scrub.

"No more lugging," said Lauren, triumphantly.

"There's a lot of water sloshing about on the floor," said Fi.

"Just fill them two-thirds and I'll drive them over in batches of three. Let's grab all the empties and give it a go."

*

They could use a full-sized JCB, Nick thought, but the Japanese mini excavator was a sturdy little beast. Nick and Dan were wielding machetes, hacking back the dried bush and grass, then Teddy, sulk over, was powering through with the little machine, clearing the debris.

Periodically, Stefi would appear with another bucket of water to drench the remaining vegetation. The gap was steadily widening at this end of the path, but the other end needed to be done, too, and the fire was getting closer. Already they could feel the heat from it and hear the fierce crackling.

"When do you think they'll get here?" Nick asked Stefi, between buckets.

"The Fire Service guys? They just promised to come as soon as they could. They'll try to call."

Nick checked his watch. It was almost three. He reckoned they had an hour before the fire would force them to abandon their efforts. Maybe less.

"You've got your phone on you, right?"

Stefi nodded.

"And it has plenty of charge."

Another nod.

"Do you have a chainsaw, Stefi? I think we need to take out the tops of the trees on the edge here. Try to widen the gap, higher up."

"I'll go get it."

Nick gave him the thumbs up and carried on swinging the machete.

*

By ten minutes to four, they had done all they could do. The wind might have lessened a tad, but the advance of the fire was relentless, moving west steadily. There was still no sign of the Fire Service. Nick reckoned they had almost doubled the width of the path as well as soaking the vegetation on the eastern side. They were vulnerable to sparks or flaming branches blowing over the path as the western side was still tinder dry, but he hoped taking out the tops of the trees on the eastern side had reduced that risk.

The heat from the fire was too much now to continue working, so they pulled back, forming a tired and sweaty band thirty metres away, towards the sea. The devastation was clear now. Stinking, black, ruins lay where the fire had consumed the eastern side of the forest. A few juniper trees were still standing but they were sticks of charcoal in a sea of ash. Lauren was stunned at the power of fire, witnessed first-hand. No amount of television news items had prepared her for this. It leapt from tree to tree, instantly engulfing. It roared as it consumed. It was unpredictable and vengeful. Worst for her was the desperation of the animals. The birds just flew away, of course, but many of the smaller mammals were confused or trapped. Occasionally, screams of terror could be heard, even above the roar of the inferno. Those sounds would stay with her forever.

"What now?" she asked her father.

"We watch and wait."

"You think our firebreak will hold?"

"I don't know, Lauren. But I don't see what more we can do."

"Chase up the Fire Service?" she responded.

"I did it already," said Stefi, "and they yelled at me. They're fighting several fires. They're fully aware of our situation and they'll get to us as soon as they can. Meanwhile, they need to keep their phone lines clear."

"Fair enough, I suppose," said Nick.

"Should I keep the water buckets coming?" asked Lauren.

"Just get all six lined up full, somewhere here, in case we need them," said Nick.

"Should we take up positions just west of the path, armed with buckets, in case any sparks cross over?"

"I think it's too dangerous, Dan. Let's see how the firebreak performs."

"I don't want anyone getting hurt," added Stefi.

"No, and, if it does make it across, I reckon we'll have at least half an hour before it becomes a threat to the rest of the place."

"Half an hour's not much. Shouldn't we be wetting those areas now?" said Dan.

"I think we need a short break, Dan, take turns to freshen up and get something to eat. This could be a very long day."

"Why don't Fi and I take the first showers, then, and sort out some lunch?" said Lauren.

"I thought you'd never ask," grinned Nick, tousling her grimy hair. "Buckets first, mind."

*

The fire reached the path at twenty past four. All four men were watching by the buckets. The girls were yet to reappear. Flames groped out into the void but found nothing to attach themselves to, though at times it was a close-run thing. The wet vegetation smoked. The fire seemed to turn inward, regrouping, intensifying and feeding on itself. The men exchanged hopeful glances, but they could see it was still strong and they could hear it fizzing and sizzling. After fifteen minutes, they were reassured. The dry vegetation had been consumed and was falling in. The intensity of the fire seemed to be lessening. Soon after, the girls arrived with a beer and a pita for each of them. The pitas were stuffed with ham, feta cheese and tomato and moistened with smeared avocado and mayonnaise. Everyone thanked them and seized their prizes gleefully.

"I'm sorry there's no rocket," said Lauren. "Hopefully it's on Roz's shopping list."

"Is it working, the firebreak?" asked Fi.

"We're hoping so," said Stefi.

"The jury's out," said Nick, looking up at the tops of the trees as he tilted back his can of Alfa.

Lauren followed his eyes. To her, not much had changed. There were still flames, though perhaps a little lazier than before, and a massive crumbling edifice of glowing debris beneath. As she watched, she heard the plastic beer cups scatter in a sudden gust. There was a crack and a tree to the right tumbled forward, plunging into the inferno. A shower of sparks flew into the air.

"Watch them," shouted Nick as twigs and leaves, glowing bright in the sharp breeze, made it across the path. Dan grabbed a bucket and went to douse a few threatening to catch on the left-hand side of the path.

"Be careful, Dan," called Stefi.

92

A second gust, fiercer still, brought a flurry of burning leaves. Soon, a dozen tiny fires had formed on the left-hand side of the path. Dan was hesitating.

"I can run to the end and back, put them out," he said.

"Don't do it, Dan," called Nick. "It's too dangerous, mate."

"They'll only form again, anyway," yelled Stefi. "You can't stop the wind. Come back."

As if confirming his remark, a third gust tore a crumbling branch, loaded with flame from the remains of a tree on the right and hurled it across the gap, sailing close by Dan's head. Behind it, another forty or fifty smouldering leaves rose in an angry cloud. Dan put his arms above his head and scampered out of the firing line. As they watched, the fire quickly took hold on the western side for the first time.

"Damn it. All that work to save just forty minutes?" said Nick.

"Nothing will stop it now," said Stefi, forlornly.

"We'll see about that," said Nick bravely but he was running out of ideas and the fire was gathering strength again. The team was looking to him for leadership, but he felt tired and defeated. His firebreak had not worked. Not really.

Lauren walked over and hugged him.

"I'm filthy," he said.

"I know, but you still deserve a hug. It was a valiant effort, and the forty minutes may yet prove crucial."

Stefi came up and stood in front of Nick.

"I want to thank you for what you tried to do, Nick. We only meet today and yet you work so hard and risk your life for me and the guys here? I owe you, big time."

"You owe me nothing, Stefi. I'll settle for a shower and a nice meal later with a glass or two of house red. But right now, we have more work to do."

*

Twenty minutes later, the fire was in full flow again, well on its way to destroying the western part of the forest, too. Lauren was back to shuttling buckets with the tractor, this time to the far western end of the forest. The rest were using them to douse the grass, scrub and bushes without any real hope of stopping the fire before it leapt across to the huts.

"What's the insurance situation?" Nick asked Stefi.

"How you mean, Nick?"

"Have you got any?"

"I hope so, but I don't know for sure. The bastards will probably say a wildfire is an Act of God and refuse to pay a cent."

"Really? What's the good of insurance if it doesn't cover fire?"

"A good question, Nick. But I had to buy insurance before the bank would lend to me so I went for the cheapest I could find."

"Ah." Nick stood up straight and rubbed his back. He surveyed the ruins of the forest, then glanced across to the huts and the equipment sheds.

"And what if the fire was started deliberately? Are you covered for arson?"

"I don't know. It will be in the small print so that probably means *No*. You think someone *did* this to me?"

"We can discuss it later, but there must be a chance of it. I checked out the local fire situation closely before I set off this morning. I went online and then I talked to a friend who is a Police Lieutenant in Chaniá. The wildfires were getting closer, but they were still eighteen kilometres from you. That's a long way for a spark to fly, my friend."

A female voice cut in, loudly.

"Keep quiet, everyone. I think I hear something."

They all turned to Fi. Her arm was raised to keep them quiet, and her head was cocked for ten, long seconds. Then she beamed.

"Can't you hear it?" she said.

There was a mixed reaction. Some thought they could, others not.

"It's a helicopter, maybe more than one. And they're getting closer."

After a few more seconds, the sound was unmistakable, and then the two red machines appeared above the wind turbines, on the highest part of the mountain. Both had giant water buckets attached. They were coming to Tamarisk Bay, no question. The six of them broke into a spontaneous cheer of relief. There were hugs. Tears streaked their grimy faces. They began waving and cheering.

They watched as the helicopters swooped down. One slowed above their heads and began to hover. The other went down to the sea. A man with a loud hailer leaned out and called to them in Greek.

"He says we must get clear of the fire now, out of their way and back towards the huts," said Stefi. He then waved his arms as if shooing sheep and they jogged away. They saw the farthest helicopter hovering in a stationary position as it lowered its bucket into the sea, then motoring forward slowly, nose down, dragging the bucket through the water to fill it before rising swiftly away, the bucket sailing below. The second helicopter followed suit and one by one they deluged the fire with the water from the buckets.

"How much water is in *those* buckets, do you think?" Lauren asked Nick.

"I'd guess close to a thousand litres. They look a similar size to my oil tank."

"That's more than all our little buckets, in one scoop!"

"Let's hope it does the trick, then."

They watched as the helicopters went back and forth. For half an hour, they concentrated on the remaining green forest to the west of the path, drenching it thoroughly. Then they completed three runs each on the path area. After fifty minutes, Stefi's cell phone started ringing. He listened intently for a few moments, covering his other ear. Then he said:

"Óchi, óchi. Endáxi. Efcharistoúme pára pára polí."

As he disconnected, they banked sharply and flew away, rising swiftly over the mountain and gradually disappearing. The sound of the rotor blades faded, leaving only the soft crash and shingle drag of the waves on the shore. The fire was out. They were saved, at least for now. *But this was not a dream destination anymore*, thought Nick. *Not for quite a while, at least.*

"It would have been good to shake their hands and share a cold beer or two," he said to Stefi.

"These guys have no time for anything now. Global warming has left them overstretched. Anyway, the beer has run out, I think. Listen, Nick. It's just after six now. Let's get cleaned up and then maybe we could talk over a drink of something before dinner. I'd like your thoughts on what's been going on here."

"Sure. Glad to help, if I can."

As they approached the huts, Lauren and Fi were waiting. The boys must have rushed to the showers.

"There's nothing much to cook, guys. When will Roz get back, Stefi?"

For a moment, he looked as if he did not understand the question or had forgotten who Roz was. Then he checked his watch again. It was still just after six; of course, it was. Then there was a dawning on his face. A realisation. Something was wrong.

"She's been gone over eight hours. It takes five or six. Maybe she had some shopping of her own? Has she called; I wonder."

He checked his phone and quickly shook his head.

"Has she called anyone?"

"Maybe Dan?" said Lauren. But, when Dan emerged from the shower and checked, he had no missed calls or messages either.

"We shouldn't have let her go alone. With this gusty wind, it would have been tough. I just didn't think."

"We've had a lot on our minds, Dan. Don't beat yourself up," said Nick.

"Okay. We start by calling her," said Stefi, punching the keys on his phone. He listened for a few moments, then shook his head. "Going straight to voicemail. Get dressed quickly and go look for the boat, Dan."

"She's got the boat *with* her."

"Let's hope so. But we start by making sure she got away okay. Then we must find out if she arrived okay, maybe call the supermarkets in Paleóchora and so on."

"I get you. Okay. I'm on my way."

"Did you give her a bank card to use for the groceries?" asked Nick. "You could check if any bills have come through."

"I gave her cash; two hundred euros."

"Ah. That's a pity. So, do you always use the same supermarket?"

"For most things, yes, we use Synka, but they won't recognise Roz. She's only been once or twice, with Dan. We'll have to send photos for them to show the staff and some of them will have finished their shifts and gone home."

"Would she need to buy anything else, go anywhere else?"

"The baker, the butcher …"

"What about wine and beer, Stefi?"

"She'd get that in Synka."

"What about fuel?"

"We'll have to ask Dan how much was in the tank."

"The girls went to Paleóchora last night, though, didn't they?"

"True, so she may well have needed a top-up."

"So, four possible places where they might remember her."

Stefi called Roz's phone again, with the same result. This time he waited and left a message asking her to call as soon as she got it. When Teddy appeared, they asked if he had heard from her. He had not. The five of them stood around listlessly. Then Stefi's phone rang.

Nick saw his face brighten but it proved to be premature.

"Oh, it's you, Dan. Hold on, I'll put you on speakerphone."

"The boat's not here, so it looks like she got away just fine. I've jogged the length of the shoreline down to the turtles. Nothing. Did you call her?"

"Not picking up."

"Oh. *That's* not good."

"No. I left a message. Better come back then, Dan."

They spent the next two hours digging out suitable photos of Roz and contact numbers for the shops and the two petrol stations. Nick suggested they start there as not many small red-headed Scottish girls would be buying petrol for a can, in cash. She would be remembered.

But she was not. Not at the petrol stations, not at Synka, not at either of the butchers nor any of the bakers. They had drawn a blank and the shops were closing now, at nine. It had been dark for a while now. They had delayed long enough.

"Stefi," said Nick, "I don't want to worry everyone but what we have here is a missing person. Roz may be in trouble and the sooner we report it, the better."

With everyone's agreement, Nick put in a call to Leo and sent him three recent photos of Roz. A missing person case was below Leo's pay grade, but he promised to alert the team at Paleóchora and put some pressure on them to be useful, for once.

"There's not much we can do in the dark, Nick, but I can make sure there's a team scouring the coastline first thing. You'll need to send me details of the boat. And we'll get some constables asking around in the town, see if anyone recognises her."

"What about the Coast Guard?"

"We'll alert them, too; standard procedure."

"And her family? I believe her father died recently but there's a mother in Scotland, somewhere."

"Send me contact details if you have them but I won't call just yet."

"No. I guess she has a right to know but what would be the point? She'd just worry herself sick."

"I will have to call later tomorrow, I think."

Nick thanked him. He knew Leo well enough by now and was confident he would get things done. It was agonising for them all, but what else could be done? With the boat gone, there was no point searching Tamarisk Bay.

CHAPTER 14
ROZ

Teddy was up early the next morning after a fitful night's sleep. With Roz absent, he would need to check on the turtle nests himself. Seeing no one else was up yet, he wandered down there before breakfast. It was a beautiful morning, the wind gone, the sun warm on his face, wavelets toying with the shingle. Parts of the forest were still smoking and three-quarters of it was ash and charcoal. One or two birds had returned, he saw, only to look around in bewilderment before flying off again. There was nothing left for them.

With all the turmoil of the previous day, it was good to see the nests looking undisturbed and peaceful. He did a few test digs to check for predators, but all seemed clear. He made a mental note to label the nest hidden behind the rocks. Then he checked the other labels for the earliest date and found it was just over five weeks earlier. It would not be long before the first hatchlings broke free, he realised. He would need to pay more attention to the night watch infrared filming and prepare some runs. It would not be easy without Roz to share the shifts.

As Teddy stood and stretched, something caught his eye, along the shore to the east. A flash of red. Was it a bird? He could not see clearly past the large tamarisk, but he knew red was not a colour much encountered in nature, at least not here in Crete. He took off his sandals and walked out into the water, curious. Now, he saw something glinting metallic in the sun, as a light breeze swayed the feathery leaves. At first, the angle confused him but then he realised. It was an outboard motor, stowed in the horizontal position but still attached to a boat. As he paddled towards it, he saw the grey form, the red stripe. It was their boat! Dan would have easily missed it, this far down and tucked behind the tree. What the hell was it doing here? With more urgency now, he ploughed through the shallow water and grabbed the side of the boat. Two things were immediately clear. The weight of the fuel tank told him it was still well over half full; so, the boat had not been to Paleóchora more than once. The shopping bags under the coiled rope confirmed this. And Roz's bag was in the boat. It was on its side and open, he saw, and a few things had fallen out. Among its contents, he found four fifty-euro notes folded and tucked into a side pocket. Standing up, he caught sight of an iPhone, face down on the floor of the boat. He picked it up and popped it in the bag. The rush of excitement he felt at the discovery had now turned to a sick feeling in the pit of his stomach. Roz was still here, somewhere. She might be hurt, and she had no phone with which to call them. They needed to find her, and soon. He called her name and searched the immediate area but there was nothing. Then he ran back to alert the others, taking her bag with him.

*

"This changes everything," said Nick. "We need to start a systematic search of Tamarisk Bay right away because she must be here. We don't understand why, but she *must* be here, agreed?"

"Unless she wandered off the property for some reason," said Dan.

"Or was taken by another boat?" said Stefi.

"I doubt she would leave her bag and phone behind," said Nick.

"She may have been given no choice," volunteered Stefi.

"All right. Let's not get too fanciful. We must assume she's here and she might have hurt herself."

They decided to work in three pairs: Stefi and Lauren, Dan and Nick, Teddy and Fi. Each pair would cover a strip of territory from west to east, working systematically and calling out to Roz at regular intervals. As they walked to their starting positions, Nick put in a call to Leo to update him.

"Doesn't sound good, does it, Nick?" he said. "I'll call off the Coast Guard and get the Paleóchora constables to help you with the search. What sort of area are we talking about?"

"Thirty or forty hectares. It's big."

"Then focus on the areas which were forest *before* the fire."

Nick was silent for a moment as the full implication of Leo's words sank in.

"You think she was caught in the fire? Oh, God, Leo!"

"Either she's immobilised somewhere or she's unconscious or dead. You know that, Nick."

He did know. Of course, he did. The facts were inescapable. As he walked, he was already asking himself why the girl would interrupt her grocery trip to come ashore. Something or someone else had to be involved, surely …

*

They searched all day but found nothing. Two constables from Paleóchora arrived by boat just before noon and then, to Nick's delight, Thaní arrived with two more from Chaniá. It was good to see him again and he told him so.

"I'm pleased to get away for a while, Nick, to be honest. Leo is frustrated with our murder case and not nice to be around."

"Not found the boyfriend, then?"

"The guy's a chef and he's gone to Iráklio, we were told. Do you know how many restaurants there are in Iráklio, Nick?"

"I can imagine. Poor Anna."

There were now eleven of them searching for Roz. Thankfully, the winds had died down, but there was a lot of ground to cover, and they needed to proceed slowly to ensure nothing was missed. As the sun went down, the police contingent asked if they might stay over and Stefi and the girls ran around, organising bedding. The shortage of groceries was becoming acute now. They would have to make a large bowl of pasta to go around. There was still plenty of wine and rakí, but the beer was running out.

As they sat around in the gathering dusk, Thaní came over to join Nick.

"An Englishman marooned without beer. How are you coping, Nick?"

"I've survived three years here without proper ale so I think I can manage a day or two without Alfa or Mythos, thanks Thaní. Anyway, it's not at the forefront of my mind right now."

"Of course, not. A frustrating day."

"You can say that again. Do you think she's out there? What's your gut feeling?"

"In my experience, young women are never far from their phones, these days. So, I think she must be close by unless she was taken somewhere else by force."

"I agree."

"May I see the phone? Do you have it here?"

Nick retrieved the iPhone from the table in Stefi's hut. It was still more than fifty per cent charged; he saw. He handed it to Thaní who found he could press the green phone symbol and flip straight to the record of recent calls.

"What happened to her passcode?" he asked.

"Er … my daughter found a way to remove it for us. On the Internet."

"This is evidence, Nick. You know better than that. Suppose we had lost all the data."

"Sorry. You're right, of course. But it's all there, I think."

Thaní was flipping through call records.

"She was in the UK recently?" he asked.

"Yes," said Nick. "She's only been back about ten days. She travelled back with my daughter."

"Okay. So, there are several UK numbers, then nothing until this number and then this number, twice, in red, which is labelled Stefanos."

Nick leaned over.

"Okay. The first one is my daughter, Lauren, a few days ago. That one must be Stefi. He called twice but she didn't answer, which is why it's in red, I think."

Thaní lost interest, returned to the main menu and selected an icon labelled Photography, then Photos.

"Have you done this already, Nick?"

"No. Not yet."

"Who is this man?" Thaní asked. "I have not seen him here."

Nick leaned over again and turned the phone to see more clearly.

"I have no idea. But it looks like it was taken here, doesn't it?"

"It does."

He flipped back through Roz's photos. There were three of this character and then what looked like a small burial mound in the sand, hands dropping round, white balls into a hole and then several of a large turtle on its back with Teddy crouched over it. Before them, there were shots of a sickly-looking older man with perhaps his wife and one with a younger, red-haired woman, too.

"This is Roz, I think?"

"Yes. With her parents, I imagine. Her dad has since died."

Nick looked for a second longer than was necessary at the attractive, dark-haired woman who must be Roz's mother.

"I think we need a chat with Stefi," said Thaní. "I want to see if he recognises this guy and find out if he has any enemies."

*

Later that evening, after a modest bowl of seafood pasta, Nick and Thaní sat down with Stefi. He asked if Dan could join them. He could.

"He has a clearer head than me at the moment, and a better memory," explained Stefi.

"Good, because we want to talk through all the troubles you've had, leading up to this," said Thaní. "I want to see if it can all be dismissed as coincidence or if something bad is happening; if someone is trying to get at you – and why."

Stefi nodded, looking grateful and perhaps relieved his burden was about to be shared.

"The first I knew was the bank turning shitty," volunteered Dan. "Why don't you start there, Stefi?"

Stefi told them about the surprising change of account manager at the bank and their sudden need to review the entire project. He described the surprising forestry claim, relating to the juniper forest, the call from Tzanakákis after the Roman coin finds and the apparent hunting incident resulting in poor Méli's demise.

By this time, Thaní had raised both hands in the air.

"Woah! Stop! Please stop, Stefi. You are joking with me. All this happened in the space of what – a few months?"

"A few weeks."

"And then the fire and Roz's disappearance?"

Stefi nodded.

"I'm sorry, but these *cannot* be coincidences. I am not a gambling man, but the probability of all these things happening *by chance* in such a short time must be close to zero, wouldn't you say, Nick?"

"Absolute zero if you ask me. And it's been escalating; the attacks are getting more personal."

Dan had been staring at Stefi steadily. Finally, he reached across and put a hand on his.

"You gotta tell 'em about the offer, Stefi," he said.

"I know, but I'm scared."

"I know you are, but you gotta tell 'em now."

"What offer?" chorused Nick and Thaní.

Stefi told them about the mysterious approach from the estate agent in Chaniá.

"You have no idea who is behind this?" asked Thaní.

"I'd guess it was a foreign buyer, but I don't really know."

"What makes you think so?"

"There has been a lot of foreign buying for development in recent years. Shadowy figures, operating through offshore companies. They make indirect approaches, through agents, lawyers, engineers."

"And is two million a fair price, in your opinion?"

"No. Tamarisk Bay is not an easy place to put a value on, but I have thirty-three hectares here. It's a mixture of terrain with five hundred metres of coastline, most of which is beach. At least twelve hectares would be buildable with the right permissions. There are not many places like this left in Crete."

"So, what is the value in your opinion, Stefi?"

"I don't have an opinion. It's not for sale. But I see people selling single plots for large villas at two hundred thousand now if they have a sea view. Twelve hectares could accommodate *thirty* such plots here – or a large hotel complex."

Nick calculated: at least six million euros by that reckoning.

"Yes, but first you must have building permissions, clearance from archaeology, forestry and so on – and then you must get electricity and water here, maybe a road, too," Thaní said.

"Of course, but this does not cost four million euros, my friend. And these guys have the politicians in their pockets. They can make things happen because they fit the big dream of touristic development which obsesses this government. They want to turn my beautiful island into another Mýkonos."

There was a pause. Nick sympathised with Stefi. It was what Háris had been griping about; foreign-owned businesses buying up beauty spots and turning them into exclusive resorts from which the tourists never ventured.

"You don't know the buyer's intentions though, do you, Stefi? Did the agent give anything away?"

"I didn't ask, Nick. When the answer is *No* there is no need to waste time on this."

Thaní had picked up Roz's phone again. Now he placed it in front of Stefi.

"Do you recognise this man? Or do you, Dan?"

They both shook their heads.

"But these were taken *here*, right?"

It was Dan who spoke.

"Yes. These two are near the end of the shingle beach. Those are the turtle nests behind him, see? And this one – with his back to us – is further along the beach, nearer to where we are now, looking west to Elafonísi. I'd guess they were taken from the same place, pretty much."

"And on the same day, less than ten minutes apart, according to the phone," said Thaní.

"I remember," said Stefi. "She said something to me about a tourist she had spotted. She didn't like the look of him. I guess this is why she took photos."

"Didn't she show them to you?"

"I thought there was nothing to worry about and told her so. She assumed I wasn't interested; I suppose."

"I don't know if these photos are good enough," said Thaní, "but I'll try to run a check with Interpol. Given what's happened, we must regard this man's presence here as suspicious."

*

The search resumed at first light, the next morning. There was still no wind and it promised to be a hot, sultry day.

Thaní decided, reluctantly, to focus on the fire-damaged forest. Apprehensive looks were exchanged as he formed them into a line with each person just two metres from their neighbour and everyone carrying a pole of some sort.

"Now, we walk forward. Slowly," he said. "Swing left and right. If you can't see, use the poles to investigate. Roz is here somewhere. Let's find her."

Nick could feel the heat from the ash. Nothing on the surface was glowing now, but underneath the forest was still simmering. Everywhere was white-grey ash, black skeletons of trees and the silence of absent birds and dead animals. They had started at the back of the juniper forest and were now walking forward in line, silent apart from the swish of poles through ash and the cracks of the occasional twig. It felt surreal, ghastly. Everyone wanted it to be over.

Of all the searchers, the one least fitted for the task drew the short straw. *Sod's Law again*, Nick would think, later. At the beginning of the third hour, Fi spotted something different. Was it just another charred log? She moved her pole and shifted some ash and debris. The constable next to her saw what she was doing and started to help. Blue began to appear amongst the ash. It was not a colour Fi had expected to see. Not a natural blue, either, but blue cloth, denim perhaps, and, below it, white. Fi stared for a moment and then shrieked and covered her face. The constable pushed her back.

"Sergeant, I think we find her. All right. Everyone must move back now," he called. "You don't want to see this. Leave it to the police now."

Nick still regarded himself as police and Thaní was not about to object, it seemed. While the five civilians gathered in a scared huddle ten metres away, the police set about securing and clearing the area around the discovery with infinite care. After doing their best with the poles, two constables were sent in with brushes to dust away the remaining ash.

The body was face-down. Dusty, denim shorts on grey-white legs belied the fact that the upper part of the body was a blackened corpse, clothes and hair burnt off, the side of the face unrecognisable. The medical examiner would need to confirm the identity of the corpse, but Nick was in no doubt. It was Roz. He wandered back to the others, hands in pockets, shaking his head.

"It's her?" said Lauren.

"I think it must be. Was she wearing cut-off jeans and trainers?"

"And a pale blue top. Is she ... *dead*?" Her voice sounded incredulous.

Nick pursed his lips and nodded. Then he hugged her and felt her chest rising and falling. Fi gave out a wail and turned to Dan for comfort. Stefi looked lost and alone until Dan roped him into a group hug.

"I don't think she suffered," said Nick. "Maybe the smoke got her first."

"Burning juniper produces very little smoke," said Stefi.

"Fumes then." Nick glared at Stefi. He did not want to discuss this here.

"And what is she doing here, Nick? Look, we are less than fifteen metres from the edge of the forest. Why not simply run away from the fire?"

"Perhaps she was already unconscious. There will be a full, forensic investigation. We're not going to know until then. Let's get away from here now, leave the police to get on with their jobs. Come on, Stefi."

Nick grabbed his shoulder and steered him away and back towards the huts. Dan followed with Teddy and the girls who were holding on to each other, wiping eyes and blowing noses.

"Maybe she just tripped and hit her head on a rock," Dan said. "And then the fire got to her before she came to."

"But what was she *doing* here, Dan?" asked Stefi. "She should have been halfway to Paleóchora."

"Maybe she saw the fire and tried to stop it? I don't know. Perhaps we'll never know."

When they reached the huts, Nick asked Stefi if they could talk. They went to his hut and opened a carton of peach juice. Stefi sat down heavily.

"I've had enough of this, Nick. I might pack this in and get out."

"That's what they want you to do, of course."

"There's a traitor here, Nick. I think it's Teddy. How else would they know about all my troubles? How else would they know I might accept a stupidly low offer for my land?"

"Easily, Stefi. They know about your troubles because they are the *cause* of them. Have you thought about it that way? Teddy may have nothing whatever to do with it."

"Who would do this?"

"Someone who wants your land at a bargain price. They start by making the project seem impossibly difficult. Suddenly, the bank has doubts – why? Then a forestry claim out of the blue for no apparent reason. Next, coins are discovered where no Romans have ever been. These moves were all about creating insurmountable obstacles for you – loss of financial support, quagmires of delays with faceless government departments. But then it gets nasty after you reject their offer out of hand. Your pet goat – sorry, I forgot the name."

"Méli."

"Right. Méli is killed. Was it a hunting accident? I doubt it. I think she was killed as a warning to you."

"That's terrible."

"Yes, it is, but not as terrible as their next move. You see, I think they started this fire. Each time, they up the ante."

"What means this? I am sorry."

"Raise the stakes. To increase the pressure – on *you*, old son."

"And Roz? You think they killed her?"

"She might have had a very unlucky accident, but I doubt it, Stefi. We know from the photos she was on to this blond guy. Perhaps he had something to do with her death?"

"But it's a week since she saw him here."

"He came back. He, or a mate of his. And more than once."

"For Méli – and then for the fire?"

"I think so."

Stefi had hardly touched his beer. He was looking bewildered.

"Why are they doing this to me, Nick?" he said.

"Again, that's easy, Stefi. Because they are unscrupulous bastards pursuing a clear objective without the normal constraints on human behaviour you or I would observe."

"What objective?"

"They want your land, and they want it for two million tops. And forget your thirty luxury villas. My guess is these guys want to build big. On your twelve hectares, they could build a hundred apartments. That's big money, Stefi."

"What should I do now, Nick?"

"Well, you don't give up on your dreams and sell for peanuts. Don't let Roz and Méli die for nothing."

It was a low blow, but Nick knew it would shame him into standing firm, at least for now.

"The police are involved now," he went on. "I don't know if you know, but I was a senior British cop a few years back. I'll talk to my contacts here and see if they'll let me work with them – and closely with you. All right?"

Stefi brightened a fraction and gripped Nick's hand.

"You would do this for me?"

"Partly for you and partly because I believe in what you're trying to do, Stefi. But also, for my daughter who has lost her new friend. I don't want these bastards getting away with murder. It's just not right, Stefi."

Whether the term *murder* was the correct one remained to be seen, but Nick was angry enough to start with the presumption.

"Now," he said, "let's go through a few questions if you're up to it."

Stefi inclined his head and, finally, took a decent sip of his beer.

"Let's start with this blond character Roz spotted. Are you quite sure you don't recognise him?"

Roz's phone was still lying there so Nick called up the three photos and ensured Stefi took a good look.

"Quite sure, Nick. We don't see many fair-haired men around here. I would remember."

"Does it mean he's not Greek?"

"No. It is possible to be fair-haired and Greek, even here in Crete. He might be from the north-west, where most of the Venetians were. Some even have blue eyes."

"But it's more likely he's not Greek at all."

"For sure. And with the way he's dressed? I would say he is from Northern or Eastern Europe."

That cuts it down to about three or four hundred million, thought Nick, ruefully. *Maybe fifty million in the right age range with blond hair.* He tried a different tack.

"Do you have any enemies, Stefi? Anyone you've seriously pissed off?"

"I've been asking myself, Nick, but almost everyone is my friend."

"Almost …"

Stefi stared out of the window for a few seconds, then picked at his hands. Nick waited, knowing not to push him at this point. Finally, he looked up.

"A couple of years ago, there was this real estate guy in Chaniá. I made the mistake of letting his firm handle my father's estate. Their job was to sell the house and some other bits of land and find somewhere smaller for my mother."

"What went wrong?"

"He was the sort of guy who spends all his time reassuring you about how hard his firm is working for you and how they're committed to the highest ethical standards when they are doing *nothing* for you because they're in someone else's pocket. In fact, they are cheating you. He sold my father's property cheaply to friends or relatives of his, we discovered later. We should have got sixty thousand more. We are not a rich family, Nick. We could not afford to miss out on that money. And, of course, he charged us three per cent of the selling price plus VAT – or about eighteen thousand euros – for his so-called work. We were grieving. We weren't paying enough attention. I wasn't."

"You put your trust in him. That's not unreasonable, Stefi."

"I wish I hadn't."

"Why did *he* come to mind? Did you hear from him again?"

"This is the man who told me about the offer. His name is Pagiánnidis."

"Ah. Okay. Did he ever come here?"

"To Tamarisk Bay? Not as far as I know."

"All right. Here, then, is a man you dislike who may also dislike you. But business is business. He will deal with you if his principals want him to."

"Yes, I see that."

"We need the link to Méli, Stefi. Who, outside the group, knew Méli was a much-loved pet and not just another goat?"

"One or two of the paying guests, perhaps. The engineer, the solar guy, the guys who built the huts a while back …"

"Any you sat down with, enjoyed a beer with? Something not purely professional."

"Only Giórgios."

"Giórgios?"

"The engineer. He is an old friend of the family. Nice guy."

"And he would know about Méli."

"What are you saying, Nick? You think Giórgios had Méli killed? Are you crazy? I know this guy all my life. He is a kind, intelligent man, not a brute. He is older and well-set, he has money and position."

"Okay, Stefi. No need to get defensive. We're just exploring possibilities here."

There was a knock on the cabin door and Thaní's face appeared.

"May I have a word, Nick?" he said.

Nick excused himself and went outside.

"I have updated Leo," Thaní said, without preamble. "He wants me to stay here and start an investigation into Roz's death. He asked if you would be available to help us again. He will call you later to agree terms if you are interested."

Nick chuckled, inwardly. Leo's *terms* would be laughable, as usual. But both knew Nick would do it anyway. How could he not?

"I'd be glad to work with you again, Thaní," he said. "My gut is telling me there are some nasty bastards behind this and nothing would please me more than to put them out of business and behind bars."

"Agreed," said Thaní, proffering a hand that Nick grasped. "Welcome aboard, Nick."

"So, what's happening?"

"It is not practical for the Medical Examiner to come here, so we have been instructed to take specific photographs and soil samples and bag up anything of interest. This will take a couple of hours and then we will take the body to Chaniá. Doctor Pánagou will conduct a post-mortem tomorrow. Also, a senior investigator from The Fire Service is coming here and will arrive between two and three this afternoon."

"Her?"

"Yes, her name is Konstantína Gavaláki. She will come with a helicopter."

"What about Roz's family, Thaní?"

"We have informed the vice consulate in Iráklio. They will be notified through the usual channels."

Nick knew what that meant. An official call. It would be courteous and precise, a carefully trained individual and a measured amount of warmth and humanity. There would be few answers to the questions which would flood the mind of the bereaved. Perhaps they would send someone – a policewoman, or a bereavement counsellor. There would be helplessness, despair, and grief. He remembered the sad, sensitive face in the photo. Two months ago, she had buried her husband. Now this. The death of her only child.

"I'll speak to Stefi," he said. "I think one of us should call. Can you give me contact details?"

"Are you sure, Nick? These people are specially trained, and you are a long way off if there's a bad reaction."

"If I were her, I'd want to know as *soon* as possible, and I'd expect to hear it from friends, the people she was working with, not some faceless Foreign Office gopher."

"I'd like to check with Leo, if you don't mind, Nick. It's rather irregular."

He *did* mind but he understood. Thaní did not want to go out on a limb in such a sensitive area.

"That's okay. Let me know, but soon, huh?"

"Sure thing, Nick. And I'm planning to interview everyone here to get a fuller picture. Maybe you'd like to sit in?"

"I'll let you know later if that's okay."

Thaní raised an eyebrow.

"You should know that Stefi thinks Teddy's their inside man, reckons he's been passing information to whoever is behind this," Nick explained.

"Do you think he's right?"

"Probably not, gut feel."

"Anything else?"

"I've been talking with Stefi, trying to find out who knew Méli was a *pet* goat. I think this is important. Whoever killed her must have known it would hurt him badly, that she wasn't just any goat."

"And?"

"And we should check out his friend, the engineer Marákis. *He* knew."

"Okay. Let me find out more about him and set up an interview."

CHAPTER 15
FRIENDLY CHATS

Thaní was keen to complete two or three of the interviews before the woman from the Fire Service arrived. Then he discovered Stefi had sent the boys off to buy groceries.

"*Both* of them?" he complained.

"I think no one should be alone, for now. Sorry," said Stefi. "I think they are back by four o'clock."

There was nothing to be done, so he started the process with the girls, but he was careful to check that they felt up to it before starting with Lauren. Nick said he would not sit in with his daughter; he did not want to inhibit her responses.

Thaní asked each girl the same questions. He started with their relationships with Roz. How had they met? How had it been between them? He was looking for any signs of latent hatred or jealousy but found none. Neither had been close to Roz; there had not been time. They found her quirky and, in Fi's case, a bit of a bore, but they both admired her spirit and strength.

He checked whether they had seen anything of the blond man in the photographs. They had not. He checked their whereabouts on the morning Roz left for the grocery run and verified they had not seen her later. He asked if they had any theories about what had happened to her, or why. Fi was reticent but Lauren had plenty to say.

"Leaving the boat where she did seems strange to me. It's not even Stefi's land there, is it? Why not just pull up on the sand by the turtle nests? Also, leaving her bag in the boat with the phone in it – why did she do it? She must have been in a big hurry or expecting to return very soon, you'd think. She must have seen something as she was going past. Maybe the fire had started already? Maybe she saw someone."

"Why would she not simply phone Stefi, if that were the case?"

"Perhaps she wasn't sure *what* she'd seen. Perhaps she was

investigating. Too bloody brave for her own good." Lauren faltered for a moment. "And then Dad said she might have been unconscious before the fire got to her. I guess you'd have to be to get half-burnt like that."

As if shocked by her own words, she gulped and choked for a moment and felt hot tears spring to her eyes.

"You okay, Lauren?" Thaní asked.

She nodded, irritated with herself.

"But, if that's right, how did she lose consciousness?" she went on. "Did she fall and hit her head? Was it from inhaling smoke or fumes? Or did someone hit her over the head? Maybe she was even *dead* before the fire came along? She could have been stabbed or strangled or something. Will the post-mortem detect any of that?"

"I don't know, but I do know Doctor Pánagou is the best Medical Examiner in Crete and we will tell her we think the death is suspicious. You can be sure she will use all her skills."

He paused, looking at her.

"Anything else, Lauren?" he said.

"No."

"You are your father's daughter, no question. Have you thought about a job with the police, in England?"

"Are you kidding? My mother would never forgive me after both husband and son."

"Jason is a police officer, too? I had not heard."

"Training to be one, yes. My mother is not best pleased."

*

The message from Leo came through in under an hour. He thought it was a good idea for Stefi or Nick to call Roz's mother, but it should be *after* the official call. He assured them they would be notified as soon as the official call had been made. Nick had mixed feelings but decided not to rock the boat, for once.

He wandered over to Stefi's hut and found him brooding over a coffee.

"We need to call Mrs Kinnear," he said.

"Oh, God," said Stefi.

"She'll know. The consulate will make their call first."

"Then she'll be in pieces."

"Which is why she'll need us to call."

"I don't think I can do it, Nick. I don't think I can handle it. Not yet."

Nick waited for Stefi to lift his head. He did not look great. His eyes were bloodshot and sunken, his hair unkempt. He had not shaved for a couple of days.

"I think it would be better coming from you – as her employer – but I can do it if you prefer. I never met Roz, of course, but God knows I've made many such calls."

The words sounded blasé but that was not how Nick was feeling. There had been many such calls, but each was different. And each one found a new way to hurt.

"Would you, Nick? I know it's feeble of me, but I need a little help at the moment."

"Sure, no problem. Maybe you could follow up in a few days?"

"Sure, if that's what she wants."

Nick gave Stefi's arm a sharp squeeze and went back to his cabin. While he waited for the prompt from the consulate, he jotted down a few points to guide himself through the conversation. Afterwards, he made himself a sandwich. As he took the first bite, the call came through.

"Mr Fisher? My name's Simon Woodruff. I'm with the British Vice Consulate in Heraklion."

"Hello, Simon. Have you made the call?"

"To Mrs Kinnear? Yes, my boss, Jonathan Beeson has, so it's all clear for you to follow up."

"How is she, do you know?"

"Hard to tell on the phone, I imagine. Jonathan said she came across as a very private person. Did you know she recently lost her husband, after a long illness?"

"I do know, yes. And Roz was her only child?"

"Yes, she was."

"Does she have any close relatives she can turn to?"

"There's a sister, I believe, and the mother is still alive, but in care."

There was little more to say. Simon gave Nick the contact information and then made his excuses and disconnected.

Nick stared at the phone, then picked up his notes and ripped them up.

The phone was answered on the sixth ring. The *Hello* sounded withdrawn, shaky.

"Mrs Kinnear?"

"Yes. I'm Alma Kinnear."

"My name's Nick Fisher. I'm calling from Tamarisk Bay in Crete."

"Oh."

"I think the consulate just called you. Is that right?"

"Hmmm. A man called Beeson."

"And I'm calling on behalf of everyone here, Alma. We're desperately sorry for your loss. The team grew very fond of Roz and enjoyed working with her. Everyone will miss her a great deal. We want you to know, she made a valuable contribution to what we're trying to do here."

There was silence for several moments. No response. Nick wondered if she had covered the microphone.

"I can't take it in," she said, finally. "It's just ten days since she left, and now they're telling me she's dead. Is she *really* dead? How could it happen, Mr Fisher?"

"We don't know yet. There was a fire here. In the forest. We don't know how it started but there have been many wildfires near here."

He paused. Silence again.

"It seems she had an accident," he went on, "a few metres into the forest. Perhaps she hit her head, or something fell on her. We don't know. But we believe she was unconscious when the fire reached her. She would not have suffered at all."

"Was she on her own? What was she doing messing around near a fire on her own?"

"We don't know. An investigation has started, and I'll be on the team. I'll keep you informed of any developments."

"Is she *badly* burned?"

He hesitated. He wasn't sure how to answer that one.

"There are burns to her upper body, yes, but she didn't suffer."

"I'm coming out there. I need to understand all this and see it for myself. Do you understand, Mr Fisher?"

"Of course, I do. If you're sure it will help, you will be welcome here. I'm sure Stefi will provide accommodation for as long as you need."

They left it that she would let him know when her flight was arriving at Chaniá, and they would help her with transit arrangements within Crete.

*

"She's coming? What, here? Oh shit, Nick. We don't need that."

"What choice did I have, Stefi? Her daughter is killed working on your site, and she wants to see things for herself and understand how and why. How could I *possibly* say *No*? How could *you*?"

"When?"

"A few days, maybe less. She'll call when she's booked flights."

"Okay, Nick. But she's not expecting me to call."

"She's not, no."

Nick was irritated with Stefi now. He wanted to avoid any responsibility for Roz's death, it seemed. He was not directly responsible, but it was his land, his project. She was working for him as a volunteer. She was not even being paid anything and now her young life was over.

"You'll need to spend some time with her when she comes, Stefi. She deserves it. Roz deserves it. And remember, Alma just lost her husband. This must be a difficult time for her."

"We can show her the turtles. Maybe some will hatch while she's here."

"Yes, that would be nice, but involve her in the whole project, not just the bloody turtles. Show her Roz was part of something magnificent. You could do your bank presentation, maybe."

"Could talk through some of the slides, I suppose."

"Have you got a date from the bank yet, by the way?"

"Still waiting. They say they will call."

Stefi made big eyes, pursed his lips, and shrugged.

"Why don't you call *them*? Tell them you're coming to Chaniá on such-and-such a date and can they see you then. You need to push them now, Stefi."

Stefi looked at him steadily and coolly. Nick had crossed a line, and he knew it. He had been brave and helpful with the fire, but Stefi's gratitude did not extend to being told how to run his business.

"Anyway," Nick said, "I'll leave the thought with you."

Outside the cabin, Lauren was waiting for him.

"Hi, Dad," she said and grabbed him so they might walk, arm-in-arm.

"Fi and I are supposed to be leaving in the morning, did you remember?"

"Of course," he lied.

"Well, I'm thinking I might stay on for a bit. I want to help you find out what happened."

"Hmmm. I'm not sure it's safe, Lauren. Who knows what's going to happen next? I think you'd better go. Your mother will be worried sick when the news gets out."

"You haven't told her about Roz?"

"No. Have you?"

"Not yet."

"Well, if you want to stay, don't tell her. But she could see something on the news. She'll be following the wildfire stories."

"We haven't seen any journalists though, have we?"

"No, but that doesn't guarantee no stories. Leaks from the Fire Service, the family in Scotland, the vice consulate ..."

"I'll take my chances. And Mum will have to cope. I want to stay – just for a week or so."

"Will you tell her?"

"Not yet. She's not expecting us back for three days yet. We were going to stay in Chaniá, remember?"

119

"What about Fi?"

"Oh, she can't wait to get home, poor thing. Can't get the sight of Roz's body out of her mind. Even the presence of Teddy is having little effect."

"Well, you're a big girl now. I can't force you to go, but I think you should. It might be dangerous here and it's a little mean to let Fi travel back alone after what she's been through."

"Teddy's going to take her back to the hire car. Then she can follow him to Chaniá. All she has to do is find the airport and the car rental place. Then she'll find someone to talk to on the plane. You know Fi."

It was a fait accomplit. Nick knew his daughter and, when she made up her mind, there was no changing it. He had given up trying long ago.

"Okay, then. But you must tell your mother no later than tomorrow and *before* Fi gets home. It wouldn't be right for Fi and her family to know when your mother doesn't."

"Okay. I see that. But I don't want to tell her about Roz or the fire."

"I don't see how you can avoid it."

"For now, I'll just text her, say I'm staying on a while."

"Don't you dare tell any fibs."

"I won't need to, Dad."

"Sins of omission are very like fibs, my girl."

"I don't want to worry her. It's just a tiny, white lie."

He shook his head and pointed a stern finger at her.

"You be careful. Or we'll both be in the poo, big time."

She peeled away from him, gave him one of her big, endearing grins and trotted off to tell Fi.

*

Leo lit a cigarette and pushed back in his chair. He skimmed through Thaní's e-mailed report with a tight smile. *The boy was doing okay but with Nick Fisher, he would do better still*, he thought. He would have no trouble getting it authorised after Nick's previous successes. Maybe he could even nudge up that pathetic daily rate?

He flipped to the attachments – three photographs of a suspect. There were two quite distant shots of a blond man and a closer shot of him from the back. Leo zoomed in on the distant shots, but the quality was poor. Perhaps the forensics team would have techniques to enhance these. Otherwise, he doubted they would be much use in identifying the man, even if Interpol had a record of the guy. Nevertheless, he filed the request for Thaní and crossed his fingers.

⋆

The Fire Investigator arrived late, at twenty past three. The engine was cut but the rotor blades were still swishing when a large woman climbed out of the cockpit and ran sideways towards them, doubled up and holding her mass of frizzy, auburn hair in place. She was breathless by the time she reached Stefi and Nick.

"I am Konstantína Gavaláki," she said.

They introduced themselves.

"They tell me a girl has died. This is true?"

They nodded.

"Then, I must see the body. I hope it has not been moved."

"The police secured the scene," said Nick. "I know they're planning to take the body to Chaniá, but hopefully not yet."

Konstantína threw her hands in the air in a pantomime of panic. "Quickly, then. You will take me there?"

Thaní had foreseen that the Fire Investigator might need to see the body in situ and, though the police had completed the work demanded of them by the Medical Examiner, they had yet to disturb the body.

After the necessary introductions, the woman put on forensic gloves and then crouched with some difficulty alongside the body, hopping and puffing as she moved around.

"I think maybe the fire did not kill her," she said, after no more than two minutes. "No one would lie there while a wildfire consumes their upper body. There seems to be nothing wrong with her legs, so obviously, she would run, no? Unless she were already dead or unconscious."

"Our thoughts, exactly," said Thaní. "Could the smoke or fumes from the fire have *caused* her to lose consciousness?"

"This is not likely. Unless she is already asleep. Would a young woman come to the forest for a sleep? I don't think it is likely. And, if she were not asleep, she would run away from fumes or smoke as she would run away from the fire."

"So, she must have hit her head, or been hit," said Thaní.

"We must ask the Medical Examiner to see if it can be established." She was looking at the blackened skull, shaking her head. "It may not be so easy," she said.

"Now, I see the fire crossed her body from right to left, so it must have started this side," she said, waving her arm to the east. "Do you know where?"

This was not a question to which they had given any thought.

"We were hoping you would tell *us*," said Nick.

"Ha!" she said. "Okay, let's see what we know. We look at the juniper forest, what is left of it, and we see it is destroyed on the eastern side and perhaps thirty per cent of it remains on the western end, yes?"

They nodded dutifully.

"We know a strong wind was blowing from the south-east all afternoon. You can confirm this?"

More nods.

"Then we start our search in the south-east corner of the forest, yes?"

"What are we looking for, Konstantína," Thaní asked, as they trudged in that direction.

"Something that could have started the fire, of course. Even wildfires don't self-combust. For that, you need special circumstances – a stack of hay bales in hot sun, for example. I don't imagine you have anything similar here."

She glanced at Stefi who was shaking his head.

"In the absence of self-combustion, there must be a trigger. Maybe hot sun on a piece of glass? Maybe lightning or volcanic activity?"

"Nothing like it in the weather we saw," said Nick, speaking on behalf of the group. "Just hot sun and wind."

"Okay. Then it was a freak set of circumstances, like a broken bottle focusing the sun's rays on a tinder-dry area of vegetation or – and this is much more likely – it was caused by human activity."

They had almost reached their destination. Konstantína stopped for a moment and addressed her remarks to the group.

"Maybe one of you did something, maybe someone else was here. I don't know. But I can tell you, more than four out of five fires are caused by human activity. Faulty electrics – often power lines – dropped cigarettes, campfires or barbecues not properly extinguished. All these things."

"And arson," said Nick.

"Yes, of course," she agreed, as if setting fire to things was the most natural thing in the world. "There are people who do this. And some are not crazy. They do it to achieve some objective."

"Such as?"

"Arson is a form of attack. It can be used to frighten people or for revenge."

"Like a vendetta."

"Exactly. And others do this to damage the land."

"To what end, Konstantína?"

"Nobody wants to buy land that looks like the moon. A fire can cut the value of the land by half. But the reality is, a fire can *benefit* the land, long-term, and there is usually a full recovery in ten to twenty years."

"So, it's a good way to destroy value in the short-term – perhaps to negotiate a lower price – knowing there will be no long-term damage."

"I will not say it is a good way. It is illegal and dangerous. But it is one way, yes."

Nick was observing Stefi throughout this exchange. His face looked grey and sweaty, and his eyes looked fearful. Both men were thinking the same thing, he suspected, but it was Nick who put it into words:

"So, Konstantína, we know someone is very interested in buying this land. If they started this fire deliberately and Roz died as a result, that would be murder, surely?"

"This is a question for the police, but I would think a charge of murder or manslaughter could be made. But then you must prove it was deliberate and find whoever did it. Now, if we're very lucky, we find an empty petrol can with fingerprints all over it …"

She moved forward again, approaching the south-eastern corner of the blackened forest.

CHAPTER 16
THE INVESTIGATION STARTS

Lauren and Fi sat on the shingle beach, staring at the horizon.

"I'm sorry about Chaniá," Lauren said.

"Aye. Me too. Your Dad says it's a beautiful, little city. But I need to get home now, after all this."

"I know you do. And it's okay."

"Are you quite sure about staying on?"

"No, but it's different for me with my dad here, and I'm curious. I want to help if I can."

"The detective's daughter," Fi grinned.

"I want to see justice for Roz. It's so unfair."

"It won't bring her back, sadly."

Lauren sensed movement and looked east, along the beach.

"Looks like they're taking her now. We should pay our last respects," she said, struggling to her feet.

Fi followed Lauren's eyes to the far end of the beach, near the turtle nests. Two constables were manhandling a stretcher towards a police boat. On it was a black body bag; all that remained of Roz.

"Where are they taking her?" asked Fi.

"Chaniá," Lauren replied. "The post-mortem. Then I guess her mum will want to get her back to Scotland. Coming?"

"What for?"

"Suit yourself."

Lauren scrunched her way along the shingle, watching the police officers stretching a gangplank from the boat to the shallow water, then struggling to drag the body bag up and into the boat. She saw them lay the black bag on the deck and stood straight, stretching. One rubbed his back, the other spat into the water. Lauren sat on the shingle again, near the boat and some eighty metres from Fi. Suddenly, her eyes filled with tears. All Roz's fervour, her youthful idealism, had been snuffed out in a moment. So full of life, now she was dead meat. A burden to be lumbered with. A bag of bones and burnt flesh. Lauren felt like shouting or crying, maybe both. She wanted to tell Roz how she wished they had become friends for life, shared good times and saved the world together. But it was too late. It would always be too late now.

Her thoughts were disturbed by a boat engine, and she looked up to see the grey hull with the red stripe battling its way across the waves. The boys were returning from Paleóchora. It would be Fi's last evening, and she would get a decent meal now, at least. After that, good riddance. Lauren would be glad to see the back of her. Silly moo.

*

There was no discarded petrol can, unsurprisingly, and the samples Konstantína took from various likely starting points revealed no traces of accelerant whatsoever. They found a broken bottle at one point, but it was shrouded in vegetation at the base of a tree. She did not think it would get enough concentrated sunlight to be the culprit.

"The trouble is," she said, standing back and cracking a twig, "when it's as dry as this, you don't need accelerant. A match will do and then the wind takes it."

"So, you think it *was* deliberate?" asked Nick.

"I did not say this. But you tell me there was nothing that could spontaneously combust. You tell me there were no lightning strikes or volcanic activity. We have found nothing, apart from the bottle, which could have intensified the sun's rays and triggered the fire. And we have discounted this bottle on account of its position. Now, I must say only that, *on the balance of probabilities*, this fire was caused by human action. I have no way of knowing whether it was deliberate or accidental."

"But we've seen no evidence of camping or cooking. There are no power lines in this area. Doesn't that tell you it *was* deliberate?"

"It makes it more likely, of course, but a spark, a cigarette end …" She shrugged.

Stefi had been listening closely to the exchange between Nick and Konstantína. Now he intervened.

"Konstantína. A girl has died. She was my responsibility. Her mother is coming here to try to understand what has happened. Can you not be more definite? You said yourself, that fires don't start themselves. We know the wildfires were not close enough to be the cause. Other than Roz, no one from my team was in this area. We also have evidence of an intruder sighted earlier."

"There was an intruder? Why did no one tell me this?"

"It was a week earlier. We have no evidence he was here on the day of the fire," said Nick, "though we suspect he did come back at some point."

"Why?"

"We don't know. Perhaps to spy on us? Or he may have been a hunter or poacher. A goat was killed," said Stefi, his voice catching.

"I have a different take on this," said Nick. "I think someone's running a campaign of intimidation against Stefi. That wasn't just any goat; it was the pet kid he adored. Before that, there were incidents aimed at wrecking Stefi's development plans. This fire looks to be the next step in the process."

"Look, gentlemen. I cannot say the fire was set deliberately; I have no evidence for this. But I can say we found no evidence of natural causes for the fire, and therefore it appears to have been caused by human action. Given Roz was the only person known to have been in the area at the time, I will say the fire appears to have been caused by her or some unidentified intruder."

"Hang on. You're saying Roz may have caused the fire that killed her?"

"We can't rule it out, can we?" replied Konstantína.

This cast a whole new light on things. Stefi's stress levels were climbing even higher.

"But you said she was dead or unconscious before the fire got to her, didn't you?"

"I said it looked that way, but the ME must confirm."

"It doesn't seem likely she would start a fire – accidentally, I assume – and then knock herself out and get burned to death. She wasn't even a smoker, was she, Stefi?"

He shook his head.

"Unlikely things happen, Mr Fisher," said Konstantína. "Somehow, she starts a fire by accident. She tries to put it out, but it spreads rapidly. She can see it's getting out of control, and she starts to run away. She trips and hits her head."

"That might make some sense if Roz had a reason for being there, but she was supposed to be taking the boat to Paleóchora to buy groceries for us all. Something made her change her plans and come back ashore."

"Hmmm. You think maybe she saw the start of the fire?"

"Or she saw the intruder starting it," said Nick.

Konstantina looked at him steadily for fully three seconds.

"Honestly? You have reasons to be suspicious," she said. "The police must investigate."

*

After Konstantína had lumbered good-heartedly back to the red helicopter, Stefi went back to help unpack the groceries while Nick sought out Thaní. He had left earlier to interview the two young men on their return from Paleóchora. Now, he found him sitting with Dan outside the latter's cabin.

"Mind if I join you?" he asked.

"We're just finishing, Nick," said Thaní. "I'll come round to your cabin in a minute."

Nick returned to his cabin where he splashed some cool water on his face and poured another peach juice. He mixed it with tonic to take away the unbearable sweetness. In less than five minutes, Thaní had joined him.

"How was it?" he asked, gesturing at the other chair.

"A waste of time," he replied. "Dan has nothing new to add."

"Have you seen Teddy yet?"

"Shortly. Do you want to sit in, Nick?"

"Not especially, thanks. Let me know if something comes up. I don't suppose he's Stefi's rat, do you?"

"I doubt there *is* a rat. I don't see the need for one."

"Nor me. Except for knowing about Méli."

"I talked with the engineer. I'm trying to nail him down for a meeting tomorrow. You and I should have a day in Chaniá. We can go with Teddy and Fi to Elafonísi, then drive up together. We can put pressure on this estate agent, too, catch up with Leo and the good doctor."

"Is she doing the post-mortem tomorrow?"

"First thing, I believe."

"Right then. Good plan, Thaní. Let's do it."

*

Maybe it was the rare treat of a larder full of groceries, beer and wine. Maybe it was the removal of Roz's body and the departure of the Fire Investigator and all the policemen, other than Thaní. Maybe it was the need to let off steam and de-stress, if only for a few hours. Or because it was Fi's last night. Whatever it was, the seven of them had a feast that night like there was no tomorrow and everyone ate and drank too much. Stefi and Dan prepared a delicious potful of chicken thighs with carrot and celery, and potatoes, baked crisp with olive oil and lemon. Lauren and Fi combined on a fruit compote with yoghurt. Recent events put a damper on frivolity, but there was plenty of warmth and camaraderie. People told stories. Everyone went to bed with a warm feeling that went some way towards supplanting the horrors of the recent past.

*

The next morning, Lauren decided to forgive Fi's behaviour and give her a proper hug goodbye.

"Now, don't forget to pick up the hire car, will you? Have you got the keys? Are you okay to drive?" she asked.

"I'll be following Teddy and the others. Even I should be able to manage that."

"And you know where to go when you get to the airport."

"I remember."

"Good! And you have some extra euros for the parking?"

Fi nodded. As the boat was about to leave, she became a little tearful.

"I'm sorry I've not been much use, Lauren," she said.

Lauren did not know what to say. It was true that she had not been much use. She had been a pain in the butt most of the time and contributed very little to the group, but standing there, with her head tilted to one side and wearing her sad, little smile, it was hard to be angry.

"Never mind. We had some fun together, before all this," Lauren managed to say.

They hugged briefly, each more circumspect about their friendship now. Then Fi climbed into the boat with Nick and Thaní. Teddy pushed off, leaping in before putting down the prop and yanking the starter cord. In a few minutes, they had disappeared around the headland and Lauren was wiping away a tear, but not for Fi. She had wanted to go with them and be part of the investigation with her dad, but it was not possible. No more than four in the boat ruled Teddy. It was not safe. Instead, she would stay with Dan and Stefi. Dan said he needed help with the turtles, and she was happy to do it, in honour of Roz. She was not sure her help was needed; he might be creating occupational therapy for her. Dan was like that. Whatever, it might be interesting.

*

Doctor Pánagou was often berated for her pessimistic outlook, but she took a different view. She was a realist, not a pessimist. If the world were a place that warranted widespread optimism, her job would not be needed. It was others' need for optimism that required her and others like her to deal with the underside of life, the dark corners, the unpleasant sights and smells. It had fallen to her to take care of these things, and she was okay with it. *Just don't expect me to grin all the time,* she would say.

This morning, her assistant informed her that the first case was another burns victim; a young girl, just twenty-one years of age. The accompanying message from the police was that the girl was thought to be unconscious or even dead before the fire got to her, so would she please verify that and search for signs of foul play? This irritated her a little. After twenty-six years, she knew her job, thank you very much.

She took a last drag on her second cigarette of the day, dropped it on the gravel and went back inside. The body was waiting under a sheet on the examination table. Her assistant, Iákovos, was waiting, expectantly.

"I have the PMCT scans," he said.

Post-mortem computed tomography scans were now standard procedure. In some areas, like identifying skull fractures, the scans were more effective than traditional autopsy methods, but it was mostly about avoiding the need for a full autopsy, where possible. If the cause of death could be established using scans, then the trauma of a full autopsy might be avoided. Pánagou was aware that some people were overly squeamish about such matters or belonged to religious groups who found the whole process unacceptable. Any thoughts she might have had about the substantial outlay on these scanners being a sycophantic pandering to minorities were, however, pushed to one side by the sheer efficiency of the things. The clarity was astonishing, the ability to section the body into one-millimetre slices astounding. In no time, she had become a closet convert and an old dog with new tricks to learn.

She went to the screen and watched as Iákovos brought the display to life.

"Also, we found something in the pocket of her shorts," he said, laying a polythene-wrapped tissue on a nearby work surface.

*

The engineer's fourth-floor office resembled a penthouse apartment. Black leather sofas, a giant pot plant and a glass-topped table were arranged in an L-shape before a picture window. There were two more leather and metal chairs in front of a large desk with a computer and a cell phone in a cradle. There were views over the tourist shopping areas to the harbour and its Venetian lighthouse. To the right, the hills rose towards the Akrotíri peninsula and the airport. Nick noticed expensive trinkets and memorabilia dotted around the room.

"Welcome, gentlemen. I am Giórgios Marákis," he said, extending a hand.

Nick and Thaní duly shook it and introduced themselves. Nick explained he was working with the Chaniá police on a temporary basis, as he had done in the past.

"The police are always welcome here," Marákis said. "Englishmen, too. So, you are doubly welcome, Mr Fisher. And you, Thanási, you are working with Leonídas?"

"He's my boss, sir."

"Did I hear that he was shot a few months ago?"

"He's recovering, thankfully, but it's taking a long time."

"You must give him my best wishes. We go way back, as the Americans say."

"I will, sir. Thank you."

Nick was studying the man. He struck him as a smooth operator. In his mid- to late-fifties, he was still good-looking and gave the air of being cultured. If the office was anything to go by, he had made money. But, if there was something dodgy about him, it was well camouflaged.

"Now, this concerns the Tamarisk Bay project, my secretary told me," said Marákis.

Thaní went on to explain. It concerned both the project and Stefi himself. Some unexplained events over the last few weeks had damaged the viability of the project and devalued the land. It appeared to be a concerted attack on Stefi. In the most recent event, a girl had died.

"A girl died? How awful for her family! And for Stefi. I had no idea any of this was going on, Sergeant. Please tell me exactly what happened."

Marákis pushed his glasses back onto the bridge of his nose and leaned forward. Putting his elbows on the desk, he made a cradle with his hands and rested his chin on it, listening calmly and attentively as Thaní talked through everything that had happened except the killing of Méli …

"I wish Stefi had confided in me. The poor man must be going through hell," he said, finally.

"Does it surprise you that he has not?" asked Thaní.

"Not especially. Stress affects people in different ways."

He was now fiddling with his watch, Nick saw, clicking open the metal strap and then securing it again. He did this several times without, seemingly, being aware of what he was doing.

"But you feel close to him, I think. How did that come about?" Thaní asked.

"I became friends with his father at university in Thessaloníki. It would have been in the late eighties. It was natural, I suppose. Two young men from Crete, looking out for each other. Then, after we both married, our children played together."

"And you're still close?"

"We see less of each other since Michális died, but the bond remains."

"Michális being Stefi's father?"

Marákis nodded.

"And this bond you still share – is this why you're the engineer on the Tamarisk Bay project?"

"Well, you'd have to ask Stefi. He appointed me, but I imagine he considered other engineers."

"But you are well-qualified for the job?"

"I have been a practising civil engineer for over thirty years, Sergeant. My formal qualifications are on the wall over there. I have a firm of engineers which occupies the third and fourth floor of this building and a firm of architects with an office on Halidon. I am also a fifty per cent partner in a development business called CretaHome. Perhaps you know of it? We built over a hundred good quality villas on Crete last year."

The statement was made without pomposity, but it was designed to impress. Thaní went on:

"Do you know who is behind the offer for Stefi's land?" he asked.

"No, of course not," he responded.

"Surely, you would have *some* idea," said Nick. "These people would be competitors of CretaHome, would they not?"

"You asked me if I *knew*. I don't. If you want me to *speculate*, that's quite a different question."

Outwardly, he remained calm, but *something had struck a nerve*, Nick thought.

"An educated guess would be welcomed."

"Some of the larger developments are foreign owned. They operate through opaque subsidiaries, often based in offshore or tax-friendly locations. It can be hard to discover who the ultimate beneficial owner is."

"What about the tactics they are using? Are these familiar to you?"

"I've come across them sometimes, I'm sorry to say, though my firm would not be a direct competitor. We build individual villas or small groups of three or four. We buy plots from four to ten strémmata, typically, up to a hectare, not thirty hectares or whatever Stefi's land is. And, when we build, we try to be sympathetic to the landscape. We adapt to the contours of the land; we build houses to fit in with the landscape. These guys just go in with the bulldozers, reshape the land for their own purposes and build apartments they know they can sell at a large profit. Personally, I hate it."

"Why are they allowed to do this?" asked Nick.

"The government is keen to encourage foreign investment in Greece. They choose to turn a blind eye – or get paid to. I don't know which."

"Sounds like you don't have much faith in the government," observed Nick.

"This is the best government Greece has ever had, Mr Fisher. They are getting things done, turning around an economy everyone thought was beyond repair. Internationally, we Greeks are raising our heads again, facing the world as equals, not as the third world country within the EU. But there is still corruption, and it is a problem."

"So, getting back to Stefi," Thaní said. "I'm guessing you would favour his plans for Tamarisk Bay rather than those of some foreign developer?"

"In every way, yes. I think his site could become a model for future developments. An example to us all."

"Do you visit the site often?"

"Not often, no. There's no need. I'm there every two or three months."

"Is it all business, or do you spend time with Stefi, socially?"

"There is always time for a rakí, Sergeant, or a cold beer. Of course, we spend a little social time together."

"So, you know his pet animal?"

Marákis looked puzzled for a moment, then suddenly brightened.

"Ha. When you said pet, I am thinking a dog or a cat, but you're talking about that goat of his."

"You know her."

"Méli? Of course, I know her. The two of them are inseparable."

"*Were*."

"What do you mean?"

"She's dead. Killed by person or persons unknown."

"Oh. I'm sorry to hear that."

Nick watched as Marákis moved up from the watch. Now, he picked up a ball-point pen and unscrewed the end stopper, causing the metal pocket grip to fall off. Then he pulled out the ink tube before reassembling it. He did this several times. *Perhaps it helped him concentrate,* Nick wondered.

Thaní went on:

"The thing is, Mr Marákis, apart from Stefi's small group of volunteers, it seems only you were aware of Stefi's closeness with the creature. Only you knew how much it would hurt him if she were killed."

"What are you saying, Sergeant?"

Nick cut in:

"He's saying whoever killed the goat, did it because they knew how much it would hurt Stefi. It was a deliberate and well-aimed act of intimidation. We're wondering how they knew. We're wondering if it came from you."

The ball-point pen was in disarray now. He left it in pieces and reverted to the watch strap. It was several seconds before he looked up and replied, in a voice that shook ever so slightly with nervousness or rage, Nick knew not which.

"I have given my time voluntarily to help you today. And now you accuse me of supplying information that would inflict harm on one of the people I care most about in this world. What kind of a man do you think I am – and why on earth would I do it?"

"It could have been accidental. It could have been under duress. But we think it came from here."

"Well, it did not. You are quite wrong. Now, if there's nothing else, gentlemen, this interview is over."

*

"Well, that was an overreaction," said Nick when they found themselves on the street again.

"He's a proud man," said Thaní.

"And did you see all the nervous fiddling about? He must be guilty of something."

"But he seems genuinely fond of Stefi, and believes in the project."

"I thought so, too. But we ruled out Méli being the victim of a hunting or poaching incident as too far-fetched, right? And no one came back for the carcass. So, with the string of other incidents, it seems clear that it was also a malicious act designed to intimidate Stefi. Agreed?"

Thaní nodded as they walked.

"Then, if it's not Marákis," Nick went on, "it would have to be Dan or Teddy who leaked the information. You interviewed those guys. What do you reckon?"

"Not Dan. He's very fond of Stefi, super-involved and wildly enthusiastic about the project. Teddy is more detached and spends more time away from the site. As you know, Stefi suspects him, so I questioned Teddy closely about it. I don't believe any leak came from him."

"Okay. Then perhaps Marákis is lying to us. Is he in financial or marital trouble? How are his businesses doing? Does he have any guilty secrets?"

"The guy is a pillar of the community, Nick. He started with very little. Now he's chair of the engineering federation, here in Crete. He is a happily married, family man. He is wealthy and settled. His businesses *must* be doing well with all the foreign buying of villas here over the last few years."

"I'm sorry, Thaní, but ask any blackmailer. We all have secrets. And what I'm hearing loud and clear is that Mr Giórgios Marákis has a hell of a lot to lose."

*

Stefi was relieved to get some *me* time. With Dan training Lauren in the art of turtle protection and the others in Chaniá, he finally had some time to get his bearings. This was time he would normally spend with Méli, and her absence felt especially poignant this morning. He was alone. He knew Dan, and now perhaps Nick and Thaní, were fighting his corner, but he also understood; the project was his, the pressure from whatever dark forces was aimed at him, and the decision about whether to continue was his and his alone.

He knew he could not proceed without finance, so he started by calling the bank. Yes, they said, they would be amenable to an appointment with Anna on Thursday, at eleven am. *Good*, Stefi thought. They would have a little time to sharpen up their presentation.

There seemed little point in calling the Forestry Department. The trees they laid claim to were smoking ruins. They might accuse him of burning them down out of spite. No, the best course was to do nothing at this stage.

Instead, he put in a call to Tzanakákis at the Ministry of Hellenic Culture and Sports.

"Ah!" said Tzanakákis. "I'm glad you called. I was on the point of calling you."

"I wanted you to know, we had a fire here. I wasn't sure if it would affect your plans."

"Yes, I saw this on the news. I am so sorry about the girl who died. Was she related to you?"

"She was one of my volunteers."

"A tragic accident. I am sorry for her family."

"Thank you."

"But, in answer to your question, I don't expect the fire to affect my plans. We will come for an exploratory dig next week. We will plan on two weeks, initially. Any future work will depend on what we discover. How does that sound?"

"Your team will be welcome if we can agree on a limited sphere of operations for your guys and if I can get on with my development plans for the rest of the site."

"Yes and no, I'm afraid. I would be happy to restrict our digging to an area of, say, one hundred metres from the coin find at this stage, but I can't have you busily destroying Roman remains elsewhere on the site."

"But I have a major development here. Everything's lined up. I need to get on with it."

"I appreciate it, but you must wait. The Greek government requires you to wait. If our excavation reveals nothing, we will review the situation."

"Meaning I could get the green light to start again in three weeks?"

"Meaning we will review the situation."

There would be no shifting him from this position, Stefi realised. He had the power. The Greek government took its duty to history seriously, these days.

They agreed that a team of three archaeologists would set up a working camp at Tamarisk Bay, starting the following Monday. They would set up a hundred-metre exclusion zone and would need some nearby land on which to camp. Stefi said they would be welcome to join the rest of the team at mealtimes and to use the toilet and shower block. Tzanakákis said Stefi would receive a modest amount of compensation for this.

"What can you share about the discovery itself?" asked Stefi.

"I already sent you those wonderful pictures of the coins."

"You did, but I'm talking about the Slovenians who found them."

"This is not information I am allowed to share with you, I'm afraid."

"I'd like to talk with them, directly."

"This won't be possible. I'm sorry."

"Did you question them at all? It seems highly unlikely to me that they would find Roman coins here. I'm sure you're very excited about a possible new site but are you certain they're telling the truth?"

"I saw no reason to doubt them – and they had the coins."

"Though no Roman artefacts have *ever* been found this far west in Crete."

"We must keep an open mind about such things. We certainly don't know everything the Romans did."

"But you have no proof the coins were found on my land."

"They took photographs of the immediate area."

"But you don't know if the coins were found here or *planted* here."

"If you'll forgive me for saying so, you are sounding a little paranoid, Spiliáki. Why on earth would someone plant two rather valuable coins on your land – a value to which you, as the landowner, will be entitled, at least in part?"

"Precisely to delay and frustrate my development project, Mr Tzanakákis."

"It seems a lot of trouble to take and would cost them several hundred euros."

"That's nothing to these people."

There was nothing Tzanakákis was prepared to add. He was sorry, but his office was *required* to investigate the find and his team would arrive on Monday. He hoped the delay would not be too much of an imposition.

On reflection, Stefi concluded that things were not so bad. If they could get the bank back on board, he could live with a three-week delay, if that's all it was. He was pleased with himself for finally getting off his backside and sorting a few things out. But what would they do next, he wondered? It was a scary thought. Thirty seconds after he ended the call with Tzanakákis, his phone started ringing.

CHAPTER 17
DIGGING DEEPER

The estate agent's office was on Daskalogiánnis, a lively street in the Old Town. It was a short walk and that was good news because the temperature was rising fast. They found it between a cannabis shop and a pharmacy.

"Very handily positioned, if you've had a bad day," Nick commented.

Thaní grinned wickedly. "Then, let's make sure he does."

The windows outside and the walls inside were covered with photographs of houses for sale. There was a wide variety, Nick saw, from old stone rebuilds for as little as forty-five thousand euros to top-end villas with infinity pools and stunning views for half a million and more. Sometimes a lot more. He spotted one at well over two million. A separate section was devoted to new builds. The name CretaHome caught his eye, and he remembered they had not asked Marákis who his business partner was.

There were just three desks, each with a desktop computer and a stack of paperwork, but only one was occupied. Nick saw the relatively young man glance at the clock and then give him a sideways look.

"Would it be Mr Fisher?"

The man remained behind the desk but stood and stretched out a hand.

"It would," confirmed Nick, "and this is my good friend, Konstantópoulos."

The man hesitated. It was not usual for two men to look for property together unless they were a couple. And yet only the younger man was wearing a wedding band. Puzzled, he gestured for them to sit.

"I'm sorry, Mr Fisher, but I can't remember which of our properties interested you."

"I didn't tell you."

"Ah. That would explain it. So, which is it?"

"None of them."

Nick smiled. The man seemed unsure how to respond.

"We are from the police," explained Thaní, laying one of his business cards on the desk. "We'd like to talk to you about Tamarisk Bay." He strolled to the door, pulled down the blind and turned the key. "I think it would be best if we were not disturbed, don't you? Perhaps you could turn off the phones, too?"

"I can't do that, Sergeant. An estate agent does all his business on the phone, you understand. And we are busy at the moment."

But Thaní was already reaching across the desk. He took the man's cell phone and switched it off. Nick crossed the room to the phone socket and pulled out the landline, none too gently, giving a reassuring smile as he did so.

"There," he said. "That wasn't so hard, was it?"

"It had better not be for long," he said.

"That rather depends on you, old son," said Nick.

"If you answer our questions openly and honestly, you'll be back in business in just a few minutes," Thaní said. "Meanwhile, I'll record our conversation, if that's all right with you."

The man shrugged and Thaní improvised with his phone.

"Now, you are Stávros Pagiánnidis, correct?" he continued.

Pagiánnidis nodded.

"I need you to respond formally for the recording."

"Ah. Yes, I am Pagiánnidis."

"We have been told you are acting for someone who wishes to acquire the Tamarisk Bay site from its present owner, Mr Stefanos Spiliákis."

"I have been appointed to assist the buyers."

"Who are they, Pagiánnidi?"

"I'm not at liberty to say. I have signed a confidentiality agreement; I'm acting as agent for undisclosed principals."

"If your clients have acted illegally, you are not bound by the terms of the agreement."

"And have they?"

"We have reason to believe they have – or you have."

"Reason to believe? What's that supposed to mean? Do you have proof of something?"

"We are pursuing our inquiries. Were you aware that a young woman was killed there, just a few days ago?"

"I saw it on the news. You mean the one who died in the wildfire?"

"In suspicious circumstances," we believe. "Are your clients aware of this?"

"Yes, I told them. Because they needed to know. I thought the damage to the forest might affect the price and they agreed."

"What do you mean?"

"They were back in touch early this morning, asking me to reduce the offer price and include a time limit for acceptance. They are losing patience, I think. I just got off the phone from telling Spiliákis. Now, I will put it in writing."

Nick and Thaní exchanged angry glances. It sounded like they were dealing with callous bastards.

"What are the new terms?" asked Nick.

"Confidential, I'm afraid."

"You might as well tell us. We can call Stefanos, and he will tell us. There's no hurry. We can sit here all day, can't we Thaní?"

Pagiánnidis glanced nervously at the clock once more. His business was at a standstill and time was money. And this was the police, after all.

"All right, I will tell you in strict confidence. They cut the price to one and a half million. Final offer. Spiliákis has ten days to accept. Then, it will be withdrawn."

"How did that go down?" asked Nick.

"He was not happy, but then he's been having a tough time of it, I gather. It's a good offer and I think it's time for him to take it. Frankly, he's not cut out to be leading such an ambitious project."

"And, if he doesn't accept, your clients will quietly walk away?"

"I imagine so. They have *other fish to fry*, I think you say in England,

Mr Fisher? If I were Mr Stefanos, I would be thinking about this seriously. One and a half million euros is better than a worthless piece
of land in the middle of nowhere."

"That sounds rather like a threat, to me."

"Not at all. I'm just observing his situation and considering what
has happened."

"All right, Pagiánnidi," said Thaní, "you can tell your undisclosed
principals that we would like to meet them, as soon as possible, or
at least hold a video call with them if they are in another country."

Pagiánnidis blinked once. Thaní went on:

"Tell them we are investigating the use of subversive tactics in their
attempted purchase of Tamarisk Bay, including the possible manslaughter – or even murder – of a young, Scottish woman. If we find
a case to answer, they should be in no doubt, we will pursue them
and bring them to justice, wherever they are."

"May I share the evidence you have for these accusations?"

"You may not. The message is that we are on to them, and they
need to tread very carefully. Once our investigations are concluded,
we may come looking for them. I expect you to communicate this
today, without fail. Is that clear?"

Pagiánnidis looked sulky but he tilted his head slightly in
acknowledgement.

"Good," said Thaní. "Now we can let you go back to work."

He handed him the cell phone and Nick went to plug the landline
back in, but before he did, he turned back to Pagiánnidis:

"One last question. I see you are selling CretaHome properties. Are
you acquainted with Giórgios Marákis?"

"Of course. He is married to my aunt."

*

They arranged to meet Leo for lunch at Oinopoieío, a smart, traditional
restaurant in a pedestrianised Old Town street called Chatzimicháli
Ntaliáni. He was sitting outside, finishing a cigarette when they arrived. They shook hands and followed him inside.

"Well, you don't look too bad," said Nick, after they sat down.

"This is what you British call a compliment, Nick?" said Leo.

"It's about as close as we get," he admitted.

"Well then, thank you. I am still weak, I have aches and pains and my guts are not working as well as I'd like but at least I'm alive, mostly thanks to you, I think."

"All part of the service."

"Thank you, 007."

Nick raised a single eyebrow and earned a chuckle from them both, *though Thani must be too young to know James Bond,* he thought. *Maybe he'd caught the endless reruns.*

"I was wondering if Sergeant Anna had given you something else for us to celebrate. Did you find your murderer yet?"

"Unfortunately, not. We think his family are hiding him."

"I thought you didn't know who his family were."

"We have a few possibilities now. We're watching two of them."

"Don't *her* family know who he was?"

"She seems to have hidden him from them, Nick. We don't know why. Or he was keeping her away from them."

"Strange. Good luck with that."

"Thank you. We'll get there in the end, I expect." Leo waved his arm at the room. "I think you will like this place, Nick. I wanted to buy you a decent lunch to compensate for the last one."

"I already like it," he said, glancing around at the polished, wooden interior and the displays of unusual wines and liqueurs, "but the last one was lovely, too."

"You know what I mean. We should have taken more time over it."

"You were hot on the trail of one Ollie Dunham, as I recall."

"The guy who got me shot."

"Indeed. What happened to him? You never told me."

"Twelve years. The judges took account of his efforts at the end."

"Which cost him a lung."

"Hmmm."

"And probably saved *my* life."

"Maybe."

"Twelve years in a Greek jail? Seems a bit rough."

"For a heroin shipper who was indirectly involved in two murders? I don't think so, Nick. And our jails aren't quite so bad, these days."

"I think he saw himself as a Schindler figure – rescuing Syrian migrants from Isis rather than Jews from the Nazis – but he was totally played by Adil."

"Schindler? Sorry, but this is a laughable comparison, Nick. Dunham was in it for the easy money needed to support a life of indolence. He turned a blind eye to Adil's evil activities. And the way he used the oil terminal guy, Lékas, was cynical and cruel. He got what he deserved."

Nick raised his hands in mock self-defence and chuckled.

"Okay, okay. Perhaps I'm going soft in my old age."

"Perhaps you are. Now, let's get some food ordered, then you can bring me up to speed with what on earth has been happening at Tamarisk Bay."

Nick loved the ambience of the place, and the service was excellent. But he was underwhelmed by the menu because it seemed too traditional. These were the dishes on taverna menus everywhere in Crete but with the occasional twist. In the end, he asked Leo to choose for him.

They shared three starters: beetroot with a garlic dip, graviéra saganáki and apákia, pieces of smoked pork with sage. Nick was familiar with all of them, but not like this. The quality of the cooking and the presentation were outstanding. For Nick's main course, Leo chose tigánia prunes – a pork tenderloin, pan-fried with prunes and cream – with a dish of crispy, golden, sauté potatoes. There was also a side dish of steamed, garlicky spinach for them to share.

"Sorry, Nick. I make a mistake. Is too much pork for you."

"No, no. I love pork, Leo and this dish is fabulous – a complete contrast to the apákia."

Leo poured red wine from a bottle of Mandilári, and they clinked their glasses together.

"Yeiá mas," he said.

"Anything from Interpol?" Nick ventured.

"They're struggling with the photo quality, trying to enhance them. The woman I spoke to was not optimistic – even if our guy's on their database."

"Have we got people out there looking for him?"

"Armed with what? Roz's photos are not enough. And where would we start looking? I don't have the manpower to cover the whole of Western Crete. We need more, a sighting, ideally."

Nick nodded sympathetically. They had little to go on.

They were still tucking into their main courses, but Thaní could not enjoy his in peace. Not on a working day.

"So, let me have your update, Thaní," said Leo, "and please add any thoughts you have, Nick."

Thaní pushed the remains of his rabbit to one side and dug out his notebook. He talked through the timetable of events leading up to that morning.

"Well, I don't think there's much doubt," Leo said, "these actions were intended to bully this man, Stefi, into selling at a low price."

"It stacks up that way, doesn't it, but it might be another matter proving it and pinning it on the guilty parties if we can identify them," said Nick.

"What's your feeling about the girl, Roz? Accident, murder, manslaughter?" Leo asked.

"We need to hear what Pánagou has to say. My gut feeling? An accident seems less likely. She must have seen *something* to go there in the first place."

Nick's phone beeped and he apologised for the interruption. It was a message from Alma, Roz's mother. She would be arriving at Chaniá airport two days from now, late on Wednesday afternoon. He would need to find someone to pick her up.

"So, how is he, this guy?" Leo continued.

Nick spotted Thaní trying to shovel in the rest of his lunch before Leo asked him another question, so he answered.

"Stefi? He's been badly shaken up by all this, but he hasn't given in. This morning won't have helped, though."

Leo raised his eyebrows in a question mark and Nick clarified.

"The would-be buyers dropped the price by half a million and gave him ten days to accept."

"Or what?"

"That's the big question, I think, Leo. The slimeball of an agent said they would just walk away but I don't see it. Not after all this. I think we have to nail them in this ten-day window or Stefi could meet with a nasty accident of some sort himself."

"I agree with you," said Leo, and Thaní, still dispatching his last mouthful, nodded vigorously.

"So, take me through this morning's interviews," Leo said, as the plates were cleared, and some perfect fresh fruit arrived. To Nick's dismay, he then waved away the accompanying rakí.

*

Later in the day, however, Nick was grateful to Leo. He needed a clear head to make sense of Pánagou. *She was looking older,* he thought, *but then he supposed they all were, in their different ways.* She was still smoking, despite various half-hearted attempts to give up, and the lines in her face had deepened, her complexion greyed. There was no grey in the hair though, cruelly scraped back into a dark bun of clinical efficiency. But that was down to the efficacy of the dye rather than the kindness of nature, Nick felt sure. The rouge on her cheeks, intended to impart a degree of warmth and humanity, had been too generously applied and gave her a scarily comical look, like a sad-eyed clown in a horror movie.

"Sergeant Konstantópoulos, or should I say *Lieutenant?*" she shook his hand firmly. "You are welcome."

"*Acting lieutenant,* apparently, but I still call myself sergeant," said Thaní.

"So, they pay you the sergeant's money and you do the work of the lieutenant. Ha!" she roared.

Thaní grinned ruefully. She was spot-on, as ever.

"And you, again! What is it with you, Nick Fisher? I can't seem to keep you away from my dead bodies."

"It's your irresistible charm," he said.

"So, how are we feeling today? Our girl is not pretty, though I doubt she ever was," she confided.

Nick winced at the callousness. *Pánagou spent too much time with the dead*, he thought. *Sometimes her remarks jarred on the ears of the living.*

They followed her into a cold, clinical room. A young, bespectacled man with longish, dark hair tied in a ponytail was backing away from a stainless-steel trolley on which a small body lay face up.

"My assistant, Iákovos," she said, throwing an arm in his direction but not bothering to introduce the police officers. Thaní inclined his head to acknowledge the young man and Nick raised his hand as he was too far away for handshaking. *Anyway, it would seem too convivial in the immediate presence of death*, he thought.

The upper half of the body was covered in a white sheet that stretched to the knees, but it was not flat against the small breasts. Something was getting in the way. The calves and feet were exposed and looked unmarked. Nick saw freckles and suddenly felt like crying. A blue tag was attached to a big toe as if she were just another number on the slab.

They stood around the trolley. Pánagou glanced at each of them, assessing their readiness, Nick supposed. Then she folded down the sheet to the navel and both men gasped involuntarily. The upper body was blackened and deformed, comprehensively on the right-hand side. In parts, it was so black as to appear almost purple. The eyes were burnt out and the skin on the face had puckered, pulling the lips above the teeth in a lop-sided snarl. Her arms were not flat against her body but raised and curled in a ghastly parody of a puny boxer. In places, a few strands of frizzy, ginger hair remained and, on her left-hand side, patches of milky-white skin with freckles. The overall impression was more of a corpse unearthed from prehistoric times than a contemporary, young woman.

Pánagou waited while they adjusted to the sight and their breathing normalised. Then she began:

"So, we start with the PMCT. You want us to look for signs of foul play, so we search for signs of skull fracture. The scan is good at finding these, but we don't find any. If she was hit over the head, then it was not hard enough to crack her skull."

"But could have been hard enough to knock her out?" asked Nick.

"Yes, possibly. But the tissue in this area has been destroyed so I cannot detect this."

"Bugger."

"It is a bugger, yes. So, next, I want to know if she died in the fire or if she was already dead. We look for soot in the respiratory tract. If she is still breathing, even if she is unconscious, she is breathing in soot from the fire, you see."

The men nodded. They were getting it.

"We don't find much soot, so we do a toxicology test, looking for COHb, carboxyhaemoglobin. It measures quite low, at eleven per cent. If she were a smoker like me, this would be normal. But she was not a smoker, so it is a little elevated. We don't care, because this is *way below* the fifty per cent or more we would expect to see if she were breathing in soot."

"Someone said juniper trees produce very little smoke when they burn," said Thani.

"Yes, but soot and smoke are not the same things, Sergeant, and the toxicology test is for carbon monoxide, which you cannot see. I suggest you leave the science to me."

Thani looked a little sheepish and gave a weak grin.

"There is also the colour of the body," she went on. "Evidence from other cases suggests strongly that the bodies of those who die in fires tend to be cherry red in colour, not purple black."

"So, she was dead before the fire got her," reasoned Nick.

"Very likely, yes."

"Why the strange boxer's pose – was she defending herself against someone?"

"This is from the heat of the fire. It is flexion deformation."

They paused and contemplated the fierceness of a blaze that could contort her limbs to such an extent. *Thank God she was not alive*, thought Nick.

"Have you searched for other possible wounds to the body, Doctor?"

"Of course. Some ribs on her right-hand side are cracked but I believe these to be *thermal* fractures of the bones, not what you are looking for."

"A fire can do this? I had no idea."

They studied the pitiful creature with a mixture of horror and reverence.

"So, where does this leave us, Doctor?" asked Thaní, eventually.

"I am almost certain she was dead before the fire engulfed her. I have a few more tests I can try, but so far, I cannot determine how she died. A fatal accident? Murdered? I'm sorry but I cannot say."

"Could she have been strangled or asphyxiated in some way?"

"She could."

"But you cannot tell?"

"I cannot."

"Could she have been hit on the head hard enough to kill her without cracking her skull?"

"Perhaps, but this is pure conjecture, gentlemen."

"Surely, the balance of probabilities must point to murder," said Nick.

"You can deal with probabilities and statistics, gentlemen, and you are welcome. I am trained to establish facts where I can. I will let you know if I can deduce anything else about this poor girl's death in the next day or two. Now, before you go, there is one more thing. Iákovos will show you."

The young man eased himself off the stainless-steel work surface and strolled over.

"We had to cut or peel off what remained of the clothes on her upper body," he said. "But her denim shorts were largely intact. In the left-hand pocket, I found this." He held up a plastic evidence bag. "It's a cigarette end. It was wrapped in a tissue."

"Interesting," said Thaní. "We know she wasn't a smoker, so why would she do this?"

"Gathering evidence," said Nick. "If Roz were murdered, I'd put my money on this being one of the killer's dog-ends. She pocketed it to try and identify him or her, knowing it could be a source of DNA."

"Clever girl," said Thaní.

"Doctor Pánagou and I were thinking along similar lines," said Iákovos. "The tissue came from one of those small packs you can buy at airports. Maybe Roz picked some up on the way through? As for the cigarette, it has a double filter: part tan with lighter-coloured chips, part white. A decorative gold ring separates the parts."

"Have you identified the brand?" asked Nick.

"I am not certain, but it looks like one of the Donskoy Tabak brands."

"I've never heard of them. Where are they made?"

"In Rostov-on-Don, Russia. But the Russian company was acquired by the Japanese."

"Can you buy their cigarettes in other countries?"

"I'm sure you can, but I don't know which countries."

"What about Greece?"

He shrugged. "There is more work to do."

"Perhaps the company would help us," said Thaní. "They could confirm the brand identity and tell us where they are available."

"Good idea," said Nick. "I'd hope a Japanese company would be ready to help. More so than a Russian one, at any rate."

"Hmmm. Let's hope so. I'll get someone onto it."

"The other thing we've done is to extract DNA from the cigarette end and profile it," Iákovos went on.

"What does it tell us?" asked Nick.

"Nothing much," said Pánagou. "We cannot say anything *about* the owner from his or her DNA, but it *is* that person. We have a unique profile, like a fingerprint. Find us a suspect's DNA and we can test for a match."

"That could be a challenge," said Nick, wryly. "Can't you tell from the *pattern* of the DNA where in the world the person comes from, their race and so on?"

"This is not a scientific technique, Mr Fisher. In the field of genealogy, they offer tests that compare DNA profiles with the collection of profiles on their databases and come to conclusions about genetic heritage, often expressed as percentages of this or that. Some are rather dubious, I would say. As to race, our knowledge of DNA has led us to conclude that race does not exist; it is merely a social construct. This is the modern thinking."

Nick was astounded.

"A social construct? How on earth …?"

"Genetically, we are *enormously* similar. Take any two humans from anywhere on the planet and their DNA sequence will be 99.9% identical."

"Really?"

"And – of the differences found in the remaining 0.1% – most diversity is found *between individuals of the same race* rather than between races. Almost 96% of it by one measure."

"This is fascinating, Doctor. So, the whole idea of racism is a nonsense."

"Some say genetics has proved it. Human perceptions are something else, of course."

"Indeed. But hang on, didn't you use DNA on the African lad for me last year? Yasir. You concluded he was from *East* Africa."

"I think I did say this, yes. I may have been able to identify his haplogroup from the Y chromosome. *The Nilotes*, perhaps."

"If you say so. Why not do it again in this case, then?"

"Last time, we had a body. It's an approximate and time-consuming procedure, Mr Fisher. I would be nervous about the outcome without a body. I fear we would be wasting our time – and I have very little of that, right now."

It was Pánagou's *subtle as a brick* way of ending the meeting. They followed her outside where the air was now cooler. Nick checked his watch and found it was ten past six. She lit a cigarette and coughed for a moment.

"I can keep Iákovos on this for a little while," she said. "He likes to explore modern techniques and is less inhibited about straying from pure science. He also knows every corner of the Internet. Don't worry, gentlemen, we will try everything to help you find your smoker."

"And maybe the killer," added Nick.

"Yes. Maybe," she said with something approaching a smile before grinding her cigarette end into the gravel and returning inside.

"We need to call Teddy," said Thaní.

"Let's grab a beer first," said Nick.

CHAPTER 18
SCALING UP

It had been a long and tiresome trip back to Tamarisk Bay the previous night, but Thaní was up early the next morning and calling in at eight thirty. He wanted to update Leo on the session with Pánagou and ask for the support he needed.

"I need resources now, boss," he said.

"Go on."

"I want a constable investigating the cigarette. We need to know whether it came from Donskoy Tabak and where it could have been bought. This might give us a clue to the identity of Roz's attacker."

"Assuming there was one. Okay."

"And I need someone to walk the pictures of our blond guy over to the engineer and the estate agent and see if they can identify him."

"Have you discussed this with Nick?"

"No. Is that something I have to do now, sir?"

"No, of course not. But it might not be such a great idea, Thaní. We *know* the agent is in touch with these guys, we *suspect* the engineer might be. We'd just be letting them know we're onto them, don't you think?"

"Is that such a bad thing, boss? Maybe they'll pull in their horns or panic, make a mistake."

"Perhaps, but I want to catch these bastards, Thaní. These guys have no idea we even know about the blond man. He may have killed Roz just to keep his identity secret, but he doesn't know we have three photographs of him, and he doesn't know we have a cigarette end we think he smoked."

"I know, sir, but it's not enough for us to identify him. I don't know where that's going to come from."

"I suggest we put a tail on the estate agent, maybe the engineer, too. I can talk to the Investigating Judge."

"We have that kind of resource available, sir?"

Thaní knew round-the-clock surveillance on two individuals would require a minimum of twelve, ideally sixteen police officers.

"No, we don't, but I'll ask the judge to make more available, from elsewhere in Crete or Athína. This looks increasingly like the murder of a British national on Greek soil, Thaní. When the authorities grasp that, or the press gets hold of the story, the pressure will be on us to solve the case. Resources will be made available. I want us to act now in recognition of that."

"So, we're going to *assume* it's murder, sir."

"Not a word I like, Thaní. Call it a working hypothesis. If Forensics can't *prove* murder, it's up to us to work with the evidence and the connections we know of, to establish the facts and build a case. Good, old-fashioned police work."

"Okay, sir. I understand. We just have to find the guy."

"Exactly. Until then, let's keep our cards close to our chests. That goes for Nick Fisher, too."

"I'll make sure of it, sir," said Thaní.

*

Nick rolled into breakfast at nine twenty, looking dishevelled. Only Stefi was there.

"Morning. Seen my daughter?" he asked.

"Turtle duty. Back soon."

Nick grabbed himself some coffee, fruit and cereal. He sat heavily on the bench opposite Stefi.

"I gather you had another call, yesterday."

"Hmmm."

"Cheeky bastards, eh?"

"They make a big mistake with this call, Nick. I was frightened before. Now, I'm angry."

"Attaboy. What did you say to them?"

"It was the agent again: Pagiánnidis. Told me how sorry he was about the wildfire and the unfortunate girl who was caught in it. Said I had his deepest sympathies. I almost believed him! Then he went on to say

155

that sadly – and inevitably – such catastrophes do impact the value of property, and he expressed the *fervent hope* my insurance arrangements would compensate me in full, financially. I said nothing, but I have no insurance as I suspect he knows. Then he says his client is aware of the fire damage and has no option but to adjust his offer accordingly. It is now one and a half million and will remain open for acceptance until midnight on the fourth of October, after which it will lapse."

"Did he say what would happen if you don't accept?"

"No, but he urged me to say *Yes*, get the hell out and do something I was better qualified to do."

"Cheeky shit."

"I told him I wasn't taking advice from the likes of him. He finished by saying he hoped I would make the right decision – and the sooner the better."

"And you're still angry?"

"What do you think, Nick?"

"Good. Keep that anger. Let's fight the bastards with everything we've got. We have to get them before they get us."

Lauren came through the door as he finished speaking.

"*Who's* going to get us, Dad? Hi, Stefi."

"No one. How are the turtles?"

"Dan reckons we'll get our first hatchlings next week."

"How exciting!"

"Yes, it is. So sad Roz won't be here to see it."

"I know … but her mum might."

"Oh. When's she coming?"

"Her name's Alma and she's arriving tomorrow night."

"Have you spoken to her?"

Nick nodded.

"What's she like? I mean, how is she?"

"She sounded a bit lost, unsurprisingly. It's just a couple of months since her husband died, remember? I think she needs to understand what happened to Roz before she can assimilate the information."

"Assimilate? Sounds very clinical, Dad."

"I mean she must go from denial to acceptance. Until she does that, she'll be unable to grieve. Coming here should help the process."

"Not that we have answers to the *what happened* bit."

"Not yet."

"You want us to pick her up, Nick? Dan and I will be in Chaniá."

"You will? Oh, the bank presentation, of course. It would be helpful, Stefi. Thank you."

*

Thaní's wife was not happy.

"Another two nights? You're kidding."

"I need to, honey; it's an important case. If it goes well, there's a good chance my promotion will be confirmed."

"I hope you're not turning into one of those men who pretends he doesn't have a family," she said.

"Now you're being silly. I'm not that sort of man and you know it."

"Don't tell me I'm silly. Two toddlers are a lot to cope with on your own and I get lonely, too."

"It's just till Thursday and we could do with the extra money, right?"

"Extra money? I'll believe it when I see it."

There was no talking to her when she was like this, and it got Thaní down. He was very much the family man. He loved his family, and he was missing them. But he was also the breadwinner, so he had to work hard to be successful and make enough money to keep them all comfortable. She knew that, yet sometimes she seemed to resent it, especially if he had to stay away. He was doing his best, but it was not enough for her, and it hurt. He thought about commuting from their Chaniá apartment to Tamarisk Bay but the need for a boat ride made it impractical. They would have to live with it for a few more days.

As soon as his wife disconnected, the phone began ringing. He did not recognise the number.

"Sergeant Konstantópoulos? Good morning. It's Iákovos from Forensics. We met yesterday."

"Ah, yes. Hello."

"I spoke to Doctor Pánagou late last night and she said I should call you."

"You have something for me?"

"Perhaps. I used my own time yesterday evening to explore the DNA pattern we found on the cigarette a little more. I used techniques genealogists use to compare the pattern with others. It's not pure science and they are all private sector initiatives, so Pánagou is sceptical, but I have friends who believe it works. Anyway, I tried it."

"Okay. Go on."

"So, I used three different companies on The Internet. They all have their own databases and I wanted to see if they confirmed each other's results or came up with three different answers. Well, it turned out the *degree* of match was different with each company, but the message was broadly the same."

"Being what exactly?"

"The DNA sequencing of the person who smoked the cigarette closely resembles a Slavic ethnic group. He or she comes from a family with origins in a Slavic country."

"This is helpful information. Thank you, Iákovo."

"It's my pleasure. I'll email my findings. I found it interesting, and I learned a lot. I should say Doctor Pánagou asks that you not place too much reliance on this. It may not stand up in court. But you might use it to confirm other theories, perhaps."

Thaní acknowledged the qualification, thanked him for his hard work and disconnected.

*

Leo's meeting with the Investigating Judge was mixed. She was not prepared to authorise phone taps or access to cell phone records for the engineer, Marákis.

"There is no case for this, Leo," she said. "The man has done nothing wrong."

"We suspect him of passing information to the criminals which helped them target their campaign of intimidation."

"He might have told them a family friend had a pet goat; I get it. It's nowhere near enough, Leo. And you know it."

"But we can put a tail on him?"

"If you can afford it and feel it's justified, do it. But expect me to deny all knowledge of it. You're on your own as far as Marákis is concerned."

Leo understood. The man was a pillar of the community, a respected architect and engineer, and an established family man. She was not going out on a limb to pursue him.

"And the estate agent?"

"Is different. We know he is in contact with these criminals and is acting as their mouthpiece. He knows of the apparent intimidation and may have been involved. He is guilty by association, at the least, and may be your only route to catching the perpetrators. I will authorise access to cell phone records for his personal and office mobiles and you may tail him for up to fourteen days if you wish."

They both knew he could not possibly afford fourteen days of surveillance.

"There's also an office landline."

"Don't push your luck, Lieutenant. Let's leave it there, for now. I imagine he'll be making calls of this nature from his mobile, anyway, maybe even a disposable mobile, wouldn't you?"

It was not all Leo wanted but it would do. He returned to the office and assigned the tasks to his small team. He told them four more constables were expected the following day, two from Réthymno and two from Paleóchora. They could get onto the phone records right away. The surveillance could start from six am the next morning.

*

Nick found Thaní, late Wednesday morning, sitting at a table under the trees. His laptop was open, and he was looking puzzled.

"Hello, Nick," he said. "We should have a catch-up."

Nick placed two mugs of coffee on the table and Thaní thanked him.

"It's only instant, not your Greek sludge, I'm afraid."

"That's okay. It's wet and it might help me stay awake."

159

Nick sat down on the wooden bench opposite.

"What have you got, then?" he asked.

Thaní had just been updated by Leo, so he was able to tell Nick about the phone records and the surveillance plans.

"He should ask for bank records, too," said Nick. "Someone's being bribed or blackmailed, I should think."

"The judge wouldn't let him have those for the engineer."

"No, I guess not. Well, we have something to get started with, at least."

Thani shared the news from Iákovos, too.

"That's a bit odd," said Nick. "I thought the word *Slav* means someone who speaks a Slavic language. I hadn't thought of it as a genetic thing."

"The DNA profile is a close match with several people who are all Slavs, as I understand it. Perhaps they all came from the same area, originally."

He spun his laptop around so that Nick could see the screen. It was a Eurasian map with Slavic areas coloured in.

"There are lots of them, unfortunately. Most of the central Europeans, former Yugoslavia, Russia."

"And this only tells us where the guy originated, genetically. It doesn't tell us where he lives now. He could be a Serb living in Italy or a Pole living in Timbuktu."

"Not much use, is it?"

"It's a piece of the jigsaw, but we need more. What about the cigarette – any news from Chaniá?"

"Not yet. I expect he's waiting for the company to get back to him."

That meant tomorrow, Nick figured, glancing at his watch and adding six hours for Tokyo time.

"And Interpol? Have they matched the photos to a famous Slavic criminal, by any chance?"

"Again, not yet. I think they're struggling with the quality of the pictures."

"We've been there before, haven't we?"

"Hmmm."

"We need to find this bastard, Thani. Any other ideas?"

"Not really. Hopefully, he'll be picked up at one of the ports or airports."

"With those photos? I doubt it."

"Then we must hope the surveillance or the phone records will lead us somewhere. That, or they try something else on poor Stefi in the meantime."

It was frustrating, but there was little they could do until there was a break or the perpetrators showed their hand a little more. Nick left Thaní with his Slavs and wandered around to Lauren's tree house. He could see her stretched out on the balcony with a book.

"I'm giving myself the afternoon off," he called. "Do you fancy some beach time with your old Dad?"

*

They packed some lunch into their beach bags. Nick hesitated about the phone but, in the end, decided he had better take it. He was being paid, after all, or at least he hoped so. Leo had not finalised the arrangements, but he assumed there would be a modest, per diem amount like before. It was enough for his conscience to insist he remain contactable.

At Nick's suggestion, they wandered towards Elafonísi for a kilometre or more to see what they could find. Someone had said there were delightful, little coves that were almost tourist-free. It felt good to escape Tamarisk Bay for a spell and have time to themselves rather than running into other members of Stefi's group all the time.

The third cove was perfect. A crescent of small shingle, partly shaded by tamarisk and juniper, it was divided from the second cove by a little promontory. They made their way to the right-hand side and Nick set up the parasol while Lauren arranged the beach towels with heavy stones on the corners to counter the breeze. There was no one there and the water was crystal clear and turquoise.

"I'm starving," said Lauren.

"Me too, but a quick dip first, I think," said Nick, stepping gingerly over the rocks and into the water.

*

The call from Chaniá came through at ten minutes to seven that evening. Thaní had retreated to his cabin in the run-up to supper and took it sitting on his bed in a bathrobe.

"Good evening, Sergeant."

It was Leftéris, one of his brighter constables. Thaní recognised his voice.

"I'm sorry it has taken so long, sir, but I have news on the cigarette."

Thaní stood and walked to the window. "Go on," he said.

"The brand *is* one of Donsky's. It's called *Russian Style* which comes in four variants, all made in their factory at Rostov-on-Don. We believe this one to be the normal strength variant. There are weaker, stronger and menthol variants, but they don't look quite the same. This variant comes in a reddish-brown pack with the name in Russian and a crest on the front of the pack."

"And the cigarettes have the double filter with the gold, decorative ring between them?"

"The normal strength ones, yes."

"How sure are they, Leftéri?"

"Oh, they're quite certain, sir. It's one of theirs all right."

"Great. And where can one buy this *Russian Style* brand?"

"They were a bit less definite about that. They ship in bulk to main distributors, but they can't control where individual packs end up. That's the bad news. The good news is, it's a relatively new brand and, so far, they've only shipped to main distributors in Russia, Japan and China."

"So, there would be none available, here in Greece."

"Not unless someone ordered them over the Internet, which is not a common way of buying cigarettes, even now."

"Or brought them with them from Russia, Japan or China."

"Right, sir."

"But Japan and China are not Slavic countries," mused Thaní.

"Er … no, I don't believe they are, sir."

*

Nick and Lauren were picking their way back across the rocks when the email from Thaní arrived. Nick saw it had been copied to Leo.

"Good probability our blond man is Russian, based on DNA profiling and cigarette brand (both of which assume it was <u>his</u> cigarette, of course). It's a bit thin but it's all we have. Is he part of a Russian syndicate? I am researching property developments in Greece where Russians have been involved. Could use your help, Nick."

"Looks like I'm going to be busy," said Nick, showing Lauren the email.

"It's okay," she said, "It was a wonderful afternoon, anyway. Thanks, Dad."

CHAPTER 19
THE HUNT BEGINS

Constable Níkos Manousákis was not happy. Grumpy at the best of times, he had been called by his boss, Investigations Sergeant Náni Samaráki, late the previous night and ordered to get himself to Chaniá by ten the next morning. He was to take fellow constable Chrístos, and they were to be part of a surveillance team. Now, they had been briefed by Acting Lieutenant Konstantópoulos who looked about thirty-five and who Níkos took to be wet behind the ears. Policing was rarely exciting, at least in Réthymno, and Níkos expected nothing more of Chaniá. And surveillance was always tedious. He found it a bit like flying; hours of boredom punctuated by moments of sheer terror.

Konstantópoulos was trying to do it on the cheap, too. You needed eight men per suspect: a team of two on six-hour shifts. Any longer and some fell asleep, usually when the suspect was making their getaway. And you needed at least two if you suddenly had to follow them. Or else you would be recognised and the whole plan would collapse. Níkos pointed this out and was told there were two suspects to be watched and resources were limited. That was why *he* was there.

Their job was to watch an estate agent called Pagiánnidis and follow him if he left his office. The guy had no criminal record – Níkos had checked – but he might be working hard to get one. Their job was to record his activities and do their best to tail him and identify any contacts he made. As simple as that. Except it was impossible to park on Daskalogiánnis and they would stick out like a sore thumb if they tried, so they would have to watch the office on foot or from the benches in the leafy square sixty metres away, on the other side of the road. At least it was handy for the café on the corner.

"You're on for six and a half hours from twelve thirty pm," they were told. "He'll probably travel back home at some point, so here's the address. Familiarise yourselves with the route from office to home."

"Where will we park?" asked Chrístos. "We don't know Chaniá well, sir."

"As you come down Daskalogiánnis – a one-way street – you'll find a tuck-in on your left. There's a restaurant on the corner just before a square on the right. Our boys will be parked there, waiting to hand over to you. Please be on time."

"How come six and a half hours, sir?"

"You can do more if you like, Constable. We're leaving the period from one thirty to six am uncovered at this stage. That way, we can do it with six constables – and without you losing your beauty sleep."

"You're very kind, sir."

*

The constables assigned to watch Marákis also faced challenges. The engineer's offices were just around the corner from one of Chaniá's main shopping streets and opposite the pedestrianised route to the harbour. As always, it was bustling with both locals and tourists. This was good news and bad news, they figured. If they had to follow him on foot, he would be unlikely to spot them, but also, it would be easy to lose him in the crowds.

His office was on the top floor of a relatively small, four-storey building. Any police presence on the fourth floor itself would be far too obvious. A lift stopped at each of the floors and at a lower floor, where the underground car park was situated. They would have to split up, they decided. One would be in the ground floor lobby, in sight of the lift, and one in their unmarked car in a shadowy corner of the parking area, in sight of the bronze-coloured Mercedes they knew belonged to the engineer. If he realised what was going on and used the fire escape, they would have no chance. If he used the stairs, the one watching the lift should spot him. The car park would see less action, so would be even more tedious, but at least it would be comfortable in the car. They decided they would switch, halfway through the shift. For now, Pandelís would take the lobby and Vangélis the car park.

*

Lauren had asked if she could help with the research. Nick suspected she was getting a little bored, so he agreed. She had finished her morning work with the turtles and Dan and Stefi had left for Chaniá early. Teddy had been assigned to tidying the vegetable and herb gardens. After an hour on their laptops, Nick and his daughter swapped notes.

"It's massive. I had no idea," said Lauren.

"What is?" asked Nick.

"The tourism industry here: the number of people who come, the size of the investments. Did you know, over thirty-three million tourists came to Greece last year? And they spent over twenty billion euros!"

"I'm not surprised, Lauren. Things bounced back after COVID. Now, the government is trying to get people to stay longer and spend more. Twenty billion sounds huge but it's only six hundred euros per tourist, which makes Greece a cheap destination, still."

"There's big money involved, too. Hines are investing. They have five hotels including the Grand Hyatt in Athens and the Out of the Blue Capsis Elite Resort, wherever that is."

"It's near Agía Pelagía, on the north coast of Crete," Nick said.

"Hines are huge, Dad. It's a private U.S. company but they have ninety-five billion dollars of assets under management and own eight hundred such properties!"

"Gosh. You have been busy."

"Then there's Blackstone. I thought they were a U.S. hedge fund, but they bought the Elounda Blu Hotel not long ago to add to the five Greek hotels they already own."

"I reckon Greece is the place to be now, Lauren. Property prices were down forty per cent with the financial crisis and then COVID, but they're starting to recover now. This government has done well with the economy and it's making all the right noises to attract foreign investment. I just hope they won't let my beautiful island be ruined in their rush for growth."

"There's a Russian one, too: Lazko. It's another privately owned outfit.

Massive. Owns a gorgeous luxury development near Ágios Nikólaos and is developing another at Eloúnda."

"There's plenty going on in the north-east."

"And Lazko have *strategic investor status* from the Greek government, whatever that means. Sounds a bit dodgy to me," Lauren added.

"I guess it's like preferred supplier status. The government works *with* them to an extent, and they get first sight of the plans and perhaps better opportunities to bid. Something like that."

"As I said. Dodgy."

"These are huge, long-established enterprises with lots to lose, though. I doubt they'd get involved in the grubby tactics used against Stefi."

"Hopefully not, but this *is* Greece, Dad."

"Have you found any other Russian outfits?"

"Some of them have backed off, I read. The war with Ukraine has stopped Russians from coming to Crete, for now. There were three hundred thousand of them at one point but it's well down now."

"But these places are not built *only* for Russians, are they?"

"Not only, no. But it must have an impact."

"Hmmm."

They turned back to their respective computers. *Last year's tourist numbers were even more impressive,* thought Nick, *if the Russians were largely absent.*

"Let's check out the regional developers," he said.

"I'm not sure we're getting anywhere, Dad. What about the estate agent you met? He must know who he's dealing with, right?"

"Oh, he knows. But he's not telling."

"He needs to be more scared of us than his principals."

"Are you suggesting we beat it out of him, daughter dear?"

"I thought that's what you did in the police."

He saw from her smirk that she was teasing.

"It would save a lot of time," she added.

"Get back to your research, you wicked girl," said Nick. "Remember, we also need to look into the family connection between Pagiánnidis and Marákis."

"You mean Stávros and his Uncle George, by marriage."

"Exactly. There are always family connections here, but this one doesn't feel healthy."

*

Thaní was wondering why he had returned to Tamarisk Bay, this time. He supposed it was to continue working closely with Nick and to be in situ if the would-be buyers had any more tricks up their sleeves, but now he felt out of it, stuck down here, knowing the surveillance teams were in action in Chaniá and both the engineer and the estate agent were based there. Not only that, but he had angered his wife into the bargain. He felt tired and irritated with himself.

Late Thursday morning, two messages came from Leo. Interpol had used all their tricks to enhance Roz's photographs of the blond man but to no avail. They were still no match with any known criminal on their extensive database. Leo asked them to focus on Slavic criminals and provide a shortlist of possibilities, but they were unable or unwilling to do this.

The estate agent, Pagiánnidis, had three cell phone numbers for which his company was billed. It looked like he used one of these as his private number. Detailed records of the calls to and from each number had been sent as a .csv spreadsheet file. Constable Dimítris was analysing the last three months. Leo asked him to start by grouping the numbers most frequently called or received and identifying the locations of any numbers outside Greece.

Leo also confirmed that the judge was allowing them to access the estate agent's bank records and they would arrive by the end of the day, with luck.

Thaní wandered over to Nick's hut, hands thrust deep into the pockets of his shorts. Perhaps *they* had found something. Anyway, at least it would be some company for lunch.

*

Going through the thick glass, security doors was like an airlock, Stefi imagined. *Hopefully, not one leading to an airless void,* he thought,

168

seeing himself for a moment jettisoned into space with only a fragile, umbilical cord attaching him to the mother ship.

"How do I look?" he asked Dan, who had squeezed in with him.

"You look like the kind of savvy entrepreneur any banker would be desperate to lend to."

"Well, I guess there's a first time for everything. Just keep me on track, will you?"

"I'll do my best, buddy."

It was five minutes before eleven. Perfect timing. Hard-hearted Anna rose from her desk when she saw them released from the airlock and indicated a side meeting room. The light flashed from her glasses but she did not smile, Stefi noticed.

She studied each of them as she shook hands with a limp wrist.

"I'll let you have five minutes to get organised, then we will start," she said. "I have asked a colleague of mine to join us. He is Mr. Kóstas."

They did not need five minutes. It was just a matter of calling up the PowerPoint presentation on the laptop and running a cable to the nearest socket, so the battery stayed fresh. Stefi took a moment to review his notes while Dan arranged the chairs.

"Remember what we said," said Dan. "Calm and confident, right?"

"Right."

Mr Kóstas was the Risk Manager for Crete, Anna explained. According to his business card, he was based in Iráklio.

"I am three days in Iráklio, one day in Réthymno and one day in Chaniá, most weeks," he said.

Stefi introduced Dan, saying:

"Dan is my lead volunteer on the project. He came for a spell last year and then he came back."

"And how long will you stay this time?" asked Anna.

"Several months, minimum," he said.

"Really? As a volunteer? How can you afford to?"

"Stefi provides bed and board and pays expenses if I go anywhere for the project. I hardly spend any money here and have a little saved, anyway."

He could see some scepticism still lingered.

"For me, it's a great opportunity to learn. We're aiming to be right at the forefront of renewable energy solutions. What I learn, here in Crete, I'll take back with me. I might start my own business in The States."

"But you could leave at any time, Dan. You have no contract. Is that correct?" asked Kóstas.

"Technically, yes. But I have no plans to. I want to stay and make this work."

"Do you have *any* regular employees?" This from Anna, directed at Stefi.

"No. All volunteers, so far. I wanted to avoid fixed costs at this stage and plenty of young people are looking for summer work. I must pay the builder and the engineer, of course."

Stefi glanced at each of them to see if they had more questions. It seemed not.

"Why don't we take you through our presentation?" he said. "It's only twenty minutes or so and I think it'll give you a good idea of what we're trying to do."

They acquiesced and pulled their chairs closer to the table and the laptop screen. The first slide showed an idyllic view of Tamarisk Bay and a slow, line-by-line reveal of the words:

Let nature recharge *your* batteries at …

TAMARISK BAY

Greece's first WHOLLY SUSTAINABLE luxury destination

"Is it true – Greece's first? What about The Ellinikón?" asked Kóstas.

This was a bit of a curve ball, but Stefi knew something about the massive development underway near Athína.

"The Ellinikón is a huge, multi-use project with apartments and shops, rather than a holiday destination. And it's keen to be *seen* as using clean energy, but I don't believe it's entirely self-sufficient as we intend to be."

This seemed to appease him somewhat, but he was not finished:

"What's your target market here, Spiliáki? Do people who care about sustainability have money to spend on luxury holidays?"

Stefi smiled inside. This was just the sort of question he relished. Many still thought the only people who cared about sustainability were young protestors, most of whom were penniless. It was not the case, and he had the research to prove it. Tamarisk Bay was the future. Pretty soon all holiday destinations will be like this.

As the presentation went on, they warmed to the task. Dan did five minutes on the technology they were planning. *Enough to excite them but not enough for them to glaze over*, as Stefi had put it. Dan knew his stuff; it was slick and well-researched. Anna and Kóstas were nodding now, understanding. Getting it. Finally, they turned to the numbers. Stefi summed up.

"The development will take two and a half years to complete but we can take guests from year two, as soon as the bulk of the accommodation and the pools have been completed. We expect to make a modest profit in year three, but it kicks in from year four."

"You can make a million euros a year?"

"From year four, pre-tax, yes."

"How many apartments, in total?"

"Thirty-two, plus twenty tree houses and a dozen yurts."

"Yurts? What the hell are they?"

"Luxury tents. From Mongolia, originally."

"Tents? On the south coast of Crete? I hope you have plenty of strong tent pegs."

"We have a more sheltered spot in mind for them, don't worry."

"What kind of occupancy rates are you hoping for?"

"We've used an average of sixty per cent in the plan, May through October."

"Sixty per cent for May or October sounds very ambitious."

"I agree. It would be, but the sixty per cent is an *average* for the whole season. It might be forty per cent in May and eighty per cent in August, but the charges are much higher then, so I think we've been conservative."

"How much would I have to pay for an apartment?"

"A two-bedroomed apartment for a week in August will be roughly two and half thousand euros."

"You can get that much?"

"We've run comparables with what's out there. We think it's very competitive."

The bank employees seemed less sure, Stefi noticed; it was probably way beyond their holiday budgets.

Kóstas turned to Anna. "What's our facility?"

"Eight hundred thousand, seventy per cent drawn. But they need three million."

He whistled softly.

Stefi checked his watch. They had been there thirty-five minutes.

"We heard you had a wildfire down there," said Anna. "How does that affect things?"

"Very little," said Stefi. "Around two-thirds of our juniper forest was destroyed. It's a bit of an eyesore, but it will soon recover. There was no damage to the development itself."

"But a girl died in the fire, didn't she?"

Stefi nodded. He wanted to speak but seemed unable to do so. Dan cut in:

"One of our volunteers. It was a terrible accident. We're still trying to understand what happened."

"Were you negligent? Could her family have a case against you?" asked Kóstas.

Stefi was shocked. He had not even considered it. But again, it was Dan who spoke.

"Stefanos told Roz to take our boat to Paleóchora to buy groceries. For some reason, she chose instead to go back onshore. This decision led to her death in the fire. I don't think there's any way Stefanos could be held responsible for a decision he neither made nor knew anything about."

"Let's hope not," Kóstas said, drily.

Anna exchanged glances with Kóstas, then steepled her fingers and looked Stefi in the eyes.

"Now, is there anything else we should know, gentlemen? Has anything happened since we last met that you need to make us aware of?"

It was a loaded question. How much did they know about what had happened at Tamarisk Bay? Or was it just a catch-all question the bank always lobbed in at this stage as they stared into the whites of their borrowers' eyes? Stefi did not know and cursed himself for not discussing what to reveal with Dan. He glanced at Dan now but found him frowning as he studied the grain on the table. Stefi decided the safest policy was to throw the dogs a bone.

"We have a small archaeological team arriving next week," he said, "from the Ministry of Hellenic Culture and Sports. I've granted them limited access to explore a small part of the site. Some tourists claimed to have found a couple of Roman coins on my land and they want to investigate. It will not inconvenience us."

"That depends on what they find, surely."

"I don't believe they will find anything of significance, Anna. My family has owned this land for over forty years, and we have never found a trace of anything Roman. It's too far west. The Romans didn't venture beyond Polyrhinnía."

"You think the tourists made a mistake?"

"I don't know what to think, but we will know when the exploratory dig has ended."

"In the meantime, it's another uncertainty for your project," observed Anna.

"These things happen. Small rocks in the river. We must manoeuvre the boat around them to reach the bountiful sea."

Anna smiled for the first time.

"And will you reach the sea, Spiliáki?"

"With your help, I believe we will."

She stood, still smiling. Kóstas did not smile but his handshake was firm, as if he had reached a place where he could trust them.

"Thank you for coming in, gentlemen," he said. "It was helpful. Now, Anna and I will discuss with our colleagues what the bank might be able to offer. This will take a few days, then Anna will be in touch."

Escaping through the airlock seemed simpler than getting in. In a few moments, they were outside, the September sunshine warm on their faces. The relief was palpable, and, for Stefi, it instantly translated into hunger.

"Let's grab some coffee and a spanakópita," he said.

*

Chrístos ambled down Daskalogiánnis again. The guy still had not come out and they needed to be sure he was still there. It was getting to the mid-afternoon point where some businesses took a break until evening. He needed to be certain it did not apply to estate agents.

The smell of spit-roasting lamb from the café at the top of the little hill was steadily replaced by grilling steak and burgers wafting up from below. His mouth was watering as he made his way down. Tourists streamed up from the harbour area. He heard American English, German, Italian, French and several Slavic languages. He crossed the road and stopped to look at the photos in the estate agent's window. Between the pictures, he could see inside but they could not see much of him. Okay. Pagiánnidis was still there, still on his cell phone. He was quite young, perhaps mid- to late-thirties, Chrístos thought, and he did not look particularly Greek. He was relatively pale with an oval face and wispy, brown hair, already thinning. He looked like he had never done a hard day's work, but seemed, nevertheless, worried and tired. For credibility, Chrístos moved along the photo boards, feigning interest, then wandered off, back up the hill. He found Níkos where he had left him, at a white, metal table under a plane tree in the square, surrounded by leaves.

"Still there," he said. "Still yakking." He sat down opposite, where he could see down the street. "D'you think we could sneak in a Gýros?" he said.

*

Pandelís was not bored. He was too busy. The lobby below the lawyer's office was in constant motion as it served all the floors of the office building and was also a walk-through to a larger building at the rear. It housed a small café, too, which served a good, iced coffee. He could testify to that. He scanned the crowds for fifty-something men with silver hair and suits and found plenty. Would he even recognise Marákis, he began to wonder and checked again the photos he had been given.

At ten minutes past three, the lift pinged yet again, and he saw three women step out. But, just as the doors were closing, he glimpsed a silver-haired man with an expensive tan, still in the lift. It was not enough for Pandelís to be sure, but it was enough for him to send an urgent text to Vangélis, in the car park below:

This MIGHT be our guy now!

He waited, picturing the lift's arrival in the car park, the man getting out and heading to his Mercedes.

A few moments later, a reply came:

It's him. Get your arse down here!

Pandelís saw the up arrow lit and rushed for the stairs instead. He hurtled down, two at a time, then paused to ease open the door to the car park. He saw the silver-haired man stepping into a bronze-coloured Mercedes and then he saw Vangélis staring at him, eyes bulging, frantically indicating for Pandelís to get into the car with him. Pandelís barrelled out of the door, sprinted the twenty metres and threw himself into the passenger seat, just as the Merc slid out of its space, heading for the exit ramp.

They saw the Merc swing left and then left again into the heavy traffic on the one-way street. They had to force their way in four cars behind, earning themselves a beep and a shout from a woman who raised both arms in bewilderment. Pandelís gave an apologetic wave, and she drew her index finger around the side of her head several times, then indicated her passenger, a boy of about ten.

"She thinks you're crazy and should be more careful," he said.

Vangélis glanced in the rear-view mirror.

"And I think the cow should have let me out. Now keep your eyes on the Merc."

The traffic lurched forward in fits and starts. Choosing a lane was problematic as double parking was prevalent and it was easy to get caught behind one of those idiots. Consequently, most of the traffic was concentrated in a broad single file grinding down the middle of the road. Motorcycles and scooters were weaving dangerously through.

When they came to the next set of traffic lights, the Merc just made it through but their unmarked Skoda and the two cars in front of it did not, despite Vangélis sounding his horn several times. They were now hemmed in on all sides.

"Shit," he said. "Watch him now."

Beyond the lights, the traffic was easier. Pandelís watched the Merc gain momentum before taking a left-hand fork off the main road.

"Do we have his home address?" asked Vangélis.

"No. I'll call in and see if they do."

"We might have to hope he's going home for the afternoon and head over there. We've lost him now, I reckon."

"Do you think he saw us?"

"I don't think so unless he spotted your antics in the car park."

*

Nick sensed Thaní's impatience. It was Thursday afternoon, and he would want to be home with his family by the weekend at the latest. He looked unhappy. Nick and Lauren took him through their limited findings on who was behind some of the larger tourist developments in Greece.

"We'll need more time to dig into the smaller guys," Nick explained, "and to make inroads into these blasted offshore companies."

"I think it's time to stand back from this for an afternoon, Nick. We need to regroup, look at what we have, and what we need to find out. Could we do that?"

"Sure, if you think it would help."

"It would help me, I think."

They made sandwiches and coffee and moved to Stefi's hut

where there was a large whiteboard with some coloured pens, Nick remembered.

"Let's remind ourselves of the various players," Nick said, picking up a pen.

"Do you want me to be scribe?" asked Lauren.

"Thanks, but no. It helps me think, as I go," he replied.

He drew a large TB in the middle of the board and beneath it wrote Stefi, Dan, Teddy, Roz, Méli the Goat and Others, then he drew square brackets around Others and a ring around everything.

"This is the Tamarisk Bay team, past and present. Do we know any of the earlier volunteers?" Thaní was shaking his head.

"Maybe we should. They could have been a source of information for the buyer."

Thaní looked sceptical, but said:

"I can talk to Stefi when he gets back."

"Good man."

Nick was creating more circles now. One for the estate agent, Pagiánnidis, one for the engineer, Marákis and one for Stefi's lawyer across the top and one for the bank, one for the Forestry Department and one for the Archaeological Department down the right-hand side.

"So, these are the players. Have I forgotten anyone?"

"The blond guy, the Russian," said Lauren.

"Nine out of ten," said Nick. "It would have been ten, but we don't *know* Blondie is Russian. We don't even know it was *his* cigarette end and we have no proof that the guy Roz photographed several days earlier was there on the day of the fire. It's all conjecture, but hope-fully, it adds up to something."

He wrote *Blond Man* in a circle to the bottom left of the board and said: "Here's what we do know."

Below, he wrote:

Smokes Russian cigarettes?

DNA profile matches Slavic groups.

Bad photos ...

"We don't know anything else about him, do we? We don't know how he got here. Did he walk from Elafonísi, or did he have a boat? We don't know if he killed Méli. We don't know if he started the fire. We don't know if he killed Roz."

"It might have been all of those," said Lauren.

"Perhaps." Nick drew dotted lines across from Blond Man to Roz and Méli, then drew a red cross over each of their names and wrote *Killer?* on each dotted line.

"Also, we don't know who he is working for, but we presume it's the would-be buyer."

Now he wrote Unknown Buyer in a circle in the top, left-hand corner and joined it to Blond Man with a dotted line with a question mark against it.

"What do we know about this unknown buyer?"

"Might be Russian," said Lauren.

"Because Blondie might be Russian?"

"And because Russian firms have been behind some tourist developments in Greece."

"All right, but it's tenuous. I think the only thing we know is this."

Now, he drew a line from the Unknown Buyer circle to the Estate Agent circle and made it into an arrow.

"We know their approach came through the agent, Pagiánnidis. This is all we know."

It was shocking but true. Everything had been conjecture. They knew nothing.

"So, what else do we *know*?" Nick stood back from the board, inviting them to contribute.

"We know Pagiánnidis has a history with Stefi," said Thaní. "They fell out over his late father's estate."

"Right." Nick drew a double-headed arrow between Stefi and the Estate Agent's circle and wrote *Friction* next to it.

"Makes one curious, that. Did the Unknown Buyer *know* about it? Did they choose Pagiánnidis *because* of it, even?"

"Why would they?"

"To make life difficult for Stefi, maybe?"

"Also, we know the engineer's wife is the aunt of the estate agent," said Lauren.

"We do." Nick drew a new line joining the two circles and wrote Mrs M, aunt of SP. "What does it tell us?"

"They know each other better than we might have expected," said Thaní.

"Being a Greek family, that's very likely," agreed Nick.

"Could they be working together on this?"

"Stefi described Marákis as an old family friend, but anything's possible, I guess."

"Blood's thicker than water, Dad," observed Lauren.

"So, I believe," grinned Nick. "Now, the lawyer."

"Why show the lawyer at all? I don't understand."

"Because Thaní, according to Stefi, *his lawyer* called him about the forestry claim. He or she was sending papers through in due course. I've not heard of those papers arriving, have you?"

"No, and I don't know who this person is. We need to find out and get in contact."

"Exactly. And then we have the bank. I gather there's a question mark over the guy who used to handle Stefi's account. What was his name? Manólis, I think. Suddenly, he was no longer there. Did the bank fire him or move him on, for some reason? We don't know, but now Stefi must deal with this woman Anna. I'll be interested to see how it goes today.

"I've put the Forestry Department up there, but we don't have a contact because it all happened through the lawyer." Nick drew an arrow from the Forestry Department's circle to the lawyer's circle. "Finally, we have the Archaeological Department, part of the Ministry of Hellenic Culture and Sports. In this case, Stefi was contacted directly by Mr Tzanakákis. He then found him online and called him back, so he appears to have been genuine. But how did he get this information about the Roman coins?"

Nick drew another bubble inside which he wrote *Slovenian Tourists*, then drew an arrow to the Archaeological Department's circle. Then, he answered his own question.

"From the Slovenian tourists we know nothing about."

"We know they're Slovenian."

"Thank you, Lauren, but we don't even know that. Neither do we know they were tourists. This is just what they told Tzanakákis."

Nick stood back from his work. "Throws up a few questions, doesn't it?" he said.

"Okay," said Thaní. "This is helpful, Nick. I can see a few things we need to do now. Let's make a list."

Nick made a box in the vacant space below Méli. "Okay. Fire away," he said.

"The lawyer – we need to call him and find out *how* he heard from the forestry people and where the follow-up paperwork is. We could also call the Forestry Department and see if they will confirm the claim."

They watched as Nick wrote 1) Lawyer and 2) Forestry Dept.

"We could try to trace this Manólis character and find out the story there. I assume the bank won't tell us anything helpful, but we should ask."

Nick wrote 3) Manólis, Bank.

"We could call Tzanakákis and ask about his Slovenian tourists and their coins."

"I think Stefi already did, and he would not divulge."

"The same question from the police should bring a different response, Nick."

"Yes, of course," he said, adding 4) Tzanakákis: Slovenian Tourists to his list. "Anything else?"

"What about the earlier volunteers?" said Lauren.

"Well remembered. Yes, we need names from Stefi, and to make contact."

He wrote 5) Stefi: prior volunteers.

"Do you want me to go on researching the developers?" asked Lauren.

"Maybe take a closer look at the Russian one you found."

"Lazko?"

"Yes. See if they have any subsidiaries focused on Greece. Even if

180

Lazko are totally legitimate, one of their subsidiary CEOs could have been a little overzealous."

"Okay."

"See if you can identify any smaller players that might stretch for an opportunity like this, particularly any with Slavic connections."

It was a big ask for his daughter and Nick knew it, but he wanted to get involved with Thaní in tackling the five things on the list he had created. Also, he had the first inkling of an idea that might make her work irrelevant, but he was not about to share it. Not yet.

*

Chrístos and Níkos were bored senseless. Their target, the estate agent, had not stirred from his office all day. It had been a complete waste of time. There were worse places to fritter away a day, watching the world go by from a leafy square next to an excellent café, but it was not a fulfilling experience, and they were getting ratty.

"Why don't we just sneak off?" suggested Níkos.

"We'd have to tell Konstantópoulos."

"We could make up some excuse."

"Hmmm. Like what?"

"Maybe your boy got hurt at school?"

"Fuck off, Níko! You're not using my family like that. Anyway, say that sort of thing and the next minute, it happens. I'd never forgive myself. What about one of your girlfriends having to go to the clinic?"

"Not urgent enough, is it?"

"What about you, then? Some nasty, little rash that's driving you insane."

"I'm not going there."

"Well, then."

"I guess we stick it out till the bastard drives home, then."

"We'll be relieved at seven, anyway. It's only an hour and three-quarters."

"Did you say *only*?"

Níkos flicked his empty paper cup at Chrístos who did not know it was empty and collided with the woman behind in his efforts to evade any liquids. It was the high point of Níkos's day.

*

"What time did we leave his office?" asked Vangélis.

Pandelís checked his phone.

"I texted you at twelve minutes past three."

"So, we would have got here by four. Obviously, he had somewhere else to go."

They had seen a rather smart woman in her fifties arrive soon after they did and watched her unload groceries from her hatchback and enter the detached, stone house. They assumed she was Mrs Marákis. Since then, very little had happened in this up-market suburb of Chaniá. A hawker selling fresh fruit and vegetables from a dishevelled pick-up truck had driven slowly past, music blaring from his roof-mounted speakers. Two girls of about ten had strolled past, arm in arm, stared in, then giggled and ran off, laughing. A small dog was yapping incessantly, fifty metres away, while an older woman admonished it in gentle, disappointed tones.

"It's no good *talking* to the bloody thing," moaned Pandelís. "It needs a good thrashing. Little bugger."

"Doing all right, isn't he? Our guy," said Vangélis, admiring the house. "Nice home, nice office with views over the harbour, I imagine. Smart wife – not bad for her age, a new hatchback and a bloody Mercedes. He's got the lot."

"Wouldn't be surprised if he had a boat in the garage or a second home at the beach, too."

"Hmmm. Both, probably."

"So, all you need, Vangéli, is to pack in this policing business. Bloody waste of time, anyway. Then, you study hard to be an architect, start a couple of businesses and run them successfully for thirty years or so."

"No chance, mate. Can't do the maths, can I?"

This was the least of his problems, thought Pandelís, but said no more. He checked his watch. Less than two hours to go, thank God.

*

Dan and Stefi sat side by side on the bright blue, plastic chairs in the Arrivals Hall at Chaniá airport. From there, they could see everyone who emerged from the baggage carousels.

"Manchester?" he said. "I thought she lived in Scotland."

"There are no direct flights from Glasgow after early September."

"That's weird when it's nice here till mid-October."

"At least. November was gorgeous, last year."

"Not in Glasgow."

"No. I suppose not," said Stefi.

"I hope you know what she looks like?" said Dan, "because I don't."

Stefi waggled his phone.

"Nick sent over Roz's photos – from the funeral."

"Let's have a look, then."

Dan saw an attractive, dark-haired woman who must be nudging fifty but looked younger. She looked sad, as might be expected, but there were laughter lines around those big, dark eyes.

"She looks okay," he said. "Sympatico."

"Her name is Alma," Stefi said.

The flight was slow to make it through the baggage area and it was already twenty past five when they spotted her. She was smaller than Dan expected, but also prettier.

"Excuse me, it's Alma, isn't it?" Dan said.

She flushed a little and managed a weak smile.

"I'm Dan and this is Stefi. We are so sorry for your loss, Alma. We were all very fond of Roz."

"Thank you. I'm not sure it's sunk in yet. The gentleman I spoke to on the phone ..."

"You'll meet Nick later. The two of us had business in Chaniá so it made sense for us to pick you up. I hope that's okay."

She looked a little disappointed, Dan thought, but soon brightened.

"I've not been to Crete before," she said.

"Well, you'll see a bit of it as we drive and then we must take a short boat trip to Tamarisk Bay. It's a lovely spot. Roz was happy there."

"I'm not sure why I'm here, to be honest. It's all very strange. Something's telling me I need to see where she lived and worked, and where she ..."

"We'll do everything we can to help you through this, Alma," Stefi cut in. "Now, let's go and find the car."

*

"We heard back from the surveillance teams," said Thaní as he walked back into the hut. "The ones tailing Marákis lost him in traffic. They assumed he'd gone home but he didn't arrive back until just before the handover, at ten to seven. We have no idea where he was."

"Good start."

"Yes. And those watching Pagiánnidis had a desperately dull day. He remained in the office until twenty past six and then drove home. He's still there."

"A waste of time, then."

"So far. We live in hope, Nick."

*

It was seven thirty when they arrived, and Alma was introduced to Nick and the others. Stefi showed her to a cabin while the youngsters, Dan, Teddy and Lauren, set about making a vegetarian moussaka.

The evening was subdued, given Alma's presence, but the food was delicious. She excused herself soon after they finished eating. She explained that, what with the long train ride down from Aberdeen, it had already been a very long day.

"Seems like a nice woman," said Lauren, after she had gone. "Does she know it might be murder?"

"No. Not yet," said Nick.

"Will you tell her?"

"Yes. She has a right to know what we're thinking."

"Would it make us more or less negligent?" asked Dan.

"That's an odd thing to ask, Dan. Her death was an accident, or she was killed by someone, accidentally or on purpose. There's no question of negligence either way, in my mind."

"The bank brought it up, Nick. I guess they're thinking employer's liability?"

"I think you can forget about that."

"I hope it's not in Alma's mind, then."

"She's here to help her grieving process, not to work out how to sue you guys."

After dinner, Nick took Stefi to one side.

"We borrowed your cabin today for the whiteboard. You'll see my scribble."

"I already did."

"Okay, well I can talk you through all that, if you like. You'll see a list of five actions; we need your help with some of those."

"Sure thing, Nick. Let me make a note."

Stefi pulled out a pen and grabbed a white, paper napkin from the table. He made notes as Nick went through the action list.

"Okay. No problem, Nick. I can get you all this by morning."

Nick thanked him and asked him how things had gone with the bank.

"Maybe this Anna has a pulse, after all. We won't know for a few days, but today seemed positive. They knew about Roz and the fire from the news, but that didn't seem to put them off. I told them about the coin find, too, and they didn't run screaming from the room."

"Did you tell them about the offers?"

"Are you crazy, Nick? No. I don't tell them this. I want to borrow three million from them so I figured telling them someone had offered me one and a half would not help. Besides, they don't need to know. We're rejecting the stupid offer, right?"

"Damned right."

Stefi reached for a carafe, filled two small glasses to the brim and handed one to Nick.

"This is old rakí, special, from my father. Yeiá mas."

"Yeiá mas," repeated Nick and they knocked the bottoms of their glasses twice on the table, then downed them in one.

CHAPTER 20
A PICTURE EMERGES

"So," said Thaní right after breakfast, Friday morning, "we work on the premise that what has happened to Stefi was not a string of unfortunate coincidences but a deliberate programme of intimidation, yes?"

"Absolutely," said Nick.

"And today, we work out how they did it."

"I have the information we need from Stefi." Nick handed him a piece of paper and Thaní ran his eyes down the page.

"Good. Let's make a start."

Nick punched in the lawyer's number.

"Is Kristína Panteláki there, please?"

A personal assistant said "One moment" in English and then put him through. A lower, contralto voice said: "Né?"

"Kaliméra, i kiría Panteláki …"

"Please, you may speak English," she interrupted. She did not say *instead of destroying my language* but there was an unspoken subtext. Nick pulled a face at Thaní but said:

"Thank you. My name is Nick Fisher and I'm working with the Chaniá police on a probable murder case."

"How may I help you?"

"I understand you were advised about a forestry claim on some land owned by Stefanos Spiliákis a few weeks ago?"

"This is correct. It was about three weeks ago, I think."

"Was this a phone call, initially?"

"Yes. He said he would mail the paperwork, but I've not seen it yet."

Nick heard her try to cover the microphone as she yelled to an adjacent room. She gave him no clue what was happening and was silent for half a minute.

"No, my assistant confirms; nothing has arrived."

"So, it was just this one phone call."

"So far, yes."

"Would it be normal, for the Forestry Department to call a person's lawyer rather than the person?"

"To be honest, I cannot tell you this. I have never before received such a call. But it is a legal matter, after all, an attempt to transfer the ownership of the land, so it did not strike me as inappropriate."

"And the expectation was that you would then make Spiliákis aware of the claim."

"Yes, he was clear about it. It was a courtesy, he said, to have me inform my client rather than just putting something in the mail."

"Do you remember the name of the caller?"

"Let's see. I am rather old-fashioned. I scribble on a daily notepad although my appointments are in an electronic diary."

Nick heard pages turning and the lawyer mumbling to herself. After less than a minute, she gave a little squeal.

"Got him!" she said. "A bit further back than I thought. He called Monday, the thirtieth of August. The name I have is Arapaï. I don't have a first name."

"Is that a Greek name?"

"I would not think so. It might be Albanian."

"And to be clear, he said he was from the Forestry Department."

"He did. He told me his position, but I can't remember for sure. Maybe Assistant to the Director, something like this?"

"And what did he say?"

"As I recall, he explained his department's brief, from our government, you understand. Then, he said they'd been mapping the southwest of the island in recent months and had now published a definitive map of the precise areas they believe should be under Forestry Department control. He explained that Mr Stefanos's juniper forest would be the subject of a claim. There was no provision for compensation, he told me. He was careful to point out that we had the right formally to object to the claim, but he warned me that if we did so, it was likely to be an extended process as they had received many objections already."

"So, in layman's terms, he told you the land was being claimed, Stefi would not be compensated, and, if you objected, it would be a long, tortuous, legal wrangle."

"Yes, exactly."

"Was there anything about his voice – style, accent, pitch whatever – you can recall?"

"He spoke Greek well, but I could tell he was *not* Greek, and I knew this anyway, from his name. I would also say he sounded like a smoker."

"And finally, was there anything about him you felt was not quite right?"

"How do you mean, Mr Fisher?"

"Were you convinced he was genuine?"

There was a momentary silence, perhaps a sharp intake of breath.

"It never occurred to me he might not be. You're saying I was tricked."

"We are exploring the possibility."

"Oh, dear. I hope I didn't cause Mr Stefanos all that angst for no good reason."

"I think this guy is a professional. Don't feel too badly about it."

"I just never thought of the possibility, and I should have. How naïve of me! I should have checked back with the Forestry Department."

"That's my next move. I'll let you know, shall I? You've been helpful, Mrs Panteláki. Thank you."

Nick ended the call and leaned back in his chair.

"I think we're onto something, Thaní," he said. "Now, you call the Forestry Department."

"Do we have a contact name?"

"Arapaï, but he may not exist. Let's start from scratch."

Thaní found contact details on a government website and called the public inquiries number.

Nick could follow part, but not all, of the quickfire Greek conversation. Thaní was put through to a different person. It was a woman's voice. He heard resistance in her tone and then Thaní introduced himself, mentioning the police and sounding more forceful. After this, she sounded more subdued and talked for two minutes or more. Finally, Thaní thanked her and disconnected.

"That was a Mrs Tsesmé. She started by saying they do not discuss individual cases over the phone. They are far too busy, and, in any case, I would need to speak to her boss, not her. When I told her it was a police matter involving a probable murder and she would be in trouble if she *didn't* help me, things got a little easier! I got her to check the Forestry Department's internal systems for me. She checked their maps and then the claims by owner's name. Nothing. There is no forestry claim relating to Tamarisk Bay or Stefanos Spiliákis. She promised to send me an email confirming it."

"So, it was a con. Just one phone call to the right lawyer, who accepted things at face value and called Stefi."

"She could have been more suspicious of the caller."

"She talked freely to me, too, just because I said I was working with the police."

"She needs to be much more careful. What's next on the list, Nick?"

"Stefi came up with an old business card for his bank guy, Manólis, so we have a full name but nothing else. He is Manólis Michailídis."

"Like Dómna, our new Minister for Labour."

"If you say so."

"She is Michailídou, of course, but it's the same. You should check her out, Nick. Very bright, rather beautiful, and only thirty-six."

"Is she any good, though?"

"We have a good government now, Nick. So yes, she probably is. Anyway, let's leave Michailídis until we've tried to trace him. Let's see if we can find out whether the archaeological find was also a con."

"Well, they convinced Tzanakákis. He's sending his team in on Monday. And the coins must have seemed real enough."

"Coins such as those can be bought over the Internet, Nick. Armed with them, someone could have made their way to Stefi's land, rubbed them in the dirt, taken a few photographs, and then gone to Tzanakákis. Simple as that."

"He might have been too excited by the find to check it out thoroughly."

"There's only one way to find out."

Thaní scanned Stefi's note and found the number for Tzanakákis. Again, Nick listened to the Greek conversation which Thaní put on speaker, this time, saying he might understand more, as the man was educated, originally Athenian, and spoke clearly.

This time, Thaní went further to explain the antecedents to the call and his role in trying to find the perpetrators of a great injustice on Stefi and probably the murder of a young girl. By the time he asked his first question, Tzanakákis was already shocked and anxious to help if he could.

"So, you will please tell me about these Slovenian tourists," Thaní said, in Greek.

"A man called me. He spoke Greek quite well, but with an accent I could not place. When he said he and his wife were from Slovenia, it made sense. They were in Crete on holiday, he said. They were staying in Paleóchora and had spent the previous day at Elafonísi. The beach got too crowded for them and so they walked east from the beach, through forests of spiky trees and rough paths over and around boulders. It was not an easy walk, he said, but they kept going because they were discovering small coves. They were looking for somewhere they could get privacy to swim naked together. But, every time they found a cove, there would be something not quite perfect: other people, difficult access, too exposed to the wind and so on. So, they kept going. Eventually, they found themselves on a much wider, shingle beach with a small, sandy cove at the end of it, sheltered by rocks. There was some development going on behind the shingle part of the beach, but it was set back and looked quiet. The sandy cove seemed ideal, so they made their way there.

"They spent a wonderful afternoon there. No one disturbed them. Later, he needed to defecate and didn't want to do it in the sea, so he walked to the forest edge. Afterwards, he didn't want to leave it like that, in such an idyllic spot, so he scraped a hole to bury the stool. The soil was loose and very dry. He reckons he went down twelve, maybe fifteen centimetres. Then, he spotted the first coin. He guessed it was Roman, got excited about his find and dug around the area with his bare hands. Ten minutes later, he found the second one at a similar depth, about three metres away from the first. His wife came looking for him and together they spent another hour digging but found nothing more. Later that evening, when they got back to their hotel, the manager helped them find out how to get in touch with us. They called me the next morning."

"And how did you respond?" asked Thaní.

"I thought fifteen centimetres was shallow for such a find. Bear in mind these coins were buried for two thousand years or more. The land builds up with deposits, you understand. But then the terrain was unusual, a thin band of forest, not far from the sea. I wasn't sure what depth I should expect. But also, I know of no Roman artefacts of any sort being found so far west in Crete. So, I was surprised, I suppose, but also excited."

"What did you do?"

"I invited them to come and see me. They had a hire car and it's not difficult to get to Chaniá from Paleóchora. That's when they told me they were flying back to Ljubljana late the next day anyway, so maybe they could swing by on their way to the airport. They asked if the coins were valuable, of course, and I told them they were probably worth a few hundred euros, not more, but I would need to inspect them."

"So, they came as planned?"

"Yes, they did."

"Could you describe them for me?"

"He was solid, quite powerfully built, between forty-five and fifty-five years old, I would guess. He was fair-haired and quite tanned. She looked older, darker and paler, almost the same height as her husband."

"Which was?"

"Oh, he was quite tall. Perhaps one hundred and ninety centimetres?"

Nick did the conversion in his head; about six foot three and solid, by the sound of it.

"Did you get eye colours?" Thaní went on.

"I can't be sure. Sorry."

"And you say they were married."

"He introduced her as his wife and they were both wearing wedding bands, so …"

"And their names were?"

"Matej and Neža … just a moment … ah – last name Žagar." He spelt it out, letter by letter for Thaní.

"Did they show ID?"

"He waved something at me, but I didn't really look at it, I'm afraid. I think it was an ID card but not a Greek one."

"Are there security cameras at your offices, Mr Tzanakákis?"

"Maybe at the entrance. I'm not sure. Certainly not in the room where we met."

"Please give me the name and number of your security chief or office manager and confirm the date and time of your meeting with these characters. Put it in an email to me today."

"I can do this."

"So, what happened next?"

"They showed me the coins."

"Do you have them now?"

"I do, but I didn't buy them. That's not what we do here. I cleaned them up, took photos of them, recorded the details of the find and, because he asked me, I put a guideline value on them, just verbally."

"Of how much?"

"One was circa two hundred and fifty euros, the other nearer six hundred."

"But they are from the same period."

"Yes. Circa 100 BCE but one is rarer than the other. Both are in rather good condition. I will be organising tests and a second opinion to confirm their origins and then they will have a provenance. After this, we will rule on the question of ownership."

"How does that work?"

"Normally, ownership is apportioned between the finder and the landowner. Often, people donate to our museum of Roman artefacts if it's not a large sum."

"So, you'd be hoping for a donation in this case."

"Yes, I would."

"You have contact details for the Slovenians, then."

"I do. I'll put those in the email too, shall I?"

"Yes. Thank you. And, overall, what did you think of their story? Did you find it believable? Did these people seem like tourists to you? Were they truly a married couple from Slovenia, do you think? Did they really find these coins?"

"That's a lot of questions, Sergeant. You obviously doubt their cred-ibility, but I had no reason to. They came to me; they had the coins, which looked like they had just been taken from the earth. They had names that sounded Slovenian, and they appeared to be married. What possible reason was there for it to be some elaborate pretence?"

"I understand you're sending a small team to Tamarisk Bay on Monday."

"It's standard procedure. An exploratory dig where a significant, new find has occurred. I don't have any choice about that."

"And, while your people are there, Mr Tzanakákis, the building project will be delayed and, if you find more artefacts, there will be a major excavation which could lead to a massive delay or even an abandonment of the project."

"I see what you mean. You think this is what they wanted to happen?"

"We think it's what they *knew* would happen. That's why they went to so much trouble."

"I guess the exploratory dig will tell us, one way or the other."

"You're likely to be wasting your time, sir, in our opinion," said Thaní.

"As I said, I have no choice in the matter."

Thaní thanked him and ended the call. While they were making themselves a cup of coffee, Nick said:

"How rare are these coins, I wonder? Perhaps we could trace their *purchase* of them. That would put the kibosh on their clever, little game, wouldn't it?"

"Kibosh? What is this, Nick?"

"An excellent question, Thaní. I have no idea. Maybe it was from

India, originally? But to *put the kibosh on* something is to bring it to an end, decisively."

"You must tell Doctor Pánagou. You know how she loves these crazy English idioms."

"Good idea."

"Especially as most of her customers had the kibosh put on them!"

Nick chuckled generously, not wanting to discomfit Thaní by saying it probably would not be used in that context.

"So, my friend, shall I move Lauren to coin trade research?" he asked.

"Isn't she researching Russian developers?"

"I think she'll have gone as far as she can, with that."

"Okay, then. She might turn up something."

When Nick had spoken with Lauren and they returned to the table with their coffees, the email from Tzanakákis had already arrived.

"At last, an efficient man!" said Nick.

They read the contact details for the Office Manager at the Ministry of Hellenic Sports and Culture, a man called Mákris, and for the Žagars. They had left an address at 7, Idrijska Ulica in Ljubljana and a cell phone number. There was no email address.

"I'll call the Office Manager, you check out the Žagars," suggested Thaní.

*

Nick went straight to his mapping software and soon found the street. It was a suburb in the south-west of the city, close to the Kulturni Center. It was a small street but there looked to be more than seven houses, so the house number could be genuine. Next, he called the mobile number. After a few seconds, a young man answered. It sounded like he was on a busy street.

"Can I speak English to you?" asked Nick.

"Of course," said the young man.

"Are you Matej?"

"Yes. Hallo."

"Matej Žagar?"

"No, I am Matej Šuštar."

"Do you know a Matej Žagar?"

"No."

"Do you know anyone who was in Greece recently?"

"I do not think so."

"May I just check the number I called?"

Nick read out the number he had been given.

"Right number, wrong guy. Sorry, mister. I can't help you."

Nick disconnected.

"Shit," he said.

Thaní looked up at him. "No good?" he said.

"Close, but no Žagar," said Nick, with a smirk that left Thaní baffled. "It's a Slovenian mobile number but it belongs to a different guy who also happens to be a Matej."

"That's odd."

"Just coincidence, I think. It's a common name in Slovenia. The address could be real, too, but I doubt very much if our guys live there. I'd go further: I doubt they're even Slovenian."

"They don't care about their share of the coins, then."

"Expenses of the con. How's your Office Manager?"

"He has just the one security camera and it's on the entrance. It's a basic service outsourced to a local security company."

"That sounds good."

"It would be, but they only keep the data for two weeks."

"And then it's archived?"

"Overwritten."

"And how long …?"

"Three or four weeks since they were there."

"Bugger it. Have you checked with them?"

"Mákris is doing that, but he was not optimistic."

"So, probably no pictures of Matej and Neža. That's a shame. I had a feeling Matej might bear a passing resemblance to our blond guy."

"So did I, but who could *she* be?"

"I don't know, Thaní. Let's move on. We know the forestry thing was a con. I think the coins were too, and probably both involved the blond guy."

"You think *he* made the call to the lawyer, then?"

"Seems likely – remember Pateláki said he had good Greek but was foreign and she thought he smoked."

"So, if you're right, Arapaï, the Albanian posing as a Forestry Department man, is also Matej Žagar, the Slovenian tourist. We know from the Tzanakákis description that he resembled the man in Roz's pictures. And he's probably Slavic and smokes Russian cigarettes."

"It's the same guy. I'd put money on it. All of it. He prepares well, he's a good actor. He could probably be any Slav you wanted him to be."

"So, what did he do at the bank, I wonder? Did he get Michailídis fired, somehow?" suggested Thaní.

"And does he have a connection to Pagiánnidis the estate agent or Marákis the engineer? Someone is hiring him, maybe the Russian developers."

"We have work to do, Nick."

Nick grinned. He was loving it. Back in the thick of it, on the trail of some serious villains with some tough problems to get his teeth into.

"Let's get on with it, then," he said.

CHAPTER 21
ALMA

Stefi was being kind to Alma. He did not share Dan's concern about potential liability. He could see she was a genuine person who faced a difficult time in her life. He avoided talking about Roz, though he answered her questions openly when they surfaced. Most of the time he spent simply showing Alma what they were doing and what they dreamed of creating. Sometimes she would listen intently, he noticed, while at others she appeared to be in a dream, staring out to sea or up at the mountains.

"I remember being pregnant with Rosie," she said at one point. "Sometimes, I felt I was doing a stupid, selfish thing, you know?"

"I don't understand," said Stefi. "Bringing a new life into the world is a wonderful thing."

She squeezed his arm.

"Yes, I felt that, too, fortunately. But I was thinking about the world I was bringing her into. Climate change was rampant and the powers that be arguing about it but doing nothing, blaming each other. The future looked bleak. We were careering headlong into the destruction of our beautiful planet. It seemed irresponsible of me to bring her into that. We caused the problem, now you deal with it, little one."

"You think it's better now, then?"

"I don't know, Stefi. Maybe it's too little, too late, but at least some things are happening now. Some governments and some people are taking it seriously and doing stuff that's making a difference. People like you."

"Thank you, Alma. But you are being too kind to me. There are few unselfish, good-hearted people in this world but many self-interested people, looking to make money from growth opportunities. The difference between now and twenty-five years ago is that businesspeople like me are seeing the growth possibilities from climate change and not just the threat it represents."

"Is that you, then? It doesn't sound like you, Stefi."

"I'm a lucky guy, Alma. My grandfather bought this land many years ago. When my father died, it came to me. Now, yesterday's useless wilderness is today's escape destination. Being difficult to get to is a bonus for the right sort of tourist. These people are searching for the real Crete, away from the crowds."

"And supportive of your efforts on climate change."

"To an extent, yes. They like the *sound* of the words *environmentally sustainable*. They don't want to harm the planet if they can help it and they'll pay a bit more to avoid doing so, but they are not activists in anoraks. Far from it. Some will know nothing of Greta Thunberg, for instance."

"So, what you're saying is climate change is going mainstream."

"It's getting there, Alma. Change takes time. But there will come a day when unsustainable is unacceptable, like smoking in a cinema or a restaurant."

He had lost her again. She was staring at their little encampment now: the tree houses, the cabins, Dan's small wind turbine. Stefi saw Nick leaving one of the cabins and heading in their direction.

"I'm proud Roz was a part of all this, Stefi, I really am, but I also need to understand how and why she died. Will you show me where it happened?"

He laid a hand on her shoulder but waited a moment for Nick to join them.

"Alma," Nick said. "I am so sorry. I've been tied up this morning. Has Stefi been looking after you?"

"He's been very sweet, thank you."

"Would it be all right if I took it from here? Thaní needs some of your time, Stefi. He's in the main cabin."

Stefi looked relieved but asked Alma if that was okay with her. She said it was, thanked him, and he ambled off.

"I want to see where it happened, Nick," she said.

"I thought you might."

As they trudged across the sandy scrub just inland from the beach, she said:

"I know it was a terrible accident, Nick, but was it avoidable? Could you explain exactly what happened? I need to know."

"Of course, you do." They stopped walking and looked at each other.

"Let's sit on this for a minute," he said, indicating a fallen tree trunk, and they sat, side by side, gazing back at the sea.

"I'm not going to be able to set your mind at rest, Alma. I wish I could. But I will tell you everything we know if that's what you want."

His eyes searched hers, then she closed her eyelids and nodded slightly. Nick went on to explain about the aborted grocery run and how Roz must have decided to come back ashore because of something she saw.

"It may have been an intruder, or she may have seen the start of the fire."

"An intruder?"

"She spotted someone a week before and took photos of him. It may have been him or someone else. Or she saw something. The fire – or something else. There's a lot we don't know."

"Why do you think this guy might have come back?"

"Because we think the fire was started deliberately. There have been many wildfires near here, but none close enough to ignite this one."

"Oh, God."

"I doubt we'll ever know exactly what happened, but I think Roz went ashore to investigate the intruder or stop the fire, perhaps both."

"But she'd have had her phone. Why didn't she call in?"

"We don't know. She left her bag in the boat."

"Ach … such an impulsive, wee thing."

"It says urgency to me, and courage."

"But she didna need to die, Nick."

"No, but at least we know she didn't suffer. The Medical Examiner says she was not alive by the time the fire reached her. There are tests which determine this with absolute certainty."

Alma looked tearful but relieved. Then, it dawned on her.

"You mean, because of the smoke?" she said, her voice wavering.

"No. Not the smoke."

"So, he killed her!"

She looked furious, suddenly.

"It could have been an accident. The Medical Examiner can't say for sure."

It was as if the sun had gone behind a cloud. A shadow across her face. The sudden realisation.

"Because she was so badly burned."

Nick put his arm around her shoulders, and she slumped, sobbing onto his chest, recognising his gesture for the confirmation it was. He had known it would come at some stage, this sudden release of grief. No one could bear the loss of a husband and then an only child with such stoicism. Not for long. They stayed like that for five minutes. Neither spoke. Nick stared out to sea, imagining how devastated he would feel if he lost Lauren or Jason. Gradually the heaving of Alma's chest subsided, and her grip changed from drowning woman to grateful friend. Eventually, she sat up and reached into her bag. She spent time blowing her nose, wiping her eyes and checking her face in a vanity mirror.

"I look a sight," she said, looking up at him.

Nick wanted to hold her and comfort her, tell her that even now she was lovely, but it was not the time. He knew it, and he did not want to take advantage. Instead, he just touched her cheek with his hand and smiled sadly.

"No, you don't," he said.

"Will you show me the photos?" she asked.

"Back at the cabin, yes. We've not been able to identify him, though. Not yet."

"Okay. And now I want you to show me where it happened."

"Are you sure? There's nothing to see."

"That's not the point, Nick. I need to do it."

*

It was after five by the time Nick got back. He had walked Alma to her cabin and hugged her as they parted, promising to meet for a drink before dinner. The sight of the blackened moonscape that had once been the juniper forest upset her again and seeing the spot where Roz died must have brought images of the horror to her mind. Nick remembered what the body looked like – even before Pánagou had taken her scalpel to it – and was relieved that Alma seemed to have no plans to view it.

"I have to get her home, though," she said.

"You might want to talk to the vice consulate about it," Nick said. "I'm afraid it's very expensive."

"Money's not a problem, now," she said. "My husband built a good-sized pension pot, and he was well insured from way back before he got sick."

"That's good," he managed to say. *Lucky you*, he could not help thinking.

Returning to the hut, he was gratified to see Lauren still hunched over her laptop.

"Ah, Dad. Where have you been? I've got stuff to tell you."

"Fire away."

"Okay. Sit down. Starting with Russian developers. There were three I managed to find but only two that operate in Crete. The third one was in The Peloponnese, mostly. And the second one doesn't seem to have done anything here recently, because of the Ukraine situation. That leaves us with Lasko as the only active Russian developer still operating in Crete."

"This is the outfit building luxury stuff in the north-east?"

"Not just the north-east. They are rumoured to be behind a major development coming to a beach near you; Triópetra."

"Oh, that's been going to happen for years. I heard some Cypriot outfit was going to build a golf complex, though how they would be able to keep it green in one of the driest parts of the island, I've no idea. Or why anyone would want to play golf in forty-degree temperatures, for that matter."

"Well, it may have been a Cypriot *shell* company that bought the land, but Lasko are behind it; trust me."

"How do you know?"

"It's on their website under a page labelled *The Future*. It's not specific but you can work out where it is easily enough, and it talks about a golf complex. There's also a planned development inland, south-east of Kíssamos, not quite so big."

"But nothing about Tamarisk Bay."

"I think they'd wait till they had the land and at least outline permissions, don't you?"

"I guess so. What makes you think it would interest them, Lauren?"

"They do luxury. Private resorts, sometimes remote locations. They reshape them as necessary and build stylish, modern apartments. Top end. We're talking holiday rentals of five to eight thousand euros *a week*."

Nick whistled.

"What they do looks very professional. Client satisfaction ratings are high," she went on, "and Tamarisk Bay is a good size. It's comparable with their larger destinations."

"What about access, though?"

"There must be a route of some sort out to those big wind turbines. Upgrade it, then drop a road down from there, maybe get the Dímos to fork out for at least some of the cost. If not, build a bigger jetty, bring everything in by sea."

"Even the guests?"

"At those prices, you could whisk them in on luxury launches."

"All sounds very expensive."

"Not if you bought the land cheap."

"Found any evidence of dodgy tactics, misdemeanours?"

"Not as such. But their board is quite a mixture: Russians and Greeks, an Italian and a Serb."

"As you'd expect, surely, for an international group operating in the Eastern Mediterranean."

"Perhaps, Dad, but they look dodgy."

"You'll have to do better than that, my girl. We need facts: criminal connections, corruption charges, use of violent means and such like, not your opinion on their mugshots, for Heaven's sake."

"I have a thing for faces. It's called intuition. Anyway, I'm not finished yet."

"Hmmm. Anything on the former volunteers?"

"There are only two, both male; an Irish guy called Declan and a Greek called Aléxis. But I was able to discount Aléxis."

"How come?"

"He pre-dates Méli. Stefi adopted her just seven months ago. Aléxis ended his spell here in November last year, nearly eleven months ago."

"And Declan?"

"It was a gap year thing for him. He went back to Ireland to finish his education. He's at University College in Cork."

"Should we speak to him?"

"I already did. He says he's not been in contact with anyone. I think he was telling the truth. He couldn't remember Méli's name, and he called Stefi *Sífis*."

"Had he been to the college bar?"

"Quite possibly. Anyway, I think we can forget about early volunteers."

"Good. One thing off the list. What about the character from the bank, Michailídis?"

"I rang the bank and asked for him. As expected, they told me he no longer worked there, but then I got chatting with one of their junior employees. I said I'd heard he was fired, and she was appalled. She said he was a very capable guy, respected for his deal-making, and she was sure he left of his own accord. There was a send-off with drinks and snacks, she said, and that doesn't happen when people get fired. The directors were very sorry to lose him, she reckoned."

"Interesting."

"That's what I thought. So, why *did* he leave, I wondered."

"For a better opportunity, presumably. Do we know what he's doing now?"

"He started his own business, she said, but she knew nothing about it. Then she hushed up on me. Must have got suspicious."

"You did well, but we need to know what he's up to now."

"Of course, but I didn't know where to go next with that, so I started digging into the family relationships instead, and using ancestry tools to work it out. Everything was in Greek, of course, but I got Teddy to help me. I found Manólis's birth certificate, then a census from thirty-odd years ago which confirmed him living with parents Níkos and María (who was born a Papadopoúlou). Looks like he was an only child. I then searched on each of the parents and found Níkos had a sister: Irína Michailídou. Later, I unearthed a marriage certificate for her."

Lauren grinned up at her father, excitement dancing in her eyes. "Guess what?"

"What?"

"She married Giánnis Pagiánnidis on the fifth of May 1986."

"That's the same surname as the estate agent, isn't it?"

"Yes. He is their son. Irína is both Stávros's mother AND Manólis's aunt. Stávros the estate agent and Manólis the banker are first cousins."

"Okay. This is getting interesting. And Giánnis, Stávros's father?"

"Died six years ago."

"What of?"

"I don't know, but he was only fifty-nine."

"But Irína is still with us."

"Very much so."

"Wasn't there something mentioned earlier about Stávros having an aunt?"

"There was. He has *two* aunts. Anna, wife of Giórgios the engineer, was born Anna Pagiannídou. To Stávros, the estate agent, she is Aunt Anna because she was the sister of his late father, Giánnis. And the banker Manólis's mother was born María Papadopoúlou. But when she married Irína's brother, Níkos Michailídis, she became Aunt María to Stávros."

"Jesus, this is convoluted. I need a darkened room and some wet towels for this. If I've got this right, then all three of our suspects have family connections to one another."

"Not quite. There's only an *indirect* connection between Manólis the banker and Giórgios the engineer in that Giórgios's wife Anna *is* a Pagiannídou and Manólis's Aunt Irína *married* one."

"So, is this all about the Pagiánnidis family or the Michailídis family?"

"I didn't know which, at this point, but then I found something else. It was in the blurb Stefi showed me about Tamarisk Bay. There's a history section saying: *The story of Tamarisk Bay began when Stefi's grandfather had the foresight to purchase the land from a local family.*"

"And?"

"And I got curious. Who was this family? So, I searched the Greek equivalent of an electronic land registry, the cadastre."

"How did you know to do that?"

"I didn't; Kristína did it for me."

"Who?"

"That nice lawyer you spoke to? After letting herself get conned by the Albanian who was nothing of the sort, I figured she owed us one."

"Clever girl. Who sold it to Stefi's grandfather, then?"

"A small, private company called Votioditiká Ktímata E.P.E. I can hardly even pronounce it, but it means something like South-Western Estates, a rather grand name for a company which owned the land at Tamarisk Bay and some strémmata of farmland around Sfinári. It had issued one hundred shares. Ninety-nine were owned by Kóstas and one by his wife."

"Now you're teasing me. Kóstas's surname being?"

"Pagiánnidis."

"Not Michailídis."

"No."

"Attagirl."

Nick went for a high five, but Lauren missed completely. The second attempt was a great slap which left her nursing her hand and giggling.

CHAPTER 22
VENDETTA

First thing the next morning, Nick was woken by a call from Leo.

"Good Lord, this is early for you," said Nick.

"I've just received a rebuke from my captain, so I thought I'd spoil your day, too."

"What have I done?"

"The captain was called by a director of the financial PR firm that represents the developer, Lasko. She told him someone – purporting to be connected to the police – has been asking questions about developments in Crete and suggesting the tactics Lasko used may have been unethical, or worse. This has the potential to be extremely damaging for a public company, she pointed out. Rumours such as these can cause reputational damage and even a run on the share price, she said. The company will release a public statement this morning to pre-empt any such damage. I am required to read it to you, and you are required to repeat it to all your team members without delay:

The Board of Lasko Developments would like it known that they have no operations whatsoever in the south-west of Crete, Greece, and none are planned or contemplated at this time. The company's operations to date have been solely in the north-east of the island where, as in every one of its worldwide operations, the company has always operated with full transparency and to the highest ethical standards."

"They're saying they're not involved in Tamarisk Bay, then."

"This is not a statement to us, Nick, it's a press release to the public markets. So, I would say they're not involved."

"Or they are distancing themselves from some wayward local employees."

"I think the *highest ethical standards* comment suggests they're not aware of anything in their company which could be described as unethical, Nick, and – unless you have clear evidence to the contrary – I strongly suggest you back off, leave them alone."

"I was heading that way, to be honest. Unless you have something from surveillance, I have nothing connecting the company to any of our suspects. All we have is a Russian-owned, private group which has developed some sites in Crete and has a dodgy-looking Board, according to my daughter."

"You're getting Lauren involved?"

"Try stopping her. Chip off the old block. But she might have been a bit too rabid about the evil, corporate angle. I'll make sure she backpedals. Anyway, I have a feeling it's much closer to home. There's another angle I want us to explore."

"Which is …?"

"A family feud; a vendetta, if you will. Let me talk the idea through with Thaní. If he buys it, we'll be in touch shortly."

"Okay, interesting. You mentioned surveillance. They've uncovered only one thing, so far. Marákis visits the same house in the Chaniá suburbs, most Mondays and Thursdays, between three thirty and six thirty, or so. The house is owned by a woman who is registered disabled."

"Could he be having an affair?"

"We don't know, yet."

"Nothing on Pagiánnidis?"

"No. He must know he's under investigation. It's too clean to be true. Just an estate agent going about his business. Even his bank records reveal nothing odd, other than a high proportion of cash transactions."

"Which is probably normal, for Crete."

"Regrettably, yes."

"Has he been observed with a guy called Manólis Michailídis, by any chance?"

"Who the hell is he?"

"He was Stefi's man at Alpha Bank, but he left a few weeks ago to start a business. I'm wondering if he and Pagiánnidis are working together now. There's a family connection, you see. They're first cousins."

"Are they now? Do you have a picture of him?"

"No."

"I'll see if I can get one and ask the surveillance teams if they've seen him."

"Great. How's your other murder going, Leo?"

Nick heard the familiar ping of the Zippo lighter and then Leo inhaling before speaking.

"We found the place where the young lovers used to meet. They were practically living there, over the last few months. It was her grandmother's until she died two years ago. The girl's body was found just over a kilometre from the house. We're still looking for the boyfriend. Anna thinks she has identified him, but she hasn't located him yet. She thinks his parents spirited him away, after the murder."

"You've questioned all the neighbours, of course."

"You *know* we have, Nick. And we have a good description of the boyfriend now – and his motorbike. It's very loud, apparently. There are a couple of kids across the road who might have seen something on the day of the murder but they're very young. Unreliable witnesses, Anna tells me."

"That's a shame. Have you interviewed his parents?"

"It's about to happen."

"Read them the Riot Act, I would."

There was a pause.

"I don't understand you, Nick. There has been no public disorder."

"Sorry, Leo. Just another English saying. It means clarifying the law and telling them they can't get away with protecting their son. Tell them they could go to jail themselves if they don't reveal where he is."

"You can be sure we will, Nick. I recall another, rather disgusting, saying of yours. Something about your grandmother sucking eggs?"

"Haha. Touché. And well remembered! Good luck with those parents. If they're good people, they'll already feel deeply uncomfortable about what they've done. It's a moral dilemma for them. He might be their son but protecting a murderer is never acceptable."

"I'll let you know what happens. And keep that daughter of yours on a much shorter rein, please. If Lasko's people call the captain again, I think he'll fire me."

"The best detective in Crete? He'd be a fool to do it."

"Is there something you want from me, Nick?"

"Now, what would make you think that?"

*

"What do you know about your grandfather buying this land, Stefi?" Nick asked, later in the day.

"Not much. It happened the year I was born. It was cheap, I believe. Tourism was something hardly anyone thought about, back then. Not around here, anyway. Paleóchora and Soúgia were hippy towns. A few people came to look at Elafonísi but nothing else was happening. He had this idea to buy it as a long-term investment."

"For you?"

"Maybe, but no one ever said so."

"And who did he buy it *from*?"

"Some local family."

"You don't know who?"

"No, I don't think I ever did. There's only a *company* name on the contract if I remember right."

"There is. But the principal shareholder was Kóstas Pagiánnidis."

Stefi sat up sharply and his mouth dropped open. Nick went on:

"His son Giánnis married Irína Michailídou, and they had a son called Stávros."

The light had dawned, Nick saw.

"It's so obvious, Nick. How did I not see it? This explains why he's always been so shitty with me, why he swindled us over my father's estate and why he's bullying me now over Tamarisk Bay. It all goes back to that!"

"Let's get together with Thaní and talk it through, Stefi. It looks like you've been on the receiving end of a slow-burning vendetta that started forty years ago when the land was sold. Your grandfather paid the drachmae equivalent of just eighty-five thousand euros for it but Kóstas Pagiánnidis would never have imagined it could be worth several million, forty years later. He sold their inheritance for a song and that must have rankled with the family ever since."

209

"And now they want it back."

"Yep. And he and his cousin Manólis hatched a plan, I'm guessing. There may be other family members involved. Hard to say, at this stage. But, if they could frighten you into selling the land at two million or less, they would be sitting on a fat, paper profit from the outset."

"The bastards. But where would they get two million?"

"At first, we thought a developer had to be involved, but now I'm not so sure. Now we know Manólis left the bank on good terms, maybe his old connections could come up with such a loan, especially in the context of an exciting, new development plan."

"Like reshaping the site and covering it with a vast number of apartments."

"Maybe."

"And to hell with the natural beauty and the turtles."

"All of that, perhaps."

"I had no idea about this, Nick."

"I can see you didn't."

"So, what happens next?"

"We go through all this with Thaní. If he agrees, we haul them into Chaniá police station and interrogate them, try to find out exactly what happened and who killed Roz."

"We still don't know who the blond trespasser was, though."

"We don't, Stefi, but we have a few ideas we can explore with the suspects."

Nick's watch confirmed what his stomach was telling him; it was time for lunch. He suggested to Stefi that they go find Lauren and Thaní and all sit down together.

*

The discovery of the family connection made all the difference, they agreed, and Leo felt the same when they called him soon after.

"We'll bring them in for questioning," he said. "Time to come back, Thaní. And Nick – you'd better come along, as well. We'll need your input, I'm sure."

After Leo ended the call, Nick turned to Lauren:

"You wanted to see Chaniá? This is your big chance."

"Fabulous. Where will we stay?"

"Somewhere in the Old Town, if we can afford it. That's your job, anyway."

"I'll get looking."

*

It was early evening when they parked the hire car near the seafront and walked to their bijou apartment, just off Daskalogiánnis. This area was a network of lanes behind the second harbour with small, multi-coloured, terraced houses mostly converted into luxury apartments for holiday letting. Most dated from the period of the Venetian occupation. Some had been embellished later with ornate, Turkish facades or panelled balconies in dark wood. Others had been recently modernised, some rather brutally, Nick thought. These featured steel doors and muted, trendy colours of sage, taupe or lilac rather than the primary colours of the more traditional houses.

Their apartment was on three floors, each about thirty-five square metres. It had been cleverly redesigned to maximise the space and they each had a double bedroom with ensuite, but on different floors. The ground floor living area was a fair-sized kitchen with a tiny lounge area close to the front door. Nick felt like Gulliver in Lilliput.

"You did remember I'm taller, didn't you?" he asked.

"You might need to be a bit careful when you move around, Dad, but it's very smart, isn't it? And it's in exactly the right place; near everything but quiet, too."

Once they had thrown a few clothes onto hangers, they headed out to get a drink and something to eat.

"What will you do, while I'm working?" asked Nick, taking a sip of his craft beer.

"Oh, don't worry about me. There's a lot to explore and some great shopping. I'll be fine."

"I'd have liked to have you along."

211

"It's a police interrogation, Dad. I'm a twenty-one-year-old former student. I never expected to be part of it."

"I'll keep you posted, anyway."

She raised her glass, in acknowledgement, and Nick saw the café lights from the black harbour water reflecting in her wine glass like coloured shooting stars.

*

Nick had been asked to arrive at the police station no later than ten. To his surprise, first up was Marákis.

"I thought he was off the hook," he said to Leo. "Isn't it Pagiánnidis and Michailídis we're gunning for?"

"It is, but Marákis can help with a couple of points, too. Don't worry, Nick. I'll lead the questioning."

"Where's Thaní?"

"I told him to spend some time with his wife."

The room was small, the windows high above their heads. It was a functional room, without trimmings. Marákis was already sitting at the Formica table in an immaculate silver-blue suit, looking far too smart for the room. The tan and the greying hair made him look rich, *as he probably was*, thought Nick. The first thing Leo did was turn up the air-conditioning.

"Lieutenant Christodoulákis *and* Mr Nick Fisher. This must be serious. Should I have my lawyer present?" Marákis said.

They sat down opposite him. Leo laid his pack of cigarettes on the table as if it were his opening chess move. Nick slopped chilled water into three plastic glasses.

"It is your right, of course," Leo said, "but we simply want to ask you a few questions. You are helping us with our inquiries, nothing more."

"I'm not a suspect, then?"

"Not at this stage."

He laid his arms on the table and entwined the fingers of each hand. It struck Nick as an attempt to control any nervous fiddling and look unruffled.

"When you talked to my sergeant, you denied giving anyone information about Stefi's pet goat. Do you remember that?"

"I do. I found the suggestion rather offensive, as I recall."

"Let me rephrase the question then. Did you *share* the fact that Stefi had a goat he treated as a pet with *anyone* – family members, for example?"

"Well, this is a quite different question, Lieutenant. Anna and I laughed about it, from time to time."

"How was it a joke?"

"We're very fond of Stefi. Don't get me wrong. But he *is* a little eccentric, in addition to being gay, of course."

This was news to Nick, but it made complete sense now he thought about it.

"So, Anna and you laughed together about gay Stefi and his pet goat."

"We did, but in a kind way. We're very fond of Stefi."

Nick imagined the sort of jokes and was not sure any of this could be done in a kind way. *Maybe Marákis was homophobic,* he thought. *Or perhaps it was just an earlier generation's attitudes, yet to be purged.*

"Your wife is the sister of the late Giánnis Pagiánnidis, I believe," Leo continued.

"Giánni? Yes, she is."

"So, Giánni's widow, Irína, would be her sister-in-law. Do they see much of each other?"

"They do. Rather more since Giánnis died. A thing like that, it's upsetting for everyone. Brings people closer together, somehow. Now, they go shopping together once or twice a month. Occasionally, she comes to tea or Anna goes there. It's not far."

"A thing like that?"

"You don't know? Giánnis hanged himself, poor devil. It all got too much for him."

"What did?"

"Everything, pretty much. He was always a depressive."

"And your relationship with them?"

"I was Giánni's friend, but I never cared for Irína. Oh, I'm polite to her and I don't mind Anna having her as a friend if that's what she wants. I have no reason to dislike the woman. We just don't have much in common."

"I imagine Anna would have shared amusing stories with Irína over tea or shopping."

"What's your point?"

"One of those would be the rather ridiculous Stefi; the man who talks to his pet goat. No?"

There was a pause while Marákis rearranged his hands.

"It's possible," he said, quietly.

"I didn't catch that," said Leo.

"It's *entirely* possible," said Marákis, more loudly, and Nick noticed again how people seldom repeat phrases exactly, preferring to embellish them, often helpfully.

"Thank you," said Leo. "So, let's assume Anna and Irína *also* shared a laugh at Stefi's expense. You know the so-called offers for Tamarisk Bay emanated from the estate agent Stávros Pagiánnidis. As you know, he is Irína's son. There must be a fair chance that the laughs extended from mother to son and perhaps to her nephew, too."

"I'm sorry, I don't know who is this nephew."

"Do you not? It is the Alpha Bank employee who, until recently, was managing the bank's relationship with Stefi: Manólis Michailídis."

"Ah! I see where you are coming from. You think they cook something up together?"

Leo was not going to be led on that one. He changed tack. He felt sure from his reactions that Marákis was not *willingly* part of this gang. But he needed to be sure he had not been coerced.

"Tell us about your Monday and Thursday afternoons," he said.

The anger was instant. An exposed nerve had been prodded, thought Nick.

"You had me followed? You had better have a warrant, Lieutenant."

Leo tilted his head to one side and stared back, daring him to pursue that argument.

"Just tell us, Maráki. We are all men of the world here. And nothing leaves this room. We just want to eliminate you from our inquiries."

"You think I'm having an affair. Is that it? Or I'm a closet gay or someone with a private fetish of some sort."

"We have no preconceived ideas. We just need to understand what it is you do, Monday and Thursday afternoons."

The hands were removed from the table. Marákis pushed his chair back a little and looked at the ceiling for several seconds, breathing deeply.

"Then I will tell you if I must," he said. "I visit a friend I have known for over forty years. We were teenage lovers until I put her in a wheelchair."

He lowered both his head and his voice as if entering a confessional.

"When we're young, we think we're invincible, don't we? Well, I wasn't, I soon found out. We weren't. I crashed the car, going much too fast. It took the Fire Service two hours to cut her free. She nearly lost her legs. Might as well have, poor thing. They were no use to her afterwards. I would have stayed with her and married her, but she flatly refused. Said she wasn't going to have the man she loved tied to a cripple for the rest of his life. Yes, I'm sorry, but that was the word she used. Insisted on me marrying Anna instead, only she wanted to be cared for, just a little. This is the deal we struck."

"Your wife *knows?*"

"Anna was part of the deal. They were best friends, you see."

"Extraordinary."

"When we meet, we talk. I bring her things. We drink tea. Sometimes we play chess or do a crossword. We hold each other now and again, a peck on the cheek when we part. Nothing sexual at all."

"Is it a secret?"

"No, but I prefer not to talk about it. People don't understand such things."

Leo stood. The short interview was over, it seemed.

*

The estate agent was scheduled for eleven thirty. Nick had disliked Pagiánnidis at the first interview, in his office. As he saw the clock creep round to eleven forty, and still no sign of the man, he started to simmer, then steam.

"Where the hell is he?" he said, finally.

"The duty officer just called him," Leo replied. "Traffic."

"It's a *walk* from Daskalogiánnis, isn't it?"

"He was out with a client, we were told."

"He's just trying to score a point. Pathetic little man."

They finally assembled at eleven forty-seven. Pagiánnidis had brought a lawyer with him, a woman of about forty, wearing rather stylish glasses with turquoise frames. The rest of her outfit was so conservative as to make the glasses seem outlandish, by contrast. She introduced herself as Marína something or other. It sounded complicated, so Nick was relieved when everyone referred to her as Mrs Marína.

"Perhaps, Lieutenant, you could start by clarifying why you wish to question my client further," Marína said.

"We are investigating the use of intimidatory tactics to buy land at Tamarisk Bay. The escalation of those tactics ultimately led to the death of a young, Scottish girl called Rosalind Kinnear. We believe your client was involved."

"What are you hoping to charge my client with?"

"We'll decide, in due course."

"I think he's entitled to know."

"The list includes misrepresentation, extortion, arson, manslaughter and murder. Now, may we proceed?"

He took their rather stunned silence for confirmation and produced a photocopy of a document, which he laid on the table.

"This is the record of a sale of the land now known as Tamarisk Bay about forty years ago. The seller is shown as Votioditiká Ktímata E.P.E. and the purchaser is Apóstolos Spiliákis. As you can see, the agreed price was almost seven million drachmae. Are you familiar with this document, Pagiánnidi?"

He pursed his lips and shook his head dismissively.

"For the recording, Mr Pagiánnidis shook his head. But, whether the document itself is familiar to you or not, I suspect you are acutely aware of its contents. Your grandfather was the principal shareholder of this company, and this document records the sale of its most valuable asset to the man who became Stefanos Spiliákis's grandfather.

"We believe this sale, by *your* grandfather, Kóstas, was something your family regretted and resented over many years. They saw the rise of tourism in Crete. They saw even the likes of Paleóchora becoming popular. They saw the millions flock to Elafonísi, Bálos and Falásarna. They saw the wealth that could and should have been theirs! And when your father took his own life and Irína was widowed, how unfair it must have felt, having to struggle for money. How you all must have resented the good fortune of the Spiliákis family."

"We do not speak of this. It's ancient history to me. We get on with our lives."

"Perhaps … Perhaps. But deep down you remembered. And then something happened, didn't it? And it was all stirred up again. Only this time you were angry."

"I'm not following you, Lieutenant."

"He's talking about your cousin, Manólis," said Nick, "and the day he shared Spiliákis's plans for Tamarisk Bay with you. Plans that had been presented to the bank, in confidence."

"I never saw any plans. The bank does not let him do this."

"But you met with him. We know you did."

It was not quite true, but it could save time, Nick figured.

"Manólis and I meet from time to time. He's a friend as well as a cousin."

"And this time he told you what Stefanos was up to, and you were incensed."

He looked at his lawyer and she shook her head, almost imperceptibly. He said nothing.

Now, Leo leaned forward and placed a photograph on the table. "Do you recognise this man?" he said.

Nick recognised the blond man who had been photographed by Roz. Pagiánnidis picked it up and studied it for two or three seconds before flipping it back across the table.

"Doesn't look familiar," he said.

"That's a *No*, is it?" said Nick.

"What do *you* think?"

"I think you're lying. This guy has been your man on the ground, or, to put it more plainly, your hatchet man, the guy who does your dirty work for you."

"Don't know him. Sorry."

"You might want to reconsider, Pagiánnidi," Leo cut in. "A girl has been murdered. This man was seen trespassing on the site. If he was working with your little team, you could find yourself facing a murder charge."

"You said the girl died in the wildfire. That's what it said on the news, too."

"I said she died in suspicious circumstances. The Medical Examiner will testify that she was dead before the fire touched her. And it was *not* a wildfire. We believe it was started deliberately."

The penny was dropping for Pagiánnidis. Nick could see the sudden realisation on his face, the beginnings of fear. Nick saw his chance to reinforce that fear.

"Where *I* come from," he said, "a jail sentence for murder *and* arson can easily run to twenty or thirty years. I doubt the Greeks are any softer, Leo?"

"We take arson very seriously here, as you would expect, but the murder of a young girl, just twenty-one years old, here to do charitable work and help save our planet? This will make the judges angry. I think thirty years is the right number. With good behaviour, you might be out for your sixtieth birthday, Pagiánnidi. Assuming you survive, that is."

Nick saw Pagiánnidis glance across at his lawyer.

"I think I need five minutes with my client," she said.

Leo spoke into the recording device and paused it and then he and Nick made their way to the police station's coffee machine.

"What do you reckon?" asked Nick as they put their coffees on a table and Leo fumbled for his cigarettes.

"I think he knows who the blond guy is. He may never have met him, I suppose. Perhaps he was brought in by one of the others."

"Do you think Blondie was following instructions when he killed Roz and burned the forest?"

"Assuming he did, you mean."

"Well, we have no one else in the frame, do we, Leo?"

"All right, assuming he did, I would say he was told to burn the forest. I'd guess Roz's death was not part of the plan. Either her death was an accident, or he killed her because he knew she could identify him."

"So, he overplayed his hand. He wasn't supposed to kill anyone, in your world."

"I think that's right. These guys are crooked businessmen, not killers."

"But this is also a forty-year vendetta, right?"

"In a way," Leo agreed, slowly, "but no one killed anyone in these families then or since, as far as we know, so it's not a vendetta, as such. This is about money and lost financial opportunity. The appropriate revenge would be to dispossess the man, sabotage his plans and take away his dream. There's no need to kill him."

"Whoever started the fire didn't much care who got killed; it seems to me."

Nick took another glug of coffee. Leo popped his dog-end into the dregs of his plastic cup with a hiss.

"It also provided a rationale for taking half a million off the price," he added.

"Hmmm," said Nick, "but simultaneously it *relieved* the pressure on Stefi by making the forestry claim irrelevant. I don't see why they would do that, after going to the trouble of making up the bloody claim in the first place."

"People aren't entirely rational, Nick."

"You'd think I'd have learned that by now," he chuckled as they ambled back to the interrogation room, but he remained unconvinced.

*

The atmosphere had changed. Nick sensed it as soon as they opened the door. Pagiánnidis was avoiding eye contact. The lawyer was in charge now, he guessed. He saw Leo set the machine to record again and then Ms. Marína spoke:

"My client wishes me to read a statement on his behalf, after which he will answer no further questions until you arrest him or charge him."

Nick looked at Leo. Leo said nothing. He clearly did not like it but waved his hands theatrically, indicating she should continue.

> *I, Stávros Pagiánnidis, wish to state categorically: I am a simple businessman and innocent of doing anything I knew to be illegal. Specifically:*
>
> *a) I have never met the man in the photograph you showed me.*
>
> *b) I have never set fire to anything nor asked anyone else to set fire to anything.*
>
> *c) I have never killed anyone nor asked anyone else to kill someone.*

It was signed and dated.

"Well, that was short and sweet," said Nick.

"Concise, yes, and to the point," said Marína, proudly.

Leo ignored them. He was angry, and Nick could sense it.

"I think it would be in your best interests to continue with our conversation, Pagiánnidi," Leo said, addressing her client directly, against the lawyer's wishes, "but if you are determined to sit there saying *Nothing* or *No Comment* then I am not prepared to waste my time."

He paused, but neither Pagiánnidis nor Marína made any move to restore the situation.

"In that case, we will end the interview. You may return to work, but you must not leave the island without my permission. We will be speaking again. I am quite sure of that."

Pagiánnidis went to say something, Nick thought, but his lawyer glared at him and then ushered him swiftly from the room.

"That was unfortunate," said Leo, when they were alone.

"Sodding lawyers," said Nick.

"I was hoping Pagiánnidis could be turned."

"Get him to shop the others to save his skin, you mean?"

"Something like that. I suspect his statement is true, but it's carefully limited."

"Like *never met*, you mean. Leaving room for messages, phone calls, even video calls, arguably."

"If he has another phone somewhere."

"Indeed."

"And the second and third statements are all about him. They don't say everyone in the gang was innocent of these things. He knows exactly who did what."

"But he's not going to tell us."

"Not yet."

It was now twelve thirty and time to interview Michailídis.

"You found him, then," said Nick.

"He was at home. Most indignant, he was."

"Ah, the protesting type, is he?" said Nick, with relish.

Leo gave him a weary, crumpled look and pressed the intercom.

"Bring him in, please, Anna."

"No lawyer?" asked Nick.

"Not yet," grinned Leo.

A female sergeant ushered him in and asked Leo if he needed her to stay. He shook his head and smiled. The man was thirty-nine but looked younger. He was typically Cretan: thick cotton, pale pink shirt, open at the neck, chinos, a neatly trimmed, dark beard and alert, brown eyes. He was also simmering with self-importance.

"Sit down please, Michailídi."

He did so, in silence.

Leo introduced himself and Nick. All very gentle and relaxed.

"Thanks for coming in. We just need to ask a few questions. It shouldn't take too long."

The body language shifted. It said: *I'm still angry but I'll cut you a little slack.*

"You worked at Alpha Bank, here in Chaniá, as we understand it, until the fourteenth of August?"

"Sounds right."

"And you were a Senior Client Relationship Manager."

"This was my final role, yes."

"Rather a good job for a relatively young man."

"No need to patronise me, Lieutenant. I was there seven years, worked my way up, worked hard."

"A good job, secure, well-paid?"

"I suppose so."

"So, why would you suddenly pack it in, resign?"

"There was nothing sudden about it. I'd been working up to it for some time. I felt I'd got as far as I was likely to get in the bank. And I was a little bored."

"Hmmm. I guess a sensible chap like you would have something else lined up."

"I wanted to start my own business."

"Doing what, exactly?"

"Touristic development. Building villas and apartments for holiday rentals."

"Woah. That's very entrepreneurial. Do you have experience in that business?"

"Is this a job interview, Lieutenant?"

"I'm sorry. It just seems a bit of a change from seven years at a high street bank."

"A change is what I wanted."

"And did you have particular projects in mind, when you left the bank?"

"I had identified a few possibles."

Nick cut in. As arranged, he was playing bad cop today.

"And were they *all* projects you knew of from confidential information given to the bank, or was that only Tamarisk Bay?"

The man looked amused. *Cocky little sod,* thought Nick.

"So *that's* what this is all about," said Michailídis.

"When did you first get the idea?" asked Nick.

"Which idea?"

"The idea of stealing the Tamarisk Bay project from Spiliákis – your *client* Spiliákis – and doing it for yourself and your mates."

"Stealing? What are you talking about? All we have done is make offers for the land which, so far, have not been accepted."

"And why have you done that? What gave you the idea?"

"Well, obviously I was aware of his plans from my time at the bank, but I left my job before I made any offer. And I took no bank files with me. As far as I'm concerned, the Chinese walls are intact, and I'm sure the bank would agree."

"You are, are you? Perhaps we should ask them. How could the so-called Chinese walls be intact when you took the knowledge – in your head? Confidential knowledge! And then used it to your advantage, and your former client's considerable disadvantage!"

"Even the banks don't wipe your memory before letting you go, so yes, of course I remembered stuff. But honestly? The only knowledge I've used is that there is a piece of land called Tamarisk Bay which Spiliákis might sell."

"And why do you think he would?"

"Because he doesn't know what he's doing. He's out of his depth and he doesn't have the skills to manage a project of such size and complexity. It will all go wrong, and I think he knows it, deep down."

"But you supported him at the bank."

"I did, but less so as time went on. The business was getting unfocused and wobbly. And the whole green thing? I wasn't convinced there was demand for it, at least not in the up-market segment."

"So, you don't want to steal his project, just his land."

"I'm not trying to *steal* anything, Mr Fisher. We *do* want the land, as an investment. If we succeed, there may be a future project, but it will bear little resemblance to Spiliákis's plan. For a start, it will be well managed by a specialist team with a proven track record, and it will maximise the commercial potential of the Tamarisk Bay site."

Nick felt his heart sinking and his anger mounting. These guys would do just what Stefi feared: reshape the land and cover it with as many apartments as they could cram in.

"Whose idea was it to kill the goat?" he asked.

"I beg your pardon."

"You heard me."

"I had nothing to do with that."

"Was it your wayward cousin, then? Did he organise the fire and the murder, as well?"

"What are you talking about? We heard there was a wildfire, and a young girl was caught up in it. I was sorry to hear it. Tragic. But nothing we had anything to do with, I assure you."

"It sounds like you don't know what your accomplices were up to so if you'll forgive me, your assurances are worthless."

Leo cut in. The good cop, clarifying, helping.

"You see, Michailídi, medical evidence proves the girl, Rosalind, died *before* the fire reached her. We also know the wildfires never got close enough to ignite the juniper forest. We have talked with the Fire Service. Someone killed the girl and lit the fire."

Nick took up the baton:

"Given the escalating campaign of terror you and your friends were putting Spiliákis through, we figured this was your next move. What other explanation could there be?"

"No … no, I'm sure they wouldn't do that."

"I'm getting the impression you're not sure about anything," said Nick.

"Maybe I should get my lawyer in here."

Nick raised his eyebrows at Leo, who took over.

"That's your right and we can suspend the questions until he or she arrives. No problem. Or we can have a chat, off the record. Clear the air. I can switch this thing off. We may have to go through it all again in a more formal way at some point but, for now, why don't you just talk us through what happened? You strike me as a reasonable guy, not the sort of man who would be comfortable with a young girl being murdered in his name."

"You're right. Totally right. I am not that man."

"We'll give you ten minutes. You can call your lawyer, or not. You can think about how you'd like to take things forward."

*

As soon as they reached the coffee machine, once again, Nick said:

"He'll call Pagiánnidis, of course."

"I'm hoping he will, Nick. I want them both worried."

"He'll tell him to keep his trap shut, get a lawyer in right away."

"I would expect that, but I'm hoping this guy is his own man. It sounds like the goat incident happened without his concurrence. Maybe he's losing control of his partner."

Leo disappeared in a shroud of blue smoke as he lit his cigarette.

"I thought the doctor told you to give them up."

"They told me a lot of things after I got shot, Nick. But they come from the presumption that we all want to live as long as possible and will make any sacrifice to do so."

"I guess they see a lot of people breathing their last and regretting stuff."

"Sure, they do, but for me, it's the *quality* of life, not its length."

"And puffing on a weed enhances the quality? Are you sure about that?"

"For me, yes it does. It helps me think and relaxes me a little."

"I used to say that, too."

Leo put his spare hand on Nick's shoulder and steered him back down the corridor.

"I never thought of you as the sanctimonious type, Nick Fisher."

"Sod's Law it'll be *me* that gets the Big C from *your* smoking, you bastard."

Leo threw him a mock punch which Nick parried, slopping his coffee as he did so, but then a constable appeared, and they quickly adopted a more serious pose. As the constable passed, he said:

"He made two calls, sir."

"Thank you, Constable," said Leo and they re-entered the interrogation room.

"Well, Michailídi, what's it to be?" he said.

"I'll talk, off the record. My partners don't like it, but I think it's the right thing to do. I want you to understand, I had nothing to do with any murder or arson. Nor did I want the goat killed and I thought I'd put a stop to that idea. I hope my openness with you will help you turn a blind eye to any minor misdemeanours I may have tolerated."

"I see," said Leo. "Well, I hear what you say, Michailídi. We'll have to see how minor they were, won't we? Now, would you like tea or coffee?"

*

Leo restarted things without preamble.

"Tell us about these partners of yours, Michailídi."

They watched him stir his tea for a long moment.

"You know about my cousin, Stávros, I think. I took the idea to him. I needed someone who understood the property market in Crete and had contacts in the building world. He was the obvious choice."

"Makes sense."

"Yes, and the first couple of meetings went well. He seemed very keen on the idea but doubted Spiliákis would sell. My view of where Spiliákis was with his project would not be shared by the man himself, Stávros pointed out. Some things needed to go wrong for that to happen. At our third meeting, his mother appeared; my Aunt Irína."

"What – she just invited herself along?"

"Stávros invited her. I was not happy about it, but he explained that she had some useful ideas and the contacts to make them happen. We would be well distanced from anything borderline in terms of ethics or legality," he assured me.

"So, anything dodgy was okay with you as long as you got away with it," said Nick.

Michailídis said nothing.

Leo slid the photograph onto the table.

"Would this be one of her contacts?" he said.

"It might be. I've never seen him."

"But you know his name?"

"No. It was someone she knew from way back. A shady character but very *talented*, if that's the right word for it. He's Bulgarian, I think. I guessed he was a former lover."

"And this is him."

226

"I don't know. As I say, I've never seen him. Iría was his contact. Neither I nor Stávros met him or even spoke to him. It was important to keep us distanced, you see."

"So, was it Iría who suggested the forestry scam?"

"Yes. And, like all good scams, it was partly true."

"How so?"

"The Forestry Department drew up maps a couple of years ago showing all the areas they felt should be *protected forestry*. They paid no attention to who the current owners were. It was an idealistic approach, I suppose. There was, I believe, some public statement advising owners to check online if they were affected, but it was low key and almost everyone ignored it. But then property transactions started hitting the buffers. The lawyers would discover a swathe of the sellers' land was on the forestry map and then it was impossible to sell without getting the forestry team to exclude it, which meant them admitting an error. Their maps included areas that had been granted building permits and even where houses had already been built, so you can imagine the chaos. Backlogs quickly developed. It would take months, often years, to resolve."

"So, finding part of your land on the forestry map was very bad news."

"Yes, certainly in terms of the inevitable delay. If you could prove pre-existing building rights, then you would normally be success-ful in revoking the claim, but it would take a long time. And if you couldn't – and Spiliákis could have no building rights over the juni-per forest – you would lose ownership to the Forestry Department. It would cease to be your land. And no compensation is given."

"So, Iría's idea was to tell Spiliákis that some of his land was on the forestry map."

"Yes. And the juniper forest was perfect for this. Junipers are quite rare in Greece, and they are fragile trees. Changes to their environment can be very damaging. They are often awarded protected status."

"Were you happy to go along with this idea, then?" asked Leo.

"It was put across as a bit of fun. I didn't think about it that much. It was just a ruse to nudge him in our direction."

"Whereas it was fraud," said Leo, "or certainly misrepresentation, and someone – probably our mysterious, Bulgarian friend – must have impersonated a government employee."

"Some nice touches from him, we noticed," added Nick. "He calls Stefi's *lawyer*, rather than the man himself. That way, when the lawyer relays the information to Stefi, it will have added weight and become *undeniable*. Secondly, he pretends to be an Albanian, long since settled in Greece. He has good Greek but, as a Bulgarian, he would sound foreign, so this works well for him. And lastly, he says he will send official papers. In the lawyer's mind, this obviates the need to verify his credentials; the official papers, when they arrive, will do that. But the information was too important to delay, so she called Stefi without pause. It takes a long time for everyone to realise no papers were forthcoming and, by that time, the damage has been done. One carefully thought-out phone call was all it took. The man's a pro. A professional, I mean."

Michailídis was not sure how to react, so he said nothing. He had not expected the man's skills to be admired.

"And then we have the discovery of the Roman coins," said Leo. "Irína again?"

"Yes. This was more involved, but it was still essentially a bit of fun, I felt. And rather clever of her."

"I doubt Professor Tzanakákis, the archaeologist arriving with his team on Monday, will share your sense of humour, Michailídi. I suppose it was our Bulgarian who bought the coins and pretended to find them at Tamarisk Bay?"

Michailídis nodded. *He was almost chuckling behind that thin beard,* Nick thought.

"And this time he was a Slovenian called Žagar and had a wife."

"Irína went with him to see Tzanakákis, I believe."

"She's hardly Slovenian."

"She said very little. It was just to add credibility to the tourist angle."

"I see," said Leo, "and, once again, this was about delay. You knew the archaeological team would get excited about a find which proved the Romans reached the far, south-west coast of Crete and you knew they have a duty to investigate and the power to bring all activity to a standstill."

"We did. And coming so soon after the forestry issue, it would seem to Spiliákis like his project was facing a bureaucratic nightmare. Better by far for him to take an escape route if offered. At least, this is what we hoped."

"But then he turned down your two million offer flat, didn't he?"

"He did. And this is when things changed. The others became much more aggressive. Nothing clever or amusing anymore. Maybe the manner of his refusal rankled. He virtually told us to fuck off. But now, some of the ideas they brought to the table were completely unacceptable to me. It was all getting very personal and unpleasant. I didn't understand where they were coming from, to be honest. It was unprofessional."

"Is this where the goat comes in?"

"Listen. I said: *No.* There was no call for that. The man does not have a partner and it must be a lonely life out there. If he has found solace in making a pet of a baby goat, then good for him. It had probably assumed even greater importance to him because of the isolated situation. It would be a very cruel thing to kill it, in terms of the man, not to mention the goat itself."

"But they ignored you?"

"They disagreed with me. They said it was necessary to raise the stakes, to frighten the man into submission."

"So, I said: what next? What if this doesn't work? Are you going to threaten *him*? Because I'm not going there. I'm not a criminal."

"You are now," said Nick and uncertainty flickered in the man's eyes.

"I'm not. Really, I'm not. If there was arson or murder, I had nothing to do with it. It was never even discussed. As for the goat, I lost control of my partners. Irína can be an evil bitch. They just went ahead and did it anyway."

"The Bulgarian again."

"I would think so. I'm sorry. I didn't think they would do it."

"How much do you know about the past ownership of Tamarisk Bay?" asked Nick.

"Nothing at all. Why?"

"Forty years ago, it was owned by the Pagiánnidis family. They believe Stávros's grandfather – Irína's father-in-law – was fooled into selling it cheaply to the Spiliákis family. If you think it suddenly got personal, it has *always* been personal for them. This is why they killed the goat and why they went on to burn the forest and kill the girl. Pagiánnidis couldn't believe his luck when you took him the idea. It gave him the perfect way to perform his vendetta and get back the land."

"My God. I had no idea."

"Why would you? But now you're caught up in a murder inquiry."

"I could believe they set light to the forest. I might even believe they could kill Spiliákis – but to murder a stranger makes no sense. It must have been an accident."

"As we told you, she died before the fire reached her. That doesn't sound much like an accident to us."

*

"I hope he's going to be okay," said Nick, as they watched Michailídis crossing the car park.

"It's all family though, isn't it?"

"He's not a Pagiánnidis."

"No, but his Aunt Irína is a Michailídou, remember. And she married a Pagiánnidis. I think he'll be okay. Anyway, he hasn't told us much we didn't already know."

"We need to interview Irína and see if we can nail Blondie."

"My thoughts exactly."

CHAPTER 23
IT GETS PERSONAL

Iría did not want to be interviewed. She made excuses, she came up with commitments that got in the way. By Monday morning, Leo lost patience and sent a car.

"We know she's behind these scams," he told the constables. "If she refuses to come with you, arrest her on the spot."

Nick was on the phone, updating Stefi. As he was finishing up, he said:

"So, we know the coin thing was a scam now, Stefi. See if you can deter Tzanakákis from wasting everyone's time. You might still catch them before they set off."

"He won't believe anything I say."

"Then have him call Leo, if he must."

"Okay, Nick. I'll call him. And thanks, man. Sounds like you're making real progress."

"Today will tell. Michailídis was useful, but we don't think he can help us with the fire or the murder. That must come from the others. Is Alma still with you?"

"She is. She's right here."

"Okay, tell her we're doing all we can, but we're not there yet. And give her a squeeze from me," he added.

"Thanks for everything you're doing, Nick. You and the guys from the police, of course. I appreciate it."

It was Alma. Stefi must have passed her the phone.

"And I'm returning your squeeze. With a big hug, too," she said.

Nick was speechless, for once.

*

She would be in her late fifties or early sixties, Nick guessed, but Iría was still a striking woman. Attractive would be going too far. Her features had been exaggerated by age, and she was more than a little

231

overweight. The perpetual scowl on her face did not help, nor did the excess of make-up. Her clothes looked expensive and might be described as glamorous but were hardly tasteful. She had made no mention of lawyers and probably had no time for them.

"Why you want see me?" she asked Leo as soon as they were all assembled in the interrogation room. "What, you think I tell you what Stávros and Manólis cannot? Is crazy."

"I think you can tell us about this man," said Leo and slid the photo across the table once again.

"Ah. This not good picture."

"You can still tell who it is though, surely."

"I mean is not good picture of him. He nicer looking than this, my Ivan."

"So, you admit to knowing him?"

"Know him? He was my husband, before Giánnis. For two years only. He comes to Crete on holiday. I am eighteen. We fall in love. But my faddah say no; Irína must marry nice, Greek boy. So, I say balls to that, and I run off to Plovdiv with him and we get married, just like that."

"But then it all went wrong?"

"He is lovely man. Very beautiful and exciting to be with but the second time he go to jail, I leave him. He broke his promise, you see."

"He was a criminal, then."

"He is small time. He's good at what he does but sometimes he gets caught."

"And what *does* he do?"

"He tricks people. He is a confidence trickster."

"So, when you turned to crime, you gave him a call."

"Tricks, no crimes, Lieutenant. We have a bit of fun with Spiliákis, is all."

"Fun designed to fool him into selling to you cheaply."

She put on a sad clown face and tilted her head to one side.

"If the man is stupid enough to fall for our little tricks, then he does not deserve to own this land."

"What you did was illegal."

"Oh, come now, Lieutenant. All is fair in love, war and business. We all know this."

"Killing the goat was not fair."

"Spiliákis was very rude to us. I got angry. Maybe it was not fair on the goat, but it made someone a nice meal, I'm sure. Anyway, after this, Ivan tells me: *Stop. It has gone far enough.* He will do no more."

"And then the fire."

"Yes. A bit of luck for us. We don't care about a few trees but now we can argue the land is worth less."

"How very convenient. We know of many cases in Crete where fires are started deliberately to reduce the value of land. I think *you* started the fire, Irína."

"You think *I* did?"

"Your ex-husband, most likely."

"I told you. He would do no more. He goes back."

"What do you mean?"

"By the time of this fire, he is back in Bulgaria. He is there now. You can check this."

"But you reduced your offer, after the fire."

"And put a time limit. We make use of the situation, Lieutenant. This is putting pressure on Spiliákis. Is good business. It does not mean we start no fire."

"Maybe you got Stávros to do it."

"I didn't get nobody to do nothing. You're making me out like some crazy woman! I don't go around setting fire to forests. People get hurt by these things."

"We know about the land and what happened forty years ago. And your second husband's suicide – was it connected? The loss of this land has been a huge thing in your family for many, many years. I believe you'd do almost anything to get it back."

"No. You wrong about this. Giánnis hanged himself because he was an idiot. All his life, he think: *I am failure.* Well, he certainly don't get everything right, but who does – honestly? He getting old, too, and say he no well. Always, he say this. Hypochondria mostly, in my view. You know this word? Is good, Greek word. Also, he think I am sleeping with Ivan again. I was not, of course, and never would.

And the land? Yes, Giánni's father did a rubbish deal, though seven million drachmae was lot of money forty years ago, you know. And Spiliákis is lucky with how things change, but we no think revenge until Manólis come with his idea."

"You're quite sure about that?"

"I tell you truth, Lieutenant. We were naughty with our tricks and a bit mean about the goat, but this is all. We don't even hate Spiliákis! Maybe there was some old resentment about the land but Kóstas was not forced to sell, was he? It is *his* fault we no longer have it."

*

Nick had arranged to meet up with Lauren on Monday lunchtime. He invited Leo along.

"It might do us both good to get out of the office for a while," he said.

The waiter erected a massive parasol for them, and they were half-heartedly studying the menus when Lauren joined them.

"Gosh, you two look a bit dispirited," she said, brightly. "Bad day at the office?"

Nick brought her up to speed while Leo poured water and lit a cigarette, much to Lauren's disgust.

"So, this woman, Irína, swears they didn't start the fire," Lauren said.

"And I don't think they did," said Leo between drags, trying to waft the smoke away from the table. "The blond guy, Ivan, was back in Bulgaria, she says. We'll check, but I'm sure it will be confirmed, otherwise she would not say this. Would the others do it for themselves? I don't think so. Michailídis wouldn't want it to happen anyway, and Pagiánnidis wouldn't want to get his hands dirty. We'll check, but they're going to have alibis."

"What *can* you charge them with, then?"

"I'll talk with the Investigating Judge, but she'll probably tell me to forget about it."

"You're kidding! And let them get away with doing all that to poor Stefi!"

"Without arson or murder, these are not significant crimes, Lauren. We'd have to try and get this guy Ivan extradited – and all for what?

A slap on the wrist, maybe a few months in jail if we're lucky. If we could prove it. And Stefi would have to relive everything in court for another year or two, maybe more, when he could be getting on with his life."

"If he's allowed to get on with his life."

"Oh, he *will* be," said Leo. "Don't worry about that. Any leniency these people are given will come with a hefty warning. We will read them the Right Act."

Lauren looked baffled.

"Ri-*ot* Act," corrected Nick, quietly. "And this is all very interesting, folks, but we're rather missing the point – and the reason for the despondency you observed, Lauren. If Irína and her gang didn't kill Roz or start the fire, then who the hell did? I, for one, have no frigging idea."

"It *must* be them, then," said Lauren.

"It's *not* them. I agree with Leo, unfortunately. One hundred per cent."

"But then we're back to square one."

"Do not pass go. Do not collect two hundred pounds."

"Fuck a duck."

Nick thrust a menu into her hand.

"You might want something to eat with your wine," he said. "I'm for the loukánika."

"Village sausages? Oh, yuk."

*

"I can't see who else would have anything to gain from starting the fire, can you?" Nick said, pouring out the rakí that had arrived with some slices of ripe watermelon at the end of their meal. Neither of the others objected to him filling their little glasses to the brim which he took as confirmation of the prevailing gloom.

"Some crazed fire lover?" suggested Leo, listlessly.

"A teetotaller set on destroying all the gin berries?" said Lauren, making a wild face.

"Come on, let's at least *try* to be sensible," said Nick.

"Well, it could have been started accidentally by someone, except there's never anyone there. If it was deliberate, then it was someone who had a grudge against Stefi, someone who wanted to devalue his land or frighten him. It's possible it was started by a nutcase who just loves to see fires raging but then they would have to go there specially, wouldn't they? There must be things to burn closer to home."

"There's another possibility."

The others set down their glasses and stared at Nick.

"We've been assuming Roz died from some freak accident or more likely got herself killed by the person who started the fire because she caught them in the act or tried to stop them – yes?"

They nodded. This was exactly what they had assumed.

"That word again. *Assuming*. Well, let's turn the assumption on its head. Maybe *Roz* was the killer's target, and the fire was started to destroy the evidence of her murder."

Leo stared at him evenly, nodding slightly. Lauren made a face.

"Why would anyone want to kill Roz?"

"Why does anyone ever want to kill? There may be reasons we are unaware of."

"Well, he didn't do a great job, did he? She was only half-burned."

"He or she did enough. It wasn't about hiding Roz's identity. It would have been obvious who she was – as it was to me – because of where she was found. No, it was about *destroying evidence*. And, in that, he or she *was* successful. The ME cannot prove it was murder, only that Roz died before the fire got to her. It's enough for the defence to argue that it was – or at least might have been – an accident. In fact, leaving her half-burned would tend to support the accident argument."

"Because anyone destroying evidence would have made certain the body was *completely* consumed," added Leo.

"Exactly. So, taking the hypothesis further, who might have had a reason to kill Roz, and why? Can we think of anyone?"

"Could it be someone working at Tamarisk Bay? That would mean Stefi, Dan or Teddy," said Lauren.

"Most murders are related to passion," said Leo. "Could one or more of them have been having an affair with her?"

236

"Well, Stefi's twice her age and gay. Dan seems more interested in his green gadgets and jazz than women. Teddy's a possible, I suppose, but he's really good-looking."

"So?"

"I don't want to speak ill of the dead, but you would not describe Roz as pretty."

"Ouch. That's a bit mean," said Nick.

"I'm just telling it how it is, Dad. Roz was not interested in *trying* to be pretty. It was not her thing, all right?"

"But you're saying Roz was not attractive enough to interest Teddy," said Leo.

"He could have almost anyone he wanted, I'd have thought."

"But there's no one there, Lauren."

"Okay. Fair point, but I saw no chemistry between them, and why on earth would he kill Roz, even if they had something going on? Seems more likely she would kill *him* for losing interest when Fi arrived."

They were silent for a few seconds. Nick topped up Lauren's and his own rakí glasses. Leo's remained untouched, he saw. He popped a piece of watermelon in his mouth.

"She came straight back here after the funeral," said Leo. "But I can't see why anyone would follow her from Scotland. If someone wanted to kill her, they would have done it there."

"So, where was she before, when she heard her father was dying?" asked Nick.

"She was here, in Crete, I think," said Lauren, "but not in Tamarisk Bay. But this was *weeks* ago. She was in Scotland nearly two months, in the end."

"Where in Crete?" he persisted.

"Oh, she was on the north coast somewhere, learning about turtles, I think she said. She had one of those blue tee shirts they all wear. She wore it here sometimes. It has something like *Ask Me About Turtles* scrawled on it. Bizarre."

"Was there a logo of any sort, do you remember?" asked Leo.

"I don't remember. Sorry."

"Are you on to something, Leo?" said Nick.

"I just need to check something. Give me a minute."

Leo took his cell phone for a walk. They could see him gesticulating in the street as tourists and passers-by weaved around him. He took the opportunity to have a cigarette at the same time without annoying Lauren, but it was annoying several other people as he waved it around, Nick noticed. At last, he stopped moving altogether, looked in their direction and blinked a couple of times. Then he trod on his cigarette end and returned to the table.

"I called Anna, my other sergeant," he said. Nick understood. He meant the sergeant who was not Thaní, the woman who had come into the interview room. "I remembered a detail from the other case – the one she's been working on."

"Go on," said Nick, impatiently.

"The girl who was murdered was a cleaner. One of the places she cleaned was the ARCHELON volunteer centre. It's on a beach near Chaniá."

"What's ARCHELON?" asked Nick.

"It's the name of a Greek turtle protection organisation. Their volunteers wear blue tee shirts."

"Was that where Roz was, Lauren?"

"Hang on."

She grabbed her phone.

"How do you spell it?" she asked Leo.

She was on their website now, Nick saw. She jumped in and out of pages. Finally, she found some pictures of volunteers in action. She zoomed in on one.

"There it is," she said. "There's the blue tee shirt. And here – do you see it? – below the logo with the turtle bobbing in the water. Is that how you write it in Greek, Leo? The word starting APX?"

"It says ARCHELON."

"Then that's where Roz was working. But let's just check."

Nick saw her click on a green tab labelled *Activity Areas*.

"Where's Glyfada, Leo?" he said.

"It's on the mainland."

"Look, Dad. There are three in the Peloponnese and three, here in Crete. I know she wasn't in Réthymno or Messará Bay, so it must have been Chaniá!"

"How do you know?"

"Roz told us. She said she had only been in south-west Crete and Chaniá."

Nick blinked a few times, looked more closely at the screen and scrolled down to a map of their sites.

"What about this other one, Sitía?"

"It's way east and it's not a volunteer site. See? It says *other sites of activity*, whatever that means. It doesn't have a blue blob like the others."

"So, it must have been Chaniá. We should speak to someone there and see if we can confirm it."

"I'll get Anna onto it," said Leo.

"So, Roz is murdered a few weeks after staying at a place where the cleaner was murdered. And it's not like you have a lot of murders here."

"Could it be the same perpetrator?"

"Could be, covering his tracks, perhaps. Did Roz know this girl, the cleaner?"

"Daphne, her name was. I'm not sure but I can find out," Leo said.

Lauren was staring at her glass, frowning, Nick saw.

"Are you all right?" he asked.

"I'm trying to remember something. I don't know if it's relevant to all this. Probably not."

"Tell us. You never know …"

"It was soon after we arrived at Tamarisk Bay. Roz was embarrassed, I think, about the reception we were given. Stefi was angry, throwing things about and ignoring us. She took it into her head to take us out for a meal in Paleóchora."

"A half-hour boat ride away?"

"At least, but she could handle the boat. It wasn't a problem. Anyway, when we got there, we went for a drink and then to this taverna on the seafront."

"Do you remember what it was called?" asked Leo.

"Um … there was this waiter guy – older man, maybe late fifties? He'd been in Ullapool."

"Where?" both men chorused.

"Ullapool. It's in Scotland, on the west coast."

"So, there we were having dinner, the three of us. Well, it turns out, the chef's a star; it was yummy. At the end of the meal, we ask the waiter to bring him out to have a rakí with us. Nothing happens. Not for ages. Finally, the waiter comes back to tell us he's gone! He doesn't know when – or even *if* – the guy's coming back. People are still arriving, though, expecting to eat something. It was weird. Oh, and he wasn't even the chef, just a trainee, the waiter told us."

"Do you remember the name of the taverna?"

"Hang on, it's coming to me. Er … It was named after the headland at the end of the bay. It was kind of a joke, I think."

"Because of what the headland looks like?" suggested Nick. "In Plakiás they have one they call *The Dragon*."

"That's clever of you, Dad. Yes. It was an alligator, I think. No, wait. A *crocodile*. The taverna was called something crocodile or crocodile something."

Leo was searching on his cell phone. After less than a minute, he said: "I have it. Cape Crocodile."

"That's right. Cape Crocodile. Of course, it was."

"So, what happened then?"

"Fi and I wanted to go on somewhere, treat Roz to coffee and cakes or whatever, but she said no, she'd rather get back, so we did. We came straight back after the meal."

"Do you remember which day this was?"

"Er … well, it was after the thing with poor Méli. That's why Stefi was in such a state. But it was before the fire. Before you came, Dad."

"How long before the fire."

"I'm just trying to think. You know, it might have been the day before."

"We need to be sure about this, Lauren."

"I'm not certain. Maybe we could check with Cape Crocodile. I think Roz reserved a table."

"We can try, or you can remember."

Out of the corner of his eye, Nick saw Leo making a call.

"Are you calling the restaurant?" he asked.

"No. I've asked Anna to wait for us at the police station. I think she needs to hear this."

They settled the bill and started walking back. On the way, Nick asked:

"If it *was* the night before the fire, it would have been the last time you saw Roz alive, Lauren. Surely you can remember. Try to recall the times you saw her after that evening."

"It wasn't the last time we saw her alive. That was breakfast the next day. And I remember now: she was boating it *back* to Paleóchora to stock up on groceries. We could have helped her the night before if she'd asked, so we felt a bit awkward about that, especially as the wind was getting up."

*

Back at the police station, they found a meeting room and Sergeant Anna Zerbáki joined them. Leo asked Lauren to repeat the story of the evening at Cape Crocodile.

"What do you remember about this guy, the chef?" asked Anna, when she had finished. "What did he look like?"

"We only caught glimpses, but it was enough for my friend Fi to get quite excited. He was *very* good-looking. Dark hair, dark beard, average height, mid-twenties, probably."

"And was the hair long or short?"

"Shortish, but thick and wavy."

"And the beard, was it shaggy, well-trimmed or just stubble?"

"Well-trimmed, I'd say."

"Any clothes you remember?"

"He was wearing chef's whites, I think. We only saw his top half."

"Did he have any means of transport you saw?"

"Nothing we noticed."

"Does this fit your guy, Anna?" asked Nick.

"If it is him, he's made changes. He had long hair, no beard and rode a motorbike. But the guy disappearing like that, in the middle of a service, it must mean something."

"Did you get the impression he recognised Roz, or she him?" Nick asked Lauren.

"Not from anything I saw, and Roz didn't say anything. It was such a strange thing to happen, I feel sure she would have. Who is this guy you're looking for, anyway, Sergeant?"

"His name is Diónysos or Dión, and he is a very dangerous young man. We believe he murdered his former girlfriend."

"The girl who cleaned at ARCHELON?"

"Yes. Daphne. And our inquiries lead us to believe that Daphne and Roz became good friends while she was staying there."

"The chef was called Michális, the waiter said, not Dión."

"Could be an assumed name. The guy is on the run."

"Did you know he was in Paleóchora?" asked Nick.

"No. His parents thought he had gone to Iráklio, they said."

"Lots of restaurants there."

"Exactly. They've not been helpful, to say the least."

"Well, Anna," said Leo, "I suggest you get down to Paleóchora, question the staff at Cape Crocodile and try to establish whether this guy Michális was, in fact, Dión. Find out if he reappeared after leaving that night. If it *was* him, we need to find him, and it sounds like we need to change the images of him we've been using."

"Sir."

"You'd better take a constable with you," Leo added as an afterthought.

"Good luck," said Nick. "Let us know how you get on."

She gave a shy grin and left the room.

"She seems capable," said Nick.

"She's not as bright as Thaní but she's diligent, thorough. And a nice woman."

Lauren looked from one to the other, unimpressed.

"What? Surely, he's allowed to say that?" Nick said.

"At least he didn't say *to boot*. It *was* a bit patronising, Lieutenant."

Nick did not know where to look. *What would Leo think of this brash daughter of his?* Then he saw Leo, grinning at his discomfort.

"Lauren is young, proud and feisty – is that the word? Nothing wrong with that, Nick. Maybe it's a genetic thing, my friend."

"Feisty I like," said Lauren.

"All right, feisty daughter of mine," said Nick, "would you like to solve the crime for us, now?"

He was putting her on the spot. Was she the chip off the old block she pretended to be? Crunch time.

"Well, I quite like the idea that this guy Michális *was* Dión and he recognised Roz but maybe not vice versa," she said cautiously. "If that were the case, he would know – if he stood right in front of her – that she *would* recognise him despite the changes to his appearance, so he did a bunk instead. But what I'm struggling with is the enormous coincidence of it. We go to Paleóchora on a whim and the restaurant we happen to choose for dinner, *Boom,* there he is."

"That depends."

"On what?"

"On why he chose Paleóchora."

"I'm not with you, Dad."

"Perhaps he found out Roz had gone to Scotland and would be returning to Tamarisk Bay sometime soon. That would be common knowledge among the ARCHELON crowd. He knew the police would not let the local murder case drop. Perhaps he figured they were waiting to interview her."

"Because she knew he did it? Maybe she even saw him doing it?"

"Yes – or so he believed."

"So, why didn't she go to the police, immediately?"

"It comes down to what she saw – or did not see. Yes, if she had seen the guy strangling her friend before her very eyes, then you'd expect her to contact the police right away. She didn't. Ergo, this is *not* what she saw. I think it was more nuanced. She saw him at or near the scene of the crime, at or near the time of the murder, maybe she saw something suspicious but didn't know quite what to make of it."

"So, there was nothing *to* report."

"No, and remember, she left the country for an extended period, soon after."

"Are you saying she didn't *know* the murder had taken place?"

"That's *exactly* what I'm saying. Local murder, local people involved, local news. It never made the international press and, even if it had, Roz was more concerned with her dad than news from Crete. I suspect she *never* learned of Daphne's fate."

"If she'd heard about it when she got back, she would have said something."

"I don't believe she did. ARCHELON was ancient history for her, by then."

"But wasn't there some incident with a pregnant turtle, before we arrived? Didn't they call ARCHELON about it? Surely, they would have told her, then."

"They might have. But it was *Teddy* who made the call, not Roz."

"Oh, I think you're right."

"Meanwhile, Dión changes his appearance, starts calling himself Michális, moves near to Tamarisk Bay and finds a job locally. And he waits. Maybe he already knew Roz was back. Perhaps he was about to make his move, but then what happens?"

"We walk into his restaurant."

"And suddenly he knows, it's now or never. Has she recognised him or not in his new disguise? He can't come to your table, far too risky, so he vanishes. But where does he go?"

"Into hiding?"

"No. I think he goes down to the harbour and waits. He knows you came from Tamarisk Bay and the only way back is by boat. I assume he has access to a boat himself or he borrows one."

"You think he followed us back? We didn't see any lights."

"You weren't looking."

"We were, actually, because the echo from the cliffs made me think there were two engines."

Nick stared at her and slowly raised one eyebrow.

"Is that your famous Roger Moore look, Dad? It only works if you're very good-looking and a tad reptilian. But okay, I get it. There *were* two engines. But no lights."

"He followed *your* lights. Easy enough."

"Shit, that's scary. And then what?"

"He couldn't kill her while you and Fi were with her. He'd have to kill all three of you."

"He could have rammed our boat. Oh, my God."

"Rather haphazard. You might not all have drowned and, in the dark, it would be difficult to make sure."

"That's comforting. So, what *did* he do?"

"Just followed you back and waited till morning. Maybe he saw the turtle cages in the moonlight and decided to wait for her there. We don't know. But, the next day, he killed her – probably strangling her like Daphne – and then dragged her to the forest and started the fire."

"But Roz wasn't doing turtles the next morning. She was getting groceries."

"He didn't know though, did he? How could he have? He saw turtle cages. Cages meant nests, and he knew they needed daily attention. He knew Roz was in Chaniá being trained in turtle procedures. What better place to lie in wait for her?"

"She must have stopped."

"Maybe he flagged her down, asking for help? Or she saw him or his boat. Stopped to investigate."

"If only she'd called in first. Wouldn't you do that? Or just ignore him and carry on."

"Doesn't sound like the Roz I've heard about. She took responsibility. She sorted things out. She knew where the buck stopped. And it stopped with her."

"It's true. Oh, Dad, it's such a sad string of events. She sees something, but she doesn't know what or doesn't understand what it means. She knows this guy Dión vaguely, but she doesn't know he's a killer because she doesn't know her friend has been killed. Then she happens to take us to *his* restaurant, allowing him to follow her and lie in wait for her. All that, and then she stops her bloody boat to give him his chance to kill her. Poor Roz."

The sound of the Zippo reminded them. Leo was still in the room.

"This is good stuff, you two. I've been paying attention while you've done my job for me, and I think you have it about right. Let's hope Michális *was* Dión, otherwise, it all rather falls apart, doesn't it? If he was, and we can find the bastard, I'll happily take all the credit – and I'm the only one getting paid for this!"

He stretched his legs, placed his feet on the table and puffed happily on his cigarette.

"Just a minute, Leo, I thought I *was* being paid something, as usual."

"Did we agree that, Nick? I'm not sure …"

"Why, you old rogue!"

"Boys!" said Lauren.

CHAPTER 24
CLOSING THE NET

There could be no doubt, Anna reported late that day, that Michális was indeed Dión. He had been paid under the counter and never shown any ID, but he had arrived on a motorbike which he still had when he left, apparently, and, although the hair was different and the beard new, he was the same height and build as Dión, as described by the few members of the ARCHELON crowd who had seen him.

"But the clincher was the eyes, sir," Anna said to Leo. "A few people have mentioned them; he had very distinctive blue-green eyes. Michális and Dión both had them."

"Unusual, in a Greek."

"Yes, sir. One person described them as startling. Because they looked so pale in contrast to his skin, she supposed."

"Roz would have picked up on that."

"You'd think so, sir."

"Did he go back, after Roz's murder?"

"No, sir. They never saw him again, even though he's owed a week's wages."

"And do we have any clues as to his whereabouts now, Sergeant?"

"Er … no, sir."

"Right. Well, you know the drill. Let's get updated images out to the airports and ports and all the police stations across the island. Highlight those eyes. And you'd better get back to the parents. Now we know they were trying to mislead us, you can threaten them with wasting police time or some other charge from your imagination. You might find they are more helpful."

"You want me to make up some laws, sir?"

"I'm happy for you to use your ingenuity, Sergeant. Let's find this bastard before he kills someone else."

"Yes, sir. Let's hope he hasn't already left Crete."

"He didn't leave the island before. I doubt he has now, Anna. Go get him."

*

The next morning an urgent bulletin went out. It featured twelve different pictures of Dión in an assortment of dark hairstyles and beards but all with those piercing, pale, blue-green eyes. It described his alleged crimes and the alias he had used to date.

"Let's hope he doesn't see these," Nick said, waving one at Lauren. "Or he'll be looking for coloured contact lenses and some hair dye, I should think."

"I'm surprised they haven't mentioned the motorbike."

"What do you reckon, shall we head back to Tamarisk Bay?"

"Hell no, Dad. We're at the sharp end here. Let's see it through if we can."

"The apartment is an arm and a leg, you know. And it's only tiny. Not designed for long stays."

"Well, let's move into a modest hotel then. It's almost October now. The prices should be returning from the stratosphere."

They got themselves organised without delay and found space at the Irída Hotel along the front to the east of Old Town. It looked clean and modern and was a bit less money. They were soon glad they had because very little happened over the next few days.

Leo set up a room at the police station with a couple of dedicated constables with direct phone lines and computers to deal with the hoped-for deluge of calls from the Cretan public and to sort the wheat from the chaff. It soon became clear that even this was overkill. No one, it seemed, apart from the odd nutter, thought they had spotted the attractive, young man with the unusual eyes.

"What would you do, if you were him," Nick asked Lauren as they sat on their hotel balcony, sipping beer, early that evening.

"I wouldn't try to leave the island. At least, not through normal channels. I suppose if I had access to a boat, like he did before, I could try for Kýthira or Santoríni or something."

"Bloody long way in a small boat."

"Right. Well, perhaps Gávdos or Chrisí islands then."

"You'd be bored shitless in a few days. They're just beaches. There's nothing there."

"All right then, if I'm staying on the main island, I'm either going to disappear into the crowd, somewhere like Iráklio, or I'm going to disappear into a remote place."

"Which?"

"The crowd is better cover but it's difficult to do without papers, these days. He won't have any ID in whatever name he's using. It's okay if you're sleeping on the beach or whatever, but most hotels won't let you in without seeing a passport."

"So, the remote option?"

"I think so. Somewhere they're unlikely to watch the news on TV or buy papers. And then lie low for a good while."

"Something like a monastery?"

"Yeah! That would do it. And there are plenty of them here."

Nick leaned across and emptied the can of Alpha into their glasses.

"There's a chance we'll never find him, you know."

"Defeatist talk, Dad. Something will come up soon. We're going to get him. For Roz. And for Alma. You wait and see."

*

The call came through on the fourth day, late morning. It was from a woman staying in Makrigiálos. She was Canadian, she said, but from a Greek family originally. She had been in Crete for two months.

Chrístos carefully wrote down her name and contact details. Then he asked her how he could help.

"The guy you're looking for. I saw it on the news in my hotel. I watch the news most nights to improve my lapsed Greek."

"Have you seen him?" asked Chrístos.

"Yes." She sounded very definite, but then they all did. "At least, I think so. Only he has real short hair now, kinda spiky, and no beard – and he's wearing glasses."

49

"So, how did you recognise him?" Chrístos asked, but he knew the answer already.

"The eyes. You don't get many Greeks with eyes that colour. They're real striking."

"Okay. Was this in Makrigiálos?"

"No. We did a little tour out east the last couple of days. It was at a taverna in Káto Zákros last night."

"He was eating in the same taverna as you?"

"No. He was *cooking* there, and rather well, I must say. My friend and I were delighted with our meals, so we went to the kitchen to say thanks and shake the chef's hand."

"And there he was."

"There he was. Indeed."

"Which taverna was this?"

"Yep. I knew you'd ask me. There are only a few and they're all back of the beach. It would be either Nóstos or Anamnésia, I have receipts from both, but I forget which."

That was ironic, Chrístos smirked to himself.

"It's okay, we'll check them both," he said. "Were you staying at the taverna?"

"No. I think they do have a few rooms, but we were up at Terra Minoiká, just on the edge of the village. Not cheap but utterly fabulous."

"I don't know this place," he said. *And on a Greek police constable's salary, I never will*, he thought. "Was there anything else about him, ma'am?"

"Well, we were rather late that night. We'd been chatting over brandy at a bar after dinner and watching the moonlight playing on the sea. My friend recently lost her husband, you see. I'm trying to help her see a way forward. Lord knows she should be thankful. He was a pig, if you ask me."

Which I didn't, thought Chrístos, tapping his pen on the desk.

"Anyway, we're walking back to Terra Minoiká. It must have been getting on for one by then when this guy on a motorbike roars past us. He had to swerve a little to miss us! I guess we were hard to see in the dark. But I think it was him. I'm not a hundred per cent on that but it looked like him. He was not wearing a crash helmet; I'm quite sure about that."

"What type of motorbike, Ma'am? Do you have any idea?"

"A loud one. And a fast one."

"Right. Well, you've been very helpful. I will pass this information on to my superiors, and I expect someone will check this out for you."

"*For me?* It's not for me, young man. The police asked for information, and I've given you some. In many ways, I feel bad sending such a great cook to jail but if he's killed some poor girl, then it must be done. Now listen to me, I'm not some foolish old bird who thinks she has seen something when she hasn't. I saw what I saw, and I expect you to act on it *now*, not sometime later if you feel like it, is that clear?"

"If I've given the imp ..."

To his astonishment, she had ended the call. *Was she just another nutter?* he wondered. He ran his eye back over his notes. If she was right, the guy had changed his appearance again, but she had caught him close-up in the kitchen, which gave her a chance to notice those eyes. He was cooking again and winning praise for it, again. He had chosen somewhere remote, on the far east coast, to hide away for a while and maybe he still owned the motorbike. Perhaps he couldn't bear to give it up.

Chrístos turned to his colleague, Pandelís.

"I might have something here, mate. I'm taking it straight to the Lieutenant."

CHAPTER 25

THE CHASE

It is about as far as you can travel, in Crete. Chaniá to Káto Zákros is over three hundred kilometres. They decided to do most of the journey the next day, spend the night at Sitía, then hook up with the local sergeant the following morning and drive the last bit.

They were in Lasíthi prefecture now. Adding Sergeant Giannakákis to the team was a nod to the local police captain. It was their case, but his prefecture. As Leo had expected, the captain wanted some representation on the team. Fair enough.

Nick's suggestion that they leave it to the Lasíthi force to apprehend the suspect had been met with derision by Leo.

"You what, Nick? There has never been a double murder on my watch. We have worked on this case for almost four months. Finally, we think we've nailed the guy and what – you think we should let the boys from Sitía or Ierápetra steal our glory and why – because it's a four-and-a-half-hour drive? Are you crazy?"

Once he knew they were going, there was no way Nick was going to miss out, and Leo accepted that readily.

"Of course, you must come," he said. "We need you, Nick."

"And Lauren?"

"That's different. You're a recently retired ex-policeman; your daughter is a student."

"She's close to this case, Leo. She's helped us out on more than one occasion. She'll be gutted if we leave her in the hotel. Can you imagine how that would feel?"

"Look, Nick. I like Lauren. She's a bright girl and she has helped, mostly, but this is a police mission to arrest a dangerous criminal, a double murderer. There's no place for her. Surely you see that."

"I'll take full responsibility, Leo. We can make sure she's out of the firing line. She would be so thrilled just to drive there and back with us, watch from a distance, feel a part of things."

"I think you're crazy, Nick, but okay. But first, you will write me something and sign it. I don't want this to come back and bite me in the backside."

"No problem. Thanks, mate."

"And you should make sure her mother is okay with it."

"I'm sure you're right," he agreed, but *should* sounded merely advisory to Nick and that was advice he was not planning to take.

*

The police Skoda Karoq with Sergeant Státhis Giannakákis from Sitía and two unmarked cars, one containing Leo, Nick and Lauren and the other Anna Zerbáki and two constables from Chaniá, came to a halt a few hundred yards outside Káto Zákros. There was just one tarmac road in and out. Leo drew up alongside the others.

"We can't just drive in, all together," he said. "This is a small place, end of season. The seven of us could double the numbers out, late morning. It's too obvious. I think we send in a small team of two or three to act like tourists. Cool and low-key. Anna, Lauren and Nick. You probably look more the part, like a family." Anna gave Nick a naughty grin and Nick hoped he didn't look too horrified at the suggestion. Lauren sniggered.

"Your job," Leo went on, "and your *only* job is to find out which taverna we're talking about and whether our man is here. Just wait around until you spot him. Drink some coffee or something. The rest of us will hang back and check out the immediate area."

*

"Should have brought our swimming gear," said Nick.

"You're brave," said Anna and she had a point. It was windy now and the heat was beginning to go out of the sun, this late in the season.

The three of them ambled into the little seaside town. Most of the accommodation seemed to be on this side of town and they passed signs for several places. Káto Zákros itself was a beach with a string of tavernas behind it. That was pretty much it. Leo was right, a task force of seven would have been painfully visible.

The first taverna looked more like a café, with round, bright blue, metal tables and canvas chairs. A blackboard in a white frame displayed their menu. The second looked more traditional, with rectangular wooden tables and wood and rattan chairs and had positioned itself as the family taverna. There were a couple of hot-looking motorbikes parked on the left and Nick wondered if either of them belonged to Dión. He saw a print of a bull he recognised from Knossós on the lintel to his left and then a blue awning advertising Taverna Gláros. Immediately beyond that, was a more discreet sign saying simply Nóstos.

There were tables on either side of the road, mostly inside, on the left, and mostly outside, on the right, just behind the beach. A giant tamarisk and some rather tired-looking parasols provided protection from the sun or, today, from the wind. Was it the cool, dark green décor or the use of French in part of the blackboard menu? Nick was not sure, but something suggested a leaning towards fish and seafood and an air of sophistication.

"I bet it's *this* one," he whispered to Anna and Lauren.

He circled, stood for a moment, hands on hips, and then ambled back to Taverna Gláros and sat down at a table on the right, fronting the road. The others followed.

"Shouldn't one of us be at the other end?" whispered Anna.

"The other place looked like a café to me. This place looks like it might be worthy of his talents. If we don't see him here by, say, twelve thirty, one of us can move closer to the other one. But I can just about see Anamnésia from here, anyway."

Nick checked his watch. It was thirteen minutes before twelve. An effusive waiter arrived but they ignored his sales pitch and ordered coffees: Greek for Anna, cappuccino for Lauren and a flat white for Nick.

Nick was able to see one or two people moving around Nóstos but no young men.

"I wonder what time he's supposed to arrive," he said.

"Some places don't start serving lunch till one," said Anna as if Nick really were a tourist, "so he has a little time."

"Maybe he only works evenings, though," said Lauren.

"Don't say that," said Nick. "I don't fancy hanging about all day."

He sent a text to Leo, confirming they were in position and promising to let him know of the first sighting. By the time the waiter returned with their coffees, Nick had weakened.

"Tell you what," he said, "let me have one of those lemon custard tarts." The waiter beamed at him and waddled off to get it.

"God, he's a bit OTT, isn't he?" said Lauren. "You'd think Jesus had handed him fifty euros from the look he gave you."

Nick was still polishing his halo when he heard a powerful motorbike, idling.

"I don't want to turn and look," he said to Lauren. "Is it him?"

She moved slightly to peer around her father.

"I think so." Nick saw Anna nodding, too. "He's on a Moto Guzzi, I think. I can see the eagle and there's a V100 badge. It's beautiful. He's not half bad, either. Oh, and here's your tart, Dad."

Lauren's fascination with motorbikes had started early, he remembered. Nick recalled the brand, but all he knew was that they were Italian and fast.

*

Once Leo knew it seemed to be Dión and he was indeed working at Nóstos, he had decisions to make. They concerned where and when. Should they arrest him at the taverna or set up a roadblock just outside the village and catch him on his way back after the lunch service? If the taverna, should they arrest him right away or wait until all the lunches had been cooked? Also, should they warn the taverna owner, or not?

As a courtesy, he discussed this with Státhis. He expressed concern for the image of police barging into a tourist taverna to arrest the chef.

"It does not look good, Lieutenant," he said. "And it's always better, in my opinion, to choose the option with the lowest number of bystanders. Then, there are fewer people at risk, of course, but also, fewer people to observe us using heavy-handed tactics or making a mess of it."

It seemed a rather defensive approach to Leo, but it was hard to argue with the logic. He had not considered that Dión might be armed, but he could easily be carrying a knife.

"So, you would favour the roadblock."

"Yes, and I have a stinger with me."

This, Leo knew, was an informal term for a TDD or Tyre Deflation Device – a spiked strip which can be thrown in the path of vehicles to puncture their tyres.

"Are they safe to use on motorcycles?"

"For whom, sir?"

"The rider, I'm talking about," said Leo with some irritation.

"They are not without risk."

"In that case, I need your loud hailer. I can warn him to stop as soon as I see him turn away from the roadblock. Then, if he pays no attention, it's his risk."

The sergeant nodded, but looked unconvinced, Leo thought.

"So, how exactly would this work?" Leo asked.

"I'm thinking we place the roadblock just around the bend as the road leaves town. He won't see it until he's twenty-five metres from it. We set it up soon and we wave cars through until we're told he's coming."

"So, we leave one person near the taverna."

"Yes. Someone we can rely on to keep alert. Two or three of us will be manning the roadblock. When he or she calls, one of us will walk back fifty metres or so with the stinger and lie in wait, concealed, if possible."

"And then what?"

"My thinking is that he will not proceed to the roadblock, sir. Even though it's the only way out of the town, he will turn back as soon as he sees it. However, by this time, I will have deployed the stinger. His tyres will deflate rapidly but not dangerously. He should remain in control of the motorcycle but unable to go anywhere."

"And then what, you arrest him single-handedly?"

The sergeant had not thought this through.

"I was thinking all three of us would do that, sir."

"But we'll be at least fifty metres away. If the man is not injured, he could run away from you or even attack you, Sergeant. I do not want a dangerous criminal running amok in your nice, little seaside town."

"No, sir. Nor me."

"I think the roadblock and the stinger are good ideas, we just need the right people in the right places. I suggest we leave Lauren near the restaurant, assuming her father agrees. She is young and should be alert, which is what we need. Also, she is a civilian; I don't want her getting involved in any rough stuff."

"No, of course not, sir."

"That leaves six of us, including Nick, who will insist on being involved if I know him."

Státhis was nodding, waiting for specifics.

"I think we need a backstop. Someone who stays near the village. Let's make it Nick. He's quite a big fellow, should it come to any rough stuff, and he can handle himself. But I would not expect him to be needed unless it all goes wrong. The remaining five, we split: two of us on the roadblock and three of us fifty metres nearer the village. You, Sergeant, will be one of the three and will deploy the stinger. You will be assisted in making the arrest by Constable Dimítris and Sergeant Zerbáki."

"So, you will be manning the roadblock, sir."

"I will, assisted by Constable Pandelís."

"And you will be in a position to arrest the man should he proceed to the roadblock."

"That's the idea."

"Are you thinking we three will be able to conceal ourselves somehow, sir? Only it might be a bit of a challenge if I remember right."

"Let's take a look, Sergeant. I want us all set up by one thirty, just in case no one turns up for lunch today."

*

"That's a pity," said Leo. "You were right, Sergeant."

There was no cover whatsoever near the bend. Státhis had remembered well. Leo glanced at his watch. It was already twelve forty.

"Okay," he said, "if you leave the stinger in its bag, how long would it take you to whip it out and deploy it?"

"Ten seconds. Fifteen, worst case, sir."

"Leo glanced up and down the road. Okay," he said. "Let's see you do it."

He stared at his watch as, out of the corner of his eye, he saw Státhis pop the catch, upend the cylindrical bag, pick up the stinger and carefully throw it across the road, keeping hold of one end.

"Eleven seconds. Well done."

"Sir. That was a good one. Sometimes it needs a little adjustment if I haven't thrown it exactly right, so best assume fifteen."

"I did the sums earlier, when we were waiting in the car. We are four hundred and forty metres from the taverna here. We'll set the roadblock at five hundred metres. If Dión rides that motorbike as it should be ridden, I could see him accelerating rapidly up to eighty or ninety kilometres an hour as he leaves the village. I doubt he'd go faster on these roads. If he *averaged* sixty kilometres an hour for the trip, he would be doing a kilometre in a minute, so he'd be here in twenty-six seconds."

"The way those things accelerate, he could average more, sir."

"Possibly. At an average of seventy, it would be twenty-three seconds. I can't see how it could be any faster."

"And then he has to slow down and turn round."

"Yes, so I think we're okay, then. We'll have Lauren make the call the second he mounts his motorbike."

Leo glanced around him. The roadside was a strip of barren grass and rocks with a vertical fall of ten metres on the seaward side and a rock face to the landward.

"Okay. There's nowhere to hide. And I think the three of you together would look suspicious to Dión. So, let's leave the stinger by the roadside in its bag, right here. We'll have Anna and Dimítris looking like tourists, coming down the hill from the roadblock, holding hands."

"Ha! He's a bit young for her, Lieutenant."

"She won't mind that," he replied, "and Dión won't have time to figure it out."

"I suppose not."

"Meanwhile, you are coming *up* the road, making for the stinger. I reckon you wait, thirty metres from the stinger, and walk steadily towards it the second we receive the call. At four kilometres per hour, it will take you twenty-seven seconds."

"It's too tight, sir."

"Then walk a little bit faster, for God's sake, but I don't want him seeing you there all together."

"Why not have the other two set off from the roadblock itself then, sir? They'll have twenty metres further to walk than me."

"Meaning they could still be twenty metres off when the shit goes down, Sergeant."

"I realise, sir, but I'm sure we'd cope. Twenty metres is nothing."

"All right then, that's what we'll do. Go measure out thirty metres and put a marker down. Then start setting up the roadblock. I'll send Dimítris and Pandélis to give you a hand."

"Yes, sir."

*

Nick was not best pleased when Leo explained his role as the backstop.

"I was hoping for a more active role, frankly," he said. "I'm more a number eight than a fullback."

"I don't know what that means, Nick, but you proved yourself in action already. This time let's try and keep you safe, especially with your daughter here, eh? Anyway, the backstop will be crucial, if it all goes wrong. Someone must save the day and protect the village. I'm trusting you with that."

"Gee, thanks. You'd better not cock it up, then, because there's only so much a pedestrian can do against a speeding motorbike. If it were me, I'd just barge into the taverna right now and grab the bastard."

"We've been through that, and the arrest needs to be outside the village. You'll be fine, Nick. We've planned all the little details. Don't worry."

"What about me?" asked Lauren. "Am I supposed to just sit around and twiddle my thumbs?"

"Yours is a vital job," said Leo. "Do you have your cell phone with you?"

"Of course."

"Is it fully charged?"

Lauren removed it from her bag and turned it on.

"Shouldn't be a problem," she said.

"Then I want you to put me into your list of contacts and call me the second Dión reaches his motorbike. This is important, Lauren."

She asked for his number, and he watched as she set it up.

"Now call me," he said.

After a few seconds, there was a bleeping in his pocket.

"Great. Now, don't get distracted, don't fall asleep and keep your eyes on him for me. The rest of the team is relying on you, Lauren."

"No pressure then," she grinned.

"And when you've made the call, stroll in my direction," said Nick. "I'll be about a hundred and fifty metres along there."

"Sure thing, Dad."

The others left Taverna Gláros and Lauren was alone. Nóstos was about a third full, so not a busy lunchtime. She could see Dión bobbing around in the kitchen. He seemed fully occupied for now and the waiters were still taking orders, she saw. She was conscious of having sat there a long time now but dared not move. She ordered herself a croissant with cheese and ham, more to seem plausible than because she was hungry. She was too nervous for that.

CHAPTER 26
THE KILL

Leo and Anna left Nick at the bottom of the hill and strolled up. Leo checked his watch. It was twenty past one. As they came around the bend, they saw the temporary roadblock was in place, with the Karoq tucked in behind. The striped bar was up and Pandelís was waving the odd car through with a friendly, *nothing to worry about* smile.

"All set?" asked Leo when all five of them were together.

Everyone nodded and gave each other encouraging smiles. They were excited, Leo saw.

"I want you in place, Sergeant," he said. "It might be a wait, I'm afraid, but the call could come through anytime and I need you there."

"No problem, sir."

"And you two," he addressed Dimítris and Anna, "need to practise being a happily married couple."

"Oooh," said Anna, "I don't think I've ever seen one of those, sir. What is it they do?"

*

Time dragged on. The waiter asked her twice if he could get her anything else after taking away the half-eaten croissant. People had stopped arriving at Nóstos, but dishes were still coming out of the kitchen. A French guy asked her pointedly if she was waiting for someone, so she said thank you, her husband had been delayed but was expected any moment. It was twenty past two. She had been there over three hours.

Nick had been walking up and down a fifty-metre stretch outside the village. A couple of young lads were working on a dilapidated scooter by the roadside. Parked nearby was a rakish-looking dirt bike. The engine would not be large, perhaps as little as 125 cc, but the spare frame and the deep tread tyres were exactly what was needed

261

for roads and tracks that had never seen tarmac. And there were quite a few in this area, Nick had observed. On the second pass, he smiled at them sympathetically. He remembered only too well the long, fruitless hours working on failing vehicles as a teenager. On the third pass, he stopped and said:

"Can you fix it?"

The older of the two stood and stretched his back.

"It's a heap of shit, mister, but yes, we fix it again, for now."

"Is this one yours?" Nick said, jerking his head at the dirt bike.

"Yes, man."

"Now that is *not* a heap of shit."

"No, man. It's cool. You wanna see?"

"Hey, we're not finished here!" called the other guy.

"I'm doing you a favour, bro, so you can wait five minutes. All right?"

He got on the motorbike, kickstarted it, and roared off in a cloud of dust. At the foot of the hill, he did a slide turn then came racing back past them, front wheel raised high in the air. When Nick turned around, he was tearing at them from the village before skidding sideways to stop half a metre from Nick's foot. He grinned, like a naughty kid with his favourite toy.

"Pretty good, mister – No?"

"Pretty good," admitted Nick.

"You wanna try?"

Nick glanced at his watch. There was still a little time, he guessed.

"Sure. Why not? I don't suppose you have a crash helmet?"

The boy stared at him like he was a pussy.

"Never mind," Nick said.

*

It took Lauren's brain a second to register that she could no longer see Dión in the kitchen. She glanced at her phone and saw two forty-three pm. When she looked up, he was right there, jogging past her in a light training jacket and jeans. As she grabbed her phone, it started ringing. An image of her mother's face appeared, just as he jumped onto the motorbike. She tried to call Leo, but the phone would not let her without dealing with her mother's call first.

"For fuck's sake," she yelled at the little screen.

"Is that you, sweetheart?" said Jen.

"No!" she yelled and cut her off, just as the motorbike roared to life.

Tears of frustration forming, her hands shook as she scrolled through her contacts and pressed Leo's name. He answered immediately.

"He's coming," she said.

"We know."

Looking up, she saw the motorbike was already a hundred metres away.

*

When his phone bleeped, Státhis started to walk. The others were out of sight, but they would have started down from the roadblock at precisely the same time, he knew. He could already hear the motorbike and glanced behind him. The guy was coming like a bat out of hell. He looked ahead to where the stinger was stashed. He was not going to make it. He started to run.

Dimítris and Anna were holding hands. They could hear the tremendous roar from the motorbike echoing from the rock walls to their left. Soon they would see it – and Dión them. Anna moved her body closer to his. But then they heard the throttle close and the revolutions drop. They glanced at each other, uncertainly. As they rounded the corner, they saw the motorbike weaving slowly. The guy was sitting on it like a jockey, half-standing, and looking in their direction. They were still thirty metres from Státhis who was a few metres short of the stinger. They saw the motorcyclist's eyes flicker between them, then he glanced over his shoulder. The sergeant was picking up the stinger, in slow motion, it seemed to them. They saw Dión's eyes change. Steely determination had replaced the uncertainty. He slewed the bike around and opened the throttle.

The machine responded instantly, and the engine howled. Státhis ripped the stinger from its case and threw himself sideways. They saw the stinger flying through the air but so did Dión and, without hesitation, he floored the bike and started to slide. He was still doing seventy kilometres an hour or more but now the bike was on its side. They heard him screaming now. He must have trapped his leg. Now he and the bike were bumping over the impotent stinger. It tore at him, and he squealed, but the tyres looked undamaged. Anna and Dimítris started to run. Státhis was on his feet now, but Dión was still sliding, a streak of bright blood glistening on the tarmac. He came to a stop twenty metres beyond the stinger. All three police officers were converging on him. Anna was wondering if this beautiful, evil boy was dead when she saw him struggle to his feet, clasping his bleeding leg. He looked back at them, staggered for a second, then shook his head. He pulled the motorbike up, almost fell astride it and managed to restart the thing. As he roared away down the hill, Anna saw his left leg trailing, dripping blood.

*

"What are you playing at, Dad?" called Lauren when she spotted him on the dirt bike.

"Just a little insurance," he said.

"Where did you get it?"

He jerked his head at the two lads. The owner had gone back to helping his brother fiddle with the scooter. Nick pressed his index finger to his lips. Lauren rolled her eyes, then Nick saw her spin her head around at the scream of the Moto Guzzi as it raced down the hill. They saw the three police officers giving up the chase. The plan had failed, and Dión was racing back towards them! But there was only one way out of the village. What was he thinking? In a few seconds, Nick saw the desperation in those extraordinary eyes. At the same time, it dawned on both Lauren and the owner of the dirt bike what was about to happen.

"Dad, no!" shrieked Lauren.

And, as he pulled away, in pursuit:

"What the fuck, man?" called the young bike owner, gesticulating.

Nick's motorbike skills were thirty-five years in the past. It had been an ancient BSA C15. A faithful, old chugger. It was utterly reliable, but he had struggled to get it beyond forty-five miles an hour, even downhill with the wind behind him. If that was a carthorse, this was a bucking bronco. It was an entirely different beast and he needed to learn fast.

He saw tourists and diners scatter in alarm as Dión roared dangerously past the string of tavernas, culminating in Nóstos where a young woman spread her arms and shrieked at him. Immediately before Akrogiáli taverna, he swung left at the last moment. Nick overshot the bend and had to slam on both brakes to avoid hitting the wall of the taverna. He had lost ground, and the Moto Guzzi was twenty metres ahead now. He saw Dión swing left again at a turn where green name signs clustered under a banner sign for ACCOMMODATION. There were bigger signs for Athéna Rooms and Yiánni's Retreat and there were two of the brown and yellow signs the Greeks use for sites of cultural interest. As he swung the bike left, he saw that one said something about archaeology.

The road was no longer tarmac, but dusty concrete that juddered the handlebars. Nick kept his head low, trying to minimise the drag from his body. To his astonishment, he found himself racing past the rubble of some Minoan settlement. A handful of tourists gathered at an information lectern turned to watch him fly by. Away to the right, he saw the church of Saint Anthony and then they were climbing, winding their way through the village of Ano Zákros. The road deteriorated further as they left the village behind them, and Nick throttled back as the track seemed to run into mid-air. Then he saw Dión navigate it with a huge lean left, into the bend, the rear wheel slithering and sliding as he accelerated around it. As he approached, Nick saw the hairpin was on the edge of a steep fall into a gorge, now at least a hundred metres below. He felt the inside of his palms moisten as he gingerly swung into it. Breathing again, he saw he had lost more ground, but the road was nothing more than a red dirt track now. His bike would come into its own. The Moto Guzzi was essentially a road racer and would struggle with the ruts and the thick dust.

As they raced uphill once more, he saw that he was gaining. The last house in the village appeared, up a driveway to his right. Beyond, there was nothing but barren hillside as far as the eye could see. They would be high now, he figured. Perhaps three or four hundred metres up. He negotiated a right-hand bend, then a sharp left and right with a faint track off to the left and then they were racing downhill. He was still gaining and now, he saw, Dión was barely holding on. There was something wrong with his left leg and, by the way he was slumped on the machine, he seemed to be losing strength. But they were still racing down the track, heading back towards the gorge.

Nick yelled: "Dión!" "Stop!" and "For Christ's sake, stop, man!" but he kept on going. Now Nick was less than ten metres behind, but the track was doing the same thing again, heading into mid-air. It must be another sharp left, close by the gorge edge, he figured. He throttled back and saw the Moto Guzzi winning back ground from him. Why was Dión *not* slowing? Was the bend not as dangerous as it looked? Nick relaxed for a moment, only to realise with a start, that he was still going way too fast. He braked hard but Dión did not. He would have to lean hard into the bend right now, to have any chance of making it. Then, it was almost as if Dión had woken up. He sat up momentarily, then hurled himself over to the left. But it was too much, surely. Nick saw the bike tilt sharply, skitter around the beginning of the bend and then fall flat on its left-hand side, crushing that wounded leg. For a long moment, Nick watched helplessly as the motorbike slid backwards towards the edge. He skidded to a halt and saw Dión groping for something, anything to grab onto but there was no vegetation in this utterly barren place.

Nick ran towards the cliff edge, but he was always going to be too late. Suddenly the noise stopped, and Dión wasn't there anymore. No screams. Just the screeching of tortured metal. The motorbike was mangling itself against the rocks as it tumbled down the walls of the gorge until, with an echoing, final bang, it stopped. A rush of dust flew up from the valley floor, then silence. Utter silence. In the sky, a Griffin vulture turned a gimlet eye in the direction of the noise.

Nick was on his stomach, two metres from the cliff edge. He raised himself to his knees and padded back three or four metres before getting shakily to his feet.

Nick suppressed an urge to throw up, but now he was wracked with self-doubt. Had giving chase been the right thing to do? Dión would still be alive if he had not. Alive and free to kill, perhaps, but maybe not. Had he pressured the boy into a fatal accident? Had the loss of blood caused him to pass out, momentarily, or had Dión not really tried to negotiate that final hairpin? Had he given up, right there? Memories of the Westminster Bridge suicide flew back into Nick's head. Had he done it again? Had he gone too far again? As he wheeled the dirt bike back up the hill, he felt the salt sting of tears, hot in his eyes.

A few minutes later, he saw the police Karoq coming up through Ano Zákros in a ball of dust. He saw Leo and Anna and the sergeant from Sitía. Lauren was not with them, and he was glad about that. As they pulled up beside him, he said:

"It's over, Leo. The boy went over the edge. I'm so sorry."

Leo was out of the vehicle in a flash, holding Nick's shoulders and looking into his eyes.

"You did your best, Nick. We all know that. This is not your fault."

"You don't know that. And neither do I. If anyone's to blame, it's me."

"A young hothead, a deeply flawed young man, burns himself out in spectacular style after killing two young women. If anyone is to blame, it's Dión, not you, Nick Fisher."

Nick stared back at him, sadly.

"I could have done more."

"It's *not* your fault," Leo repeated. "Now, are you up to showing us where it happened?"

CHAPTER 27

ON THE SHELF

Nick abandoned the dirt bike and joined them in the Karoq for the long haul back up the side of the mountain. A few minutes later, as they approached the second hairpin, he said:

"It was here. Right here."

They parked up and got out. They saw Státhis stride towards the cliff edge and gingerly lean over. He called out to them:

"The boy's still here," he said. "The bike's gone down a thousand metres or more, smashed to pieces on the valley floor, but our boy only fell about ten metres. There's a grassy shelf of rock and it caught him. He's hanging off it, dead or unconscious. I don't know which."

They joined the sergeant and hesitantly peered over the edge.

"One thing's for sure," said Leo. "If he *is* unconscious and comes to in that position, the first thing he's going to do is fall."

Nick looked and saw Dión's left arm and the mangled left leg hanging over the edge. If his body made the smallest shift to the left, he would fall.

"It might be for the best, sir," said Státhis.

"We are police officers, Sergeant," said Leo. "We have a duty to preserve life."

"Even the life of a double murderer, sir?"

"Yes."

"Even if it involves great personal risk, sir?"

"That's a judgment call, but yes. Risk comes with the job. You know it."

"I don't know about you, sir, but I don't fancy putting my life in grave danger to save a double murderer, especially when he might already be dead."

"As the senior police officer present, it's my responsibility."

"With respect, sir, I am the senior police officer in this prefecture."

Nick had heard enough. He turned to Anna.

"I don't suppose there's a winch on that thing?" He nodded towards the Karoq.

"No, Nick. It's an SUV. Anyway, Greek police budgets don't stretch that far. There might be some rope or something."

"Let's go check."

They left the others and went to the Karoq. Miracle of miracles, there was a coil of nylon rope. Eight millimetre or so, Nick reckoned. He uncoiled it and stretched it out. It was about eight metres long.

"Is there any more?" he asked.

Anna shook her head.

"Just the stinger," she volunteered.

"The what?"

"The thing we throw across the road to stop cars."

"How long is it?"

"About five metres, I guess."

Anna took it out of its bag and Nick came over and looked at it. It looked like a spiky garden trellis. It was made of metal but did not look particularly robust.

"Would it take my weight?" he asked.

"I've no idea, Nick. I wouldn't bet my life on it."

Nick lifted it. It had some weight to it, perhaps two or three kilos.

"Here, grab one end," he said.

She did, and they pulled on it, tug-of-war style, for several seconds. It held.

Now she saw Nick put a knot in the rope before attaching the end to the stinger using a special knot which he tied with some care.

"I hope you won't need this, later," he said. "This may never come undone."

Now she saw him slip under the Karoq and tie the other end of the rope to a chassis member.

"How's your driving?" he asked.

Anna looked nervous.

"I need you to take the vehicle to within a metre of the cliff edge. I'll show you where."

"No. I don't think I can do it, Nick."

"Of course, you can. I'll be guiding you."

Anna felt the sweat break out on her palms.

"The other sergeant, Státhis. It's his regular ride, sir. Wouldn't it be better to ask him?"

Nick glanced over to where the other two seemed still to be discussing the ethics and morality of the situation.

"What's going on, guys?" he yelled.

"We're deciding who goes down."

"*I'm* going down. It's my fault he's there at all. No argument."

"But you're a *civilian*, Nick," said Leo.

"And you're a semi-invalid, the sergeant is overweight and poor Anna is already terrified, so let's just get on with it, shall we? The boy could regain consciousness at any moment."

The relief from the police officers was tangible. Someone else was going to do it. A biggish man in his late fifties, but undeniably fit. He would be okay. And they could see it would be cathartic for him. He needed to do it. They understood. Thank God.

"All right, Nick," said Leo. "How can we help?"

Nick dragged the stinger with the rope attached so it ran back under the centre of the Karoq, away from the wheels. Then he asked Státhis to drive it forward to the cliff edge.

"No, *don't* put your seat belt on, you idiot," he called, "you might need to jump."

The sergeant went pale and looked desperately nervous, but he started the engine and inched forward steadily with Nick and Leo posted on either side of the vehicle, pacing with him, towards the edge.

"Just two more metres," called Nick. "There's not much rope. We need to get close. Very slowly now."

Finally, Nick was able to call:

"Now stop! Now apply the handbrake. All the way. Now put it in neutral and switch off. Now engage reverse."

Státhis had to be helped out of the driving seat. He was shaking and his shirt was drenched. Nick carefully led him around to the rear of the vehicle, well away from the edge.

"Well done, mate. That was bravely done," he said.

"You haven't got a smoke, I suppose," the sergeant said.

"Sorry, mate, I gave up."

"So did I."

Leo was looking over the edge again.

"I think I saw him move," he said. "Just a twitch of the right foot, but I think he's alive."

"Not for long, if he moves the wrong way," said Nick.

And now there was added urgency in Nick's movements as he crawled around the front bumper, working in the single metre between that and oblivion, trying not to think about it. *Stay practical* he said to himself. He held onto the bumper with one hand and used the other to tug through the rope, and eventually the stinger. Then he let it all drop over the edge.

"You're joking with me, Nick," said Leo, in shocked tones. "You're not going down on that, surely?"

"It's all there is, Leo. You don't have a winch. Any other suggestions are welcome. I think it's strong enough, and, if I'm lucky, I might not have to use the stinger end."

"But how will you grip the rope?"

"By gripping it. There's no magic, Leo. No crampons around, are there? I think I'm strong enough. I put a knot in above the stinger to hold onto in case I'm not. Then you guys might have to haul me up."

"What about him? We can't haul both of you up."

"You might have to – one at a time."

"But that would leave you on the ledge without a rope, Nick. It's windy and the ledge is no more than four or five square metres."

"Then I'll keep my head down and whistle till you drop the rope back."

"It's crazy, Nick. I forbid it."

"Shut up, Leo, for God's sake. Just tell me whether the rope reaches the ledge. Can you see?"

Leo leaned tentatively over the edge, once more.

"No. I'd say it's about three metres short. But, with the stinger, it's hanging around two metres below the ledge."

"Okay. That'll have to do. Now, keep your eyes on the rope where it runs between these rocks. I think it's smooth enough but let me know right away if it starts to fray or chafe."

Leo was wide-eyed, shaking his head. He did not understand.

"Tell me immediately if the rope gets damaged. Okay?"

"All right, Nick."

"Now you'd best get the two sergeants here. And when you pull on the ropes, do it with your backs to the vehicle, rather than leaning over the cliff, or we'll all fall off. And that would be rather embarrassing."

It was not the word Leo would have chosen, but he summoned the nervous-looking sergeants as requested.

"Right," said Nick. "Here we go." And, with that, he grabbed the rope with both hands and lowered himself over the edge.

The wind was immediately stronger, hot and gusty, but Nick did not mind. It was something tangible to fight against. He glanced below him and tried to focus on the grassy shoulder rather than the sheer drop to the valley floor, hundreds of metres below. It was just ten metres down. He could almost jump it. All he needed to do was stay focused. He hooked his legs around the rope to reduce the strain on his hands and then brought one hand down about thirty centimetres before bringing the other down to join it. He then moved his legs down a similar distance and clamped them around the rope again. This was not difficult, he decided. He just needed to keep on doing it and try not to think about where he was.

He kept his eyes on the cliff face with the occasional glance up at Leo and kept going. Right hand down, left to join it, then both legs. He resisted all temptation to increase the thirty centimetres and he did not look down. He counted each thirty-centimetre descent. It was agonisingly slow, but he was getting there. *Sigá-sigá* he repeated to himself, like a mantra. After twenty iterations, he glanced down. He was three or four metres above the ledge now, but the wind had pushed him to one side, away from Dión. If he carried on down, he would miss the ledge by a metre or more. He had made no allowance for the strong, offshore wind when deciding where to drop the rope. Nevertheless, he carried on, hand over hand until his feet found the knot.

Now, he lowered himself a few times more until his hands were grasping the knot, legs flailing rather than attempting to grip the stinger. Decision time. He looked again. He was less than two metres higher than the ledge and could drop to it without using the stinger, but first, he needed to be directly above the ledge, rather than to one side of it. Without any support from his legs, the strain on his hands was much worse. He clamped his fingers together around the rope, resting all his weight on the knot. He looked again at the ledge. He could swing the rope sideways, to get himself above it, he reckoned, but then he would have to time his jump with great care. Too early and he would fall, too late and he would collide with Dión and knock him off, maybe them both. Too risky, he decided. Instead, he needed to swing, not just to his right, but *both* to his right *and* away from the cliff face. He could then jump on the return swing. That way, he would slam into the cliff face, rather than hitting Dión. It was still risky. He would have to make damned sure he stayed on the ledge and didn't bounce off it into oblivion. He glanced up at Leo, who must have sensed this was the moment because he raised a clenched fist. Nick swung into the cliff face, then kicked off with his legs.

He started with a couple of straight swings to gauge the distance, then tried a partly sideways kicking motion to take him over the ledge. It worked! He did it twice more, each time estimating the point at which he would jump. He saw that the momentum of the rope dragged part of the stinger onto the ledge each time, before pulling it away. That was important. He would need to turn around and grab it, once landed, otherwise, the rope might settle out of reach. He did not relish having to leap from the ledge into mid-air to catch a dangling rope. That might be too much for his poor, old heart.

Now he listened to the wind, felt the rhythm of its gusts. A sudden, huge gust could be a problem. Then he wiped his wet hands one by one on his shorts, changed his hands back to one above the other rather than interlocked, so he could get free in an instant, glanced one final time at Leo and kicked off from the cliff. As he swung out, he thought he heard cheering from above. It seemed odd. As he started the backswing towards the ledge, he saw Dión getting to his feet. Somehow, he had survived regaining consciousness, and now those eyes were tracking Nick's trajectory.

Nick's brain screamed *Abort*, but the momentum was in the rope. It carried him to the cliff face about a metre above Dión's head. He kicked off again, but now something felt very different. He looked down and saw Dión gripping the stinger. *You crazy bastard*, he thought. He saw blood streaming from the killer's hands. Would he be able to hold on? Or would the stinger break and plunge him to the valley floor? Would the rope cope with the weight of them both?

The boy did not want to die. Nick could see it in his tortured, desperate face. But what could they do now? The added weight had caused the rope to lose momentum. Now they were hanging at the mercy of the wind, one or two metres to the left of the ledge. To get back there, they would need to work together on the slanted kick-offs and agree on who was to attempt the jump and when. Then, once landed, that person would need to grab the rope and help the other one in. Except that Dión might not do that. He might leave him dangling, so Nick would have to be the jumper. But Dión would need to understand what the hell Nick was trying to do, or he could panic or try to fight. Nick did not have enough Greek. He would have to shout above the roaring wind in English and hope like hell Dión understood what he was saying.

Nick felt rising terror. He knew it had to be controlled, otherwise his mind would turn to mush. He took a deep breath and concentrated on the cliff face, despite the agony in his hands. He forced himself to register each sand-coloured rock, every little patch of scree, every one of the tiny, immaculate, blue flowers. He would get out of this. They would get out of this. He just needed to stay calm. Think. He closed his eyes for a moment.

When he looked again, the blue flowers were not in the same place. Was he dreaming or were they lower? Just a fraction. And then he felt an unmistakable tug on the rope and the flowers dropped ten centimetres. Slowly but surely, they were being hauled up.

Státhis was sweating profusely again, but at least he was driving *away* from the cliff edge this time. Immediately Leo witnessed Dión's extraordinary leap onto the stinger, he knew something had to be done, or both Dión and Nick would be killed. He ordered the sergeant back into the Karoq and told him to reverse it slowly and steadily away from the cliff edge.

"Remember, it's already in reverse, so you need to depress the clutch, *then* switch on and get the revs up before releasing the clutch and letting off the handbrake. If you stall, it could be the last thing you do in this world," he told the terrified officer who did not even want to climb back in, so close to the edge. "Get a grip, man," he added, "and be quick about it. At least *you're* not dangling from the end of a rope."

Leo hoped to God Nick's knots were good and the rope could handle the weight. He watched closely for any fraying or chafing of the fibre as Státhis reversed. As soon as he saw Nick's hands appear above the edge, he yelled at the sergeant to stop. Grasping the rope behind them with one hand and one of Nick's wrists each with the other, Leo and Anna hauled him clear of the edge. He lay on his stomach for a moment and then rolled himself further away from the edge. Leo raised his hand to the sergeant and the vehicle continued backwards. Leo saw the top of the stinger appear and then catch on a rock. The rope was pulling it out of shape, stretching the metal.

"Stop!" he yelled, raising his hand again. This time, Státhis left the Karoq and came back to join them.

"We're going to have to pull him up this last bit or the stinger will break," cried Leo.

He leaned over and spoke to Dión in Greek. The boy looked utterly shattered, defeated. He would give them no trouble now.

Still gripping the rope with their other hands, Státhis and Leo reached over and hauled the twisted stinger up until they could make a grab for the boy's wrists. As soon as they did so, the stinger broke in half and the rear section careered away in the wind. Sergeant Anna joined them and grabbed a handful of the boy's clothing to help drag him over the top.

Nick was on his feet now, they saw, as they handcuffed the boy and read him his rights. Anna was already calling for medical assistance; the boy's left leg was a mangled mess, and he could put no weight on it without yelping like a wounded hound.

"We'll get them to take a look at those, too," she said, prising open Nick's red raw hands.

"Pah!" he said, "a little antiseptic cream and I'll be right as rain. Might stay away from cliffs for a while, though."

"You'll be having nightmares, I should imagine."

Nick strolled over to Leo.

"Thank you, my friend," he said.

"What for?"

"Finding reverse gear."

"That was Státhis."

"Ah. Then I think he'll be needing one of your cigarettes."

CHAPTER 28
LOGGERHEADS

As the boat puttered into the shallows, Teddy cut the engine and jumped out. Now he was hauling the boat to the shingle while the others waited to greet them.

"Welcome back, guys," called Dan, beaming.

Alma was smiling, too, Nick saw, and Stefi seemed quite overcome. As their feet hit the shingle, he buried his head in Nick's shoulder and sobbed. It was several seconds before he surfaced, but now he was grinning through the tears. He stretched out his arm to include Lauren in the embrace.

"My saviours," he said. "I owe you so much."

"You owe us nothing, Stefi," said Nick. "Just make the dream work now. That will be our reward."

"I think I can now, Nick. I really think I can."

*

With the cooler weather, Dan had prepared a feast of lamb giouvétsi for them. The aromas of the spices and the rich, tomato sauce filled their senses as they entered the communal hut. And there was a fine red wine, too, Stefi added.

"It's the best I have, as befits the occasion," he said, handing a bottle to Nick. "It's a blend of Syrah and Kotsifáli grapes. Cretan white grapes can stand on their own but the reds, like Kotsifáli, benefit from mixing with foreign varieties."

"Like Syrah."

"Yes, Nick. The grapes are *grown* here but Syrah is not indigenous. It is not a Cretan grape."

Nick was turning the dark bottle in his hand. He saw it was already seven years in the bottle. On the label, he saw three swallows in flight.

"Philoxenía. This is the name?" he asked.

"Yes, my friend. And you know what means this?"

"It's the Greek welcome, isn't it? Showing great hospitality to others."

"Yes, but it is more than this, even. And we are not entirely altruistic in this. It means show hospitality to strangers *and you will benefit from this.*"

"Like the grapes?"

Stefi slapped him on the back.

"We make a Greek of you yet, Nick Fisher," he bellowed.

As they tucked into the hearty chunks of lamb and the slippery pasta, Nick went through everything that had happened.

"What was he like, this Dión?" asked Alma.

The room hushed. She was asking about her daughter's murderer.

"Just another wild, young man, in many ways, Alma," said Nick. "Despite his good looks and his cooking talents, I think he was deeply insecure. Losing a leg and spending twenty years in jail won't improve that, I'm afraid."

"I didn't know he was losing his leg."

"There's still a chance the doctors can save it, but I have my doubts."

There was a protracted pause.

"Let's talk about something more cheerful," said Lauren. "Where are you with the project now, Stefi? Did the bank ever get back to you?"

It was Dan who answered.

"The bank are on board. No question," he said. "They liked what they heard from us, this time around, and made us a substantial loan offer on quite reasonable terms."

"But not quite substantial enough," added Stefi.

"It wasn't everything we wanted, but it's a serious, long-term commitment," Dan added.

"They offered a facility of up to two and a half million euros, Nick," continued Stefi. "We can draw on it over the next three years. But we needed three million."

He was looking at Alma, Nick noticed. She gave him the tiniest of nods, accompanied by a slow closing of those delightful eyelids.

"That's when Alma came up with the rest – as equity, rather than debt."

Nick raised his eyebrows and looked enquiringly at Alma.

"I've put in half a million euros, Nick, for fifteen per cent of the shares and a seat on the board. It's most of the insurance money but I wanted to do it in Roz's memory. This project is something she truly believed in."

"It's a lot of money, Alma. I hope you took some financial advice."

"My financial adviser didn't want me to do it but then she's never done anything entrepreneurial in her life. And I don't *need* the money. Not really. If it all goes pear-shaped, I won't starve. I wouldn't have done it if I didn't think it was a sound investment, mind you."

"Spoken like a true Scottish widow," he said. "Well, I think that's fantastic, guys."

"Thank you," chorused Dan and Stefi.

"And there's some other news, I think ..." said Alma, looking expectantly at the two of them.

Dan and Stefi looked at each other and smiled.

It was Dan who spoke first.

"I've agreed to stay on indefinitely, Nick. Perhaps you know already; Stefi and I are an item. It's been that way for a little while now."

An item. *How little it said about the love in their eyes and the hands which now gripped each other on the table rather than under it,* Nick thought.

"Ha! I didn't know *for sure,* guys, but I'm delighted for you both," he said.

"Me too," said Lauren.

"And we've set a date for next year," said Stefi. "We hope you'll come Nick, Lauren, too."

"You're getting married?"

"Something like that. Neither of us is religious so it will be a humanist thing, on the beach here; a ceremony, a declaration of love and commitment to each other."

"And then, we party," added Dan, with a wicked grin.

"Fabulous. Congratulations, guys," Nick said.

Nick tapped his glass with his teaspoon a few times, then raised it and everyone clinked their glasses together.

"To Stefi and Dan," he called.

"Stefi and Dan," they responded.

Then Stefi reached for the second bottle of Philoxenía and Dan excused himself and headed off to the kitchen.

"He make galaktoboúreko for you, Nick," Stefi said.

"No wonder you're marrying him," said Nick.

*

As the light seeped from the sky and the dinner wound down, Nick went looking for Alma and found she had already gone to bed. Mildly disappointed, he found himself sitting next to Teddy.

"What about you, Teddy?" he said. "What are *your* plans now?"

"Now I'm playing gooseberry to these lovebirds, you mean?"

Nick was surprised to hear the idiom coming from a Greek.

"Your English is remarkable, you know."

"I used to have an English girlfriend. Her little brother was our gooseberry."

Teddy stretched out his legs and sighed.

"I'll stay until spring, at least. I promised them that. And I want to learn more about renewable energy, so I'll help Dan with his projects. Then, who knows? I might go back to ARCHELON."

"Back to the turtles."

"They feel a part of me now, somehow. And I've learned so much, I think I could teach new volunteers. I'd like that."

"Good for you," Nick said.

They saw Lauren approaching them.

"I might go to bed now, Dad, if that's all right," she said.

"You're a big girl now. You get to decide for yourself," said Nick.

"I know, but I don't want to be a party pooper."

"If you're pooped, you're allowed to be a pooper, I think." Nick raised an eyebrow at Teddy, for confirmation, but he was peering at his watch.

"Before you do, there's something you might want to see," he said. "It should only take a few minutes."

The adjacent cabin was dark but there was an electronic glow from a far corner. Teddy ushered them to seats in front of two computer screens but only Lauren sat.

"We've been watching for more than two weeks now," he said and pressed a button. "And this is the very last one. We weren't sure anything was going to happen but now there are signs. It's very close."

The left-hand screen lit with an infrared image of the sandy area immediately around a solitary turtle nest, adjacent to a boulder. Nothing was happening. Lauren turned to Teddy.

"Wait," he said.

After a few minutes, the sand began to twitch and subside.

"What's happening?" asked Lauren, but Teddy was just smiling. Nick moved in to stand close behind Lauren.

A moment later, they saw the end of a tiny flipper appear above the surface of the sand, feeling for more sand and finding none. Then the turtle's head appeared, along with the other front flipper and it peered around with twitchy, staccato movements.

"Wow," said Lauren.

"Just wait," said Teddy.

Now, as they watched, the surrounding area sank and churned and several more, tiny turtles, speckled with sand, battled their way to the surface. The frontrunners were now hoicking themselves over the wall of the mini crater they had made and starting a run for the sea. *They could not be more than ten centimetres long*, Lauren thought.

Teddy pressed some more buttons and an image appeared on the second screen. He must have placed a camera above the expected run because now they could see thirty or forty turtles, their flippers propelling them on a methodical, determined march to the sea. After less than twenty seconds, he stopped the film.

"This has been happening every night. But *this* nest was extra special for us. The eggs came from a dead turtle Roz found and it was *she* who insisted we save the hatchlings and give them a chance at life. Every turtle you've seen owes its existence to Roz."

"How wonderful is that?" said Lauren, tears welling as she turned to her father.

"Life *is* wonderful," said Nick, putting a hand on her shoulder. "And then you die."

"Oh, Dad! Why do you have to spoil *everything*?"

THE END

LEAVING A REVIEW

If you have enjoyed reading my book, it would be wonderful if you could find a minute to complete a short review of *Tamarisk Bay* on your chosen retailer's website. Thank you!

Alex

THANK YOU

Those of you expecting another 'stone' in the title may feel disappointed. We can call the first three novels *The Stone Trilogy* if you like but I felt it was time to escape the stricture and move to a wider array of geographic features! I hope you will forgive me.

Two years between books is a long time in today's breathless rush to publication, so I would like to thank you for your patience. I hope you find my fourth novel worth waiting for. Please let me know – or leave a review.

As always, special thanks are due to my partner, Leonie Carter McMahon. She helped me devise plot outlines at the outset of the series and the back story for *Nick Fisher*. She also provided a detailed critique of the final draft of this novel and came up with ideas and changes, some of which I was happy to adopt.

I must also thank my doughty beta readers: Sarah Toonen, Terri Jones, George Schrijver, Alexandra ("Sandy") Smithies, Roger Collins, Christine Hoare, Kathrina Valters, Catherine Stead, Kenrick Ghosh, Camilla Ghosh and Emma Wilson. I asked more of them this time by sending them a book that needed work. I put my timetable before the needs of the book. Big mistake. Their hard work and considerable input helped me rescue the book and restore the quality of the finished article.

Thanks again to my newsletter subscribers and all those who have been kind enough to leave reviews or comments on Amazon, Facebook, Instagram, X, BookBub, Goodreads, or anywhere else. It's challenging for a self-published author to gain traction in today's fiercely competitive market and telling the world you enjoyed my books is extremely helpful and important to me.

And lastly, thank you for buying and reading *Tamarisk Bay*. I hope you enjoyed it and will seek out more Nick Fisher novels and anything else I write. You can see all my published work at www.alexdunlevy.com.

ABOUT THE AUTHOR

Alex abandoned a career in finance at the age of forty-nine and spent a few years staring at the Mediterranean, contemplating life and loss. Finally, he accepted what his heart had always known. So, he joined some writing groups and he began to write.

He has now completed four novels in a series of crime thrillers set on the island of Crete and featuring British protagonist Nick Fisher. *The Unforgiving Stone* was the October 2020 debut. *Beneath the Stone* followed in 2021, *The Stone Skimmers* in 2022 and *Tamarisk Bay* in 2024. The first three have been awarded medallions of quality by B.R.A.G. (Book Readers Appreciation Group in the USA) and Amazon UK readers rate them 4.5 (out of 5) on average.

Alex has also published a collection of short stories, *The Late Shift Specialist*. These are quite different from his crime writing.

Recently, he has been working on a darkly comic novel set in the world of 1990s corporate finance and a bitter-sweet coming-of-age story, set in the 1960s.

Born in Derbyshire, England, Alex now lives in The Apokóronas, a fertile region in the north-west Crete, between the White Mountains and the nearby Cretan Sea.

CONTACT

You can find out more about Alex on his website: www.alexdunlevy.com. Here, you can join his newsletter group, listen to him read, learn more about his writing or buy his books. You are also very welcome to email: alexdunlevyauthor@gmail.com. He would love to hear from you.

He can also be found on Facebook, X and Instagram.

ALSO BY ALEX DUNLEVY

The Unforgiving Stone
(the first novel in the Nick Fisher series)

Beneath the Stone
(the second novel in the Nick Fisher series)

The Stone Skimmers
(the third novel in the Nick Fisher series)

The Late Shift Specialist
(a collection of short stories)

Printed in Great Britain
by Amazon